Water churned near the rowboat. Up came Cadderly, standing on the water! Seeming more surprised than Danica, Cadderly took a few gulps of air. He looked back toward the approaching assassins' boat and saw the crossbowman preparing another shot.

"Get in!" Danica cried, but Cadderly did not hear her. He was chanting and slowly waving a hand to and fro.

* * * * *

The second volume in the classic adventure series from the *New York Times* best-selling author of *The Dark Elf Trilogy* and *The Demon Wars Trilogy*.

* * * * *

"We've talked a lot over the years about what makes a good fantasy. It's a hard definition to settle on, but I think Bob's fantasies are good because he makes you believe so completely in his characters and story."

—**Terry Brooks**

W9-AZI-157

The Cleric Quintet
R. A. Salvatore

Book I
Canticle

Book II
In Sylvan Shadows

Book III
Night Masks

Book IV
The Fallen Fortress

Book V
The Chaos Curse

Night Masks

R. A. Salvatore

The Cleric Quintet - Book Three

NIGHT MASKS

Distributed to the hobby, toy, and comic trade in the United States and Canada by regional distributors.

Distributed worldwide by Wizards of the Coast, Inc. and regional distributors.

Forgotten Realms and the Wizards of the Coast logo are registered trademarks owned by Wizards of the Coast, Inc.

All Wizards of the Coast characters, character names, and the distinctive likenesses thereof are trademarks owned by Wizards of the Coast, Inc.

All rights reserved. Made in the U.S.A.

Cover art by Daren Bader
First Printing: August 1992
Library of Congress Catalog Card Number: 99-69446

9 8 7 6 5 4 3

ISBN: 0-7869-1606-0
620-T21606

U.S., CANADA,	EUROPEAN HEADQUARTERS
ASIA, PACIFIC, & LATIN AMERICA	Wizards of the Coast, Belgium
Wizards of the Coast, Inc.	P.B. 2031
P.O. Box 707	2600 Berchem
Renton, WA 98057-0707	Belgium
+1-800-324-6496	+32-70-23-32-77

Visit our web site at www.wizards.com

To Aunt Terry, who'll never know
how much her support has meant to me.

Impresk
Lake

Carradoon Isle
(Estates)

Sunset Inn
(Visiting Nobles)

Carradoon
Castle

Cadderly's
Private Place

Dragon's
Codpiece

Tide
Wall

Snoozing
Dwarf
Inn

Lakeview
Street

Westward
(Guilds)

To Mountains
And
Library

West
Gate

Market
Square

East
Gate

Order of
Sune

Cemetery

To Tower
of
Belisarius

Stables

South
Gate

South
Park

Temple
of Ilmater

Boulevard
of the Bridge

Carradoon

★ City Militia
O Tree
◠◡ hedge

0   500
      Feet

N

Prologue

The large fighter shifted uneasily in his seat, looking all about the nearly empty tavern.

"Not so busy this night," the slender, drowsy-looking man across the table remarked. He shifted back lazily in his seat, crossed his legs in front of him, and draped a skinny arm over them.

The larger man regarded him warily as he began to understand. "And you know all in attendance," he replied.

"Of course."

The burly fighter looked back just in time to see the last of the other patrons slip out the door. "They have left by your bidding?" he asked.

"Of course."

"Mako sent you."

The weakling man curled his lips in a wicked grin, one that widened as the burly fighter regarded his skinny arms with obvious disdain.

"To kill me," the large man finished, trying to appear calm. His wringing hands, fingers moving as if seeking something to keep them occupied, revealed his nervousness.

He licked his dried lips and glanced around quickly, not taking his dark eyes from the assassin for any length of time. He noticed that the man wore gloves, one white and one black, and silently berated himself for not being more observant.

The thin man replied at length, "You knew Mako would repay you for his cousin's death."

"His own fault!" the large man retorted. "It was he who struck the first blow. I had no choi—"

"I am neither judge nor jury," the puny man reminded him.

"Just a killer," the fighter replied, "serving whoever gives you the largest sack of gold."

The assassin nodded, not the least bit insulted by the description.

The little man noticed his target's hand slipping casually into the hidden pouch, the fitchet, in the V cut of his tunic, above his right hip.

"Please, do not," the assassin said. He had been monitoring this man for many weeks, carefully, completely, and he knew of the knife concealed within.

The fighter stopped the movement and eyed him incredulously.

"Of course I know the trick," the assassin explained. "Do you not understand, dear dead Vaclav? You have no surprises left for me."

The man paused, then protested, "Why now?" The large man's ire rose with his obvious frustration.

"Now is the time," replied the assassin. "All things have their time. Should a killing be any different? Besides, I have pressing business in the west and can play the game no longer."

"You have had ample opportunity to finish this business many times before now," Vaclav argued. In fact, the little man had been hovering about him for weeks, had gained his trust somewhat, though he didn't even know the man's name. The fighter's eyes narrowed with further frustration when he contemplated that notion and realized that the man's frail frame—too frail to be viewed as any threat—had precipitated that acceptance. If this man, now revealed as an enemy, had appeared more threatening, Vaclav never would have let him get this close.

"More chances than you would believe," the assassin replied with a snicker. The large man had seen him often, but not nearly as often as the killer, in perfect and varied disguises, had seen Vaclav.

"I pride myself on my business," the assassin continued, "unlike so many of the crass killers that walk the Realms. They prefer to keep their distance until the opportunity to strike presents itself, but I—" his beady eyes flickered with pride, "—prefer to personalize things. I have been all about you. Several of your friends are dead, and I now know you so well that I can anticipate your every movement."

Vaclav's breathing came in short rasps. Several friends dead? And this weakling threatening him openly? He had defeated countless monsters ten times this one's weight, had served honorably in three wars, had even battled a dragon! He was scared now, however. Vaclav had to admit that. Something was terribly wrong about this whole set-up, terribly out of place.

"I am an artist," the slender, sleepy man rambled. "That is why I will never err, why I will survive while so many other hired murderers go to early graves."

"You are a simple killer and nothing more!" the large man cried, his frustration boiling over. He leaped from his seat and drew a huge sword.

A sharp pain slowed him, and he found himself somehow sitting again. He blinked, trying to make sense of it all, for he saw himself at the empty bar, was, in fact, staring at his own face! He stood gawking as he—as his own body!—slid the heavy sword back into its scabbard.

"So crude," Vaclav heard his own body say. He looked down to the figure he now wore, the killer's weak form.

"And so messy," the assassin continued.

"How . . . ?"

"I do not have the time to explain, I fear," the assassin replied.

"What is your name?" Vaclav cried, desperate for any diversion.

"Ghost," answered the assassin. He lurched over, confident that the seemingly androgynous form, one he knew so well, could not muster the speed to escape him or the strength to fend him off.

Vaclav felt himself being lifted from the floor, felt the huge hands slipping about his neck. "The ghost of who?" managed the out-of-control, desperate man. He kicked as hard as his new body would allow, so pitiful an attempt against the burly, powerful form his enemy now possessed. Then his breath would not come.

Vaclav heard the snap of bone, and it was the last sound he would ever hear.

"Not 'the ghost,' " the victorious assassin replied to the dead form, "just 'Ghost.' " He sat then to finish his drink. How perfect this job had been; how easily Vaclav had been coaxed into so vulnerable a position.

"An artist," Ghost said, lifting his cup in a toast to himself. His more familiar body would be magically repaired before the dawn, and he could then take it back, leaving the empty shell of Vaclav's corpse behind.

Ghost had not lied when he had mentioned pressing business in the west. A wizard had contacted the assassin's guild, promising exorbitant payments for a minor execution.

The price must have been high indeed, Ghost knew, for his superiors had requested that he take on the task. The wizard apparently wanted the best.

The wizard wanted an artist.

One

Placid Fields

Cadderly walked slowly from the single stone tower, across the fields, toward the lakeside town of Carradoon. Autumn had come to the region; the few trees along Cadderly's path, red maples mostly, shone brilliantly in their fall wardrobe. The sun was bright this day and warm, in contrast with the chilly breezes blowing down from the nearby Snowflake Mountains, gusting strong enough to float Cadderly's silken blue cape out behind him as he walked, and strong enough to bend the wide brim of his similarly blue hat.

The troubled young scholar noticed nothing.

Cadderly absently pushed his sand-brown locks from his gray eyes, then grew frustrated as the unkempt hair, much longer than he had ever worn it, defiantly dropped back down. He pushed it away again, and then again, and finally tucked it tightly under the brim of his hat.

Carradoon came within sight a short while later, on the banks of wide Impresk Lake and surrounded by hedge-lined fields of sheep and cattle and crops. The city proper was walled, as were most cities of the Realms, with many multi-story structures huddled inside against ever-present perils. A long bridge connected Carradoon to a nearby island, the section of the town reserved for the more well-to-do merchants and governing officials.

As always when he came by this route, Cadderly looked at the town with mixed and uncertain feelings. He had been born in Carradoon, but did not remember that early part of his life. Cadderly's gaze drifted past the walled city, to the west and to the towering Snowflakes, to the passes that led high into the mountains, where lay the Edificant Library, a sheltered and secure bastion of learning.

That had been Cadderly's home, though he realized that now it was not, and thus he felt he could not return there. He was not a poor man. The wizard in the tower he had recently left had once paid him a huge sum for transcribing a lost spell book—and he had the means to support himself in relative comfort.

But all the gold in the world could not have produced a home for Cadderly, nor could it have released his troubled spirit from its turmoil.

Cadderly had grown up, had learned the truth of his violent, imperfect world, too suddenly. The young scholar had been thrust into situations beyond his experience, forced into the role of hero-warrior when all he really wanted was to read of adventures in books of legend. Cadderly had recently killed a man, and had fought in a war that had blasted, torn, and ultimately tainted a once-pristine sylvan forest.

Now he had no answers, only questions.

Cadderly thought of his room at the Dragon's Codpiece, where the *Tome of Universal Harmony*, the most prized book of the god named Deneir, sat open on his small table.

It had been given to Cadderly by Pertelope, a high-ranking priestess of his order, with the promise that within its thick bindings Cadderly would find his answers.

Cadderly wasn't sure he believed that.

The young scholar sat on a grassy rise overlooking the town, scratched at his stubbly beard, and wondered again about his purpose and calling in this confusing life. He removed his wide-brimmed hat and stared at the porcelain insignia attached to its red band: an eye and a single candle, the holy symbol of Deneir, the deity dedicated to literature and the arts.

Cadderly had served Deneir since his earliest recollections, though he had never really been certain of what that service entailed, or of the real purpose in dedicating his life to any god. He was a scholar and an inventor and believed wholeheartedly in the powers of knowledge and creation, two very important tenets for the Deneirian sect.

Only recently had Cadderly begun to feel that the god was something more than a symbol, more than a fabricated ideal for the scholars to emulate. In the elven forest Cadderly had felt the birth of powers he could not begin to understand. He had magically healed a friend's wound that otherwise would have proved fatal. He had gained supernatural insight into the history of the elves, not just their recorded events, but the feelings, the eldritch aura, that had given the ancient race its identity. He had watched in amazement as the spirit of a noble horse rose from its broken body and walked solemnly away. He had seen a dryad disappear into a tree and had commanded the tree to push the elusive creature back out—and the tree had heeded his command!

There could be no doubt for young Cadderly: mighty magic was with him, granting him these terrifying powers. His peers called that magic Deneir and called it a good thing, but in light of what he had done, of what he had become, and the horrors he had witnessed, Cadderly was not certain that he wanted Deneir with him.

He got up from the grassy rise and continued his journey to the walled town, to the Dragon's Codpiece, and to the *Tome of Universal Harmony*, where he could only pray that he would find some answers and some peace.

* * * * *

He flipped the page, his eyes desperately trying to scan the newest material in the split second it took him to turn the page again. It was impossible; Cadderly simply could not keep up with his desire, his insatiable hunger, to turn the pages.

He was finished with the *Tome of Universal Harmony*, a work of nearly two thousand pages, in mere minutes. Cadderly slammed the book shut, frustrated and fearful, and tried to rise from his small desk, thinking that perhaps he should go for a walk, or go to find Brennan, the innkeeper's teenage son who had become a close friend.

The tome grabbed at him before he could get out of his seat. With a defiant but impotant snarl, the young scholar flipped the book back over and began his frantic scan once more. The pages flipped at a wild pace; Cadderly couldn't begin to read more than a single word or two on any one page, and yet, the *song* of the book, the special meanings behind the simple words, rang clearly in his mind. It seemed as though all the mysteries of the universe were embedded in the sweet and melancholy melody, a song of living and dying, of salvation and damnation, of eternal energy and finite matter.

He heard voices as well—ancient accents and reverent tones singing in the deepest corners of his mind, but he could not make out any of the words, like the written words on the pages of the book. Cadderly could see them as a whole, could see their connotations, if not the actual lettering.

Cadderly felt his strength quickly draining as he continued to press on. His eyes ached, but he could not close them; his mind raced in too many directions, unlocking secrets, then storing them back into his subconscious in a more organized fashion. In those brief transitions from one page to another, Cadderly managed to wonder if he would go insane, or if the work would consume him emotionally.

He understood something else, then, and the thought finally gave to him the strength to slam the book shut. Several of the higher ranking Deneirian priests at the Edificant Library had been found dead, lying across this very book. Always the deaths had been seen as by natural causes—all of those priests had been much older than Cadderly—but Cadderly's insight told him differently.

They had tried to hear the song of Deneir, the song of universal mysteries, but they had not been strong enough to control the effects of that strange and beautiful music. They had been consumed.

Cadderly frowned at the black cover of the closed tome as though it were a demonic thing. It was not, he reminded himself, and, before his fears could argue back, he opened the book once more, from the beginning, and began his frantic scan.

Melancholy assaulted him; the doors blocking revelations swung wide, their contents finding a place in the receptacle of young Cadderly's mind.

Gradually the young scholar's eyes drooped from sheer exhaustion, but still the song played on, the music of the heavenly spheres, of sunrise and sunset and all the details that played eternally in between.

It played on and on, a song without end, and Cadderly felt himself falling toward it, becoming no more than a passing note among an infinite number of passing notes.

On and on . . .

"Cadderly?" The call came from far away, as if from another world perhaps. Cadderly felt a hand grasp his shoulder, tangible and chill, and felt himself turned gently about. He opened a sleepy eye and saw young Brennan's curly black mop and beaming face.

"Are you all right?"

Cadderly managed a weak nod and rubbed his bleary eyes. He sat up in his chair, felt a dozen aches in various parts of his stiff body. How long had he been asleep?

It was not sleep, the young scholar realized then, to his mounting horror. The weariness that had taken him from consciousness was too profound to be cured by simple sleep. What, then?

It was a journey, he sensed. He felt as though he had been on a journey. But to where?

"What were you reading?" Brennan asked, leaning past him to regard the open book. The words shook Cadderly from his reflections. Suddenly terrified, he shoved Brennan aside and slammed the book.

"Do not look at it!" he answered harshly.

Brennan seemed at a loss. "I . . . I am sorry," he apologized, obviously confused, his green eyes downcast. "I did not mean—"

"No," Cadderly interrupted, forcing a disarming smile to his face. He hadn't intended to wound the young lad who had been so kind to him over the last few weeks. "You did nothing wrong. But promise me that you will never look into this book—not unless I am here to guide you."

Brennan took a step away from the desk, eyeing the closed tome with sincere fear.

"It is magical," Cadderly acknowledged, "and it could cause harm to one who does not know how to read it properly. I am not angry with you—truly. You just startled me."

Brennan nodded weakly, seeming unconvinced.

"I brought your food," he explained, pointing to a tray he had placed on the night table beside Cadderly's small bed.

Cadderly smiled at the sight. Dependable Brennan. When he had come to the Dragon's Codpiece, Cadderly had desired solitude and had arranged with Fredegar Harriman, the innkeeper, to have his meals delivered outside his door. That arrangement had quickly changed, though, as Cadderly had come to know and like Brennan. Now the young man felt free to enter Cadderly's room and deliver the plates of food—always more than the price had called for—personally. Cadderly, for all his stubbornness and the icy demeanor he had developed after the horrors of Shilmista's war, had soon found that he could not resist the unthreatening companionship.

Cadderly eyed the plate of supper for a long while. He noticed a few specks of crumbs on the floor, some from a biscuit and some darker—the crust of the midday bread, he realized. The curtains over his small window had been drawn and his lamp had been turned down, and then turned back up.

"You could not wake me the last three times you came in here?" he asked.

Brennan stuttered, surprised that Cadderly had deduced that he had been in the room three times previously. "Three times?" he replied.

"To deliver breakfast and then lunch," Cadderly reasoned, and then he paused, realizing that he should not know what he knew. "Then once more to check on me, when you turned the lamp back up and drew the curtains."

Cadderly looked back to Brennan and was surprised again. He almost called out in alarm, but quickly realized that the images he saw dancing on the young man's shoulders—shadowy forms of scantily clad dancing girls and disembodied breasts—were of his own making, an interpretation from his own mind.

Cadderly turned away and snapped his eyes shut. An interpretation of what?

He heard the song again, distantly. The chant was specific this time, the same phrases repeated over and over, though Cadderly still could not make out the exact words, except for one: *aurora*.

"Are you all right?" Brennan asked again.

Cadderly nodded and looked back, this time not so startled by the dancing shadows. "I am," he replied sincerely. "And I have kept you here longer than you wished."

Brennan's face screwed up with curiosity.

"You be careful at the Moth Closet," Cadderly warned, referring to the seedy private club at the end of Lakeview Street, on the eastern side of Carradoon, near where Impresk Lake spilled into Shalane River. "How does a boy your age get into the place?"

"How . . ." Brennan stuttered, his pimpled face blushing to deep crimson.

Cadderly waved him away, a wide smile on his face. The dancing shadow breasts atop Brennan's shoulder disappeared in a burst of splotchy black dots. Apparently Cadderly's guesses had knocked out the teenager's hormonal urgings.

Temporarily, Cadderly realized as Brennan headed for the door, for the shadows already began to form anew. Cadderly's laugh turned Brennan back around.

"You will not tell my father?" he pleaded.

Cadderly waved him away, stifling the urge to burst out in laughter. Brennan hesitated, perplexed. He relaxed almost immediately, reminding himself that Cadderly was his friend. A smile found his face, and a dancing girl found a perch on his shoulder. He snapped his fingers and swiftly disappeared from the room.

Cadderly stared long and hard at the closed door, and at the telltale crumbs on the floor beside his night table.

Things had seemed so very obvious to him, both of what had transpired in his room while he was asleep, and of Brennan's intentions for a night of mischief. So obvious, and yet, Cadderly knew they should not have been.

"Aurora?" he whispered, searching for the significance. "The dawn?" Cadderly translated, and shook his head slowly; what could the dawn have to do with silhouettes of dancing girls on Brennan's shoulder?

The young priest looked back to the tome. Would he find his answer there?

He had to force himself to eat, to remind himself that he would need all his strength for the hours ahead. Soon after, one hunger sated and another tearing at him, Cadderly dove back into the *Tome of Universal Harmony*.

The pages began to flip, and the song played on and on.

Two

Mopping Up

Danica blew a lock of her strawberry-blonde hair from in front of her exotic, almond-shaped brown eyes and peered intently down the forest path, searching for some sign of the approaching enemy. She shifted her compact, hundred-pound frame from foot to foot, always keeping perfect balance, her finely toned muscles tense in anticipation of what was to come.

"Are the dwarves in position?" Elbereth, the new king of Shilmista's elves, asked her, his strange, almost eerie, silver eyes looking more to the trees surrounding the path than to the trail itself.

Two other elves, one a golden-haired maiden, the other with black hair as striking as Elbereth's, came to join the friends.

"I would expect the dwarves to be ready in time," Danica assured the elf king. "Ivan and Pikel have never let us down."

The three elves nodded; Elbereth could not help but

smile. He remembered when he had first encountered the gruff dwarves, when Ivan, the tougher of the pair, had found him bound and helpless as a prisoner of their enemy. Never would the elf have believed that he would soon come to trust so implicitly in the bearded brothers.

"The dryad has returned," the black-haired elf wizard, Tintagel, said to Elbereth. He led the elf king's gaze to a nearby tree, where Elbereth managed to make out Hammadeen, the elusive dryad, as her tan-skinned, green-haired form peeked from around the trunk.

"She brings news that the enemy will soon arrive," remarked Shayleigh, the elven maiden. The anxious tone of her voice and the sudden sparkle that came into her violet eyes reminded Danica of the fiery maiden's lust for battle. Danica had seen Shayleigh "at play" with both sword and bow, and she had to agree with Ivan Bouldershoulder's proclamation that he was glad Shayleigh was on their side.

Tintagel motioned for the others to follow him to the rest of the gathered elves, some two score of Elbereth's people, almost half of the remaining elves in Shilmista. The wizard considered the landscape for a moment, then began positioning the elves along both sides of the path, trying to properly distribute those better in hand-to-hand combat and those better with their great bows. He called Danica to his side and began his spellcasting chant, walking along the elven lines and sprinkling white birch bark chips.

As he neared the end of the spell, Tintagel took up his own position, Danica moving to her customary spot beside him, and sprinkled chips upon himself and his human escort.

Then it was completed, and where Danica and forty elven warriors had been standing now stood rows of unremarkable birch trees.

Danica looked out from her new disguise to the forest about her, which seemed vague and foggy to her now, more like a feeling than any definite vision. She focused on the path, knowing that she and Tintagel must remain aware of their surroundings, must be ready to come out of the shape-changing spell as soon as Ivan and Pikel began the assault.

She wondered what she looked like as a tree, and thought, as she always thought when Tintagel performed this spell, that she might like to spend some quiet time in this form, viewing the forest around her, feeling its strength in her feet-become-roots.

But now there was killing to do.

*   *   *   *   *

"Oo," moaned Pikel Bouldershoulder, a round-shouldered dwarf with a green-dyed beard braided halfway down his back and open-toed sandals on his gnarly feet, as he watched the distant spectacle of Tintagel's spell. The longing gaze was plain to see, and Pikel almost toppled out of the tree in which he sat.

"No, ye don't!" his brother whispered harshly from across the way, disdaining Pikel's druidic tendencies. Ivan tucked his yellow beard into his wide belt and shifted his dwarven-hard buttocks about on the tree branch and his deer-antlered helmet about on his head, trying to find a comfortable position in this very undwarvenlike perch. In one hand he held a club made from the thick trunk of a dead tree. A heavy rope had been tied about his waist and looped up over a branch halfway across the trail.

Ivan had accepted the high seat, knowing what fun it would bring, but he drew the line at being turned into a tree—above his would-be druid brother's whining protests. Ivan had offered a compromise, enquiring of Tintagel about a variation of his mighty spell, but the elf wizard had declined, explaining that he had no power to turn people into rocks.

Across the path, in a perch opposite Ivan, Pikel seemed much more comfortable, both with his tree seat and tree-trunk club. He, too, sported a rope about his waist, the other end of Ivan's. Pikel's comfort with the perch could not defeat his frown, though, a frown brought on by his longing to be with the elves, to be a tree in Shilmista's soil.

Guttural goblin grumbling down the path alerted the dwarves of the enemy's approach.

"Sneaksters," Ivan whispered with a wide smile, trying to brighten his brother's surly mood. Ivan didn't want Pikel pouting at this critical moment.

Both dwarves tightened their grip on their clubs.

Soon the enemy band passed directly under them, spindle-armed and ugly goblins mixed in with pig-faced orcs and larger orogs. Ivan had to force himself not to spit on the wretched throng, had to remind himself that more fun would be had if he and his brother could hold their positions just a short while longer.

Then, as the dryad Hammadeen had told them it would, a giant came into view, plodding slowly down the path, seemingly oblivious to its surroundings. By the dryad's words this was the last giant remaining in Shilmista, and Ivan wasn't about to let the evil thing go crawling back to its mountain home.

"Sneaksters," Ivan whispered again, the title he had chosen for him and his brother, a title he knew that the giant, above all others, would appreciate in just another moment.

The huge head bobbed steadily closer. One goblin stopped suddenly and sniffed the air.

Too late.

Ivan and Pikel leveled their clubs and, with a nod to each other, hopped off their high perches, swinging down at the path. Their timing proved perfect and the oblivious giant stepped between them, its gaze straight ahead, its head bobbing at just the right height.

Pikel connected just a split-second before Ivan, the heavy dwarves sandwiching the monster's head in a tremendous slam. Ivan immediately dropped his bloodied club and tore out his favored double-bladed axe instead.

On the path below, the smaller monsters went into a frenzy, pushing and shoving, diving to the dirt, and running in all directions. They had lost many companions in the last few weeks, and they knew what was to come.

The wizard, Tintagel, cried out the dispelling syllable; Danica and forty elves behind her reverted to their original forms, drew back their bowstrings, and charged with gleaming swords waving high.

The dazed giant wobbled, but stubbornly, stupidly, held its balance, and Ivan and Pikel, dangling nearly twenty feet above the forest path, went to work.

Ivan's axe took off an ear; Pikel's club splattered the monster's nose all over its cheek. Again and again they smacked at the beast. They knew they were vulnerable up there, knew that if the giant managed to get even a single hit in, it would probably knock one of them halfway back to the Edificant Library. But the brothers didn't think of that grim fact at the time; they were having too much fun.

Below the hanging dwarves came the sound of elven bows loosing hail after hail of arrows deep into goblin, orc, and orog flesh.

Creatures died by the score; others cried in agony and terror, and the merciless elves came on, swords in hand, hacking at the squirming forms of these vile invaders, the monsters that had so tainted the precious elven home.

Danica spotted one group of monsters slipping away through the trees to the side. She called to Tintagel and sped off in pursuit, taking up her crystal-bladed daggers, one with a golden pommel carved into the likeness of a tiger, the other, with a hilt of silver, carved into a dragon.

* * * * *

Pikel's club knocked the giant's head backward so brutally that the dwarves heard the sharp crack of the huge
monster's neck bone. The giant somehow held its balance
for just a moment longer, looking dazed and confused, and
then became quite dead. It rolled up on the balls of its huge
feet and toppled forward like a chopped tree.

Ivan quickly surveyed the path ahead of the falling beast.

"Two!" the dwarf yelled, and the giant's body buried two
unfortunate goblins as it landed.

"Ye owe me a gold piece!" Ivan roared, and Pikel nodded
happily, more than willing to pay the bet.

"Ye ready for more?" Ivan cried.

"Oo oi!" Pikel replied with enthusiasm. Without a word
of warning to his brother, Pikel grabbed a nearby branch
and quickly pulled the loop around his waist, freeing his
end of the rope.

Ivan did manage to open his eyes wide, but the inevitable
curses aimed at his brother would have to wait as he took a
more direct descent to the ground. To Pikel's credit, the
plummeting Ivan did clobber a goblin beneath him.

The yellow-bearded dwarf hopped back to his feet, spitting dirt and curses. He casually dropped his heavy axe
onto the back of the wounded goblin's head, ending its
complaints, and looked back up to his brother, who was
making a more conventional way down the tree.

Pikel shrugged and smiled meekly. "Oops," he offered,
and Ivan silently mouthed the word at the same instant
Pikel spoke it, fully expecting the all-too-common apology.

"When ye get down here . . ." Ivan began to threaten, but
goblins suddenly closed in around the vulnerable dwarf.
Ivan howled happily and forgot any anger harbored against
Pikel. After all, how could he possibly stay mad at someone
who had dropped him right in the middle of so much fun?

* * * * *

The fleeing band's lead goblin scrambled through the thick underbrush, desperate to leave the slaughter behind. The monster hooked one ankle on one of many crisscrossing roots in this overgrown region, and stubbornly pulled itself free. Then it got hooked again, and this time the grasp was not so easily broken.

The goblin squealed and pulled, then looked back to see, not a root, but a woman, smiling wickedly and holding fast to its ankle.

Danica twisted her arm in a sudden jerk and charged up and ahead from her low concealment, tripping the unfortunate creature. She was atop the thing in an instant, her free hand pushing away the frantic beast's futile slaps while her other hand, holding the golden-hilted dagger, came slashing in for a single, vicious strike.

Danica rarely needed more than one.

The young woman pulled herself up from the slain creature, openly facing its surprised comrades, who weaved in and out of the trees behind and to the sides. The band eyed her curiously and looked all about, not really knowing what to make of the woman. Where had she come from, and why was she alone? Not another leaf or bush in this area moved, though the fighting continued back on the trail.

With that thought in mind, an orog cried for a charge, eager to claim at least one victim amidst the disaster. The monstrous band came crashing in at Danica from three sides, through the bushes and brambles, gaining confidence and resolve with every step.

Elbereth dropped from a tree limb above Danica, his gleaming sword and shining armor revealing his prominent stature among the elven clan. Some of the monsters halted altogether, and the others slowed, looking back and forth curiously from the elf and woman to their less brave comrades.

A short distance to the side, Shayleigh appeared from

behind a tree and set her bow immediately to work, dropping the creature closest to her companions.

The orogs cried out to run away, a command goblins were always ready to follow. Elbereth and Danica moved first, though, catching the nearest goblins in a furious rush, while Shayleigh concentrated her fire on the orogs.

Those monsters not engaged ran wildly, picking their escape routes through the thick trees and brush.

A wall of mist rolled up before them. Terrified goblins skidded to a stop. The orogs, right behind, prodded them, knowing that to halt was to die.

An arrow thudded into the back of an orog; another bolt followed its flight just a split second later, and the remaining two orogs shoved the lead goblin into the fog.

Watching from the boughs above, Tintagel quickly launched another spell, throwing his voice through a rolled-up cone of parchment into the area of the vapors. His fog wall was a harmless thing, but the cries of agony that suddenly emanated from within made the hesitant creatures think otherwise.

Three arrows took down the second orog. The remaining brute scrambled about, seeking cover behind its goblin fodder. It came out the side of the group, thinking to circle around the fog wall . . . but it found Elbereth, and Elbereth's sword, instead.

* * * * *

"It's about time ye got here!" Ivan growled when Pikel finally made his way down the towering tree to come to his side. Many yards from the host of elves, and with many monsters between him and them, Ivan had been sorely pressed. Still, the tough dwarf had managed to escape any serious injury, for the bulk of the monsters were more interested in escaping than in fighting.

And it had quickly become obvious to the goblins that any who ventured near Ivan's furious axe swipes would not long survive.

Now, back to back, the dwarven brothers elevated the battle to new heights of slaughter. They overwhelmed the nearby monsters in mere minutes, then shuffled up the path to overwhelm another group.

The elves cut in just as fiercely, swordsmen driving the monstrous throng every which way, and archers, just a short distance behind, making short work of those creatures that broke out of the pack. The goblinoids had nowhere to run and nowhere to hide. Already, more monsters lay dead than those standing to continue the fight, and that ratio came to favor the elves more and more with every passing second.

* * * * *

Tintagel watched as the first goblin that had been pushed into the wall emerged from the other side unharmed. The elf wizard resisted the urge to blast the thing down, for his role in this fight was to contain the monsters so that Elbereth, Shayleigh, and Danica could finish them. He pulled more dried peas from his pouch and tossed them to the ground, perpendicular to the mist wall. Uttering the proper chant, the wizard summoned a second fog wall to box in the monsters.

Danica followed Shayleigh's next three arrows into the confused horde. She whipped her daggers into the nearest targets, killing one goblin and dropping a second in screaming pain, and came in with a fury that her enemies could not match.

Nor could the remaining orog match Elbereth's skill. The creature parried the elf's initial, testing swing, then brought its heavy club across wickedly. Elbereth easily sidestepped the blow and waded in behind, jabbing his fine sword repeatedly into the slower beast's chest.

The creature blinked many times as though it was trying to focus through eyes that were no longer seeing clearly. Elbereth couldn't wait for it to decide its next move. He whipped his shield arm about, slamming the shield—which had belonged to his father not so long ago—against the orog's head. The monster dropped heavily, star-shaped welts from the embossed symbols of Shilmista crossing the side of its piggish face.

Shayleigh, now with a sword in hand, came up beside the elven king and together they waded confidently into the goblins.

With no options readily before them, the trapped goblins began to fight back. Three surrounded Danica, hacking wildly with their short swords. They couldn't keep up with her darting movements, dips, and dodges, though, and weren't really coming very close to connecting.

Danica bided her time. One frustrated creature whipped its sword across in a harmlessly wide arc. Before the goblin could recover from its overbalanced swing, Danica's foot snapped straight up, connected under its chin, and drove its jaw up under its nose. The goblin promptly disappeared under the brush.

A second beast rushed at the distracted woman's back.

Bolts of magical energy flashed down from the tree above, burning into its head and neck. The goblin howled and grabbed at the wound, and Danica, fully balanced at all times, spun a half-circle, one foot flying wide, and circle-kicked it across the face. Its head looking far back over one shoulder, the goblin joined its dead companion on the ground.

Danica managed to nod her thanks to Tintagel as she waded into the lone goblin facing her, her hands and feet flying in from all sides, finding opening after opening in the pitiful creature's defenses. One kick knocked its sword away and, before it could cry out a surrender, Danica's stiffened fingers rifled into its throat, tearing out its windpipe.

Suddenly, it was over, with no more monsters to hit. The four companions, three of them covered in the blood of their enemies, stood solemn and grim, surveying their necessary handiwork.

* * * * *

"Ye know, elf," Ivan said when Elbereth and the others came back to the group on the trail, "this is getting too easy." The dwarf spat in both hands and grasped his axe handle, the blade of his weapon buried deeply into an orog's thick head. With a sickening crack, Ivan pulled the mighty weapon free.

"First fight in a week," Ivan continued, "and this group seemed more keen on running than fighting!"

Elbereth couldn't deny the dwarf's observations, but he was far from upset at what the goblins' retreat indicated.

"If we are fortunate, it will be another week before we find the need to fight again," he replied.

Ivan balked, and drove his gore-stained blade into the earth to clean it. As Elbereth moved away, the dwarf muttered to his brother, "Spoken like a true elf."

Three

Heartfelt

Y ou sit here and wait while all of our dreams—all of the dreams Talona herself gave you—fall to pieces!" Dorigen Kel Lamond, second most powerful wizard in all of Castle Trinity, sat back in her chair, somewhat surprised by her uncharacteristic outburst. Her amber eyes looked away from Aballister, her mentor and superior.

The hollow-featured, older wizard seemed to take no offense. He rocked back in his comfortable chair, his stick-like fingers tap-tapping in front of him and an amused expression upon his gaunt face.

"Pieces?" he asked after a silence designed to make Dorigen uncomfortable. "Shilmista has been, or soon will be, reclaimed by the elves, that much is true," he admitted. "But their insignificant number has been halved by all reports—less than a hundred of them remain to defend the forest."

"And we lost more than a thousand soldiers," Dorigen

snapped sharply. "Thousands more have fled our dominion, gone back to their mountain holes."

"Where we might reclaim them," Aballister assured her, "when the time is right."

Dorigen fumed but remained silent. She brushed a bead of sweat from her crooked nose and again looked away. Sporting two broken hands, the woman felt vulnerable with both unpredictable Aballister and upstart Bogo Rath in the private room, to say nothing of Druzil, Aballister's pet imp. That was one of the problems in working beside such evil men, Dorigen reminded herself. She could never be certain when Aballister might think he would be better off without her.

"We still have three thousand soldiers—mostly human—at our immediate disposal," Aballister went on. "The goblinoids will be brought back when we need them—after the winter, perhaps, when the season is favorable for an invasion."

"How many will we need?" he asked, more to Bogo than to Dorigen. "Shilmista is but a semblance of itself, and the Edificant Library has been severely wounded. That leaves only Carradoon." The tone of Aballister's voice showed clearly how he felt about the farmers and fishermen of the small community on the banks of Impresk Lake.

"I'll not deny that the library has been wounded," Dorigen replied, "but we really do not know the extent of those wounds. You seem to have underestimated Shilmista as well. Must I remind you of our most recent defeat?"

"And must I remind you that it was you, not I, who presided over that defeat?" the older wizard growled, his dark-eyed gaze boring into Dorigen. "That it was Dorigen who fled the forest at the most critical stages of the battle?" Seeing her cowed, Aballister again rocked back in his chair and calmed.

"I sympathize with your pains," he said quietly. "You have lost Tiennek. That must have been a terrible blow."

Dorigen winced. She had expected the remark, but it stung her nonetheless. Tiennek, a barbarian warrior she had plucked from the northland and trained to serve as her consort, had replaced Aballister as her lover. Dorigen didn't doubt for a minute the older wizard's satisfaction upon hearing that the great warrior had been killed. A woman nearly two feet shorter than Tiennek and barely a third of his weight had done the deed. In reporting the incident, the imp Druzil had purposely downplayed the young woman's prowess, Dorigen knew, just to fan the flames that had come between the two wizards.

Dorigen wanted to fight back, wanted to shout in the wizard's face that he could not understand the power of that young woman, Danica, the monk escort of Cadderly, and of all the enemies she had met in Shilmista. She looked to Druzil, who had been there beside her, but the imp covered his doglike face with his leathery wings and made no move to support her.

"Wretched, cowardly creature," Dorigen muttered. Since their return to Castle Trinity, Druzil had avoided contact with Dorigen. He held no loyalty to Aballister, she knew, except that Aballister was in control here, and the prudent imp always preferred to be on the winning side.

"Enough of this bantering," Aballister said suddenly. "Our plans have been delayed by some unexpected problems."

"Like your own son," Dorigen had to put in.

Aballister's smile hinted that Dorigen might have overstepped her bounds. "My son," the wizard echoed, "dear young Cadderly. Yes, Dorigen, he has proved the most unexpected and severe of our problems. Do you agree, Boygo?"

Dorigen looked to the youngest of Castle Trinity's wizards, Bogo Rath, whom she and her mentor routinely called "Boygo."

The young man narrowed his eyes at the insult, not that he hadn't expected it. He was so very different from his two peers, and so often the butt of their jokes. He jerked his head back and forth, flipping his long, stringy brown hair over one ear, away from the side of his head that he kept shaved.

Dorigen, tiring of Bogo's outrageous actions, almost growled at his ridiculous haircut.

"Your son has indeed proved to be quite a problem," Bogo replied. "What else might we expect from the off-spring of mighty Aballister? If young Cadderly must fight on the other side, then we would be wise to pay attention to him."

"Young Cadderly," Dorigen mumbled, her face locked in an expression of disgust. "Young Cadderly" had to be at least two or three years older than this upstart!

Aballister held up a small, bulging bag and shook it once to show the others that its thickness came from many coins—gold, probably. Dorigen understood the bag's significance, understood what it would buy for Aballister, and for Bogo as well. Bogo had come from West-gate, a city four hundred miles to the northeast, at the mouth of the Lake of Dragons. Westgate was notable as a bustling trading town, and it was known, too, for an assassin band called the Night Masks, who were among the cruelest killers in the Realms.

"Even your Night Masks will have a difficult time striking at our young scholar, whether he is in Shilmista or has returned to the Edificant Library," Dorigen asserted, if for no better reason than to take some of the bite out of Aballister's icy demeanor concerning his son. For all that she hated Cadderly—he had broken her hands and stolen several magical items from her—Dorigen simply could not believe Aballister's viciousness toward his own son.

"He is not in Shilmista," Bogo replied with a grin, his brown eyes flashing with excitement, "nor in the library." Dorigen stared at Bogo, and her sudden interest obviously pleased the young wizard. "He is in Carradoon."

"Rousing the garrison, no doubt," Aballister added.

"How can you be certain?" Dorigen asked Bogo.

Bogo looked to Aballister, who shook the bag of gold once more. Its tinkling coins sent a shiver along Dorigen's spine. Bogo's assassin connections with Westgate, his one claim to any prestige in Castle Trinity, were already on the trail.

Even though her hands continued to throb, Dorigen felt pity for the young scholar.

"One problem at a time, dear Dorigen," Aballister said, a thought he had iterated before, when he had first told Dorigen of his plans for his son. Again the older wizard shook the bag of gold, and again a shiver coursed along Dorigen's spine.

* * * * *

Elbereth and Danica sat atop Deny Ridge, a defensible position that the elves had taken as their base. Few of the elven folk were about this starry night, and there was no longer any danger demanding an alert garrison. Indeed, according to Hammadeen—and dryad's tree-gotten information had been accurate since Cadderly had pressed her into service weeks earlier—no monsters were within ten miles of the ridge.

It was peaceful and quiet, not the ring of swords or the cries of the dying to be heard.

"The wind grows chill," Elbereth commented, offering Danica his traveling cloak. She accepted it and lay in the thick grass beside the elf, looking up to the countless stars and the few black forms of meandering clouds.

Elbereth's soft chuckle led her to sit up once more. She followed the elf's gaze to the base of the sloping hill. Squinting, she could just make out three forms—one elven and the other two obviously dwarven—darting in and out of the shadows along the tree line.

"Shayleigh?" Danica asked.

Elbereth nodded. "She and the dwarves have become great friends in the last few weeks," he noted. "Shayleigh admires their courage and is not ungrateful that they have remained to aid in our fight."

"Is the elf king ungrateful?" Danica asked slyly.

Elbereth managed a smile at her good-natured sarcasm. He recalled his first meeting with the dwarves, and how he had come close to trading serious blows with Ivan. How long ago that seemed now! Elbereth had been just a prince then, in disfavor with his father, the king, at a time when the forest was in peril.

"I am not ungrateful," he replied softly. "I will never forget the debt I owe the dwarves . . . and you." He locked stares with Danica then, his silver eyes catching the woman's rich brown orbs in an unblinking gaze.

Their faces lingered, barely an inch apart.

Danica cleared her throat and turned away. "The fighting nears its end," she remarked, stealing the romance from the moment. Elbereth knew at once where her comment would lead, for she had hinted at her plans for several days.

"We will be ridding Shilmista of the goblin vermin for the rest of the season," the elf king said firmly. "And I fear that a new attack might begin in the spring, after the mountain trails are clear."

"Hopefully by then Carradoon and the library will be roused," Danica offered.

"Will you help that process?"

Danica looked back down the grassy slope, where the three forms were now steadily approaching.

"Never did care much for trees," they heard Ivan complaining as he rubbed at his nose.

"I would have thought that one as short as a dwarf would be able to avoid low-hanging branches," Shayleigh replied with a melodic laugh.

"Hee hee hee," added Pikel, prudently swerving out of Ivan's backhanded reach.

"The time has come for me, and Ivan and Pikel, to depart," Danica blurted, hating the words but having to say them. Elbereth's smile was gone in an instant. He looked long and hard at the woman and did not respond.

"Perhaps we should have left with Avery and Rufo for the library," Danica went on.

"Or perhaps you should trust them to handle the affairs at the library and in Carradoon," Elbereth put in. "You could remain, all three. The invitation is open, and I assure you that Shilmista takes on an entirely new beauty under winter's white blanket."

"I do not doubt your words," Danica replied, "but I fear I must go. There is—"

"Cadderly," Elbereth interrupted, smiling despite his disappointment that his three friends would soon leave.

Danica did not reply, was not even sure of how she felt. She looked back to the slope, where Ivan and Pikel still tried to make their way to where Shayleigh waited. They almost made it this time, but apparently Ivan muttered something that offended his brother, for Pikel sprang upon him and the two rolled down once more. The elf maiden threw up her hands in surrender and sprinted the rest of the way to Danica and Elbereth.

As soon as she joined the two, her smile was replaced by a curious expression. She studied Danica's face for a moment, then commented matter-of-factly, "You are leaving."

Danica did not respond, could hardly look the elven maiden in the face.

"When?" Shayleigh asked, her tone still calm and composed.

"Soon—perhaps tomorrow," Danica replied.

Shayleigh spent a long moment considering the bittersweet news. Danica was leaving after the victory, with the forest secured. She could return, or the elves could go to her, freely, with little threat of goblins and orcs.

"I applaud your choice," Shayleigh said evenly. Danica turned to regard her, caught off guard by the elf's approval.

"The fight here is won, at least for now," the elf maiden continued, gaily spinning a turn in the clean and crisp evening air. "You have many duties to attend to, and, of course, you have studies back at the Edificant Library."

"I expect that Ivan and Pikel will accompany me," Danica replied. "They also have duties at the library."

Shayleigh nodded and looked back to the slope, where the brothers were trying a third time to get all the way up. At that angle, in the clear starlight, Danica could see the sincere admiration in the elf maiden's violet eyes. Danica understood that Shayleigh had put on her carefree attitude because she believed Danica's decision was the right one, not because she was pleased that Danica and the dwarves would soon depart.

"If the fight begins anew in the spring . . ." Shayleigh started to say.

"We will be back," Danica assured her.

"Back where?" Ivan finally came up, shook from his yellow beard the twigs and leaves that had gotten caught up in it from his two rolls down the hill, and tucked it into his wide belt.

"Back to Shilmista," Shayleigh explained. "If the fighting begins anew."

"We going somewhere?" Ivan asked Danica.

"Uh-oh," moaned Pikel, beginning to understand.

"The first blows of winter will be upon us soon," Danica replied. "The trails through the Snowflakes will become impassable."

"Uh-oh," Pikel said again.

"Ye're right," Ivan said after thinking things over for a moment. "Things're settling here—not much left to hit. Me and me brother'd get bored soon enough, and besides, them priests at the library probably ain't had a good-cooked meal since we left!"

Shayleigh slapped Ivan on the side of the head. Ivan turned to stare incredulously into her wistful smile, and even the gruff dwarf could recognize the pain hidden beneath the fair maiden's delicate features.

"You still owe me a fight," Shayleigh explained.

Ivan snorted and cleared his throat, sneakily moving his shirt sleeve high enough to wipe the moisture from his eyes as he ran his sleeve across his nose. Danica was amazed by the obvious chink in the dwarf's callous demeanor.

"Bah!" Ivan growled. "What fight? Ye're just like the other one!" He waggled an accusing finger at Elbereth, whom he had battled to a draw in a similar challenge just a few weeks before. "Ye'd dance all about and run in circles until we both fell down tired!"

"Do you think I would release you from the insult you gave my people?" Shayleigh snarled, hands on hips, and moved over to tower above the dwarf.

"Ye think I'd let ye?" Ivan retorted, poking a stubby finger into Shayleigh's belly. "Bah!" Ivan snorted, and he turned and stormed away.

"Bah!" Shayleigh mimicked, her voice too melodic to

properly copy the dwarf's grating tone.

Ivan spun back and glowered at her, then motioned for Pikel to follow him away. "Well, ye got yer wood back, elf," Ivan said to Elbereth. "Ye're welcome!"

"Farewell to you, too, Ivan Bouldershoulder," Elbereth replied. "Our thanks to you and your splendid brother. Know that Shilmista will be open to either of you if you choose to pass this way again."

Ivan smiled Pikel's way. "As if that one could stop us anyhow!" he roared, and he slapped Shayleigh across the rump and darted away before she recovered enough to respond.

"I must go as well," Danica said to Elbereth. "I have many preparations to make before dawn."

Elbereth nodded but could not reply past the lump in his throat. As soon as Danica was gone, skipping down the slope to catch up with the dwarves, Shayleigh took a seat beside the silver-eyed elf king.

"You love her," the elf maiden remarked after a few silent moments.

Elbereth sat quietly for a while, then admitted, "With all my heart."

"And she loves Cadderly," said Shayleigh.

"With all her heart," Elbereth replied somberly.

Shayleigh managed a weak grin, trying to bolster her friend's resolve.

"Never would I have believed that an elf king of Shilmista would fall in love with a human!" Shayleigh spouted, nudging Elbereth in the shoulder.

The elf turned his silver-eyed gaze upon her and smiled wryly. "Nor I that an elf maiden would be enchanted by a yellow-bearded dwarf," he replied.

Shayleigh's initial reaction came out as an incredulous burst of laughter. Certainly Shayleigh had come to know Ivan and Pikel as friends, and trusted allies, but to hint at anything more than that was simply ridiculous. Still, the elven maiden quieted considerably when she looked down the now empty slope.

Empty indeed did it seem with the Bouldershoulder brothers gone from view.

Four

A Long Time to Dawn

Bogo Rath tentatively knocked on the door of the small conference room. He was never secure in his dealings with the dreaded Night Masks. A score of assassins had accompanied the two Night Mask leaders into Castle Trinity that same morning, many more trained killers than Bogo had anticipated for such a seemingly simple execution.

Black-robed sentries searched the young wizard before he was allowed entry. These two were unremarkable enough, Bogo noted, probably beginners in the dark band. They wore the customary dress of Westgate's assassin guild, nondescript yeoman's clothes and silver-edged black eye masks. One sentry's tusky grin made Bogo think his heritage might be more orc than human, something common in the underground band, and that thought sent a shudder along the young wizard's spine.

Whether these two were human or not, though, Bogo would not have been comfortable. He knew that, while the assassins openly displayed no weapons, each of them carried many and were trained to kill with their bare hands as well.

When the searching was done, the two guards led the young wizard into the room, then stepped back to the door, standing impassively on either side of the portal.

Bogo forgot about them as soon as they were behind him, for the young wizard found the two persons inside the comfortable room much more interesting. Closest to him sat a puny man—if it was a man—effeminate and obviously weak, issuing a steady stream of phlegm-filled coughs. The man showed no beard at all, not even stubble; his face was too clean and soft-looking to be an adult's. His heavy eyelids drooped lazily, and his lips, too thick and too full, seemed almost a childlike caricature.

Across the way sat the man's opposite, a thick-muscled, robust specimen with a full, thick beard and shock of hair, both flaming red, and arms that could snap Bogo in half with little effort. Still, this powerful man seemed even more out of place (from what Bogo knew of the Night Masks) than did the weakling. He brandished a huge sword on his girdle and bore the scars of many battles. His dress, too, was far from that preferred by assassins. Wide, studded bracers, glittering with dozens of small jewels, adorned the man's wrists, and his snow-white traveling cloak had been cut from the back of a northern bear, albeit a small one.

"You are Bogo Rath?" the large man asked in a smooth baritone, with an articulation that was sharper and more sophisticated than Bogo had expected.

The wizard nodded. "Well met, fellow Night Mask," the young wizard replied with a low bow.

The red-haired man gave him a curious look. "I was not told you retained any connection to the guild," he said. "I was informed that you left the band of mutual consent."

Bogo shifted nervously from foot to foot. He had paid a huge sum to be allowed out of the Night Masks three years earlier, and even with the bribe, if it hadn't been for the fact that his father was an influential merchant in Westgate—one with political associations and ties to the dark guild—Bogo would have been given the customary send-off for one who could not meet the Night Masks' standards: death.

"It is unusual to see a person who can claim that he once belonged to our beloved brotherhood," the red-haired man teased, his cultured voice dripping with sarcasm.

Again Bogo shifted, and he had to remind himself that this was Castle Trinity, his home, and that Aballister and Dorigen, for all their taunts, would look out for him.

"It was an unusual circumstance," the young wizard replied, revealing his nervousness with an uneasy flip of his stringy brown hair. "I had another calling, one that took me far from Westgate. As you can see, my departure has done us both some good. I have attained a level of power that you cannot comprehend, and you shall be paid well for doing me this one small task."

The huge man grinned, seeming to mock Bogo's claims of power, and looked to his puny companion, who seemed none too pleased by this whole business.

"Do sit with us," the large man bade Bogo. "I am Vander, the taskmaster for this small bit of business of which you speak. My associate is Ghost, a most unusual and talented man."

Bogo took a seat between the two, alternating his gaze to try to find clues about his untrusted associates.

"Is there a problem?" Vander asked him after studying Bogo's actions for a moment.

"No," Bogo blurted immediately. He forced himself to calm down. "I am just surprised that so many have been sent for so simple an execution," he admitted.

Vander laughed aloud, but then stopped abruptly, a curious expression crossing his face. His glower fell over Ghost as his body went into a series of convulsions, and then, to Bogo's amazement, Vander and his possessions began to grow.

The sword, huge to begin with, took on gigantic proportions, and the northern bear that comprised the fine cloak no longer seemed a cub. Because Vander was seated, Bogo couldn't tell just exactly how large the man became—at least ten feet tall, he guessed.

"Firbolg?" he asked as much as stated, recognizing the giant for what it was. Now Bogo was at a loss. Having a huge, red-haired man, so easily distinguishable, in the Night Masks, was stunning enough, but a firbolg?

Vander's angry glare did not relent. His dark eyes peered intently at Ghost from under his bushy brows. He regained his composure quickly, though, and rested back in his seat.

"Forgive me," he said unexpectedly to Bogo. "I am indeed of the race of giant-kin, though I do not openly reveal my more-than-human stature."

"Then why—?" Bogo began to ask.

"An indiscretion," Vander quickly interrupted, the tone of his deep voice indicating that he did not wish to continue.

Bogo wasn't about to argue with an eight-hundred-pound giant. He crossed his hands defensively over his lap and tried hard to appear relaxed.

"You question our number?" Vander asked, going back to the wizard's original inquiry.

"I did not expect so many," Bogo reiterated.

"The Night Masks take no chances," Vander replied evenly. "Often executions appearing so simple prove the most difficult. We do not make mistakes. That is why we are so well rewarded for our efforts." He cocked his giant head to one side—a curiously ungiantlike action, Bogo thought—and looked to the pouch on Bogo's rope belt.

Taking the cue, the young wizard pulled the bag of gold from his belt and handed it to Vander. "Half payment," he explained, "as was agreed to by your superiors."

"And by yours," Vander was quick to remark, not willing to give Bogo the upper hand, "a wizard named Aballister, I believe."

Bogo did not respond, did not confirm or deny the claim.

"And you will accompany us as a representative of Castle Trinity in this matter?" Vander stated as much as asked. "Another unusual circumstance."

"That, too, was agreed upon," Bogo replied firmly, though the way he continually moved his fingers defeated the conviction in his tone. "By both parties," he prudently added, "most likely because I was once a member of your guild and understand your ways."

Vander stifled his urge to deflate the pretentious young man's swelling ego. The giant knew that Aballister had paid a considerable amount of extra gold to get Bogo included, and that the young wizard's assignment had nothing to do with Bogo's past employment with the assassin band.

"I will journey to Carradoon beside you," Bogo continued, "to offer a full report to my sup—associates."

Vander smiled widely, catching the slip. "Whatever role you might play in the death of Cadderly does not change the sum owed the Night Masks," he said grimly.

Bogo nodded. "My role will be as observer, nothing more, unless, of course, you, as taskmaster, decide otherwise," he agreed. "Might I enquire of your own role?" Bogo paused. He knew he might be overstepping his bounds, but he could not let Vander have such an obvious advantage in their dealings. "It seems unlikely that a firbolg could parade through the streets of Carradoon. And what of the Ghost?"

"He is called Ghost, not 'the Ghost,' " Vander snapped.

"You would do well to remember that. My own role," he continued, mellowing a bit, "is none of your concern."

It struck Bogo as more than a little curious that Vander took more offense at his concerns for Ghost than for himself, particularly since Bogo had directly questioned the firbolg's value.

"Ghost will lead the way in, gather information, and prepare the target," Vander went on. "I have twenty skilled assassins at my disposal, so we will need to secure a base near, but not within, the walls of Carradoon."

Bogo nodded at the simple logic.

"We will leave in the morning, then," Vander continued. "Are you prepared?"

"Of course."

"Then our meeting is concluded," Vander stated abruptly, flatly, motioning to the door. Immediately the two black-robed sentries moved to each side of Bogo to escort him from the room.

Bogo looked back at the door many times as he made his way slowly down the corridor. A firbolg and a weakling? It seemed very unusual, but then, Bogo had been in the Night Masks only a day more than a month before he had begged to leave, and he had to admit, at least to himself, that he knew very little about the band's methods.

Bogo soon dismissed all thoughts of Vander and Ghost, concentrating instead on another meeting he had planned. At Aballister's request, Bogo would meet with Druzil to learn all he could about Cadderly and his cohorts. The imp had dealt with Cadderly on two occasions—both disastrous for Castle Trinity—and knew as much about him as anyone.

Bogo desperately wanted that knowledge. He was a bit dismayed that so many Night Masks had been assigned to this task, not because he wanted Cadderly to have a chance to escape, but because he wanted to be in on the action. More than anything else, Bogo Rath wanted to play a vital role in the kill, wanted to gain the respect of Aballister and, particularly, Dorigen.

He was tired of the taunts, of being referred to as Boygo. How would mighty Dorigen, who returned from Shilmista stripped of her valuable possessions and with her hands broken and swollen, feel when Bogo delivered the head of Aballister's troublesome son? Cadderly, after all, had been the source of Dorigen's humiliation.

Bogo dared to dream that he might ascend within Castle Trinity's hierarchy to become Aballister's second. Dorigen's hands were slow to heal; the fortress's clerics doubted that many of her fingers would ever straighten. Given that precise movements played a vital role in spell casting, who could guess the implications to Dorigen's power?

Bogo rubbed his soft hands together eagerly and sped off for the meeting room, to where Druzil, his guide to a better life, waited.

* * * * *

"How dare you do that to me!" the firbolg growled at his companion as soon as Bogo had gone. A nod from him sent the two guards scrambling from the room. The giant leaped from his seat and threateningly advanced a step.

"I did not know that my . . . that your . . . body's size would return to normal," the little man protested, trying to sink deeper into the cushions of his soft chair. "I believed the enchantment would last longer, at least through the meeting." The firbolg grabbed the little man by the collar and hoisted him into the air. "Ah, Vander," the giant purred, his features too calm, "dear Vander." The firbolg's face contorted suddenly in rage and he punched the little man in the face, destroying his nose. A backhand slap raised a welt on one cheek; a second slap did likewise on the other.

Then, with an evil grin, the firbolg grabbed the little man by one forearm and snapped his bone so severely that the man's fingers brushed against his elbow.

The beating went on for many minutes, and finally the firbolg dropped the barely conscious man back to his seat.

"If you ever deceive me so again . . ." the red-haired giant warned. "If ever again you humiliate me in front of one such as Bogo Rath, I will torment you until you beg for death!"

The smaller man, the real Vander, curled up in a fetal position, cradling his shattered arm, feeling terribly vulnerable and afraid trapped inside the puny body of the weakling, Ghost.

"I want my body back," Ghost said suddenly, tugging uncomfortably at his firbolg trappings. "You are so hairy and itchy!"

Vander sat up and nodded, eager to be back in his own form.

"Not now," Ghost growled at him. "Not until the wounds heal. I would not accept my body back in less than perfect condition," he said wryly. "As it was when I gave it to you."

Vander slumped back. This game had grown quite old over the last few years, but what options lay before him? He couldn't escape Ghost's evil clutches, couldn't resist the demands of Ghost's magic. Vander wanted nothing more than to get back into his firbolg form and pound the little man, but he knew that Ghost would simply initiate a switch back, and then Vander would feel the pain of his own attacks. Ghost would continue the beating, Vander knew, for hours sometimes, until poor Vander broke and wept openly, and begged his master to stop.

The trapped firbolg put a hand to his broken human nose. Already it was on the mend; the pain was no more and the blood flow had stopped. The broken forearm had straightened again and Vander could feel tingling as the bones knitted. Just a few more minutes, he thought to comfort himself, and I will have my body back, my own strong body.

"I will be leaving this hour," Ghost said to him. He pointed a threatening finger Vander's way. "Remember that you are my spirit-mate," he warned. "I can come back for you, just for you, Vander, from any distance, at any time."

Vander averted his eyes, unable to deny the threat. Once he had tried to flee this nightmare, had gotten all the way home to the Spine of the World Mountains, but Ghost, thousands of miles away, had found him and forced a body switch. Merely to show Vander the folly of his actions, Ghost mercilessly had slaughtered several of Vander's fellow firbolgs, including his brother, on a little-used mountain trail east of Mirabar. Vander vividly remembered the terrible moment when Ghost had given him back his body, holding his oldest son's left arm in his gigantic hand.

Vander had killed Ghost when he returned to Westgate, had nearly torn the little man's head from his shoulders, but, a week later, Ghost had walked into Vander's camp, smiling.

Vander came out of his contemplations and regarded his hated companion. Ghost towered above him, a black glove on one hand, a white one on the other, and wearing a familiar golden-edged mirror hanging on a golden chain around his neck.

At the clap of the firbolg's hands, Vander felt himself floating. His noncorporeal spirit looked back to the weak, drowsy form on the floor with contempt, then looked ahead to the giant receptacle. There came a flash of burning pain as Vander entered his firbolg body. His spirit twisted about and shifted to reconfigure itself to the proper form, to reorient Vander to his new coil.

Ghost had come out of the spirit-walk faster than Vander, as always, and was sitting comfortably in a chair, watching the firbolg intently, as Vander came back to consciousness.

The puny body now wore the gloves and mirror; the magic device always transferred with its master. As soon as it became obvious that Vander would not attack him, Ghost clenched his hands and closed his eyes. The gloves and mirror disappeared, but Vander knew from bitter and painful experience that they were well within immediate recall.

"You will depart as planned with the band and the young wizard," Ghost instructed.

"What of this Bogo Rath?" Vander asked. "I do not trust him."

"That is of no consequence," Ghost replied. "After all, you do not trust me, either, but I know you are enamored of my warm personality."

Vander wanted to smash the smug smile off Ghost's sleepy-eyed face.

"The wizard is to accompany us," Ghost instructed. "Aballister paid us handsomely to take Rath along, a fine cache of gold for so minor an inconvenience."

"To what purpose?" Vander had to ask, always amazed at the webs of seemingly pointless intrigue created by less than honorable people.

"Aballister believes that sending an emissary will keep him informed," Ghost replied. "The wizard has a weakness for knowledge. He cannot tolerate the occurrence of anything that affects him, directly or even indirectly, without his knowledge."

Vander did not disagree. He had met Aballister only once, and Ghost had spoken with the hollow-featured wizard no more than three times. But the firbolg didn't doubt Ghost's perceptions. The little man possessed an uncanny understanding of character, particularly of character flaws, and always found a way to use that to his advantage.

* * * * *

The young scholar blinked at the morning brightness, shining across Impresk Lake and through the windows of his room's balcony doors. Breakfast sat on the table next to Cadderly—extra portions, he noted, and he smiled. They were a bribe, Brennan's way of saying thank you for Cadderly's continued discretion. Fredegar wouldn't be happy with his son if he knew where Brennan had spent the evening.

Cadderly was indeed hungry, and the food looked good, but when the young scholar noticed the *Tome of Universal Harmony* sitting open on his desk by the window, he realized a more profound and demanding hunger. He took a single biscuit with him as he went to the desk.

Like so many times before, Cadderly devoured the pages, the blurred words, faster than his eyes could follow. He was through the tome in a matter of minutes, then turned it back over and began again, rushing, almost desperately, to keep the mysterious song flowing uninterrupted. How many times Cadderly went through the work that day, he could not know. When Brennan came in with his lunch, then his supper, he did not look up from his reading, from his listening to the song.

The daylight waned, and still Cadderly pored on. His first thought, when the room became too dark to read in, was to go and light his lamp, but he hated to waste the time that action would take. Hardly considering his actions, Cadderly recalled a page in the tome, a particular melody, and uttered a few simple words, and instantly the room was filled with light.

The stream of the song was broken. Cadderly sat blinking in amazement at what he had done. He retraced his mental steps, recalled that same page, its image clear in his mind. He uttered the chant again, changing his inflections and alternating two of the words.

The light went out.

Shaking, Cadderly slipped out of his chair and over to his bed. He threw an arm across his eyes, as though that act might hide the confusing memory of what had just occurred.

"I'll see the wizard in the morning," he whispered aloud. "He will understand."

Cadderly didn't believe a word of it, but he refused to listen to the truth.

"In the morning," he whispered again, as he sought the serenity of sleep.

The morning was many hours and many dreams away for the troubled young man.

*   *   *   *   *

Percival hopped up to the room's window—no, not the window, but the terrace doors. Cadderly considered the strange sight, for the squirrel's sheer size made the doors look more like a tiny window. It was Percival, Cadderly knew instinctively, but why was the squirrel six feet tall?

The white squirrel entered the room and came beside him. Cadderly extended his hand to pat the beast, but Percival recoiled, then rushed back in, his not-so-tiny paws ripping tears in the pouches on Cadderly's belt. Cadderly began to protest, but one of the pouches broke open, spilling a continual stream of cacasa nuts onto the floor.

Hundreds of cacasa nuts! Thousands of cacasa nuts! The gigantic squirrel eagerly stuffed them into his bulging mouth by the score and soon the floor was clear again.

"Where are you going?" Cadderly heard himself ask as the squirrel bounded away. The doors were closed again somehow, but the squirrel ran right through them, knocking them from their hinges. Then Percival hopped over the balcony railing and was gone.

Cadderly sat up in his bed—but it was not his bed, for he

was not in his room. Rather, he was lying in the inn's common room. It was very late, he knew, and very quiet.

Cadderly was not alone. He felt a ghostlike presence behind him. Mustering his courage, he spun about.

Then he cried out, the scream torn from his lungs by sheer desperation. There lay Headmaster Avery, Cadderly's mentor, his surrogate father spread across one of the room's small circular tables, his chest opened wide.

Cadderly didn't have to examine the man to know he was dead and that his heart had been torn out.

* * * * *

Cadderly sat up in his bed—and now it was indeed his bed. His room was quiet, except for the occasional rattling of the balcony doors, shivering in the night wind. A full moon was up, its silvery light dancing through the window, splaying shadows across the floor.

The serenity seemed hardly enough to chase away the dreams. Cadderly tried to recall that page in the tome again, tried to remember the chant, the spell, to bathe the room in light. He was weary and troubled and had not eaten all that day, and hardly at all the day before. The image of the page would not come, so he lay still, terrified, in the dim light.

There was only the quiet light of the moon.

Dawn was a long while away.

Five

Home Again

A steady stream of shouts led the way for Danica and the Bouldershoulder brothers as they walked the halls in the southern section of the Edificant Library's second floor. All three companions knew the source of the ruckus was Headmaster Avery even before they approached his office, and they knew, too, from whispers that had greeted them on their arrival, that Kierkan Rufo bore the brunt of the verbal assault.

"It is good that you have returned," came a voice to the side. Headmistress Pertelope strode toward the three. She smiled warmly and wore, as had become her norm, a full-length, long-sleeved gown and black gloves. Not an inch of skin peeked out below her neck, and, between the dark robes and the tightly cropped salt-and-pepper hair, her face seemed almost detached, floating in an empty background. "I'd feared you had lost your hearts to Shilmista—something perfectly reasonable," the headmistress said sincerely, with no hint of judgment in her perpetually calm tone.

"Ye're bats!" Ivan snorted, shaking his head vigorously. "An elfish place, and not for me liking."

Pikel kicked him in the shin, and the brothers glared long and hard at each other.

"Shilmista was wonderful," Danica admitted. "Especially when we sent the monsters in full flight. Already it seems as if the shadows have lightened in the elven wood."

Pertelope nodded and flashed her warm smile once more. "You are going to see Avery?" she stated as much as asked.

"It is our duty," Danica replied, "but he does not seem to be in a good mood this day."

"Rufo'd spoil anyone's day, by me reckoning," Ivan put in.

Again Pertelope nodded, and she managed a somewhat strained smile. "Kierkan Rufo's actions in the forest will not be easily forgotten," she explained. "The young priest has much to prove if he wishes to regain the favor of the headmasters, particularly Headmaster Avery."

"Good enough for him!" Ivan snorted.

"Oo oi!" Pikel added.

"I've heard that Rufo has already received some punishment," Pertelope continued wryly, looking pointedly at Danica's fist.

Danica unconsciously slipped her guilty hands behind her back. She couldn't deny that she had slugged Rufo, back in the forest when he was complaining about his companions' deficiencies. She also couldn't deny how much she had enjoyed dropping the blustering fool. Her actions had been rash, though, and probably not without consequence.

Pertelope sensed the young woman's discomfort and quickly moved on to a different subject. "When you are done talking with Headmaster Avery," she said to Danica, "do come and see me. We have much to discuss."

Danica knew that Pertelope was speaking of Cadderly, and she wanted to ask a hundred questions of the headmistress then and there. She only nodded, though, and remained silent, conscientious of her duty and knowing that her desires would have to wait.

The perceptive headmistress smiled knowingly and said, "Later," then gave the young woman a wink and walked on.

Danica watched her go, a thousand thoughts of Cadderly following kind Pertelope's every step. Ivan's tapping boot reminded her that she had other considerations, and she reluctantly turned back to the dwarves. "Are you two ready to face Avery?"

Ivan chuckled wickedly. "Not to worry," the dwarf assured her, grabbing her by the arm and leading her to the portly headmaster's office. "If the fat one gets outta line with ye, I'll threaten him with smaller portions at the dinner table. There's a measure of power from being a place's cook!"

Danica couldn't disagree, but that offered little comfort as she neared the door and heard more clearly the level of Avery's rage.

"Excuses!" the headmaster roared. "Always excuses! Why do you refuse to take responsibility for your actions?"

"I did not—" they heard Rufo begin meekly, but Avery promptly cut him off.

"You did!" the headmaster cried. "You betrayed them to that wretched imp—and more than once!" There came a pause, then Avery's voice sounded again, more composed. "Your actions after that were somewhat courageous, I will admit," he said, "but they do not excuse you. Do not presume for a moment that you are forgiven. Now, go to your tasks with the knowledge that any transgression, however minor, will cost you dearly!"

The door swung open and a haggard Rufo rushed out, seeming displeased to see Danica and the dwarves.

"Surprised?" Ivan asked him with a wide grin.

The angular man, tilting slightly, ran his fingers through his matted black hair. His dark eyes darted about as if in search of escape. With nowhere to go, Rufo shoved his way between Danica and Pikel and scurried away, obviously embarrassed.

"Yer day just got better, eh?" Ivan called after him, enjoying the tall man's torment.

"It took you a while to find your way to me," came a surly call from the room, turning the companions back to Avery.

"Uh-oh," muttered Pikel, but Ivan merely snorted and strode into the room, right up to Avery's oaken desk. Danica and Pikel came in a bit more hesitantly.

Avery's bluster seemed to have played itself out. The chubby man pulled a handkerchief from his pocket and rubbed it across his sweaty, blotchy face. "I did not believe you would come back," he said, huffing with labored breath. He alternated his glance from Ivan to Pikel. "I had even suggested to Dean Thobicus that we begin to search for new cooks."

"Not to worry," Ivan assured him with a bow that swept the dwarf's yellow beard across the floor. "The masters of yer belly have returned."

Pikel piped up in hearty agreement, but Avery's renewed glare showed he did not enjoy the boisterous dwarf's smug attitude.

"We will, of course, need a full report of your time in Shilmista—a written report," he said, shuffling some papers about on his large desk.

"I don't write," Ivan teased, "but I can cook ye a goblin ear stew. That'll fairly sum up me time in the wood." Even Danica couldn't bite back a chuckle at that.

"Lady Maupoissant will help you then," Avery said, articulating each word slowly to show them he was not amused.

"When will you need this?" Danica asked, hoping he would give her the whole winter. Her thoughts were on Carradoon, on Cadderly, and she was beginning to suspect that perhaps she should have continued through the mountains and gone straight to him.

"You are scheduled to meet with Dean Thobicus in three days," Avery informed her. "That should give you ample time—"

"Impossible," Danica said to him. "I will meet with the dean this day, or in the morning, perhaps, but—"

"Three days," Avery repeated. "The dean's schedule is not for you to manipulate, Lady Maupoissant." Again he used her surname, and Danica knew it was to emphasize his anger.

Danica felt trapped. "I am not of your order," she reminded the portly man. "I am under no obligation—"

Again Avery cut her short. "You will do as you are told," he said grimly. "Do not think your actions in Shilmista have been forgotten or forgiven."

Danica fell back a step; Ivan, as angry as he was confused, hopped to his toes and glowered at Avery.

"Huh?" was all that stunned Pikel could mutter.

"As I said," Avery declared, slamming a heavy fist on the desk. "You all played the role of hero, both in Shilmista and before that, when the evil priest and his insidious curse fell over the library, but that does not excuse your actions, Lady Maupoissant."

Danica wanted to scream "What actions?" but she couldn't get a sound past the mounting rage in her throat.

"You struck him," Avery finally explained. "You attacked Rufo, a priest of Deneir, a host of the Edificant Library, without provocation?"

"He had it coming," Ivan retorted.

Avery managed a bit of a smile. "Somehow, I do not doubt that," he agreed, for a moment seeming his old, likable self. "Yet there are rules concerning such behavior." He looked straight into Danica's brown eyes. "You might well be banned from the library for life if I were to pursue Rufo's charges.

"Think of it," Avery continued after giving Danica and the dwarves a moment to absorb his meaning. "All of your texts are here, all of the known works of Grandmaster Penpahg D'Ahn. I know how dear your studies are to you."

"Then why do you threaten me like this?" Danica snapped. She flipped a lock of her unkempt hair from in front of her face and crossed her arms before her. "If I erred in striking Rufo, then so be it, but if the same situation was repeated—if, after so many trials and so much killing, I had to listen to his endless whining and berating of me and my friends—I cannot honestly say that I would not punch him again."

"Oo oi!" Pikel readily agreed.

"Had it coming," Ivan said again.

Avery waved his hand in a patting motion to try to calm the three. "Agreed," he said, "and I assure you I have no intention of letting Rufo's accusations go beyond this point. But in exchange, I demand that you give me these few things I have asked. Prepare the report and meet with Thobicus in three days, as he desires. On my word, Rufo's accusations will never again be mentioned, to you or to anyone else."

Danica blew the stubborn strand of hair away from her face, an action Avery understood as a resigned sigh.

"Cadderly is all right, by all reports," the headmaster said quietly. Danica winced. Hearing the name aloud brought fears and painful recollections.

"He stays at the Dragon's Codpiece, a fine inn," Avery went on. "Fredegar, the innkeeper, is a friend, and he has looked after Cadderly, though that has not been difficult since our man rarely leaves his room."

The portly headmaster's obvious concern for Cadderly reminded Danica that Avery was no enemy—for her or for her love. She understood, too, that most of Avery's surly behavior could be attributed to the same fact that had been gnawing away at her: Cadderly had remained at the library only as long as it took to retrieve his possessions. Cadderly had not, and might not ever, come home.

"I leave for Carradoon this afternoon," Avery announced. "There is much business to be handled between the headmasters and the town's leaders. With this threat of war hanging over us and . . . well, worry not about it. You three have earned at least a few days of relaxation."

Again Danica understood the implication of the portly headmaster's words. Certainly there was business between the library and the town, but Danica thought it unlikely that Avery, whose duties were to preside over and guide the younger priests, would be chosen as the library's representative in town matters. Avery had volunteered to go, had insisted, Danica knew, and not because of any threat to the region. His business in Carradoon was an excuse to look in on Cadderly, the young man whom he loved as dearly as he would his own son.

Danica and the dwarves took their leave, the brothers protectively flanking Danica as they exited the room.

"Not to worry," Ivan said to Danica. "Me and me brother'll have to go to town soon anyway, to stock up for the winter. Get yer business and yer meeting done and we'll set off right after. It's not a long road to Carradoon, but 'tis better, in these times, that ye don't go down it alone."

Pikel nodded his agreement, then they parted, the dwarves heading down the stairs for the kitchen and Danica toward her room. Ivan and Pikel missed Cadderly, too, the young woman realized. She gave a flip of her strawberry-blonde hair, which now hung several inches below her shoulders, as though that symbolic act would allow her to put her troubles behind her for the moment. Like the stubborn hair that inevitably found its way back around to her face, though, Danica's fears did not stay away.

She desperately wanted to see Cadderly, to hold him and kiss him, but at the same time she feared that meeting. If the young scholar rejected her again, as he had in Shilmista, her life, even her dedication to her studies, would fail to have meaning.

* * * * *

"I did not see much," Danica admitted, adjusting her position on the edge of Headmistress Pertelope's cushioned bed. "I was guarding against the approaching battle. I knew Cadderly and Elbereth would be vulnerable while they cast their summons to the trees."

"But you are convinced that Cadderly played a role in that summoning?" Pertelope pressed, repeating the question for perhaps the fifth time. Pertelope sat near Danica and was clad in her usual modest garments. "It was not just the elf prince."

Danica shook her head. "I heard Cadderly's chant," she tried to explain. "There was something more to it, some underlying power . . ." She struggled to find the words, but how could she? What had happened back in Shilmista, when Cadderly and Elbereth had awakened the great oaks, had seemed almost miraculous to the young woman. And miracles, by definition, defied description.

"Cadderly told me he had played a role," a flustered Danica responded at last. "There was more to the summons than simply repeating the ancient words. He spoke of gathering energy, of a mindset that brought him into the trees' world before awakening them and coaxing them to ours."

Pertelope nodded slowly as she digested the words. She held no doubts about Danica's honesty, or about Cadderly's mysterious, budding power. "And the elf wizard's wound?" she prompted.

"By Elbereth's description, the spear had gone a foot or more into Tintagel's side," Danica replied. "So very much blood covered his clothing—I saw that much for myself—and Elbereth had not expected him to survive for more than a few moments longer. Yet when I saw him, just half an hour after he was wounded, he was nearly healed and casting spells at our enemies once more."

"You have seen spells of healing at the library," Pertelope said, trying to hide her excitement. "When the Oghman priest broke his arm in wrestling you, for example."

"Minor compared to the healing Cadderly did on Tintagel," Danica assured her. "By Elbereth's word, he held the wizard's belly in while the skin mended around his fingers!"

Pertelope nodded again and remained quiet for a long while. There was no need to go over it all again. Danica's recounting had been consistent and, Pertelope knew instinctively, honest. Her hazel eyes stared into emptiness for a time before she focused again on Danica.

The young monk sat quietly and very still, lost in her own contemplations. To Pertelope's eyes, a shadow appeared on Danica's shoulder, a silhouette of a tiny female, trembling and glancing nervously about. Extraordinary heat emanated from the young monk's body, and her breathing, steady to the casual observer, reflected her anxieties to Pertelope's knowing and probing gaze.

Danica was full of passion, yet full of fear, the headmistress knew. Merely thinking of Cadderly stirred a boiling turmoil within her.

Pertelope shook the insightful visions away, ended the distant song that played in the recesses of her mind, and put a comforting hand on Danica's shoulder. "Thank you for coming to sit with me," she said sincerely. "You have been a great help to me—and to Cadderly, do not doubt."

A confused look came over Danica. Pertelope hated that she had to be cryptic with someone so obviously attached to Cadderly, but she knew Danica would not understand the powers at work on the young priest. Those same powers had been with Pertelope for nearly a score of years, and Pertelope wasn't certain that even she understood them.

The bed creaked as Danica stood. "I have to go now," she explained, looking back to the small room's door. "If you wish, I can come back . . ."

"No need," the headmistress answered, offering a warm smile. "Unless you feel you would like to talk," she quickly added. Pertelope intensified her gaze again and bade the song begin, searching for that insightful, supernatural, level of perception. The trembling shadow remained upon Danica's shoulder, but it seemed calmer now, and the young monk's breathing had steadied.

The heat was still there, though, the vital energy of anticipated passion for this young woman, no more a girl. Even after Danica had departed, the door handle glowed softly from her touch.

Pertelope blew out a long sigh. She slipped one of her arm-length gloves off to scratch at the shark skin it hid and tried to recall her own trials when Deneir had selected her—had cursed her, she often believed.

Pertelope smiled at the dark thought. "No, not a curse," she said aloud, lifting her eyes toward the ceiling as though she were addressing a higher presence. She played the song more strongly in her mind, the universal harmony that she had heard a thousand times in the turning pages of the tome she had given to Cadderly. She fell into the song and followed its notes, gaining communion with her dearest god.

"So you have chosen Cadderly," she whispered.

She received no answer, and had expected none.

"He could not otherwise have accomplished all of those 'miracles' in the elven wood," Pertelope went on, speaking aloud her conclusions to bolster her suspicions. "I pity him, and yet I envy him, for he is young and strong, stronger than I ever was. How powerful will he become?"

Again, except for the continuing melody in Pertelope's head, there came no response.

That was why the headmistress often felt as though she had been cursed; there never were any answers granted. She had always had to discover them for herself.

And so, too, she knew, would Cadderly.

Six

A Beggar Man, A Thief

Cadderly purposely avoided looking at the guardsman as he moved through the short tunnel and under the raised portcullis leading out of the lakeside town. All along his route to the western gate the young scholar had observed people of every station and every demeanor, and the variety of shadowy images he had seen leaping from their shoulders had nearly overwhelmed him. Again the song of Deneir played in his thoughts, as though he had subconsciously summoned it, and again, *aurora* remained the only identifiable term. Cadderly could not make sense of it all; he feared that this new insight would drive him mad.

He grew more at ease when he had put the bustle of Carradoon behind him and was walking along the hedge- and tree-lined roads, with nothing more to attract his attention than the chatter of birds and the overhead rustle of squirrels gathering their winter stores.

"Is mine the curse of the hermits?" he asked himself aloud. "That it is!" he proclaimed loudly, startling a nearby

61

squirrel that had frozen in place on the camouflaging gray
bark of a tree. The rising volume of Cadderly's voice sent
the critter hop-skipping up the tree, where it froze again, not
even its bushy tail twitching.

"Well, it is," Cadderly cried to the rodent in feigned exas-
peration. "All those poor, wretched, solitary souls, so
frowned upon by the rest of us. They are not hermits by
choice. They possess this same vision that haunts me, and it
drives them mad, drives them to where they cannot bear the
sight of another intelligent thing."

Cadderly moved to the base of the tree to better view the
beast. "I see no shadows leaping from your shoulders, Mr.
Gray," he called. "You have no hidden desires, no cravings
beyond those you obviously seek to fill."

"Unless there be a lady squirrel about!" came a cry from
down the path. Cadderly nearly leaped out of his boots. He
spun about to see a large, dirty man dressed in ragged, ill-
fitting clothes and boots whose toes had long ago worn
away.

"A lady squirrel would get his mind from those nuts," the
stubble-faced man continued, advancing easily down the
road.

Cadderly unconsciously brought his ram-headed walking
stick up in front of him. Thieves were common on the roads
close to the town, especially in this season, with winter fast
approaching.

"But, then . . ." the large man continued, putting a finger
upon his lower lip in a contemplative gesture. Cadderly
noted that he wore mismatched fingerless gloves, one
black, one brown leather. "If the lady was about, the squirrel would still have no 'hidden desires,' since the unabashed
beast would seek to fill whatever his heart deemed necessary, the call of his belly or the call of his loins.

"I'd be one to choose the loins, eh?" the dirty man said
with a lascivious wink.

Cadderly blushed slightly and nearly laughed aloud, though he still hadn't figured out what to make of this well-spoken vagabond, and he still wasn't comfortable near the dirty man. He peered closer, trying to find a revealing shadow on the man's shoulders. But Cadderly's surprise had stolen the song fully, and nothing rested there, except the badly worn folds of an old woolen scarf.

"It is a fine day to be about, talking to the beasts," the man went on, seeing no response forthcoming from Cadderly. "A pity, then, that I must get myself inside the gates of Carradoon, in the realm of smells more unpleasant, where high buildings hide the panorama of beauty so easily taken for granted on this most lovely of country roads."

"You will not easily pass by the guards," Cadderly remarked, knowing how carefully the city militiamen were protecting their home, especially with rumors of war brewing.

The vagabond opened a small pouch on the side of his rope belt and produced a single silver coin.

"A bribe?" Cadderly asked.

"Admission," the beggar corrected. "'One must spend gold'—or silver, as the case may be—'to make gold,' goes the old saying. I will accept the lore as true, since I know I will indeed secure some gold once I am within the town's wall."

Cadderly studied the man more closely. He wore no insignia of any lawful guild, showed no signs of any money-making talents whatsoever. "A thief," he stated flatly.

"Never," the man asserted.

"A beggar?" Cadderly asked, this word coming out with the same obvious venom.

The larger man clutched his chest and staggered back several steps, as though Cadderly had launched a dagger into his heart.

Now Cadderly did notice some shadows. He caught the

flicker of a pained look beneath the man's sarcastic, playful facade. He saw a woman on one shoulder, holding a small child, and an older child on the man's other shoulder. The images were gone in an instant, and Cadderly noticed for the first time that the man had a slight limp and a blue-green bruise on his wrist just above the edge of the brown glove.

Waves of nausea nearly overwhelmed the young scholar; as he focused his senses, he felt the emanations of the disease clearly and knew beyond doubt why this intelligent, articulate man had sunk to his lowly station.

He was a leper.

"M-my pardon," Cadderly stammered. "I did not know . . ."

"Does anyone . . . ever?" the large man asked, in a snarling voice. "I do not appreciate your pity, young priest of Deneir, but I'll gladly accept your pittance."

Cadderly clenched his walking stick tightly, mistaking the remark as a threat.

"You know of what I speak," the beggar man said to him, "the coins you inevitably will throw my way to alleviate your guilt."

Cadderly winced at the biting remark, but couldn't deny his pity that one so intelligent had sunk so low. He was surprised, too, that the beggar had discerned his order, even though he wore his holy symbol prominently on the front of his wide-brimmed hat. The large man studied Cadderly intently as the tumult of emotions rolled through the young priest.

"Pig," the man said with a sneer, to Cadderly's surprise. "How terrible that one such as I should have sunk to the level of a street beggar!"

Cadderly bit his lip in the face of such dramatics.

"To wallow in the mud beside the wretches," the man continued, throwing one arm out wide, the other still clutching at his mock-wounded chest.

He stopped suddenly in that pose and turned a confused expression Cadderly's way. "Wretches?" he asked. "What do you know of them, arrogant priest? You, who are so intelligent—that is the weal of your order, is it not?

"Intelligence." The beggar spat with distaste. "An excuse, I say, for those such as you. It is what separates you, what elevates you." He eyed Cadderly dangerously and finished, deliberately, "It is what blinds you."

"I do not deserve this!" Cadderly declared.

The man threw his hands above his head and blurted a mocking, incredulous shout. "Deserve?" he cried. He jerked the sleeve up on one arm, revealing a row of rotting, bruised skin.

"Deserve?" he asked again. "What, pray tell me, young priest who is so wise, do those kneeling before, and crawling from, the alleys of Carradoon deserve?"

Cadderly thought he would burst apart. He felt an angry energy building within him, gathering explosive strength. He remembered when he had awakened the trees in Shilmista, and when he had healed Tintagel, had held the elf wizard's guts in while a similar energy had mended the garish wound. A page from the *Tome of Universal Harmony* flashed in Cadderly's head, as clearly as if he held the open book before him, and he knew then the object of his rage. He eyed the bruises on the large man's arm, filled his nostrils with the stench of the disease that had so tormented this undeserving man's soul.

"*Pieta pieta, dominus* . . ." Cadderly began, reciting the chant as he read the words from the clear image in his mind.

"No!" the large man cried, charging ahead. Cadderly halted the chant and tried to throw up his arms to block, but the man was surprisingly fast and balanced for one so tall, and he caught hold of Cadderly's clothing and shook the young priest thoroughly.

Cadderly saw an opening, could have jammed his walking stick up under the man's chin. He knew, though, that the frustrated beggar meant him no real harm, and he was not surprised when the man released him, shoving him back a step.

"I could cure you!" Cadderly growled.

"Could you?" the man mocked. "And could you cure them?" he cried, waggling a finger toward the distant town. "Could you cure them all? Are all the world's ills to fall before this young priest of Deneir? Call to the wretched, I say!" the beggar cried, whirling about and shouting to the four winds. "Line them up before this . . . this . . ." He searched for the word, his dirty lips moving silently. "This godsend!" he cried at last.

A nearby squirrel broke into a dead run along the branches across the path.

"I do not deserve this," Cadderly said again, calmly.

His tone seemed infectious, for the large man dropped his hands to his sides immediately and his shoulders visibly slumped.

"No," the leper agreed, "but accept it, I pray you, as but a small penance in a world filled with undeserved penance."

Cadderly blinked away the moisture that suddenly came into his gray eyes. "What are their names?" he asked quietly.

The beggar looked at him curiously for a moment, then his lips curled up in his first sincere smile. "Jhanine, my wife," he answered. "Toby, my son, and Millinea, my young daughter. None have shown signs of my infection as yet," he explained, guessing Cadderly's unspoken question. "I see them rarely—to deliver the pittance I have gained from the guilty arrogants of Carradoon."

The beggar chuckled, seeing Cadderly's blush. "My pardon," he said, dipping into a low bow. "I, too, am sometimes blind, seeing the well and fortunate in a similar light."

Cadderly nodded his acceptance of that inevitable—and excusable—fault. "What is your name?"

"Nameless," the beggar answered without hesitation. "Yes, that is a good name for one such as me. Nameless akin to all the other Namelesses huddled in the squalor between the towers of the wealthy."

"You hold such self-pity?" Cadderly asked.

"Self-truth," Nameless answered immediately.

Cadderly conceded the point. "I could cure you," the young priest said again.

Nameless shrugged his shoulders. "Others have tried," he explained, "priests from your own order, and those of Oghma as well. I went to the Edificant Library—of course I went to the library—when the signs first appeared."

The mention of the Edificant Library brought an unconscious frown to Cadderly's face. "I am not like the others," he asserted more forcefully than he had intended.

The beggar smiled. "No, you're not," he agreed.

"Then you will accept my aid?"

Nameless did not relinquish his smile. "I will . . . consider it," he replied quietly. Cadderly caught an unmistakable glimmer of hope in his dark brown eyes, and saw a shadow appear atop the man's shoulder, a shadow of the beggar himself, gaily tossing a small form—Millinea, he somehow knew—into the air and catching her. The shadow fell apart quickly, dissipating in the wind.

Cadderly nodded somewhat grimly, suspecting the dangers of false hopes for one in this man's position. Suspecting the risks, but not truly understanding them, Cadderly now knew, for he was not, for all his sympathy, standing in the beggar man's holey shoes.

The young priest tore the pouch from his belt. "Then accept this," he said forcefully, tossing it to the large man.

Nameless caught it and eyed Cadderly curiously, but made no move to return the coin-filled purse. Here was an offering holding no false hopes, Cadderly understood, an offering of face value and nothing more.

"I am one of those arrogants," Cadderly explained, "guilty, as you have accused."

"And this will alleviate that guilt?" the beggar man asked, his eyes narrowing.

Cadderly couldn't hold back his chuckle. "Hardly," he replied, and he knew that if Nameless believed the purse would alleviate his guilt, then Nameless would have thrown it back at him. "Hardly a proper penance. I give it to you because you, and Jhanine, Toby, and Millinea, are more *deserving* of it than I, not for any lessening of the guilt. That guilt I must carry until I have learned better." Cadderly cocked his head to the side as a thought came to him.

"Call the gold a tutor's fee if that helps you to lessen your own guilt for waylaying one as innocent as me!" he said.

The beggar man laughed and bowed low. "Indeed, young priest, you are not like those of your order who greeted me at the library's great door, those who were more concerned with their own failings to cure me than with the consequences of my ailment."

That is why they failed, Cadderly knew, but he did not interrupt.

"It is a fine day!" Nameless went on. "And I pray you enjoy it." He held up the purse and shook it. His whole body shaking in a joyful dance, he smiled at the loud jingle of coins. "Perhaps I will as well. To the Nine Hells with Carradoon's stinking alleys this day!"

Nameless stopped his dance abruptly and stood stock-still, eyeing Cadderly gravely. Slowly, he extended his right hand, seemingly conscious, for the first time, of his dirty, fingerless glove.

Cadderly understood the action as a test, a test he was glad he could pass so easily. Without a thought for superstitious consequences, the young priest accepted the handshake.

"I pass by here often," Cadderly said quietly. "Consider my offer of healing."

The beggar man, too touched to reply verbally, nodded sincerely. He turned about and walked briskly away, his limp more pronounced, as though he no longer cared to hide it. Cadderly watched him for few moments, then turned and continued away from Carradoon. He smiled as more squirrels scrabbled overhead, but he hardly looked up to see them.

It seemed to the young priest that the day had grown finer and less fine at the same time.

* * * * *

Nameless smiled as a squirrel nearly lost its balance on a small branch, catching hold and righting itself at the last moment. The beggar man tried to use that simple, natural movement as a symbol of what had just transpired between him and the curious young priest, viewing himself as the branch and Cadderly as the creature righting its course. The thought made the leper feel good, valuable, for the first time in a long, long while.

He couldn't brood on it, though, and could hardly hope to meet enough people like this curious Cadderly, who would care to see their arrogance laid out before them. No, Nameless would have to continue as he had for more than a year, struggling daily to gain enough trinkets to keep his wife and children from starving.

He had at least a temporary reprieve. He tossed the purse into the air, caught it gingerly, and smiled again. It was indeed a fine day!

Nameless spun about, prepared to pay Jhanine and the children a long overdue visit, but his smile fast became a frown.

"So sorry to startle you, good friend," said a puny man, his drooping, thick eyelids open only enough for Nameless to make out his small, dark eyes.

Nameless instinctively moved the coin-filled pouch out of sight and kept his arms in front of him.

"I am a leper," he growled, using his disease as a threat.

The smaller man chuckled and gave a wheezing laugh that sounded more like a cough. "You think me a thief?" he asked, holding his hands out wide. Nameless blinked at the man's curious gloves, one white, the other black. "As you can see, I carry no weapons," the little man assured.

"None openly," Nameless admitted.

"I see we both wear a mixed set of gloves," Ghost remarked. "Kindred spirits, eh?"

Nameless slipped his hands under the folds of his badly fitting clothes, embarrassed for some reason he did not understand. Kindred spirits? he thought. Hardly. The fine gloves this little man wore, matched or not, must have cost more than Nameless had seen in many months, the young priest's pouch included.

"But we are," Ghost asserted, noticing the frown.

"You are a beggar, then?" Nameless dared to ask. "Carradoon is but a mile down the road. I was going there myself. The take is always good."

"But the young priest changed your mind?" the stranger asked. "Do tell me about that one."

Nameless shrugged and shook his head slightly, hardly conscious of the movement. Ghost caught it, though, and the beggar man's confusion told the wicked man much.

"Ah," Ghost said, his arms still wide, "you do not know young Cadderly."

"You do?"

"Of course," Ghost replied, motioning to the pouch Nameless tried to hide. "Shouldn't all those of our ilk know one as generous as Cadderly?"

"Then you are a beggar," Nameless reasoned, relaxing a bit. There was an unspoken code among the people of squalor, an implied brotherhood.

"Perhaps," Ghost answered cryptically. "I have been many things, but now I am a beggar man." He wheezed another chuckle. "Or soon I will be," he corrected. Nameless watched as the man unbuttoned the top of his surcoat and pulled the woolen folds aside.

"A mirror?" the beggar man muttered, then he said no more, transfixed by his own image in the silvery device.

Nameless felt the intrusion. He tried to pull away, but could not, held firmly by the strange magic. He saw nothing except for his own image, lined in black as though he had been transported to some other place, some dark, otherworldly place. Nameless tried desperately to look around at his surroundings, tried to make sense of them, find some familiarity.

He saw only his image.

He heard a clap, then he was moving, or he felt as though he was moving, even though he knew that his physical body had not stirred in the least. There came a brief, sharp pain as his spirit exited his body and floated helplessly toward the effeminate vessel that awaited it.

The pain came again.

Nameless blinked, consciously fighting against the heavy droop of his eyelids. He saw his own beggar's image again, wearing gloves, black and white. His confusion lasted only until he realized that it was no longer a reflected image he saw, but his own body.

"What have you done to me?" the beggar man cried, reaching for the stranger in his body. Every movement seemed to drag; his arms had little strength to convey his fury.

Ghost snapped his fingers, and the black and white gloves disappeared, leaving his newly acquired hands half exposed in the fingerless gloves. Half-heartedly, he pushed the weakling back. How useful that lax body had proven to Ghost. How benign and unthreatening, a body that even a young boy could defeat. With an almost resigned shrug, he advanced on the whimpering and sorely confused wretch and wrapped his dirty hands about the skinny neck.

Nameless fought desperately, as desperately as Ghost's puny form had ever battled, but there was no strength in his arms, no power to loosen the larger attacker's hold. Soon he stopped struggling, and Ghost knew the beggar's resignation was founded in grief for those he would leave behind.

The wicked man contemplated the change with amusement, thinking it curious, even humorous, that one as obviously wretched as this leprous beggar would lament the end of his life.

There was no mercy in Ghost, though. He had killed this body a hundred times, perhaps, and had killed his previous body a like number, and the body he had used before that as well.

The corpse slumped to the ground. Ghost immediately brought back his magical device and called upon its powers to watch the beggar man's spirit step out of the slain form. Ghost quickly pulled off the fine black glove and placed it on his unoccupied body. He closed his eyes and stiffened his resolve against the ensuing pain, for the simple act had transferred a part of his own spirit back into the corpse.

It was a necessary step for two reasons. The body would heal—Ghost had a powerful magical item concealed in one boot to see to that—and if the receptacle remained open, then the beggar man's spirit would find its way back in. Also, if Ghost allowed the body to die, if he allowed the item in his boot to call back a spirit, the item's regenerative powers would partially consume the form. Considering how many times Ghost had made this switch, the item would have burned up the puny form long ago.

But that wouldn't happen. Ghost knew how to use the items in conjunction; the *Ghearufu*, the glove-and-mirror

device, had long ago shown him the way, and he had spent
three lifetimes perfecting the act.

Ghost looked both ways along the empty road, then
pulled the slender body far from the trail, into some covering brush. He felt the disease in this new form that he had
taken. It was an unpleasant sensation, but Ghost took heart
that he would not wear this disguise for long—just long
enough to meet this young Cadderly for himself.

He hopped back out to the road and wandered along,
wondering how much of the day he would have to watch
pass him by before young Cadderly returned down the
road.

After the thief in the beggar's body had departed, Nameless's spirit stood beside the puny corpse, confused and
helpless. If Cadderly, with his new insight, had gazed upon
the spirit then, he would have seen the shadows of Jhanine,
Toby, and Millinea scattering to the four winds, fading like
the images of hope that Nameless had never dared to sustain.

Seven

The Maze

Cadderly approached the steep-sided, round hillock and the tower of Belisarius tentatively, fully expecting that the wizard, as knowledgeable as he was, would offer him little insight into the strange things that had been happening to him. Actually, Cadderly had no idea if the wizard would grant him an audience. He had done some valuable penning for Belisarius on several occasions, but he couldn't really call the man a friend. Furthermore, Cadderly wasn't sure that Belisarius would be home.

The young scholar relaxed a bit when a wide line up the nearly seventy-degree incline transformed from unremarkable grass to a stone stairway with flat and even steps. The wizard was home and apparently had seen Cadderly coming.

Seventy-five steps brought Cadderly to the hillock's flat top and the cobblestone walkway that encircled the tower. Cadderly had to walk nearly halfway around the base, for

Belisarius had placed his steps far to the side of the entrance this day. The steps never appeared on the same spot on the hillock, and Cadderly hadn't yet figured out if the wizard created new steps each time, had some way of rotating the grassy knoll under the stationary tower, or simply deceived visitors of the steps' actual location. Cadderly thought the last possibility, deception, the most likely, since Belisarius used his magic primarily for elaborate illusions.

The tower's iron-bound door swung open as Cadderly approached (or had it been open all along, only appearing to be closed? Cadderly mused). Cadderly paused as he started over the threshold, for there came the sound of grating stone and an entire section of the stone wall in the foyer shifted and swung out, blocking the inner entry door and revealing a cobwebbed stairway winding down into the blackness.

Cadderly scratched the stubble on his chin, his gray eyes flashing inquisitively at the unexpected invitation. He remembered the days when he had come to the tower with Headmaster Avery. Every time, the skilled wizard presented the duo with a new test of cunning. Cadderly was glad for the diversion, glad that Belisarius had apparently come up with something new, something that might take the young man's mind from the disturbing questions the beggar man had raised.

"This is a new path, and a new trick," Cadderly said aloud, congratulating the wizard, who was no doubt listening. Always curious, the young scholar promptly pulled a torch from its sconce on the foyer wall and started down. Twenty spiraling steps later, he came to a low corridor ending at a thick wooden door. Cadderly carefully studied the portal for a long moment, then slowly placed his hand against it, feeling the solidity of its grain. Satisfied that it was real, he pushed it open and continued on, finding another descending stairway behind it.

The next level proved a bit more confusing. The stairway ended in a three-way intersection of similar, unremarkable stone passageways. Cadderly took a step straight ahead, then changed his mind and went to the left, passing through another door (after repeating his pause and study test), then another after that. Again he had entered an intersection, this one much more confusing, since each of the ways revealed many side passages, both left and right. Cadderly nearly laughed aloud and he silently congratulated the clever wizard. With a helpless shrug, he let his walking stick fall to the floor, then followed the path determined by the unseeing gaze of the carved ram's head. Any way seemed as good as another as the young priest moved along, left, and then right, right again, and then straight ahead. Three more doors were left open behind him; one passage sloped down at a noticeable angle.

"Excellent!" Cadderly exclaimed when he passed a sharp corner, and found himself back where he had started, at the bottom of the second stairway. His torch was beginning to burn low, but the curious young priest pressed ahead once more, consciously selecting different avenues than on his first time through.

The torch burned away, leaving Cadderly in utter blackness. Calmly he closed his eyes and recalled a page in the *Tome of Universal Harmony*. He heard a few notes of Deneir's endless song and muttered the appropriate chant, pointing to the tip of his burned-out torch. He blinked many times and squinted against the glare as the magical light came on, much brighter than the flickering torch flame had been. When his eyes at last adjusted, he went on, turning corner after corner.

A scuffling, scraping sound made him pause. It was no rat, Cadderly knew; the animal, if it was an animal, that had made the sound was much larger.

An image of a bull came into Cadderly's thoughts. He

recalled a day as a youngster, out with Headmaster Avery, when he had passed a pasture full of cows. At least, Avery had thought they were cows. Cadderly couldn't help but smile when he remembered the image of portly Avery huffing and puffing in full flight from an angry bull.

The scuffling came again.

Cadderly considered extinguishing his magical light, but reconsidered immediately, realizing the predicament that act would leave him in. He crept up to the next corner, took off his wide-brimmed hat, and slowly peeked around.

The scuffler was humanoid, but certainly not human. It towered seven feet tall, shoulders and chest wide and impossibly strong, and its head—no mask, Cadderly knew—resembled the bull in that long-ago field. Wearing only a wolf pelt loincloth, the creature carried no weapon, though that hardly brought a sense of relief to the minimally armed young scholar.

A minotaur! Cadderly's heart nearly failed him. Suddenly he wasn't so sure that this whole trek through the tower's catacombs was inspired by Belisarius. It occurred to Cadderly that something pernicious might have happened to the congenial mage, that some dark force might have overcome the tower's formidable defenses.

His thoughts were blown away, along with his breath, a moment later, as the bull-headed giant scraped one foot on the stone again and charged, slamming into Cadderly and launching him across the corridor. He cracked his shoulder blade as he smashed into the stone, and his torch flew away, though of course the magical light did not diminish.

The minotaur snorted and stormed in. Cadderly took up his walking stick defensively, wondering what in the Nine Hells the minuscule weapon could do against this awesome beast. The minotaur seemed none too concerned with it, striding right in to meet its foe.

Cadderly swung with all his might, but the skinny club broke apart as he connected on the brute's thick-skinned chest.

The minotaur slapped him once, then leaned its horned head in, squashing Cadderly against the stone. The young man freed one arm and punched the beast, to no avail. The beast pressed more forcefully and Cadderly could neither squirm nor breathe.

His estimate of how long he had to live shortened considerably when the minotaur opened its huge mouth, putting its formidable teeth in line with Cadderly's exposed neck.

In that split second, the young priest recognized the fields of energy floating about him. He looked down to the floor, to his unbroken walking stick.

Cadderly jammed his free arm into the gaping maw, and plunged his hand down the minotaur's throat. A moment later, he retracted the hand, holding the bull-headed monster's beating heart. The creature fell back a step, not daring to do anything at all.

"I have traveled down two stairways, which actually went up," Cadderly announced firmly. "And through six doors, two of which were illusionary. That would put me in the west wing of your library, would it not, good Belisarius?"

The illusionary minotaur disappeared, but, strangely, Cadderly still held the pumping heart. The scene reverted to its true form, the west wing, as Cadderly had guessed, and Belisarius, a confused, almost frightened look on his bushy-browed, bearded face, stood across the room, leaning heavily on a bookcase.

Cadderly winked at him, then opened his mouth and moved as though to take a bite of the thing in his hand.

"Oh, you!" the wizard cried. He turned away and put a hand to his mouth, trying to keep his stomach's contents down. "Oh, do not! I beg, do not!"

Cadderly dismissed the gruesome image, willed it away, though he was not certain how he had brought it into being in the first place.

"How?" the wizard gasped, finally composed.

"My magic has shifted recently," Cadderly tried to explain, "grown."

"That is no clerical magic I have ever heard of," Belisarius insisted. "To create such perfect illusions . . ." Just the words made the wizard picture the heart, and he gagged yet again.

Cadderly understood something that Belisarius apparently did not. "I did not create the image," the young scholar explained, as much to himself as to the wizard, "nor did I collect the magical forces necessary to create the image."

The wizard dismissed any remaining revulsion, too intrigued by what Cadderly was hinting at. He moved quietly across the room toward the young priest.

"I saw the energies gathered," Cadderly went on. "I discovered the trick for what it was and . . . perverted . . . your grand imagery."

"Couldn't you have dispelled it altogether, as most priests would have?" Belisarius asked dryly.

Cadderly shrugged. "I thought I had," he replied with a wry smile, "in a grand fashion befitting your illusions."

Belisarius tipped his floppy woolen cap to the young priest.

"But I am not sure," Cadderly admitted. "Actually, I am not sure of much where my magic is concerned, and that is why I have returned."

Belisarius led the young man to the adjoining sitting room where they both nestled into comfortable chairs. The wizard produced four items—three rings and a slender wand—that Cadderly had given him three weeks before, and laid them aside, anxious to hear Cadderly's revelations.

It took Cadderly a while to begin his many tales—so much had happened to him! Once he began, though, he went on and on, covering every minute detail. He told Belisarius about summoning Shilmista's trees, about healing Tintagel, and about watching the gallant horse Temmerisa's spirit depart. Then he spoke of the more specific and recent incidents, of creating light and then darkness in his room and in Belisarius's maze. Most disturbing of all to the young priest were the shadowy images he had seen dancing atop shoulders. Cadderly said nothing immediately about his dreams, though, not quite certain of how they fit into anything, and also a bit afraid of what they might reveal.

"The spells you speak of are not so unusual to one of priestly magic," the wizard said when the obviously exasperated young man had finished his worrisome tale. "Many can be duplicated by a wizard as well, such as the manipulation of light. As for the shadows, well, clerics have been able to determine the general weal of individuals for centuries."

"Aurora," Cadderly replied, speaking the one word he had been able to decipher from that particular chant. "I do not understand how 'the dawn' would affect such a spell."

Belisarius scratched his graying beard. "That is unusual," he said at length. "But is 'the dawn' the only meaning of the word? When was this wondrous tome penned?"

Cadderly thought for a moment, then had his answer. "Aurora," he said firmly, "aura." He looked up to the wizard and smiled widely.

"Aurora means aura," Belisarius agreed, "or at least it used to, referring to the emanation of light, of good, surrounding an individual. There you have it, then, a clerical spell to be sure. Perhaps that is what has happened to you, only you have not yet learned to interpret what you see."

Cadderly nodded, though he did not really agree. He certainly knew how to—or *felt* how to—interpret the dancing and fleeting shadows; that was not the problem.

"I have witnessed extreme examples of clerical magic," Cadderly replied, "but these powers, I fear, are different. I do not study the spells before I call on them, as do the priests at the library. I make no preparations at all—as with the illusion that I defeated before your eyes. I did not expect you to challenge me so. I was not even expecting you to know I had come to visit."

Cadderly had to pause for a long moment to compose himself, and during the silence, Belisarius mumbled almost constantly under his breath and scratched at his bushy beard.

"You know something," Cadderly declared, his words sounding like an accusation.

"I suspect something," Belisarius replied. "Since the Time of Troubles, there have been increasing reports of individuals with internal magical powers."

"Psionics," Cadderly said immediately.

"You have heard of them, then," the wizard said. He threw his wiry arms out wide in heightened resignation. "Of course you have," he muttered. "You have heard of everything. That is what is so very frustrating about dealing with you."

The dramatics pulled a smile out of Cadderly and allowed him to relax back in the comfortable leather seat.

Belisarius seemed truly intrigued, as though he desperately hoped his guess was correct. "Might you be a psionicist?" he asked.

"I know little about them," the young priest admitted. "If that is what is happening to me, then it is happening without my assistance or approval."

"The powers are not so different from those of a wizard," Belisarius explained, "except that they come from the individual's mind and not the external powers of the universe. I am well acquainted with your mental abilities." He snickered, obviously referring to his spell book, which Cadderly had replaced from memory alone. "That type of prowess is the prime element of a psionicist's power."

Cadderly considered the words and gradually began to shake his head. "The power I manipulated in this tower was external," he reasoned. "Could psionics interact so with a wizard's spell?"

Belisarius patted a knobby finger against his lower lip, his frown revealing the snag in the logic. "I do not know," he admitted. The two sat quietly, digesting the details of their conversation.

"It does not fit," Cadderly announced a moment later. "I am the receptacle of the power and the transmuter of the power to the desired effect, of that much I am sure."

"I will not argue," Belisarius replied, "but such power must have a conduit—a spell, if you will. One cannot simply tap into the external energies of the universe on a whim!"

Cadderly understood the growing excitement in the wizard's voice. If Belisarius was wrong, then the wizard's entire life, his hermitlike devotion to his magical studies, might be revealed as an exercise in futility.

"The song," Cadderly muttered, suddenly realizing the truth of it all.

"Song?"

"The *Tome of Universal Harmony*," the young priest explained. "The book of Deneir. Whenever I have used the powers, even unconsciously, as with the dancing shadows, I have heard the song of that book in the recesses of my mind. My answers are in that song."

"Song of the book?" Belisarius could not begin to understand.

"The rhythm of the words," Cadderly tried to explain, though he knew he could not, not really.

Belisarius shrugged and seemed to accept the simple explanation. "Then you have found your conduit," he said, "but I fear there is little I can tell you concerning it. This book would seem to be more a matter to take up with the headmasters at the Edificant Library."

"Or with my deity," Cadderly mumbled.

Belisarius shrugged noncommittally. "As you will," he said. "I can tell you this much, though, and I know I am right simply by looking at your haggard features."

"I have not been sleeping well," Cadderly promptly put in, fearing what the wizard would say.

"Magic, the transference of such energies," Belisarius went on, undeflected by Cadderly's announcement, "exacts a toll on the practitioner. We wizards are very careful not to exceed our limitations. Normally we could not anyway, since the memorization of any spell is when those limits are revealed.

"Likewise, a cleric's granted powers stem from his or her faith and are tempered by agents of the gods, or even by the gods themselves where the high priests are sometimes concerned," Belisarius reasoned. "I warn you, young Cadderly, I have seen foolish mages consumed when trying to cast the spells of those more powerful than they, spells beyond their abilities. If you have found a way to avoid the normal boundaries and limitations of magic use, whatever type of magic might be involved, then I pray you will find the wisdom to moderate your activities, else it will consume you."

A thousand possibilities began their progression through Cadderly's thoughts. Perhaps he should go back to the library with his dilemma. He could speak to Pertelope . . .

"Now for some items that I know more about," Belisarius said. The wizard reached for the rings and the wand. He first held up a signet ring inscribed with the trident-and-bottle design of Castle Trinity. It once had belonged to the evil mage Dorigen.

"There is no detectable magic in this, as you believed," the wizard said, tossing it to Cadderly.

"I know," Cadderly said, as he caught it and put it into his pouch.

The declaration made Belisarius pause and consider the young man. "This ring," he said slowly, holding up the gold band set with a large onyx stone, "is indeed magical, and powerful."

"It evokes a line of flame," Cadderly said, "when the possessor utters '*Fete*,' the elven word for fire. I have seen it in use," the young priest added quickly, noticing Belisarius's deepening frown.

"Indeed," muttered the wizard. "And have you ever heard of a wizard named Agannazzar?"

Belisarius smiled as Cadderly shook his head. "He is a mage of no large fame born two centuries ago," the wizard explained.

"Now dead," Cadderly reasoned.

"Perhaps," Belisarius said wryly, flashing a wink. "One can never be certain where wizards are concerned."

"And was this his ring?" Cadderly asked.

"I cannot be sure," Belisarius replied. "Either he or one of his associates created it with this specific power imbued. It is not too powerful, but you may find it useful." He tossed it to Cadderly and took up the wand. The young priest suspected that Belisarius had purposely saved the remaining ring for last.

"This is a common device," the wizard began, but Cadderly stopped him with an upraised hand. At first the wand seemed an unremarkable, slender shaft of black wood just over a foot long, but, as he looked at it, Cadderly heard the notes of a distant song playing in his mind.

Cadderly studied deeper, sensed, and then saw clearly, the magic of the item.

"Light," he said to the wizard. "The wand's power has to do with the manipulation of illumination."

Belisarius frowned again and looked at the wand, as if ensuring that there were no runes visibly etched on its smooth side. "You have seen it in use?" the wizard asked hopefully, already tired of being upstaged.

"No," Cadderly said absently, not releasing his attention from the revelations. In his mind, he saw lights forming different images and dancing about.

"*Domin illu*," he muttered. The light he pictured became constant and of the same intensity as the light he had conjured in his room and in the maze.

"*Illu*," an arcane word for light, escaped his trembling lips. The light intensified, brightened to where Cadderly squinted against the glare in his mind.

"*Mas illu*," he said, the literal translation being "great light." The image burst forth in all its splendor, a fiery green explosion of light spewing golden rays and blazing in Cadderly's mind. Cadderly cried out and looked away, nearly shouting, "*Illumas belle!*" as he fell out of his chair.

Cadderly sat up and looked at the wizard, who was still sitting, holding the unremarkable wand in his extended hand.

"What just happened?" Belisarius asked bluntly.

"I saw the powers—four distinctly," Cadderly stammered, "in my mind."

"And you repeated the triggering phrases," the perturbed wizard added, "exactly."

"But how?" Cadderly asked him, honestly perplexed.

"Go see a priest," Belisarius said with a snarl. "Why did you waste my time and effort on things you already knew?"

"I did not," Cadderly insisted.

"Go see a priest," Belisarius repeated, tossing the wand to Cadderly.

The young man accepted the item and looked to the floor beside the wizard's chair. "We have one more ring to explore," he remarked, backing away into his chair as he spoke.

Belisarius scooped up the remaining ring, a gold band lined with diamond chips, and held it out for Cadderly to see. "You tell me," the wizard insisted.

Again Cadderly heard the distant song playing, but for the sake of his valued friend's pride, he consciously pushed it away.

"It is not magical," he lied, extending his hand to accept it.

"Hah!" the wizard snapped and pulled back his hand. "This is the most potent item of all!" He held it close to his sparkling, admiring eyes. "A ring for wizards," he explained, "to heighten their powers. It would be quite useless to you."

An alarm went off in Cadderly's head. What was sneaky Belisarius up to? The young priest concentrated not on the ring, but on the wizard himself, and saw a shadow image of Belisarius perched on the wizard's shoulder, waggling its eager fingers and rubbing its hands anxiously as it peered at the ring. But Cadderly realized that the wizard's greed was indeed for a wizard's item. The bent of the shadow told him beyond any doubt that Belisarius had not lied to him, and he privately berated himself for thinking differently.

"Keep it," he offered.

The wizard nearly toppled from his chair. His smile seemed as though it would engulf his ears. "I will," he said, his voice an unintentional shriek. "What might I pay you in return?"

Cadderly waved the thought away.

"I must insist," Belisarius continued, undaunted. "This is too valuable a gift—"

"Not to me," Cadderly reminded him.

Belisarius conceded the point with a nod, but still searched for some way to give something back to the young priest.

"Your walking stick!" he proclaimed at last.

Cadderly took up the item, not understanding.

"You use it as a weapon?"

"If I must use anything at all," Cadderly answered. "It is harder than my hand." The mere mention of open-handed combat inevitably brought an image of Danica to Cadderly's mind.

"But not as sturdy as you would like?" Belisarius went on, not noticing the cloud of despair that briefly crossed Cadderly's face.

"Do not deny it," the wizard insisted. "You revealed your fears for the feebleness of the weapon in your fight with the minotaur, when you readily accepted the image of it breaking."

Cadderly didn't argue.

"Leave it with me, my boy!" Belisarius cried. "Give me a few days, and I promise you that you will never consider it a feeble weapon again."

"So you are an enchanter as well?" Cadderly remarked.

"There are many wizardly talents that a cleric would not understand," the wizard replied with an exaggerated air of superiority.

"Especially a cleric who does not understand his own talents," Cadderly replied, his simple admission stealing the wizard's bluster.

Belisarius nodded and managed a weak smile, then left Cadderly with a final thought: "Moderation."

* * * * *

Cadderly was a bit surprised to find Nameless still wandering the road between the wizard's tower and

Carradoon, expecting that the beggar would either have gone to Carradoon to further his day's take, or to his wife and children to enjoy a reprieve from the unenviable lifestyle that had been forced upon him.

Cadderly grew even more surprised when the beggar looked at him and gave him an exaggerated wink, holding up and jingling the purse of gold with a lascivious smile on his dirty face.

Something about that gesture struck Cadderly as badly out of character for Nameless, an act of open greed or open thanks, neither of which applied to the proud, unfortunate man Cadderly had met earlier on the road.

Then Cadderly saw the shadows.

He could not make them out distinctly, as he had the images of Jhanine and her children. They were hunched and growling things, their forms shifting continually, but always emanating a clear and unrepentant wickedness to the young priest. One imaginary claw reached out from the beggar's shoulder and raked the air in Cadderly's direction.

Suddenly Cadderly was very afraid. His neck hair stood on end; his heart began to drum rapidly. A sickly sweet smell came to him then; he thought he heard the buzz of flies. Cadderly shook his head vigorously, feeling that he must be going insane. It seemed as if his senses had heightened, become animal-like, and the sudden intrusion of so much stimulation nearly overwhelmed the young priest.

Then he was calm again and looking at the innocent beggar man. He wished that he had his walking stick, and glanced back to the distant tower.

"Fine day!" the beggar said, seeming cheery, though Cadderly instinctively knew better.

Fete. The word came into Cadderly's head and he almost uttered it. He looked down to his hand, the onyx ring upon one finger, and saw that he had subconsciously angled it the beggar's way.

"Must you be gone so soon?" the beggar man asked, sounding innocent, almost wounded.

Cadderly saw the black shadows crouched upon the man's shoulder, saw the claws and venom-dripping fangs. He nodded briskly, pulled his cloak tightly around his shoulders, and hurried on his way.

He caught a whiff of that sickly sweet scent again and heard the flies. If he had been alone and not so unnerved, he would have stopped and sought out the source. He glanced to the side only briefly as he passed, to the bushes lining the road.

If he had looked closer, Cadderly would have discovered the body, already bloated after just a few hours in the late summer sun. And if he had found the strength to work his magical perceptions, Cadderly would have seen, too, the spirit of Nameless, helpless and hopeless and pitifully wandering until the gods came to claim it.

Eight

Unnecessary Evils

The young priest had noticed the change! Ghost cursed himself and considered the implications of the unexpected occurrence. He had never really believed that he would be able to kill Cadderly so easily—according to every piece of information he had been given, this young priest was a deadly opponent—but when he had seen Cadderly coming down the road, alone and with no obvious witnesses around, Ghost had briefly wondered if the purse might be earned quickly, if his artistry had so easily paid off.

The beggar man had gained Cadderly's confidence; that much Ghost knew from eavesdropping on their conversation. Now, posing as that man, the assassin thought he could get close, could catch Cadderly with his guard down. But the young priest had noticed the change!

Ghost replayed the brief encounter, trying to discern where his act had failed. Nothing obvious came to him; certainly nothing so blatant as to justify sending a defensively huddled Cadderly running on his way. A singular fear came to the assassin then: if Cadderly proved as formidable as the reports had indicated—and as Ghost was now beginning to suspect—then he might be strong enough to fend off the magic of the *Ghearufu*. It had been done only twice before, both times by wizards, when Ghost's attempts at possession had been mentally blocked.

"There are other options," Ghost said aloud, reminding himself of his many allies and of the fact that both of those resisting wizards had wound up as worm food. One of those times, Ghost had possessed a victim that the unsuspecting mage could not suspect—his wife. What a sweet kill that had been! On the other occasion, Ghost had served the attending Night Mask band as an infiltrator, providing them with such an enormous amount of information that the targeted wizard, as powerful as he was, had been among the society's easiest kills.

"Either way, young Cadderly," the merciless assassin whispered to the wind, "I shall paint my picture, and you shall be dead before the first of winter's snows."

With an evil snicker, the assassin in a beggar's body went to the bushes and retrieved his own form. The magical ring had nearly completed its healing work on the limp-muscled figure by then; the stench was fast fading and the flies had gone away.

"Do you wear a ring such as mine?" the evil man teased to the formless spirit he knew would still be wandering the area. Ghost willed the *Ghearufu*, white glove and mirror, back into sight and took the black-gloved hand from the hand of the corpse. He fell back into his mind, connecting with the powers of the magical device.

The eyes of the assassin's more familiar form blinked open just in time to watch the beggar's body fall stiffly to the side. Ghost spent a moment reorienting himself to his customary form, then propped himself up on his elbows.

"No magic ring?" He laughed at the beggar man's corpse. "Then you will stay dead, pitiful fool, though whoever finds your body will have no idea of how you died!"

The thought widened Ghost's smile. In his earliest days with the *Ghearufu*, more than a hundred years before, he had hacked up his unmarked victims. His confidence had quickly grown, though, and Ghost had soon changed tactics, thinking in his budding arrogance that the mysteries surrounding the demise of an apparently healthy body would serve as an appropriate calling card.

Ghost willed the *Ghearufu* away and brushed the dirt from his clothes. He started down the road immediately for the distant gates of Carradoon, for his room at the Dragon's Codpiece.

* * * * *

The firbolg noted with distaste the apparently normal situation at the farmhouse on the outskirts of Carradoon. A few hens clucked and strutted, pecking at discarded seed here and there; the three horses in the stable beside the barn showed no signs that they had been spooked in the least; and the house itself seemed perfectly secure, not a broken window or even a visible scrape mark on any door.

Vander knew better. It was always this way, always done in absolute secrecy. It all seemed so perfectly cowardly to the warrior giant.

"We could have stayed in the forest," Vander muttered, flipping his white-furred cloak back over his muscular shoulders.

The black-and-silver-outfitted assassins at the firbolg's sides looked at each other curiously. "It was by your orders . . ." one of them began to reply, but Vander's upraised hand silenced him.

Not by my orders, the firbolg thought, remembering

when Ghost, in Vander's magnificent body, had set the troupe into motion, while Vander could only sit and watch helplessly from inside Ghost's weak form.

"We must get inside," offered the assassin after a few moments of uncomfortable silence. "This yard can be seen from the road."

"The light of day offends you," the firbolg remarked.

"It reveals us," the Night Mask replied obstinately.

Vander cast him a threatening scowl but did follow the two men to the door. The portal was large enough so that Vander did not have to alter his size, and he was glad, for he did not enjoy wearing a human frame, especially not around the treacherous murderers. He liked the imposing strength of his giant body, the long and muscled limbs that could reach an enemy from across a room and easily throttle him.

Vander hesitated at the threshold.

"The house is secure," one of the assassins inside assured the firbolg, misunderstanding his dismay. "Only the elder daughter remains alive, and she is held—" the lewd way the man spoke that word irritated Vander profoundly, "—in the bedroom."

Vander strode in. "Where?" he demanded, purposely redirecting his gaze from the bloodied male and female bodies in the corner of the small kitchen. The human assassin, obviously unbothered by the gruesome sight, sat at the table, casually eating breakfast. He motioned to a door at the back of the room.

Propelled by his mounting rage, Vander was across the kitchen and through the door in an instant. He nearly tripped over a smaller bloodied form just inside the second room, and that moved him along only faster, more determinedly.

This room connected to a side bedroom, its door open a crack. A whimpering sound came from within, revealing to

Vander what was going on before the firbolg even shoved the door wide.

The girl lay on the bed, half-dressed and securely tied to the posts by her wrists and ankles, with the sides of her mouth pulled tightly back by a cloth gag. An assassin lay on each side of her, teasing her and taking delight at her terrified movements.

Vander had to stoop low in this room to avoid the ceiling beams, but that didn't slow him. He swept aside the three Night Masks standing in his way with a single movement, then stepped to the foot of the bed.

One of the prone assassins looked up and grinned wickedly, misconstruing the firbolg's urgency. The fool motioned for Vander to join in the fun.

Vander's great hands caught both the men by their collars and sent them flying across the room to collide heavily with the wall on each side of the door. The firbolg quickly threw a blanket over the exposed young woman and turned to face his hated associates.

The three on the side of the room looked to each other nervously; one of the men who had hit the wall lay crumpled in a heap at its base. The other, though, was up and outraged, a short sword in one hand.

Vander couldn't help but grin as he considered the situation. Might this be the long-awaited showdown? A nagging thought stole his mirth. He could kill these men, all five, and probably the other dozen or so that were in and about the house, but what about Ghost?

Always, the firbolg had to remember Ghost.

"You three," he commanded to the men on the side of the room. "Your associate has drawn a weapon on your master."

The three understood the implications immediately, as did the man holding the short sword, if his suddenly fearful expression correctly revealed his thoughts. The

Night Masks were a vicious and evil band, but within the organization existed strict codes of conduct and horrible forms of discipline that even the hardiest assassin feared. The three by the wall drew their own weapons and faced the traitor.

The man with the short sword fumbled to put his weapon away. He jerked once, then again, a confused expression on his face.

His accomplice, crumpled at the base of the wall, was not as dazed as he had appeared, and he was eager to regain the taskmaster's favor. In his hand he held the last of three daggers, and this one, too, he whipped across to find a place in the traitor's side.

Anxious to show their respect and loyalty to their powerful leader, the other three promptly rushed the dying man. A club slapped the short sword from trembling hands, and all four loyal soldiers set upon the doomed man, hacking and crushing until he lay in a bloody heap on the floor.

"Put him with the other dead," Vander said to them. He looked back to the bed. "And find a proper prison for this girl."

"She is a witness and must be killed," an assassin replied. "That is our way."

"On my word alone," Vander growled back, his voice carrying tremendous influence now, considering the grim fate of the one who had dared to oppose him. "Now take her!" The same man who had questioned the decision started immediately for the bed, sheathing his weapon but not relenting his steely-eyed glare.

Vander caught him in one hand by the throat and easily lifted him from the floor.

"You are not to touch her." The firbolg snarled in his face. He noticed the man's hand inching toward his belt. "Yes," Vander purred, "do draw your little knife!"

The three remaining men seemed at a loss.

"She must be killed," one of them dared to offer in support of his threatened colleague.

The man in Vander's grasp twisted free enough to growl defiantly at the firbolg.

Vander heaved him through the nearest wall, back into the kitchen. Several assassins who had gathered in the other room stared through the hole in disbelief at the angry firbolg.

"On your word alone," the three men by the door said obediently.

"I will make my place in the barn," Vander said to them all. "It is more fitting to my size and there I will not have to deal with your impertinence. I warn you just one more time," he growled ominously. "If the girl is harmed in any way . . ."

Vander left it at that, preferring to end the threat by leading the others' gazes to the squirming and groaning Night Mask caught fast by broken, stabbing planks halfway between the bedroom and the kitchen.

* * * * *

Fredegar Harriman, proprietor of the Dragon's Codpiece, shook his thick-jowled face in disbelief at the request for yet another private room. The inn had only eight such rooms, and while the much less expensive common room was nearly empty, all of the private rooms were occupied. That alone seemed amazing enough, but what struck Fredegar as even more odd was the makeup of his guests. Five of the rooms belonged to visiting merchants, as was common. A sixth had been paid for until the end of the year by Cadderly, and a seventh had been reserved by the Edificant Library for use by a soon-to-arrive headmaster. Even more unexpectedly, the last room had been rented that very day, to a stranger nearly as curious-looking as this brown-haired lad.

"Common room won't do?" the flustered innkeeper asked. "At least for a few nights? It's on the back side of the building. Not much of a view, but quiet enough."

The young man shook his head, his stringy brown hair flopping to one side, revealing that half of his head had been shaved. "I can pay you well," Bogo offered, giving his purse a quick shake to accentuate the point.

Fredegar continued to wipe the bar and tried to find a way around the dilemma. He didn't want to put the young man out, more for the innkeeper's reputation and his sincerity than for the lost coins, but he didn't see a way around it. The hearth room was teeming this night—it had been full every night since the rumors of impending war had spread through Carradoon—mostly with locals. Fredegar peered through the throng, trying to see if any of his private guests were in attendance.

"I have just one room empty," he explained, "but it won't be for long—might even be filled this night."

"I am here now to fill it," Bogo argued. "Is my gold not as good as another's?"

"Your gold is fine," Fredegar assured him, hoping to keep the tension low. "The one open room has been reserved for more than a week by priests from the Edificant Library. I have assured them that it will be available, and, well, if you are from the area, you know that it is not wise for an honest merchant such as myself to alienate the Edificant Library."

Bogo perked his ears up at mention of the place and the notion that other priests were on their way to town.

"Headmaster Avery and Kierkan Rufo will be in soon," the talkative innkeeper went on. "I haven't seen the good, fat headmaster for almost a year now. I expect he and Rufo have come to town to meet with young Cadderly, another of my guests and another of their priests, and to prepare for this potential war that everyone seems to be talking about."

Bogo scrutinized every word, all the while trying to appear unconcerned. The news about Rufo seemed almost too good to be true. Having the two-time stooge so close at hand could aid his plans to make the kill on Cadderly.

Fredegar, as usual, rambled on in many unimportant directions, speaking mostly of the outrageous rumors that had been circulating. Bogo put in an occasional smile or grunt to make it appear that he was listening, but his mind was whirling down the many avenues the newest information had opened to him.

"I have it!" Fredegar announced suddenly, so loudly that several patrons at the nearest tables of the hearth room stopped their conversations and turned to regard the innkeeper.

"Malcolm," Fredegar called across the room. An older gentleman, a merchant by his rich and fanciful dress, looked up from his table.

"Half price if you will share a room with my Brennan," Fredegar offered.

The old gentleman smiled and turned to talk with his companions at the table, then stood and came over to the bar.

"I have only one more night in town," he answered when he arrived. "I leave for Riatavin in the morning." He winked conspiratorially, both at Fredegar and the odd-looking young man standing at the bar. "One can make fine trades with such grim news filling the air, eh?"

"A night with my Brennan?" Fredegar said hopefully.

The merchant gazed across the room to a younger woman, fine in stature and looking back at him with obvious interest. "I had hoped to be accompanied on my last night in town," he explained. Again came his wink, this time even more lecherous. "After all, back in Riatavin tomorrow night, I will be forced to spend some time with my wife."

Fredegar, blushing, joined him in his laughter.

"I could spend a single night in the common room," Bogo interjected, not at all amused by the worthless bantering, "if you will guarantee me this man's room by midday tomorrow." Bogo turned his thin lips up in a wry smile, thinking it best to play the conniving buddy game. "Free of charge this night?" he asked coyly.

Fredegar, never one to bicker (especially not when the inn was so full), readily agreed. "And an ale with my compliments, young stranger," the innkeeper offered as he filled a tankard. "And one for your intended?" Fredegar asked Malcolm.

"I will meet it at the table," the lecherous merchant replied, going back to his seat.

Bogo accepted the drink with a smile and turned about, leaning with his elbow propped on the bar. The crowd buzzed and played; it was a jovial and warm inn, its atmosphere not at all hindered (perhaps even enhanced) by the still-distant rumors of war. The perfect cover, Bogo thought as he watched the bustle, and he nearly laughed aloud as he considered how the events of the next few days might steal a bit of the mirth.

"So good that you have returned!" he heard Fredegar say a short while later. Bogo's eyes widened and he purposely shifted farther down the bar as a young man, of above average height and solid build, moved to join the innkeeper.

He wore a blue, wide-brimmed hat lined with a red sash. Set in its middle was a porcelain brooch bearing the holy symbol of Deneir. There could be little doubt as to this one's identity—Dorigen's description of Cadderly had not included the beard, but Bogo could see that it was newly grown, and the unkempt sand-brown hair and gray eyes certainly fit.

"Headmaster Avery and Kierkan Rufo are coming in," Fredegar explained, "perhaps this very night."

Bogo noticed the young man flinch at that remark, though the priest had tried to cover his reaction. "Do they know I am staying here?" he asked.

Fredegar seemed at a loss by his guest's obvious discomfort.

"Why, Cadderly," he replied slyly, "have you done something wrong?"

The young priest smiled noncommittally and started for the staircase beside the bar. Distracted, Cadderly did not even notice the odd-looking young man as he passed by.

But Bogo certainly noticed Cadderly. He watched the priest go, thinking how easy this all might be.

Nine

Evil Visions, Evil Deeds

He stood in a lighted room, the sitting room of Belisarius's tower perhaps, holding a beating heart in his hand. The slain minotaur lay at his feet and all his closest friends, Danica and the dwarven brothers, stood by it, laughing wildly, uncontrollably.

Cadderly, too, joined in the laughter but as soon as he did, he realized that his friends were not laughing at all. Rather, they were crying, sobbing great tears that streaked their cheeks and fell in impossibly large puddles at their feet.

He did not understand.

Something was logically wrong; Cadderly sensed that something about the entire scene was out of place. He felt the warm blood running down his arm, soaking his tunic, but in his perversion of the wizard's minotaur and maze illusion, there had been no blood! Slowly, fearfully the young scholar looked down.

The minotaur was not a minotaur any longer, nor had

it vanished like some insubstantial illusion, as Cadderly had expected. It was Avery—Cadderly knew it was Avery, though he could not see the face of the man who lay on his back across a table, arms and legs splayed wide and his chest savagely torn open.

Cadderly held Avery's still-beating heart.

He tried to scream but could not. There came a rapping noise, sharp but distant.

He could not scream.

* * * * *

Cadderly sat up. The rapping came again, more insistently, followed by a voice that Cadderly could not ignore. At last he dared to open his eyes and sighed deeply when he learned that he was in his own room, that it had all been another terrible dream.

"Cadderly?"

The call was not a dream, and his recognition of the commanding, fatherly voice could not be wrong. He closed his eyes again, tried to pretend he was not there, or that Avery was not there.

"Cadderly?" The knocking did not diminish.

What time was it? Cadderly wondered. The moon was up, though beyond its zenith, for no direct silvery light played through the young priest's east window.

Resignedly, Cadderly pulled himself out of bed, straightened his nightshirt, and went to the closed door.

"Cadderly?"

He cracked open the portal and winced at the sight of Headmaster Avery. Kierkan Rufo, leaning as always in his customary position, leered over the headmaster's broad shoulder.

"It is late," Cadderly mumbled through the cottony sensation and the lump of revulsion in his mouth. He could not look at Avery without the gruesome dream image coming clearly to his thoughts, could not regard the man without the warm sensation of blood running along his arm. Unconsciously, he rubbed one hand against his night-shirt.

"So it is," Avery replied, somewhat embarrassed, "but I thought you would be pleased to learn that Rufo here, and I, have arrived in town. We shall be staying at the inn, just four doors down from you, across from the stairway." The portly headmaster glanced that way, his expression clearly revealing an invitation for the young priest.

Cadderly only nodded, then winced again as another drop of imaginary blood ran the length of his forearm.

Avery did not miss the sour expression. "Is something wrong, lad?" the headmaster asked with compassion.

"Nothing," Cadderly replied curtly. He mellowed immediately, guessing that his demeanor would inspire further curiosity. "I am just tired. I was sleeping . . ."

"My pardon," Avery said, straining to be lighthearted, "but you are not sleeping now." He took a step forward, as though to push his way into the room.

Cadderly shifted to block the door. "I will soon be sleeping again," he said evenly.

Avery stepped back and, for the first time since he had arrived, regarded Cadderly with a less than appreciative glint in his puffy eyes.

"Still stubborn?" Avery asked him sharply. "You tread on dangerous ground, young priest. Your absence from the library might be overlooked. Dean Thobicus has promised that he will allow you to make up your missed duties and studies."

"I do not care for his promise."

"If you continue on your wayward path," Avery went on, his voice a growl against Cadderly's biting remark, "then you may move beyond the order altogether. I am not certain even kind Thobicus could forgive your transgressions against Deneir. . . ."

"What do you know of Deneir?" Cadderly asked. In his mind he saw Avery again, lying dead across the table, but he shook the evil thought away, realizing how much he loved this man who had been a surrogate father to him. "And why would you care for me? Did you not once call me a 'Gondsman'?" Cadderly asked sharply, referring to the order of inventive priests who created without conscience, without regard to the implications of their creations.

His tirade exhausted, Cadderly looked at the headmaster, the father he had just terribly wounded with his impertinence. Avery couldn't respond to his last statement and seemed more on the verge of tears than an explosion of anger. Behind him, Kierkan Rufo wore an almost amused expression of disbelief.

"I am sorry," Cadderly stammered. Avery put a large hand up to halt him.

"I am tired, that is all," Cadderly tried to explain. "I have had some terrible dreams of late."

Avery's expression shifted to one of concern, and Cadderly knew his apology had been accepted, or would be soon.

"We are but four doors down," the portly headmaster reiterated. "If you feel the need to talk, do come and join us."

Cadderly nodded, though he knew he would not go to them, and shut the door the second Avery had turned away. He fell back against the door heavily, thinking how flimsy a barrier it was against the doubts and confusion of the outside world. He looked to his table by the window, to the open tome. When was the last time that book had been closed?

Cadderly couldn't even muster the strength to go to it; he slipped over to his bed and collapsed, hoping that he had put this night's evil dreams behind him.

* * * * *

Bogo Rath released his spell of clairaudience and cracked open the common room's door. The common room was on the southwestern wing of the inn's second level; almost directly across from him, over the hearth room, loomed Cadderly's door, closed once more. Avery and Rufo rounded the corner diagonally to Bogo's right, moving toward the door directly opposite the wide staircase. The hearth room was quiet now and Bogo could hear their conversation clearly.

"His surliness has not relented one bit since he passed through the library," Rufo said in an accusatory tone.

"He appeared weary," Avery answered with a resigned sigh. "Poor lad—perhaps Danica's arrival will brighten his mood."

They entered their room then, and Bogo considered using his eavesdropping magic to hear the rest of their discussion.

"Who is Danica?" came a quiet, monotone question from behind Bogo. The young wizard froze, then slowly managed to turn about.

There stood Ghost, in the otherwise empty common room. The puny man held no weapon and made no move toward Bogo, but the wizard felt vulnerable nonetheless. How had Ghost come in so easily behind him? There was but one door to the room, and it had no outside balcony, as did the more expensive private rooms.

"How did you get in here?" Bogo asked, managing to steady his voice.

"I have been in here all along," Ghost replied. He turned and pointed to a pile of blankets. "In there, awaiting your return from the hearth room."

"You should have told me."

Ghost's wheezing laughter mocked him and showed him how ridiculous he had sounded.

"Who is Danica?" the evil little man asked again, more determinedly.

"Lady Danica Maupoissant," Bogo replied, "from West-gate. Do you know of her?"

Ghost shook his head.

"She is Cadderly's dearest friend," Bogo went on, "a beautiful wisp of a woman, by all descriptions, but formidable." Bogo's expression and tone grew grave. "This is not good news, my associate," he explained. "Lady Maupoissant has been a terrible foe to Castle Trinity in the fight thus far. If she arrives soon, then you would be well advised to finish your business with Cadderly promptly and be gone from here."

Ghost nodded, considering the warning. "From where will she come?" he asked. "The library?"

"That would seem likely," Bogo replied. He flipped his brown hair to one side and smiled slyly. "What are you thinking?"

Ghost's glare stole the wizard's mirth. "That is none of your concern," he rasped with sudden anger, pushing past Bogo to the door. "If you are thinking of making any moves against Cadderly on your own . . ." He let the implication hang in the air.

"Well, let us just say that the consequences of failure can be terrible indeed," Ghost finished, and he started away. He turned back immediately, though, his gaze directing Bogo to the pile of blankets that had hidden Ghost. "Do watch your back, young wizard," Ghost said evenly, then he coughed a wheezing laugh and went to his room, in the corner of the north wing, halfway between Cadderly's room and the room occupied by Avery and Rufo.

"From the library, from the mountains," Ghost mused, closing the door behind him. "Well, we shall see if Lady Maupoissant follows her path all the way to Carradoon." Ghost sat on his bed and summoned the *Ghearufu*. Using its powers, he sent his thoughts out of the town, to Vander, in the farmhouse.

Ghost felt the firbolg's typical revulsion and knew from its depth that Vander was angry both with the situation at the farm and with Ghost's intrusion.

Let me in, Vander, the wicked man teased, confident that the firbolg could not deny access even if he tried. Vander was Ghost's chosen victim, his special target, and with Vander alone, Ghost could make the body transfer from almost any range. He felt the sharp, burning pain as his spirit stepped out of his body, and then he was floating, flying on the winds, propelled straight for the firbolg's shell. As he entered the giant body, he knew that Vander had entered his, back in the room at the Dragon's Codpiece.

Do not leave the room, Ghost instructed telepathically through the continuing mental link. *Admit no visitors, particularly not that foolish wizard, Bogo Rath!*

Ghost willed away the *Ghearufu* and considered his surroundings. Curiously enough, he was in a barn, surrounded by stabled horses and cows. The man in the firbolg's body shook his head at Vander's continuing surprises and made his way to the large door.

The farmyard was quiet under the light of the westering moon, and the house, dark; not a single candle burned in any window. Ghost made his way across to the porch and heard a shuffle up above.

"It is only the master," he said to the unseen guards. "Gather the others and come into the barn, all of you. The time has come to tighten our noose."

Just a few minutes later, the entire band of nineteen remaining Night Masks assembled around their leader. Ghost noted that one of his henchmen was missing, but he said nothing about it, realizing that Vander probably knew what had happened to the man and that he might confuse them all by questioning the absence while wearing Vander's form.

He drew a quick map on the ground in front of him. "I have word that a woman is on her way to Carradoon from the Edificant Library," he said, indicating the location of the mountain structure. "There are only a few trails down the mountains, and they all exit in this general area. She should not be hard to find."

"How many should we send?" one of the assassins asked.

Ghost paused as much to consider the angry edge to the man's tone as to consider the question itself. Perhaps the missing Night Mask had met an unfortunate demise at Vander's impulsive hands.

"Five," Ghost said at last. "The woman is to be killed, as are any who travel beside her."

"It could be a large and formidable band," the same assassin argued.

"If so, then kill only the woman and be gone from there," Ghost snapped back, his firbolg-strength voice resounding off the barn's walls.

"Which five?" asked one of the group.

"Choose among yourselves," Ghost replied, "but do not take this woman lightly. She is, by all reports, formidable indeed.

"Another group of five is to strike within the town," Ghost went on. "Our information was correct. Cadderly stays at the Dragon's Codpiece. Here," he said, extending his map to show the lakeside section of Carradoon and indicating the lane running along the shore, "on Lakeview Street. Secure positions near the inn, where you will be at my . . . at Ghost's call. But take care to be far enough out of reach so as not to arouse suspicion."

"With five stringers to open a line of contact to the group within the city?" the same questioning assassin put in.

"That is our usual method," Ghost answered calmly.

"That will leave only four here at the farmhouse, excluding yourself," the angry assassin reasoned. Ghost did not understand the problem. "If we are forced to maintain a continual guard over the girl—"

"The girl?" Ghost didn't mean to sound so startled.

The assassin, and several others, cocked an eye curiously. "The girl that Mishalak died for," he said contemptuously. Ghost saw a problem building, and he scowled immediately to force the upstart back on the defensive.

"I do not question your decision to let her live," the assassin quickly explained. "Nor do I deny that Mishalak deserved death for drawing a weapon against you, the taskmaster. But if only four of us remain to guard the farmhouse, then the girl becomes a threat."

It all made perfect sense to the cunning impersonator. Vander's soft heart had caused problems before now. Oftentimes the firbolg was too intent on honor, placing the foolish notion above his duty. Ghost spent a moment considering how he might punish the giant, then smiled widely as a typically fiendish idea came into his head.

"You are correct," he said to the assassin. "It is time for you to end that threat." The man nodded eagerly, and Ghost's smile widened, the wicked man thinking how furious Vander would become, and how helpless, impotent, Vander would be. The proud firbolg would hate that most of all.

"End that threat this night," Ghost purred, "but, first, you and your friends might have your way with her." All about the ring, the evil assassins smiled. "We cannot survive on duty alone!"

That brought a cheer from the group.

"Go for the mountains this night as well," Ghost continued. "I do not know how many days away this Lady Maupoissant is from Carradoon, but she cannot be allowed to enter the town."

"Maupoissant?" one of the assassins, an older killer with salt and pepper hair, piped in.

"You know the name?"

"Nearly a decade ago, we killed a wainwright by that name," the man admitted, "a wagon maker and his wife. And we were paid handsomely for the task, I must say."

"The name is unusual and she is, by my informant's words, from Westgate," Ghost reasoned. "There could be a connection."

"Good," said the man, drawing a dagger and running the flat of the blade slowly along his bony cheek. "I always like to keep it in the family."

The nineteen Night Masks were pleased to see their unpredictable firbolg taskmaster joining in the laughter, the giant's heartfelt roars smothering their own. They were nervous; the time to kill was drawing near, and adding this "Lady Maupoissant" to the victim list was akin to smearing icing on an already delicious cake.

Ten

Professionals

"What time is it?" Ivan asked, rolling out of his blankets and giving a profound stretch.

"It is hours past the dawn," Danica answered sharply, privately berating herself for being foolish enough to take the last watch.

"Ye should've woked me up," Ivan complained. He started to sit, then changed his mind and fell back into the bedroll in a heap.

"I have," Danica muttered, though the dwarf was no longer listening. "Six times!

"But not again," the fiery woman whispered. This time she was prepared. She took up two small buckets, filled with the icy cold water of a nearby mountain stream. Stealthily, she slipped up to the dwarves, their bedrolls having merged from their typically wild slumber during the night into a single large tangle. Danica sorted out the mess and moved the blankets aside enough to reveal the backs of hairy necks.

111

Pikel's presented the most problem, since the dwarf wore his beard pulled back over his ears and braided with his long hair (which he had recently redyed forest green) halfway down his back. Gently Danica moved the tousle aside, drawing a semiconscious "Hee hee," from the snoozing dwarf, and lifted one of the buckets.

The next thunderous roars resounding from the camp sent animals for nearly a mile around scurrying for cover. Even a fat black bear, out to catch some morning sunshine, raced through a tangle and up the side of a thick oak, sniffing the air nervously, fearfully.

The dwarves ran about in circles, crashed into each other several times, and threw their blankets into the air.

"Me weapon!" Ivan cried in distress.

"Oo oi!" Pikel wholeheartedly agreed, unable to locate his tree-trunk club.

Ivan calmed first, noticing Danica standing next to a tree, her arms folded across her chest and her grin spreading from ear to ear. The dwarf stopped his running altogether and regarded her with dart-throwing eyes.

He should have looked out for his brother instead.

Pikel hit him broadside, and the two flew away into some brambles. By the time they extricated themselves and had stomped back into the camp, their beards were thrown wildly about and their nightshirts seemed almost furry with burrs.

"Yerself did that to us!" Ivan shouted accusingly at Danica.

"I wish to be in Carradoon no later than tomorrow," the woman replied just as angrily. "I welcomed your company, but did not know it would mean holding camp until after noon each day! I thought dwarves were industrious!"

"Oooo," Pikel moaned, ashamed of his perceived laziness.

"Not our fault," Ivan muttered, also on the defensive.

"It's the ground," he blurted. "Yeah, the ground. Too hard and comfortable for a dwarf to want to get himself up in the morning!"

"You have forfeited breakfast," Danica scolded.

"When halflings shave their feet!" Ivan roared, and Danica suspected—correctly—that she was overstepping her bounds. Throwing ice-cold water down the backs of sleeping dwarves was one thing, but denying them food was something altogether different, something downright dangerous.

"A quick meal then," she conceded, "then we are off."

Sixteen trout, four tankards of ale (each), half a sack of biscuits and three bowls of berries (each) later, the dwarven brothers gathered their belongings and skipped off down the mountain trails behind Danica. Impresk Lake was clearly visible whenever they came to an open ridge, and Carradoon soon came into sight as well, far below.

Despite Danica's desire for haste, the trio took all caution in their trek. The Snowflake Mountains were a dangerous place, even in their southern reaches, where the charges of the Edificant Library dominated the region. With war brewing in the north and battles continuing back to the west, in Shilmista, the companions had to assume that the trails would now be even more dangerous.

Danica led the way, bending low to inspect every track, every bent blade of grass. Ivan and Pikel bobbed along behind her, Ivan in his deer-antlered helmet and Pikel wearing a many-dented cooking pot for lack of any true headgear. Even though Danica continually searched the ground as she traveled, the speedy monk had little trouble outpacing the dwarves and forced them to scurry along just to keep up.

Danica slowed considerably; Ivan and Pikel nearly ran her down.

"Uh-oh," Pikel muttered, seeing Danica's curious expression.

"What'd ye find?" Ivan asked quietly, pulling his brother along behind him.

Danica shook her head, unsure. "Someone has passed this way," she declared.

"Avery and Rufo," Ivan replied.

"More recently," Danica said, standing straight again and taking a long, hard look at the nearby brush.

"Coming or going?" Ivan pressed.

Danica shook her head, unable to decide. She was confident that her guess had been correct, but what bothered her was the nature of the tracks, the scratching marks made over the apparent boot prints. If someone had crossed this trail earlier that morning, then they had gone to great lengths to conceal their tracks.

Ivan looked down at the unremarkable ground and, scratching confusedly at his yellow beard, produced yet another stubborn burr. "I don't see tracks," he huffed.

Danica pointed out a slight depression in the ground, barely visible, then indicated the pattern that made her believe that brush had been scraped over the ground.

Ivan snorted in disbelief. "That all ye got to go on?" he asked loudly, no longer afraid of the volume of his voice.

Danica didn't even try to hush him. She remained confident of her guess; she could hope only that some ranger, or one of Elbereth's elven kin, perhaps, was in the region. If not a ranger or an elf, then Danica felt certain that these tracks had been made by someone intent on concealing himself.

In the wilds of the mountains, that rarely boded well for travelers.

A few hundred yards down the trail, Danica found further signs of passage. This time even Ivan could not discount the obvious boot print in the soft trail, though half of it had been just as obviously brushed away.

The dwarf put his hands on his hips and looked about,

focusing on the crook of a low branch hanging over the trail.

"I seen some rocks aside the trail just a dozen yards back," the dwarf began.

"Uh-oh," muttered Pikel, suspecting what his brother was getting at.

"Got some big enough trees hanging over the trail," Ivan continued, not hearing Pikel's flustered sigh. He looked at Danica, who seemed not to understand.

"Could set us a trap," Ivan spouted. "Could haul a rock up one of them trees and—"

Pikel slapped him across the back of the head.

"You've tried that before," Danica reasoned from the sour look on Pikel's face.

Pikel groaned and Ivan glared at him, but the yellow-bearded dwarf took no retribution against his brother. They had indeed tried that trap before. Although Ivan stubbornly, if with little real conviction, insisted that it had been a success (they had clobbered an orc with the rock), Pikel just as stubbornly insisted that the meager kill had hardly been worth the terrific effort of putting the rock in the tree in the first place.

Knowing that this time there would be another witness, Ivan would have conceded the point and gone along without further mention of the trap and Pikel's assault—it was only a slap, after all—but then, without explanation, Pikel whipped his club up in front of Ivan's face. To Danica, standing to the side, it seemed clear that Pikel tried to halt the weapon's momentum short of Ivan, but the club still connected with Ivan's great nose. It knocked him back several steps and sent a stream of warm blood flowing over the dwarf's hairy lip.

"What'd ye . . ." Ivan stammered, hardly believing the attack. He took up his double-bladed axe, snarled, and stepped toward his frantically squeaking brother.

Pikel couldn't explain the action to either Ivan or Danica, but he did manage to turn his fat club around in time, revealing a heavy dart buried halfway into the hard wood.

Now came Ivan's turn to do his brother a good deed. Looking to the thick bushes past Pikel, to where his warrior instincts immediately told him the dart had come from, he saw a crossbow leveled Pikel's way.

A tall form fell from a branch to land softly behind Danica.

Ivan's pointing finger made Pikel turn about.

"Uh-oh," the green-bearded dwarf squeaked, knowing he had no time to get out of harm's way.

Ivan hit him just before the quarrel, though, taking him down in a perfect tackle as the bolt flew harmlessly past. Ivan did not relent. As he rolled, he heaved Pikel right over him, and Pikel understood the tactic, likewise heaving Ivan back over him. Like a rolling boulder, the dwarven brothers barreled into the brush, forcefully enough to tangle the two men concealed there.

The Night Mask behind Danica, his sword bared and held high, had no reason to believe that the woman, intent on the spectacle of the dwarves, even knew that she was about to die. His surprise was complete when Danica snapped into a bend at her waist, her leg shooting out behind her, high enough to connect on the man's chest.

He flew back several feet, slamming into a tree trunk heavily, but managed to regain his dropped sword. More wary, he began backing away defensively, step for step with the dangerous woman's approach.

Danica broke into a run and came in hard and fast, but skidded suddenly to her knees and dipped her head as another form appeared from behind the trunk and launched a shoulder-high swipe at her with a short, slender staff. The weapon banged hard against the tree, spitting flakes of bark.

Danica slipped one foot back under her and kicked out with the other, thinking to break this second enemy's knee. He got his staff down in time to deflect the attack, though, then countered with several sharp and furious thrusts.

The young monk knew at once that she was in trouble. These were not ordinary highwaymen, though their dress seemed ordinary enough. She managed to fall out of the way as the other's sword flashed at her skull, but took a hit on the hip from the fast-flying staff.

Then she was up in a crouch a few feet away from the two men, taking careful measure of their tempered approach, looking for an opening where there seemed to be none.

* * * * *

Ivan bit down hard, and continued to bite, until he realized from the steady stream of "Ooooo's" that it was Pikel's calf, not an enemy's, in his mouth.

The dwarf scrambled to gain his footing in the tight quarters, branches and brambles grabbing at him with every move, and the nearest man landing no less than three punches on his already wounded nose.

Then Ivan was up, as was Pikel, with weapons ready. Ivan launched a vicious swipe with his axe, but his arm slipped through another thin but tough branch, shortening his reach so that he never got close to hitting the man.

Pikel yelped in terror and dove aside as his brother followed through, the wild flying axe nearly connecting. Again, albeit unintentionally, Ivan had saved his brother's life, for as Pikel leaped aside, another crossbow bolt soared in, cutting the air between the dwarves with a sizzling sound and thudding heavily into the shoulder of the man facing Ivan.

Both brothers paused long enough to look behind them to the crossbowman, who was frantically recocking the weapon. Pikel went back at his attacker, who had finally extricated himself from the brush tangle, and Ivan turned to where his closest enemy had been standing.

The man was not to be seen, and Ivan suspected from the still-shaking bushes that he had been laid out flat. Not to argue with good fortune, the dwarf howled and bolted back the other way, crunching out of the brambles to find the clear path leading to the crossbowman.

*   *   *   *   *

The swordsman was wounded; that was something at least. Danica's kick apparently had done some damage, for he winced with every circling step he took. Danica had already come to the conclusion that the staff-wielder was the more formidable of the two, though. His salt-and-pepper hair showed experience, and the perfect balance of his measured strides made her realize that this one had spent his lifetime training in the fighting arts. His staff seemed puny compared to the other's sword, but in his hands it was a deadly weapon indeed.

A sword cut sent the woman low; the staff clipped her shoulder and she had to dive over backward, rolling back to her feet just in time to prevent a killing follow-up attack.

Danica had used the roll to her advantage. Crouched in a ball on the way over, the monk had slipped one of her crystal-bladed daggers from her boot sheath.

The swordsman came on again, seeming more confident.

Danica planted her right foot out in front of her and pivoted on it, launching her left foot high and wide behind her as she twirled. She knew that her circle-kick attack would have no more effect than to force the swordsman's blade out wide, and knew, too, that she had left herself vulnerable to the other attacker. She threw her supporting leg out from under her and completed her circuit as she crashed down to the ground, hearing the whiz of the staff as it flew inches above her head.

Danica broke her fall with one arm and kept her torso high enough from the ground for her to snap her other arm underneath her, releasing the dagger. Its short flight ended in the swordsman's belly, and he fell back, eyes wide in disbelief and mouth wide in a silent scream.

The staff-wielder laughed and congratulated Danica for the cunning move, then came on relentlessly.

* * * * *

Pikel's attacker, too, wielded a club, but he faced two serious disadvantages. First, Pikel's club was much larger than his, and, second, he couldn't possibly hit the thick-skinned and thicker-headed dwarf hard enough with a blunt weapon to do any serious damage. Lightning fast, he smacked Pikel twice on the shoulder and once on the pot helmet, which rang loudly.

Pikel hardly cared, accepting the three hits for the one he returned. His tree-trunk club caught the man's exposed side and sent him flying from the brush to roll hard against the base of a tree.

The man's face could not have reflected a greater terror if he had been tied to a stake in the path of a horse stampede when Pikel came rushing out in pursuit, his pot all the way down over his face, but his club leveled perfectly to squash the man between the tree and its thick end.

The man rolled aside and Pikel slammed in, snapping the young tree down and going headlong over its broken trunk.

"Oo," the dwarf grunted as he skidded to a stop along the felled tree's rough bark. Then came that loud ring again as his stubborn attacker rushed back in and planted a two-hander on the top of his helmet.

* * * * *

Ivan realized he would not get to the crossbowman before the man had the weapon readied, so he hoisted his axe above his head in both hands and roared, "Time to die, ye thieving dog!" as he let the weapon fly.

The man dove over backward, thrusting his crossbow up in front of him as a makeshift shield. The axe took it solidly, tearing it from the man's hands and carrying it along on its flight until the whole connected with a tree, the crossbow falling in two pieces and the axe burying several inches into the trunk.

Ivan slowed his charge as the man came back up to his feet, drawing a long, thin sword, and not at all unnerved by the fine throw. In fact, the killer smiled widely at the now unarmed dwarf's approach.

"I could be wrong," Ivan admitted quietly, his ferocious charge withering to a halt.

* * * * *

Danica punched and punched again, both attacks deflected harmlessly wide by the small staff. Her attacker countered with a straight thrust and Danica threw her forearm up at the last moment to push it out of line with her face. She countered with a snapping kick, but her attacker had his staff back in place quickly enough to slow the blow so that it did no real damage.

A groan drew Danica's attention to the side. There stood the swordsman, his trembling hand at last closed around

Danica's bloodied dagger. The man's face contorted in obvious agony, but also in obvious rage, and Danica suspected that he would soon be back in the fray. No matter how ineffective he might prove, she feared she could not handle both of these men at once.

Her temporary distraction cost her; the staff connected on her side. Danica rolled sidelong with the blow, diminishing its painful sting, and grabbed at her other boot as she went over and came back up to a crouch.

The staff-wielder leaped and spun in a flurry of defensive movements, anticipating another dagger throw. Danica pumped her arm several times, delicately shifting her angle with each forward movement. Each time, her intended victim placed himself in a position to block the throw or dodge aside.

The man was good.

Danica carefully aligned herself, pumped her arm once more, and threw. The staff-wielder easily slipped to the side, his expression revealing confusion that this skilled woman would have missed him so cleanly. He understood a moment later, when his companion groaned again, loudly.

The swordsman's trembling hand slipped free of the golden tiger hilt of the dagger in his belly and inched upward to the silver dragon protruding from his chest. Helplessly, he fell back against a tree and slid down to the ground.

"You and I," said the staff-wielder, and he accentuated his point with a furious rush and a blinding, dizzying series of thrusts and swipes.

* * * * *

Pikel looked mournfully at the tree he had felled, his pause for sorrowful contemplations costing him yet another ringing slam on his pot helmet.

The druidic-minded dwarf felt nothing but a most profound rage welling inside of him. Pikel had always been regarded by those who knew him as among the most even-minded of people, the slowest of the slow to anger. But now he had killed a tree.

He had killed a tree!

"Ooooooo!" the groan issued out of his trembling lips, between gnashing, gritted teeth.

"Ooooooo!" He turned around to face his attacker, who backed off a step at the sheer strength of the dwarf's bared fury.

"Ooooooo!" Pikel tripped over the tree stump as he charged, diving headlong. His attacker turned to flee, but the sprawling dwarf caught him by the ankle. The man's club came down hard on Pikel's grasping fingers repeatedly, but the enraged dwarf felt no pain.

Pikel dragged the man in, grabbed him in both hands, and hoisted him into the air. Gaining his feet, the powerful dwarf held the man above his head and looked around curiously, as though he was wondering what to do next.

The club rang again on Pikel's cooking pot helmet.

Pikel decided he had had enough. He impaled the man on the jagged edge of the broken tree stump.

* * * * *

Ivan whipped off his backpack, fumbling with the straps as his enemy rushed in. The dwarf blocked a sword thrust with the pack, tangling the sword in its straps long enough for Ivan to get out a package, six inches square and carefully wrapped.

The swordsman yanked away and tore the pack from his blade, then looked back to the dwarf curiously.

Ivan had ripped open the box and removed its contents:

a toy he had been making for Cadderly ever since the young priest's heroics against the evil Barjin.

The black adamantite border of the spindle-disks contrasted mesmerizingly with the semiprecious crystal center. The swordsman paused, wondering what purpose these twin disks, joined in their center by a small rod, might possibly serve.

Ivan fumbled to get his fat finger through the loop in the string wrapping that small rod. He had seen Cadderly use this type of toy a thousand times, had marveled at how the young priest so easily let the disks roll down to the end of their cord, then casually, with a flip of his wrist, sent them spinning back to his waiting hand.

"Ye ever seen one of these?" Ivan asked the curious swordsman.

The man charged; Ivan flung the disks out at him. The man got his sword in the way to block, then eyed his weapon incredulously, regarding the ample nick the harder adamantite had caused.

Ivan had no time to gloat over the integrity of the craftsmanship, though. His throw had been strong, but, unlike Cadderly, he had no idea of how to recall the spinning disks. They hung near the end of the string, spinning sidelong.

"Ooooooo!" Pikel's rush from the side turned the swordsman about. He sidestepped the raging dwarf and regained his balance as Pikel swung about, scraping one foot on the ground for leverage to begin yet another furious charge.

This time, the green-bearded dwarf stopped short of passing the man, instead launching a series of furious blows with his heavy club. The swordsman worked hard, but managed to keep out of harm's way.

Ivan shoulder-blocked Pikel aside.

"This one's mine!" the gruff dwarf explained.

The swordsman smiled at the dwarf's apparent stupidity—together these two could have easily finished him.

His smile went away—literally—when Ivan suddenly hurled the spindle-disks again. This time, surprisingly, the small weapon was not attached to the dwarf's finger, had no encumbrance at all as it zipped past the swordsman's futile attempt to block.

The man's head snapped backward viciously and his face seemed to melt away when the adamantite disks connected squarely, removing every visible tooth, smashing apart his nose and both cheekbones, and neatly tucking his chin up under his upper jaw.

"Didn't think a dwarf could throw like that, did ye?" Ivan bellowed.

The man stood staring in disbelief; his sword fell to the ground.

"Oo," Pikel muttered as the man's head lolled freely to one side, for only then did either of the brothers realize that Ivan's powerful throw had snapped the man's neck.

Ivan reiterated Pikel's grim thought. "Oo."

* * * * *

Kick and swipe, punch and spearing thrust.

Danica and the staff-wielder moved in vicious harmony, attacking and parrying with incredible speed. For seconds that stretched into minutes, neither scored any hit at all.

But in the heightened competition, the adrenaline pumping fiercely, neither seemed to tire in the least.

"You are good, Lady . . ." the staff-wielder remarked, his voice trailing off as though he had meant to say more. "As I expected you would be."

Danica could hardly reply. Had the man just teased her, almost uttering her name? How could he know? A hundred

thoughts raced through Danica's mind with the sudden
suspicion that this was not a random ambush. Was Cadderly safe? she wondered frantically. And what of Avery and
Rufo, who had come down this same path just a couple of
days before?

Thinking her distracted, the Night Mask came in viciously.

Danica dropped straight to the ground and kicked out,
connecting on the man's knee hard enough to halt his rush.

Danica stepped ahead, coming up right in the man's
face. She took a painful hit on the shoulder for her efforts,
but got in one of her own, a snapping chop to the man's
throat. In the single instant the man was forced to pause
and gulp for breath, Danica got one hand planted on his
chin and the other around the back of his head to grab a
clump of hair.

The man dropped his staff and clamped his hands desperately onto Danica's wrists, preventing her from twisting
his head around. They held the pose for several moments,
with Danica simply not strong enough to continue the intended maneuver.

The man, sensing his superiority, smiled wickedly.

Never releasing her grip, Danica leaped and rolled right
over his shoulder, letting her weight do what her strength
could not. They twisted and squirmed, Danica bending her
knees to keep her full weight on the hold. The man wisely
dropped to the ground, but Danica rolled again, under and
to the side, now with her forearm locked tightly under the
man's chin.

He gasped futilely for breath, scratched and clawed at
Danica's arms, then shoved his own hand into Danica's
face, probing for her eyes.

Danica felt the hardness of a stone under her hip and
she quickly shifted again, putting the man's head in line.
Frantically, brutally, the young monk realigned her grip on

the man's hair, leaving the back of his head exposed, and began slamming him down to the stone.

Still, he could not breath; all the world disappeared in a darkening fog.

"He's dead!" Ivan cried, and Danica realized only then that the dwarf had been uttering the words over and over.

Horrified and sorely bruised, the young woman released her grip and rolled away from the man, fighting back her nausea.

"That one'll be gone soon, too," Ivan said calmly, indicating the man slumped against the tree, two daggers protruding from his bloody torso. "Unless we tend his wounds."

The man seemed to hear and looked pleadingly at the three companions.

"We must," Danica, composed again, explained to the dwarves. "I think this one knew my name. There may be a conspiracy here and he—" she pointed to the man against the tree, "—can tell us what it is."

Ivan shrugged his agreement and took a step toward the man, who seemed to take some comfort in the fact that his life would be spared. But there came a click from the side, and the man jerked violently a moment later, a crossbow quarrel next to the silver-hilted dagger.

* * * * *

The lone surviving Night Mask, wounded with a crossbow quarrel protruding from his shoulder, crashed through the brush, on the edge of delirium from the searing pain and the loss of blood. One thought dominated his thoughts: hehad failed in his mission. But at least he had stopped his cowardly comrade from revealing the greater mission—rule number one to the merciless band.

The man didn't know where to run. Vander would kill him when the firbolg learned that Lady Maupoissant had survived—the man regretted now that he had chosen his one remaining shot to finish the potential informant instead of trying again for Danica. Then he took heart as he reminded himself that even if he had been able to hit Danica, even if he had killed her, the dwarves would have had their informant and the more important plan to eliminate Cadderly would have been in jeopardy.

Still, the man regretted the decision, all the more when he heard the pursuit. Even wounded and weakened, he was confident that he could outrun the short-legged dwarves. When he looked back over his shoulder, though, he saw the young monk, flying effortlessly through the brush, gaining on him with every sure-footed stride.

The trees and brush opened up to more barren, rocky ground, and the desperate man smiled as he recalled his immediate terrain. He was a Night Mask to the bitter end, loyal and proud. His duty, wicked though it often was, had been his all, a dedication bordering on obsession.

The cruel monk was only a few strides behind him, he knew.

Loyal and proud, he never slowed as he came upon the edge of the hundred-foot cliff, and his scream as he leaped into the air was one of victory, not terror.

Eleven

What the Shadows Say

Long shadows of the day's last light streaked across the barn's floor and walls. Gray webs glistened across gaps in the rafters, then went dark as the sun slipped farther away. Vander leaned against the wooden wall, glad to be back in his body again, but not so glad to learn what had transpired in the few short hours that Ghost had taken his form.

The farmer's girl was dead, and her end had been most unpleasant.

Memories of the time he had fled to his homeland, the Spine of the World, when Ghost had caught up to him and taken his body, coursed through Vander's thoughts, forcing the firbolg lower against the wall. For the proud firbolg, the defeat was complete. To Vander's warrior sensibilities, this was the ultimate humiliation. He could accept being defeated in honest battle, could kneel to a rightful king, but Ghost had dared to take that one step further; Ghost had taken Vander's valor, his honor, his very identity.

"Have they returned?" the firbolg snapped at the black-and-silver robed man as soon as he appeared at the barn door.

"The trip to the mountains would have taken them all of last night," the Night Mask replied, as if he sensed Vander's frustration. "Likely, they have not yet even encountered Lady Maupoissant."

Vander looked away.

"The line has been set up to Carradoon, and the group has taken position near the Dragon's Codpiece," the assassin went on hopefully.

Vander eyed the man for a long moment. He knew what the human was thinking, knew that the man had only blurted that information in the hopes that the news would be well received and would spare him from the firbolg's unpredictable wrath.

Unpredictable! Vander nearly laughed at the vicious irony of that thought. He waved the man away, and the Night Mask seemed more than happy to follow the silent command.

Vander sat alone once more in the deepening shadows. He took some measure of solace in the fact that the noose was apparently tightening around their latest target and that this business might soon be concluded.

Vander hardly began to smile before a frown again captured his visage. The business would be finished and another would soon begin. It would not end, Vander knew, until Ghost decided that the firbolg had outlived his usefulness.

The sun was gone, leaving Vander in the darkness.

* * * * *

"You have indicated that you wanted to be of help," Ghost said to the surprised wizard. "Now I offer you that chance."

Bogo Rath's beady green eyes seemed to grow even smaller as he studied the sleepy-eyed man. He had just moved his small pack of belongings to the private room that Fredegar had provided, only to find the mysterious assassin sitting on his bed and waiting for him.

Ghost understood the wizard's suspicion and his hesitation. Bogo did not trust Ghost (and rightly so) and Bogo's agenda was his own. Surely Bogo wanted Cadderly dead, but Ghost knew that the opportunistic and ambitious young wizard was not working with the assassin band. Rather, he was working independently, hopeful that he might use them to meet his own ends. Ghost, above all others, could understand that self-serving methodology and, above all others, the wicked man knew the dangers that might accompany such actions.

"I am to serve as sentry?" Bogo replied, incredulous.

Ghost thought it over, then nodded—that was as good a description as he could think of. "For this minor exploration only," he answered. "The time has come for us to learn a bit more about Cadderly's room and personal defenses. I can do that, do not doubt, but I would not be pleased to have the other two priests of the library return to the inn while I am otherwise engaged."

Bogo spent a long moment staring at the man. "You are so filled with riddles," he said at length. "You can get near Cadderly, hint that you can get even closer, and yet, the young priest lives. Is it caution or macabre pleasure that makes you play the game?"

Ghost smiled, congratulating Bogo for his perceptiveness. "Both," he answered honestly, more than willing to tout his own prowess. "I am an artist, young wizard, and not a common killer. The game, for that is what it is, must be played on my terms and by my rules." Ghost carefully chose his emphasis for that last sentence, letting it sound just enough like a threat to keep Bogo on edge.

"It is early for the hearth room," Bogo reasoned. "The sun is just down. Most of the patrons are still at home, finishing their dinners. And I am not yet settled into my new quarters," he added, a hint of dissatisfaction in his tone.

"Do you consider that so very important?" Ghost asked bluntly.

Bogo found no immediate reply.

"Take your dinner down in the hearth room," Ghost replied. "It is not so unusual a practice for guests of the inn."

"The priests went to the Temple of Ilmater," Bogo argued. "It is unlikely they will return within the hour you say you will need."

"But they might," Ghost said, his voice hinting of mounting anger. "Artist," he reiterated, voicing each syllable slowly and clearly. "Perfectionist."

Bogo gave up the argument and resignedly nodded in agreement. Ghost had indicated that he wouldn't yet kill Cadderly, and the young wizard had no reason to believe otherwise. Certainly, if the weakling assassin had wanted to strike against the young priest, he could have done so at almost any time over the last few days, and he would not have had to go out of his way and engage Bogo to stand watch in the hearth room.

They left Bogo's room together, Ghost stopping Bogo at the door and whispering to him, "Do inform young Brennan, the innkeeper's son, that Cadderly wishes to take his dinner now." Bogo cocked an eyebrow at him.

"It will get the door open," Ghost explained, a perfectly reasonable lie.

Ghost turned into his own room, with Bogo continuing on to the stairway. The puny assassin silently congratulated himself for so easily handling the potentially troubling wizard. He willed the *Ghearufu* into sight as he slipped behind the protection of his partly opened door.

The industrious Brennan came hopping up the stairs a short while later, carrying a dinner tray balanced easily in one hand and a long and narrow package in the other. Ghost admired the spring in the teenager's step, the vigor and boundless energy of awakening manhood for the handsome, if a bit slender, Brennan.

"Boy!" Ghost called out softly as Brennan turned the corner past Avery's room and headed past the assassin's door. Brennan stopped and turned to regard the curious man, following the waving motion of Ghost's white-gloved hand.

"Let me deliver this and then I'll get you whatever . . ." Brennan began, but Ghost cut him short with his upheld hand, this one, Brennan noted curiously, adorned with a black glove.

"My business will take only a moment," Ghost said, the significance of his wry smile lost on the unsuspecting youth.

A split second later, Brennan found himself staring back into his own face, and to the hallway beyond. At first, he thought that the strange man had put up some sort of mirror, but then the image, his image, moved independently. And he, or at least his image, was now wearing the black and white gloves!

"What?" Brennan stammered, on the verge of panic.

Ghost shoved the trapped man back into the room and waded in, closing the door behind him, dropping the narrow bundle—he knew it now to be some sort of staff or rod—and setting the tray on his own night table.

"It is just a game," Ghost purred, trying to keep the terrified victim from calling out. "How do you like your borrowed body?"

Brennan's eyes darted about in search of some escape. Gradually, his terror shifted to curiosity; the man standing before him, wearing his body, certainly did not seem so ominous.

"I feel weak," he admitted bluntly, then cringed, realizing that he might have offended the man.

"But you are!" Ghost teased. "Do you not understand? That is the point of the game."

Brennan's face crinkled in further confusion, then his eyes popped open wide as Ghost, moving with the speed of youth, clenched his borrowed fist and launched a round-house punch. Brennan tried to dodge, tried to block, but the weak body did not respond quickly enough. The fist slipped through the pitiful defenses, slamming Brennan between the eyes, and he was falling helplessly, with no strength to resist the waves of blackness closing over him.

Ghost regarded the body for a long while, trying to discern his next move. The prudent act, he knew, would be to strangle Brennan then and there, as he had done with the beggar on the road, and put one glove on the body to prevent the regeneration process from recalling the lad's wandering spirit.

Other sensations argued against that course. The wretched assassin felt wonderful in the youth's body, full of barely controllable energy, and with his passions fluctuating almost violently, beckoning him urgently toward base actions he had not seriously considered for decades. The impulsive notion came to Ghost to reach over and remove the boot and the magical ring, to kill Brennan in the weakling body and leave him dead. Ghost could then claim this form as his own until he had burned it out as he had nearly burned out the effeminate mantle.

He again wore the black and white gloves when his hands went around the weakling's neck.

Ghost realized that he must not do it—not yet. He berated himself for even beginning to act on such a rash notion. Moving methodically, he tied and gagged his victim securely, dragged him behind the bed, and wedged him between the bed and the wall.

The ring had already begun its work, and young Brennan's eyelids fluttered with the first signs of consciousness.

Ghost smashed him again, and again after that.

Brennan groaned through the gag and Ghost leaned in close, putting his lips to the trapped boy's ear. "You must be quiet," he purred, "or you will be punished."

Brennan groaned again, more loudly.

"Would you like me to tell you the punishments I have planned for your disobedience?" Ghost asked, putting a finger into Brennan's eye.

The terrified Brennan made no sounds and no movements at all.

"Good, wise lad," Ghost cooed. "Now let us see what you have brought." The assassin moved away and quickly unwrapped the bundle, revealing a ram-headed walking stick, finely crafted and perfectly balanced. Ghost had seen the marvelous item before, in Cadderly's hands when the priest had gone to the wizard's tower outside Carradoon. Only then did Ghost realize that the young priest had not been carrying the stick when he had returned down the road.

"How convenient!" he said, moving back over to Brennan. "I said I would tell you of the punishments, but here, let me show you instead," he said, patting the formidable club against his open palm.

Ghost's face contorted with sudden rage, and he launched a two-handed overhead chop. He felt the magic of the weapon thrumming when he slammed the ram's head down on Brennan's shoulder, and smiled even more widely when he saw the skinny limb crumble under the weapon's tremendous enchantment. Ghost had never fancied weapons, but he thought of keeping this one.

Ghost considered the wisdom of turning the walking stick over to Cadderly. The assassin was left in a quandary, for if the young priest was expecting the weapon's return, he might seek out Fredegar, or the wizard in the tower, and either would likely pose larger, more dangerous, questions.

That would be the worst of the possibilities.

The artist-killer left the room a few minutes later, bearing the tray and the retied bundle for Cadderly, and leaving the crumpled, unconscious Brennan hidden behind the bed in a pool of blood. Ghost had beaten Brennan severely, and the young man in the pitiful body would soon have died, except for the persistent healing magic of the ring concealed under the boot.

Semiconscious, Brennan almost hoped he would die. A thousand fiery explosions seemed to be going off within him; every joint ached, and the evil man with the club had paid particularly painful attention to his groin and collarbone.

He tried to move his head but could not; tried to wriggle his body out of the tight cubby, despite the pain, but found he was securely bound in place. He reflexively coughed up another gout of blood, his survival instincts barely managing to force the warm liquid past the gag so that he would not choke on it.

Broken, Brennan prayed that this torment would soon end, even if that end meant death. He did not know, of course, that he wore a magical ring, that he would soon be healed once more.

* * * * *

Cadderly wasn't thinking of dinner, wasn't thinking of anything at all beyond the alluring song playing in his mind as he turned the pages of the *Tome of Universal Harmony.* The book had offered him shelter once again, had chased away the images of Avery and Rufo—they had come back to see Cadderly that morning, and had again been abruptly turned away—and all the other troubles weighing heavily on the young priest's shoulders.

Under the protection of the sweet song of Deneir, Cadderly felt none of that weight, but sat straight and tall. He worked his arms out to the sides when they were not engaged in turning the pages, in a manner similar to the meditative techniques Danica had once shown him back at the Edificant Library. Back then, these movements had been simple exercise, but now, with the song flowing through his every movement, Cadderly felt the strength, his inner strength, coursing through his limbs.

"I have your supper!" he heard Brennan call from behind him, and he knew from the young man's volume that Brennan had probably called him several times and knocked loudly on the door before that. Embarrassed, Cadderly closed the great book and turned to meet the young man.

Brennan's eyes opened wide.

"Excuse me," Cadderly apologized, looking around helplessly for something with which to cover up. He was naked from the waist up, his well-muscled chest and shoulders glistening with sweat, and the rippling muscles of his waistline, newly trim from the meditative exercises over the tome, quivering from the recent exertion.

Brennan quickly composed himself, even flipped Cadderly a towel from the dinner tray with which he could rub down.

"It would seem that you could use the meal," Ghost offered. "I did not know that reading could be so strenuous."

Cadderly chuckled at the witticism, though he was a bit confused that Brennan had made such a remark. The young man had seen him at his reading many times before, and many times involved, as he was now, in the meditative exercises.

"What have you there?" Cadderly asked, seeing the long and narrow bundle.

Ghost fumbled with the item, still unsure if the young priest had expected it or not. "It came in just this afternoon,"

he explained, "from the wizard, I would assume." He unwrapped the bundle and handed the fine walking stick to
Cadderly.

"Yes, Belisarius," Cadderly replied absently. He waved
the walking stick about easily, testing its balance, then
tossed it casually on the bed. "I had nearly forgotten about
it," he remarked, and added with obvious sarcasm, "I
wonder what mighty enchantments my wizard friend bestowed upon it!"

Ghost only shrugged, though secretly he was gnawing
at his lower lip, angry now that he had decided to return
the unlooked-for present.

Cadderly gave the young man a wink. "Not that I will
ever find use for it, you understand."

"We never know when a fight might fall our way," Ghost
replied, sliding the tray onto Cadderly's small table and arranging the silverware. Cadderly eyed him curiously,
caught off guard by the grim tones and uncharacteristically
reflective thought of the passion-driven youth.

The young man held a serrated knife in his hand for just
a moment, with his hand only inches from Cadderly's bare
chest. For some reason, that dangerous image suddenly
mattered to Cadderly; silent alarms went off inside him.
The young priest fought them away, as easily as he rubbed
the sweat from his neck, rationally telling himself that he
was letting his imagination run wild.

The song played in the back of Cadderly's mind. He
almost turned about to see if he had left the tome open, but
he had not; he could not. Shadows began to form atop Brennan's slender shoulders.

Aurora.

For some reason he could not understand, Cadderly
sensed again the unfathomable possibility that Brennan was
considering striking him with the knife.

Suddenly, Brennan dropped the knife to the tray and

fumbled about with the small bowl and plate. Cadderly did not relax; Brennan's movements were too stiff, too edgy, as if Brennan was consciously trying to act as though nothing unusual had occurred.

Cadderly said nothing, but held the small towel around his neck with both hands, his muscles tight and ready. He did not concentrate on the man's specific actions; rather, he shifted back to the young man's shoulders, to the misshapen, growling shadows huddled there, black claws raking empty air.

Aurora.

The song played in the distant recesses of his mind, revealing the truth before him. But Cadderly, still a novice, still unsure of his power's source, did not know if he should trust in it or not.

Cadderly could not recognize the shadows any more than to equate them with the same fearsome things he had seen perched upon the shoulders of the beggar on the road. He sensed that they boded evil, both then and now, sensed that they were images resulting from vile thoughts. Considering that Brennan had just been holding a cutting knife, that a short stroke could have driven the serrated instrument into Cadderly's bare chest, those sensations did not put the young priest at ease.

"You must go," he said to the youth.

Ghost looked up at him, confused, but again, the expression did not seem right to Cadderly. "Is something wrong?" the slender youth asked innocently.

"Go," Cadderly said again, his scowl unrelenting, and this time the word held the strength of a minor magical enchantment.

Surprisingly, the young man held stubbornly to his position. The shadows on Brennan's shoulders dissipated and Cadderly had to wonder if he had misread the signals, if those shadows represented something else altogether.

Brennan gave him a curt bow—another unexpected movement from the young man that Cadderly thought he knew quite well—and then prudently slipped from the room, closing the door behind him.

Cadderly stood staring at the door for a long time, thinking that he must be going mad. He looked back to the *Tome of Universal Harmony*, wondering if it was a cursed book, a book inspiring lies and a discordant song that sounded true to the foolish victim's ear. How many priests had been found dead, lying across its open pages?

Cadderly labored for breath for a few crucial moments, at a crossroad in his life, though he did not realize it.

No, he decided at length. He had to believe in the book, wanted desperately to believe in something.

Still he remained in the same position, looking back to the door, to the tome, and lastly to his own heart. He realized that his meal was getting cold, then knew he did not care.

The emptiness within him could not be sated by food.

* * * * *

Bogo had given Ghost more than the hour the evil man had asked for, but the eager wizard decided to stay in the hearth room anyway, to see what he might learn. The talk among the growing number of patrons settled always on the rumors of war, but, to Bogo's relief, none of the gathering seemed to have any idea of the depth of the danger that hung over their heads. When Aballister decided to march, most likely in the early spring, the army of Castle Trinity would have little trouble in bringing Carradoon to its knees.

The night deepened, the warm fires and the many conversations blazed, and Bogo, despite his fears that Ghost had already dispatched Cadderly, remained in the room, listening and chatting. Every time the door to the foyer opened, the young wizard looked up, anxious to note the return of the two priests, thinking that perhaps they would provide him with better information than the misinformed townsmen.

Bogo's smile curled up when Kierkan Rufo entered a short while later, for the more formidable headmaster was not beside the angular man. Rufo headed right for the stairs, but Bogo cut him off.

"You are of the Edificant Library?" he asked, his tone sounding hopeful.

Rufo's sharp features seemed sharper still in the flickering firelight, and his dark eyes did not blink as he regarded the curious-looking young man.

"Might I buy you some ale, or fine wine perhaps?" Bogo pressed, seeing no answer forthcoming.

Rufo's answer dripped of suspicion. "Why?"

"I am not of the region," Bogo replied without the slightest hesitation. The ambitious mage had played this scene out a dozen times in his mind, along with several other potential scenarios concerning the priest who would be stooge. "All the night, I have been assailed with rumors of war," he explained. "And all the rumors hint that the one hope lies in the Edificant Library."

Again Rufo did not respond, but Bogo noticed the vain man straighten his shoulders with some pride.

"I am not without skills," Bogo went on, confident that Rufo was falling into his trap. "Perhaps I might aid in those hopes. Surely I would try.

"Let me buy you some wine, then," Bogo offered after a short pause, not wanting to break his budding momentum. "We can talk, and perhaps a wise priest can guide me to where my skills would be most helpful."

Rufo looked back to the foyer door, as though he expected, and feared, that Headmaster Avery would come pounding through at any moment. Then he nodded curtly and followed Bogo to one of the few empty tables remaining in the hearth room.

The talk remained casual for some time, with Bogo and Rufo sipping their wine, and Bogo quickly losing any hope that he would be able to get too much of the drink into the angular man. Rufo, who had been through many torments these last few weeks, remained cautious and guarded, covering his half-filled glass whenever Brennan, waiting on tables, made one of his frequent visits.

Bogo noted several times that the innkeeper's son seemed to be regarding him suspiciously, but he attributed it to the lad's natural curiosity that a stranger would have business with a priest from the library, and thought no more of it.

Bogo wasted little time in shifting the conversation to more specific topics, such as the Edificant Library and the ranking of Rufo's portly friend. Gradually, casually, the wizard led the talk to include the other priest who was a guest at the inn. Rufo, cryptic from the start, backed off even more and seemed to grow somewhat suspicious, but Bogo did not relent.

"Why are you in town?" Bogo asked, rather sharply.

Rufo seemed to note the subtle shift in the increasingly impatient wizard's tone. He rested back in his chair and regarded Bogo silently.

"I must go," the angular priest announced unexpectedly, bracing himself on the table and beginning to rise.

"Sit down, Kierkan Rufo," Bogo snarled at him. Rufo looked at him curiously for a moment, and realized he had not, in the course of the conversation, told the man his name. A small whine escaped the angular man's thin lips as he fell back into his chair, now almost expecting what was to come.

"How do you know my name?" Rufo demanded with as much courage as he could muster.

"Druzil told it to me," Bogo answered bluntly. Again came that almost imperceptible whine.

Rufo began to ask another question, but Bogo promptly silenced him.

"You will answer and obey," Bogo explained casually.

"Not again," Rufo growled with defiance that surprised even himself.

"Dorigen thinks differently," Bogo replied, "as does Druzil, who has been in your room for both nights you have been in town," Bogo lied. "The imp has been in your room since before you and Avery occupied the room. Did you think to escape so easily, Kierkan Rufo? Did you think the battle was won despite the minor setback we were given in Shilmista Forest?"

Rufo found no words with which to respond.

"There," Bogo said calmly, settling back into his chair and flipping his stringy brown hair over to one side. "Now we understand each other."

"What do you require of me this time?" Rufo asked, his voice sharp and a bit too loud for Bogo's liking (especially since Brennan was nearby again, regarding the two men with open curiosity). Rufo's visage continued to appear defiant, but Bogo was not concerned. The man was weak, he knew, else Rufo would have already left, or struck out against his revealed enemy.

"As of now, nothing," Bogo answered, not wanting to set too many things into motion until he better understood what Ghost and the Night Masks were planning. "I will be nearby, and you will remain available to me. I have some specific things planned for my visit to Carradoon, and you, Rufo, will play a role in those, do not doubt." He tipped his glass to the angular man and drained it, then rose from the table and started away, leaving Rufo lost in yet another unresolvable trap.

"Be wary, young mage," Bogo heard from the side as he

took his first step up the stairs beside the hearth room's bar. He turned to see young Brennan, casually wiping down the bar and regarding him dangerously.

"Are you addressing me?" Bogo asked, trying to sound superior, though he was indeed becoming a bit unnerved by the innkeeper's son's sudden attention.

"I am warning you," Ghost, appearing as Brennan, clarified. "And know that it is the only warning you will receive. Your business here is as observer—that position determined by Aballister himself. If you interfere, you might find yourself lying in a hole beside Cadderly."

Bogo's eyes widened in shock, an expression that brought a satisfied smile to Ghost's borrowed lips.

"Who are you?" the wizard demanded. "How . . . ?"

"We are many," Ghost replied cryptically, obviously enjoying the spectacle of the squirming mage. "We are many and we are all about you. You were told that we do things properly, Bogo Rath. You were told that we take no chances." Ghost let it drop there and turned back to his work at the bar.

Bogo understood the reason behind the sudden break in the conversation when Avery, just returned to the inn, and Kierkan Rufo walked past him up the stairs, heading for their rooms.

Bogo followed them at a safe distance, no longer certain that he would have further instructions for Kierkan Rufo, no longer certain of anything.

Twelve

Mortality

T he dawn found Cadderly at his meditation, at his exercises, reaching his arms far to the side one at a time, muscle playing powerfully against muscle. He eyed the open book on the table before him as he moved, heard the song in his head, and felt in tune with it. Sweat lathered his bare chest and streaked the sides of his face, and the young priest felt it keenly, his senses heightened in this meditative state.

When at last he finished, Cadderly was thoroughly weary. He considered his bed, then changed his mind, thinking that he had been spending too much time in his room the past few days. The day would be bright and warm; outside his window, Impresk Lake glittered with a thousand sparkles in the morning sun.

Cadderly closed the *Tome of Universal Harmony*, but, looking upon the waters of that lake, so serene and inspiring, he still heard the song acutely. It was time to take the knowledge (the emotional strength, he hoped) that he had gained from the book out into the world. It was time to see how his new insights might fit into the everyday struggles of the people around him.

Cadderly feared those revelations. Could he control the shadows he would inevitably see dancing atop the shoulders of the many people of Carradoon? And could he decipher their meaning—truly? He thought back to the events of the night before, when he had turned young Brennan away, frightened at the implications of the squirming, growling manifestations he had seen.

The young priest washed and toweled off, strengthening his resolve. The choices seemed clear: go out and learn to assimilate in light of his newfound knowledge, or remain in his room, living a hermitlike existence. Cadderly thought of Belisarius, alone in his tower. The wizard would die there, alone, and, most likely, his body would not be discovered for weeks.

Cadderly did not wish to share that grim fate.

* * * * *

Still wearing the mantle of young Brennan, Ghost, absently replacing the candles on the lowered chandelier at the top of the staircase, watched the young priest leave the Dragon's Codpiece. He had heard Cadderly tell Fredegar that he would not return until late, and Ghost thought that a good thing. The Night Masks were in town and ready; Ghost had to meet with them this day. Perhaps young Cadderly would have a rather unpleasant surprise waiting for him when he returned that evening.

A patient killer, an artist, Ghost would have preferred to wait a few more days before arranging the strike, would have liked to get even closer to this curious young man, to know everything about him so that there could be no mistakes. The assassin considered this especially important in light of the potential problems arising from the arrival of the two other priests. Powerful priests had been known to resurrect the dead, and under normal circumstances, Ghost would prefer to take the time and discern exactly how much magical interference might be expected from the newcomers, particularly the priest bearing the title of headmaster. Might the Night Masks slay young Cadderly, only to have Avery locate his body and bring him back to life?

Bogo Rath presented even more complications. What might the upstart wizard be planning? the assassin wondered. Bogo had spoken with the other, lesser priest on the previous night, and that could not be a good thing.

Ghost did not like loose ends. He was a consummate professional who prided himself on being a perfect killer with never a lingering problem left behind. But while this operation seemed ragged to him, he had to believe that the problems could be circumvented—or eliminated. A new wrinkle had come into this picture, a new desire for Ghost that, in his mind at least, justified his seeming carelessness. Ghost felt the vitality coursing through his limbs, felt the powerful urges of adolescence, and remembered the pleasure those urges might bring.

He did not want to give up his new body.

But he knew, too, that he could not continue to play this charade much longer. With a single meeting, Cadderly had come to suspect that something was amiss, and Ghost did not doubt that those suspicions would only increase with time. Also, in this form, Ghost was severely restricted. His other body remained alive, and it would until the assassin fully committed himself to the idea of taking Brennan's body as his own, a dangerous action indeed until this mission was completed. And while that other, puny form drew breath, Ghost could not use the *Ghearufu* on any new victims. Even to get to Vander, his chosen victim, Ghost would have to go through his own body, and doing that would release young Brennan.

Things would become so much simpler when Cadderly lay dead, he knew. Ghost had considered trying the strike the night before, when he had held a cutting knife in his hand just inches from Cadderly's bare chest. If his aim had been good, the game would have ended then and there, and he could collect his gold, and seriously consider his immediate impulse to retain this young and vital body, to kill the trapped spirit of the young man back in his own room and remove the magical ring from the corpse's foot. In just a few days, his spirit would become acclimated to this new form, and then the *Ghearufu* would be his to use again. Vital youth would be his once more.

Hesitance had cost the assassin his chance. Before he had resolved to move, Cadderly was again intent upon him. The loose ends—his ignorance of Cadderly's powers, his ignorance of the other two priests—had held him back.

"Brennan!" Fredegar's cry startled the assassin from his contemplations.

"What are you waiting for?" the innkeeper bellowed. "Get that chandelier cranked back to its place, and soon! The hearth room needs cleaning, boy. Now get to it!"

More restrictions accompanied the pleasing young form. Ghost did not even argue. The Night Masks were not far—he had plenty of time to get to them—and in truth, he was glad for the delay so that he could better sort through the many potential problems and the many interesting questions.

About an hour later, the assassin was even more grateful for the delay that had kept him at the inn, when a young woman, strawberry-blonde hair bouncing gaily about her shoulders, entered the Dragon's Codpiece, looking for Cadderly and introducing herself as Lady Danica Maupoissant.

Another wrinkle.

* * * * *

"There's the lad!" Ivan called, pointing back toward the front of the Dragon's Codpiece and roughly spinning Pikel about.

"Oo oi!" Pikel piped as soon as he spotted Cadderly, more concerned with getting Ivan's hands off him so that he might stop his spin. Dizzied, the green-bearded dwarf shuffled from foot to foot, struggling to straighten his cooking pot helmet.

Ivan started for Cadderly, who had not yet noticed them, but Danica put a hand on the dwarf's shoulder. As soon as the startled dwarf turned about and looked into Danica's pleading eyes, he understood.

"Ye want to go to him yerself," Ivan reasoned.

"Might I?" Danica asked. "I do not know how Cadderly will respond to seeing me. I would prefer . . ."

"Say no more, Lady," Ivan bellowed. "Me and me brother got more than a bit of work afore us, and it's getting late in the day already. I'll get us some rooms there." He pointed to the sign of an inn two doors down from where they stood, and two doors shy of the Dragon's Codpiece. "Ye can come and get us when ye want us.

"And ye can give him this from me and me brother," Ivan added, pulling the adamantite spindle-disks from a deep pocket. He started to give them to Danica, then pulled them back, embarrassed. As discreetly as he could, the gruff dwarf rubbed off a chunk of the weapon's first victim's face. Danica could not miss the movement. With a helpless shrug, Ivan tossed the disks to her.

Danica bent low and kissed the understanding dwarf on the forehead, drawing a deep blush from Ivan.

"Hee hee hee," Pikel chirped.

"Aw, what'd ye go and do that for?" the flustered dwarf asked Danica. He slapped his chuckling brother across the shoulder to set them both into motion, moving away from the inn and away from Cadderly. Ivan knew that if the young scholar saw them all, he would probably invite them in, thus ruining Danica's desires.

Danica stood alone in the crowded street, watching Cadderly's every step as he made his way into the Dragon's Codpiece. Across from her, the waters of Impresk Lake sparkled in late afternoon sunlight, and she almost followed their spellbinding allure and ran away from her fears. Truly, Danica did not know how Cadderly would react, did not know how final their parting in Shilmista Forest had been.

If Cadderly rebuked her now, Danica did not know where she would turn.

For the young monk, who had faced many challenges, many enemies, no moment had ever been so trying. It took every measure of courage that Danica could muster, but, finally, she skipped off toward the waiting inn.

Cadderly was on the stairs, heading up, when Danica entered. He held his familiar walking stick in the crook of one elbow and was looking at some wrinkled parchment, apparently oblivious to the world around him.

Quiet as a cat, the agile monk crossed the room and made the stairs. A boy of perhaps fifteen years eyed her curiously as she passed, she noted, and she half expected the lad to stop her, for she was not a paying guest. He did not, though, and soon Cadderly, still too busy with the parchment to notice her, loomed just two steps ahead of her.

Danica studied him a moment longer. He looked leaner than he had just a few weeks ago, but she knew it was not for lack of eating. Cadderly's boyish form had taken on the hardness of manhood; even his step seemed more sure and solid, less inclined to skip aside from his chosen path.

"You look good," Danica blurted, hardly thinking before she made the comment. Cadderly stopped abruptly, stumbling over the next step. Slowly, he lifted his gaze from the parchment. Danica heard him gulp for breath.

It seemed like many minutes had passed before the young priest finally mustered the courage to turn and face her, and when he did, Danica stared into a confused face indeed. She waited for Cadderly to reply, but, apparently, he either could not find his voice, or had nothing to say.

"You look good," Danica said again, and she thought herself incredibly inane. "I . . . we, had to come to Carradoon . . ."

She stopped, her words halted by the look in Cadderly's gray eyes. Danica had many times before stared intently into those eyes, but she saw something new there now, a sadness of bitter experiences.

Again, it seemed like many minutes slipped by.

Cadderly's walking stick fell to the stairs with an impossibly loud thud. Danica looked to it curiously, and when she looked up again, Cadderly was with her, his arms wrapped about her, nearly crushing her.

Danica was independent and strong, arguably one of the very finest fighters in all the land, but never in her life had she felt so secure and warm. Gentle tears made their way down her smooth cheeks; there was no sadness in her heart.

*   *   *   *   *

Still wearing Brennan's body as his own, Ghost watched the pair from the bottom of the stairs as he absently pushed a broom back and forth. His devious mind continued its typical whirling, formulating new plans, making subtle adjustments in the old plans. Ghost had to get things moving quickly now, he knew. The complications were undeniably piling up.

The skilled killer, the artist, was not afraid. He liked

challenges, and compared to the many dead heroes he had left in his wake, this action, this victim, Cadderly, did not seem so much a problem.

* * * * *

Danica.

Cadderly had not seen her in more than five weeks, and while he had not forgotten her appearance, he was nonetheless surprised by her beauty. She stood inside the closed door of his room, her head cocked patiently to the side, strawberry hair dancing against one shoulder, and her exotic eyes, rich and brown, tender and knowing, gazing at him.

He had initiated their breakup. He had been the one who had left—had left Danica, the war, and Shilmista. He still was not certain of Danica's intentions in coming to see him, but whatever they might be, Cadderly knew it was surely his turn to speak, to explain.

"I did not expect you to come," he said, moving beside his reading table and gently closing the *Tome of Universal Harmony*. A nervous chuckle escaped his dry lips. "I feared I would receive an invitation to Shilmista Forest to witness the wedding of Danica and Elbereth."

"I do not deserve that," Danica replied, keeping her melodic voice even-toned and steady.

Cadderly threw up his hands helplessly. "I would have deserved it," he admitted.

Danica produced Ivan's gift and tossed it to him. "From the dwarves," she explained as Cadderly caught the heavy disks. "They began it long ago, a present to the one who saved the Edificant Library."

Cadderly could feel the strength of the weapon, and that horrified him as much as thrilled him. "Always weapons," he muttered resignedly and tossed the spindle-disks to the floor at the foot of his bed, where they bounced against a small clothes chest, dented the hardwood, and rolled to a stop inches from Cadderly's newly enchanted walking stick.

Cadderly regarded the fitting image and nearly laughed aloud, but he would not let Danica's obvious distraction keep him from his point. "You loved the elf prince," he said to her.

"He is now the elf king," Danica reminded him.

Cadderly did not miss the fact that she did not respond to his accusation.

"You did . . . do love Elbereth," Cadderly said again, quietly.

"As do you," Danica replied. "He is a dear friend, and among the most extraordinary and honorable people I have ever had the privilege of fighting beside. I would give my life for the elf king of Shilmista, as would you."

Her words did not come as any revelation to Cadderly. All along, beneath the veil of his fears, he had known the truth of Danica's relationship with Elbereth, had known that her love for the elf—and it was indeed love—was irrelevant to her feelings for the priest. Danica and Elbereth had bonded in a common cause, as warriors with shared values. If Cadderly loved Danica, and he did with all of his heart, then how could he not also love Elbereth?

But there remained a nagging question, a nagging doubt, and not one about Danica.

"You would give your life for him," Cadderly replied with all sincerity. "I wish I could claim equal courage."

Danica's smile was not meant to mock him, but he felt it keenly anyway.

"I ran from there," Cadderly pointedly reminded her.

"Not when you were needed," Danica replied. "Neither I nor the elves have forgotten what you did at Syldritch Trea, or in the height of the fight. Tintagel is alive because of you.

Shilmista is back in the hands of Elbereth's people because of you."

"But I ran away," Cadderly argued. "Do not doubt that."

Danica's next question, tinged with innocence and honest trepidation, caught the young priest off his guard. "Why did you run?"

She dropped her traveling cloak on the small night table and moved over to sit on Cadderly's bed, and he turned about to look out of his window, over the still-glittering lake in the dying light of day. Cadderly had never asked himself that question so bluntly, had never considered the cause of his distress.

"Because," he said after a moment, then he paused again, the words still not clear in his mind. He heard the bed creak and feared for a moment that Danica was coming to him; he did not want her to see the pain on his face at that moment. The bed creaked again and he realized that she had only shifted and had not risen.

"Too much was spinning about me," he said. "The fighting, the magic, my dilemma over Dorigen's unconscious form and the fear that I did wrong in not killing her, the cries of the dying that would not leave my ears." Cadderly managed a soft chuckle. "And the way you looked at Elbereth."

"All of that would seem cause to remain beside those who love you, not to run away," Danica observed.

"This madness has been mounting for some time," Cadderly explained, "perhaps even before the evil priest began his assault on the library. Perhaps I have been troubled all of my adult life. That would not surprise me.

"I must face these troubles and get beyond them," he continued, stealing a look at Danica over his shoulder. "I know that now."

"But again . . ." Danica began, but Cadderly, facing the lake again, cut her off with an outstretched palm.

"I could not face them beside you, do you not understand?" he asked, his voice pleading, hoping that she would forgive him. "Back in the library, whenever the many questions threatened to overwhelm me, all I had to do was seek out my Danica, my love. Beside you, watching you, there were no troubles, no unanswerable questions."

He turned to face her squarely, saw the joy emanating from her beautiful face.

"You are not my answer," Cadderly admitted, and he winced as Danica's light went out, a great pain washing through her almond eyes.

"You are not my cure," Cadderly quickly tried to explain, lamenting his initial choice of words. "You are a salve, a temporary relief."

"A plaything?"

"Never!" The word was torn from Cadderly's heart, bursting forth with the sureness that Danica needed to hear.

"When I am with you, then all the world and all of my life is beautiful," Cadderly went on. "In truth, it is not, of course. Shilmista proved that beyond doubt. When I am with you, I can hide behind my love. You, my Danica, have been my mask. Wearing it, I could even hide from the horrors of that continuing battle, I am sure."

"But you could not hide from yourself," Danica put in, beginning to catch on.

Cadderly nodded. "There are troubles in here," he explained, pointing to his heart and then to his head, "that will remain beside me until I can resolve them. Or until they destroy me."

"And you could not face them while your mask was there to hide behind," Danica reasoned. There was no malice in her quiet tones. Honestly sympathetic for Cadderly, she asked softly, "Have you found your answers?"

Cadderly nearly laughed out loud. "I have found more

questions," he admitted. "The world has only become more confusing since I delved into myself." He pointed to the *Tome of Universal Harmony*. "You would hardly believe the sights that book has shown to me, though whether they are true sights or clever deceptions, I cannot tell."

By the way Danica's posture seemed to shrink back from him, Cadderly realized that he had said something revealing. He waited long moments for Danica to respond, to share the revelation with him.

"You question your faith?" she asked bluntly.

Cadderly spun away, his gaze again searching for the dying light on the lake. She had hit the mark squarely, he only then realized. How could he, as a priest of Deneir, doubt the vision and magic shown to him by the most holy book of his god?

"I do not doubt the principles espoused by the clerics of Deneir," Cadderly asserted with conviction.

"Then it is the god himself," Danica reasoned incredulously. "You question the existence of such beings?" her voice nearly broke apart with the words. "How can one who was raised among priests, and who has witnessed so much clerical magic, claim to be agnostic?"

"I claim nothing," Cadderly protested. "I am just not certain of anything!"

"You have seen the magic bestowed by the gods," Danica argued. "You felt the magic . . . in healing Tintagel."

"I believe in magic," Cadderly reasoned. "It is an undeniable fact on the soil of Faerûn. And, yes, I have felt the power, but where it comes from I cannot say."

"The curse of intelligence," Danica muttered ironically. Cadderly regarded her over his shoulder once more. "You cannot believe anything you cannot prove beyond doubt," she said to him. "Must everything be tangible? Is there no room for faith in a mind that can unravel any of the lesser mysteries?"

A wind had kicked up across the lake. Ripples rolled to the shore, carrying the last daylight on their crests.

"I just do not know," Cadderly said, regarding the rolling water, trying to find some fitting symbolism in its transport of the dying light.

"Why did you run?" Danica asked him again, and he knew by her determined tone that she meant to force him through this, whatever the cost to them both.

"I was afraid," he admitted. "Afraid to kill any more. Afraid that you would be killed. That I could not bear." Cadderly paused and swallowed hard, forced to come to terms with this difficult realization. His silence went on, Danica not daring to interrupt his train of thought.

"I was afraid to die." There it was. Cadderly had just admitted his own cowardice. He tightened his arms against his sides, fearing Danica's stinging rebuttal.

"Of course you were," she said instead, and there was no sarcasm in her remark. "You question your faith, question that there is anything beyond this existence. If you believe there is nothing more, then of what worth is honor? Bravery rides the crest of a cause, Cadderly. You would die for Elbereth. You have already proven that. And if a spear were aimed for my heart, you would willingly take it in my stead. That I do not doubt."

Cadderly continued to stare out the window. He heard Danica shifting on the bed again, but was too lost in contemplations of her wisdom. He watched the last gasps of light riding the waves, riding the crest, and knew that there was truth in Danica's description. He had been afraid to die in Shilmista, but only because the justification for continuing that fight was founded in a cause of principles, and those principles were, in turn, founded in faith. And he had been so angry at Danica and Elbereth, and all the others, because he had feared for them and could not appreciate their dedication to those higher principles, their willingness to continue a course that might easily lead to their deaths.

"I would take the spear," Cadderly decided.

"I never doubted you," Danica replied. There was something in the ring of her voice, something softer and mysterious, that made Cadderly turn back to her.

She lay on her side comfortably on his bed, her clothes dropped in a pile at the bedside. If Cadderly lived a thousand years, he would never forget the sight of Danica at that moment. She rested her head against her hand, propped at the elbow, her thick strawberry-blonde locks cascading down her arm to dance on the single pillow. The minimal light accentuated the curves of Danica's soft skin, the shine of her sculpted legs.

"Through all the weeks, I never doubted you," she said.

Cadderly sensed the slight tremor in her voice, but still could not believe how brave she had been. Without blinking, he unbuttoned his shirt and started to her.

A moment later, they were together. The song played again in Cadderly's mind. No, rather, he felt it, thrumming with urgency through every facet of his body, guiding him through every subtle motion, and convincing him that nothing had ever been so right.

Cadderly's mind whirled through a dizzying jumble of thoughts and emotions. He thought of Danica bearing his child, and considered the implications of mortality.

Most of all, Cadderly focused his thoughts on Danica, his soul mate, and he loved her all the more. Perhaps once she had been his shelter, but only because he had made that her role. Now, Cadderly had revealed his vulnerability, his deepest fears, and Danica had accepted them, and him, with all her heart, and with the sincere desire to help him resolve them.

Later, as Danica slept, Cadderly rose from the bed and lit a single candle on his table, beside the *Tome of Universal*

Harmony. Not bothering to dress, he looked back to Danica on the bed, and felt a surge of love course through his veins. Strengthened by that security, Cadderly sat down and opened the book, hopeful that, in light of this night's revelations, he would hear the song a different way.

* * * * *

Many hours before Cadderly lit that candle, Ghost had slipped away from the young priest's door, confident from his eavesdropping that the arrival of Danica Maupoissant would do little to deflect his solidifying plans. Actually, Ghost had come to the conclusion that he might be able to use Danica—her body, at least—to substantially increase the pleasure offered by this kill.

If he could possess the body of Cadderly's lover, he might catch the young priest with his guard about as far down as it could possibly go.

But for all the eagerness reflected when Ghost rubbed his hands together, every step of the way back to his own room, he was wise enough to realize that things had become dangerously complicated.

Still bound in the cubby between bed and wall, poor, beaten Brennan looked up pleadingly.

"I will release you this night," Ghost promised. "I have decided that I cannot afford to keep your body—and a pity that is, for the body is fine!"

Brennan, desperate to hope, almost managed to smile right up until the point when Ghost's hands—Brennan's own hands—closed around his borrowed throat. There was no pain this time for the beleaguered innkeeper's son; there was only blackness.

The task completed, Ghost sat down on the bed, untying the weakling form and waiting impatiently for when he could take back his own body. He lamented that he had lost his chance at this fine young form, but reminded himself of the pressing business and pressing danger. He assured himself that he would find another suitable body soon enough, when Cadderly lay dead.

Thirteen

The Stooge's Stooge

Kierkan Rufo eyed the stocked shelves with open contempt. Shopping! For more than a dozen years, he had labored in the Edificant Library, had meticulously attended to his duties, and now Headmaster Avery had sent him shopping!

This entire trip to Carradoon had been one humiliation after another for poor Rufo. He knew his actions in Shilmista had angered Avery (though he had convinced himself by this time that none of it had really been his fault), but he never would have believed that the headmaster would degrade him so. Through all the many meetings, with the priests of Ilmater, with several of the other religious Sects in the city, and with the city officials, Rufo had been ordered to stand behind Avery and remain silent. These meetings were vital to the defense of the region, vital to the survival of the Edificant Library, yet Rufo was, for all purposes, left out of them. Not only was his input not wanted by Avery, the headmaster had outright forbidden it!

And now he was shopping. Rufo stood before the shelves for many moments, fantasizing that the other side had won in Shilmista Forest, thinking that he would have been better off if Dorigen's forces had slaughtered the elves and had taken him into their ranks as the imp had promised. Perhaps the world would be a better place for Kierkan Rufo if Cadderly had fallen in the sylvan shadows.

Cadderly! The word screamed out in Rufo's mind like the most damning of curses. Cadderly had apparently forsaken the library and the Order of Deneir, had virtually slapped Headmaster Avery and all the other priests in the face with his desertion—there could be no other word for the young priest's actions. Cadderly had never been a good priest—not by Rufo's estimation—had never attended to the many duties given the lesser clerics with any kind of dedication. And yet, in Avery's eyes at least, Cadderly ranked far above Rufo, far above any except the ruling order in the library.

Rufo grabbed a sack of flour and pulled it to him so forcefully that a small white puff burst up at him, covering his face.

"Someone's not seeming a bit too happy," came a gruff, gravelly voice beside him.

"Uh-uh," agreed a voice on the other side.

The angular priest did not have to look sidelong or down to know that the Bouldershoulder brothers had flanked him, and that fact did little to improve his sour mood. He had known that the dwarves were coming to Carradoon, but he had hoped that he and Avery would be well on their way back to the library before these two ever arrived.

He turned toward Ivan and started to push past the dwarf, through the narrow aisle of the cramped store. Ivan did little to aid the angular man, and with the dwarf's considerable girth, Rufo had nowhere to go.

"Ye're in a hurry," Ivan remarked. "I thinked ye'd be glad to see me and me brother."

"Get out of my way, dwarf," Rufo said grimly.

"Dwarf?" Ivan echoed, feigning a mortal wound. "Ye saying that like it's an insult?"

"Take it for what you will," Rufo replied evenly, "but do get out of my way. I am in Carradoon on important business, something you obviously could not understand."

"I always figured flour to be important," Ivan replied sarcastically, giving the bag a rough pat that sent another white burst into Rufo's face. The angular man trembled with mounting rage, but that only spurred Ivan to further taunts.

"Ye're acting like ye're not so glad to see me and me brother," the dwarf said.

"Should I be?" Rufo asked. "When have we ever claimed friendship to one another?"

"We fought together in the wood," Ivan reminded him, "or at least, some of us fought. Others figured to hide in a tall tree, if me memory's working proper."

Rufo growled and pushed ahead, dislodging several packages in his attempt to get beyond Ivan. He had nearly made his way past when the dwarf threw out one strong arm, stopping Rufo as completely as a stone wall.

"Danica's in town, too," Ivan remarked, his other hand held high and balled into a fist.

"Boom," Pikel added grimly behind the angular man.

The reference to Danica's humiliating attack made Rufo's face flush red with rage. He growled again and shoved past Ivan, stumbling all the rest of the way down the narrow aisle and knocking many more items from the shelves.

"A fine day to ye," Ivan called behind him. Rufo dropped the sack of flour and passed right by the counter, fleeing for the street.

"Good to see him," Ivan said to Pikel. "Adds a bit of flavor to a dull trip."

"Hee hee hee," Pikel agreed.

Ivan's face went serious once more as he noticed a tall

man selecting goods from a shelf behind Pikel. The man's gait and movements were easy and graceful, his eyes sharp and steady, and he hoisted a twenty-pound bag of meal easily with one hand. His tunic moved up from the back of his trousers as he moved, revealing a dagger tucked securely in the back of his belt.

That alone would not have fired off any alarms in Ivan; many people carried concealed weapons in Carradoon, and Ivan himself had a knife in one pocket.

But the dwarf was certain he'd seen this man before, in a different guise. He watched the man for a few moments longer, until the man noticed him, snarled, and headed off the other way down the aisle.

"Eh?" Pikel asked, wondering what problem so obviously bothered his brother.

Ivan did not immediately reply, for he was too busy searching his memory. Then it came to him: he had seen a man closely resembling the shopper in the alley beside the Dragon's Codpiece. The man had been more disheveled then, wearing tattered clothing and seeming like an ordinary street beggar, of which Carradoon had its share. Even then, though, Ivan had noted the grace of the beggar's movements, a skilled and measured step.

The dwarf hadn't thought much about it, and wouldn't even have given it more than a passing thought now, except for the unpleasant incident on his journey into the city. Danica was convinced that the would-be bandits were not ordinary highwaymen and had been waiting to ambush the three companions. Ivan had little proof either way, and, while he held many private doubts, he knew Danica better than to openly disagree with her reasoning. An inspection of the bodies had revealed little, though, for the men carried no obvious marks, not even the familiar trident-and-bottle insignia of the enemy, which the companions had expected to find.

By all appearances, they had been simple robbers, coincidentally stumbling into the companions' path, and that had seemed even more plausible when Ivan and the others had arrived in Carradoon to find Cadderly, Avery, and Rufo safe and secure at the Dragon's Codpiece.

But prudent, battle-tested Ivan had not let his guard down, not one bit.

"We should go find Cadderly and Danica," he said to Pikel.

"Tut tut," Pikel argued, blushing with embarrassment and waggling a stubby finger Ivan's way. Danica had not returned to her room the previous night, and the dwarves didn't have to struggle to figure out where she had stayed, and why she had stayed there.

"We won't bother them if we don't need to," Ivan growled back. "Just want to keep an eye on them, that's all." Ivan nodded to the end of the aisle, where the suspicious shopper was gathering more goods. "I'm not so sure we seen the last of the group that hit us on the road."

"Eh?" Pikel balked.

"Sure, that bunch is dead," Ivan said as Pikel finally hopped around to regard the man, "but me thinking's that they got friends, and me fear's that we were more than accidental targets."

"Uh-oh," Pikel whined. He looked back to Ivan, crestfallen and obviously worried.

"We'll just watch 'em, that's all," Ivan said comfortingly. "We'll just watch 'em close."

* * * * *

Vander paced nervously about the barn on the outskirts of town. Ghost had telepathically contacted him using the power of the *Ghearufu* that morning to set the plans into motion; the strike against Cadderly would come before the next dawn. All of the other assassins were gone from the

farm, sent into position with their remaining associates in
Carradoon. There had still been no word of the five who
had gone into the mountains, but word of the arrival of
Danica and the dwarves into the city did not bode well for
the missing Night Masks.

Still, fourteen expertly trained assassins should prove an
ample number for a single, unsuspecting kill. At least, that had
been Ghost's reasoning when he had told Vander, the most
powerful of the group, to remain at the farm, out of the way.

Truly the firbolg did not mind the specifics of the instructions; executions had always left a sour taste in the
honorable giant's mouth. What bothered Vander now was
Ghost's motivations in keeping him beyond the immediate
action. The only times the devious little assassin ever used
this method of attack was when Ghost sincerely respected
the powers of his intended victim. On those occasions,
Vander became no more than a secret escape route for
Ghost. If the assassin got into serious trouble, he could just
summon his magical item and flee to Vander's body . . .
leaving Vander back in Ghost's body to suffer whatever
peril the assassin had gotten himself into.

How long would it continue? the firbolg wondered for
about the ten thousandth time. How long would he remain
the plaything of that wicked, honorless little weakling?

For all of his pacing and all of his painstaking thought,
Vander could see no end and no escape. He could find consolation only by telling himself that in the morning Cadderly would be dead, and this wretched chapter of his
miserable life would be at an end.

* * * * *

"You seem in a hurry," the young wizard commented
when Rufo, his face chalk white with flour, entered the
Dragon's Codpiece and made his way straight for the stairs.

Rufo looked at Bogo Rath and snorted derisively, but didn't have the courage to ignore the young wizard's hand gesture that Rufo should go over and join him.

"What do you need?" Rufo snapped, angry at all the world and especially impatient in yet another situation in which he was forced to serve. Everywhere the angular man turned, he found someone more than willing to give him orders.

Bogo laughed heartily and flipped his stringy hair over to the side, out of his green eyes. "How go your meetings?" the wizard asked.

Again Rufo snorted. "You should ask Avery," he replied, venom dripping from every word. "Certainly I, the errand boy, would not know!" As evidence to his point, Rufo held up the few small sacks of purchases he had made in the first stores he had visited that day.

"You deserve better treatment than this," Bogo commented, trying to sound like an honest friend.

"From you as well," Rufo replied sharply.

Bogo nodded and did not argue. In truth, the young wizard, "Boygo" to his older associates, could sympathize with Rufo's dilemma.

"Well, have you a task for me, or are you merely wasting my time?" Rufo asked. "Not that my time is such a precious thing."

"Nothing," Bogo replied. Immediately, the angular man spun away, heading back for the stairs. "As of yet," Bogo remarked after him, stealing some of the ire-filled thunder from Rufo's determined steps. The priest looked back one final time.

"You will be informed when you are needed," Bogo said evenly, his visage stern and unyielding. The young wizard might sympathize with Rufo, but that would offer the priest little reprieve from the duties Bogo would eventually require of him.

*   *   *   *   *

"You met with the priest again this day," Ghost said to Bogo when the young wizard entered his room later that afternoon. He really wasn't surprised to find the sneaky assassin waiting for him, or by the fact that Ghost knew of his meeting with Rufo.

"I have warned you once of your meddling," Ghost went on. Bogo's face twisted curiously, and Ghost realized that he had made a mistake. He hadn't warned Bogo of any such thing; the innkeeper's son had done that, at least as far as Bogo was concerned.

"You?" Bogo questioned, his lips turning up in a smile. "I have not seen young Brennan today," he remarked cryptically. "Actually, his father is quite worried about him."

Ghost settled back on the bed and nodded silent congratulations to the observant wizard. "Let us just say that the young man outlived his usefulness," he explained. "A very dangerous thing to do."

Neither man spoke for a very long while, but there remained little tension between them. Ghost studied Bogo long and hard, and the young wizard seemed to sense that the assassin was forming some plans—plans that Bogo could only hope would include him.

"The time is close then," Bogo remarked. "The disappearance of young Brennan is a question that you cannot let hang unanswered for a very long time."

Again, Ghost nodded his silent appreciation of Bogo's reasoning powers. "The time is nearly upon us," he confirmed, "but it would seem that some things have changed."

"The arrival of the priests and Danica?" Bogo asked.

"Complications," Ghost replied.

"And what else has changed?"

"Your role," Ghost answered immediately. Bogo initially took a cautious step back, fearing that he, too, might have outlived his usefulness.

"I had said you were only an observer," the assassin explained, "and, so, by Aballister's measure, you were meant to be. But you never believed that, did you, Rath? You never planned to sit back and watch while the Night Masks had all the fun of killing this young Cadderly."

Bogo cocked his head curiously at the assassin, obviously unsure of what that plain fact might mean.

"And you have proven to me," Ghost continued, "both by your astute conclusions and your ability to get close to our enemies, that your value extends beyond your assigned role."

"I thought you did not want me talking with Rufo," Bogo replied, still a safe distance from the dangerous man.

"I just explained to you that things have changed," Ghost retorted. "We have a headmaster from the library to deal with and a formidable young woman, it would seem. I intend to handle the latter problem personally, and for that I will need to borrow your stooge."

Bogo moved over to the bed, now more curious than afraid.

"A simple matter," Ghost explained. "A simple, innocuous task for Kierkan Rufo that will allow me to get at the Lady Maupoissant."

"You will kill her?"

"In a manner," Ghost replied. "First I will use her so that when the Night Masks come for Cadderly, the one he believes is his closest ally will, in truth, be his enemy."

Bogo's smile widened, mimicking Ghost's devious expression. The assassin's plan was beautifully simple, with Bogo, and more particularly, Rufo, being the only potential trouble areas that he could foresee. To that end, the assassin then delivered a secure hook.

His smile abruptly disappeared, causing Bogo's visage to assume a similarly grim tone.

"I offer you a part in this execution," Ghost explained, "something you have craved since before we left Castle

Trinity. I assure you that your role will be well received by Aballister.

"But," Ghost continued slyly, and this was the real hook, "my pay will be as originally agreed."

"Of course . . ." Bogo started, but Ghost didn't pause long enough to let him continue.

"And if Aballister does not deliver to me the full amount," Ghost went on grimly, "then you must make up the difference—to the gold piece."

Bogo nodded eagerly, more than happy to pay such a pittance in exchange for the prestige, and also beginning to understand for the first time, how very bad it might be to get on the wrong side of this wicked little man.

They spent another hour together, with Ghost detailing the plans and the role Bogo would play. To the ambitious young wizard, the plan and his part seemed safe enough (Rufo would actually be doing most of the work) and rewarding enough to satisfy him.

Just as Ghost had known it would.

Fourteen

To Capture a Soul

Cadderly and Danica had slept very late that day. Brennan did not appear with Cadderly's breakfast, and Cadderly, in his modesty, was glad of that. He suspected that the innkeeper's son had probably come to the door, then had turned away, blushing, at what he had heard inside. With a private smile, Cadderly thought no more about it.

The lovers left their room shortly after noon, taking a meal together in the hearth room. Fredegar served them himself—an unusual occurrence that Cadderly realized was out of sorts only when the innkeeper asked him if he had seen anything of Brennan that morning.

Still, Cadderly was too consumed by the presence of Danica to appreciate the implications of the missing youth. He promised to keep an eye out for Brennan when he and Danica went out walking. Fredegar nodded his thanks, but he was plainly worried.

"The mistakes of adolescence," Cadderly explained to

Danica, not too concerned for the welfare of the youth. He figured that Brennan had been out late in pursuit of some young lady, and that maybe this time Brennan had made the catch. For all of Cadderly's inner turmoil, all the world seemed calm that morning, with Danica beside him again, and the young priest couldn't even begin to think dark and ominous thoughts.

They left the inn together, crossed the wide way of Lakeview Street, and moved down to Impresk Lake's sandy shore. The breeze was stiff off the water, chill but not cold, and long-winged birds zipped about at impossible angles and cut sharply in daring maneuvers all about them. The normal morning mist had long since dissipated, leaving the two with a grand view of the island that comprised the wealthier section of Carradoon, and the wide, arching stone bridge that led to it. Several multistory structures peeked up above the trees, and a fleet of boats, both pleasure and fishing, meandered around the land mass.

"I suppose I might come to accept the beard," Danica said after many minutes of quiet watching. She moved over and tugged at an exceptionally long strand. "As long as you keep it trimmed!"

"And I love you," Cadderly replied with a contented smile. "Will you stay beside me?"

"Are you certain you want me to?" Danica said in a teasing tone, but there was a subtle undercurrent of dread in her question.

"Stay with me," Cadderly said again, more forcefully.

Danica looked back to the water and did not answer. The request seemed so simple and obvious, and yet, the woman realized that many obstacles remained. She had gone to the Edificant Library to study the ancient works of Grandmaster Penpahg D'Ahn, the Most Holy One, prophet and founder of her order. Only in the library could Danica continue her work, and that work was very important to her, the culmination of all her personal goals.

As important as Cadderly?

Danica was not honestly sure, but she knew that if she gave up her goals to remain beside her lover, then she would forever look back to this time and wonder what might have been, what level of perfection she might have achieved.

And there remained, too, the war. The last few days had come as a reprieve to the battle-weary woman, despite the attack on the road, but Danica knew that this quiet time was only temporary. More fighting would break out, if not now, then in the spring, and Danica had long ago resolved to be a part of that.

Cadderly, though, had run away from it, and the woman now did not know if he would change his mind.

So Danica did not answer the question, and Cadderly, wise enough to understand her hesitancy and her fears, did not ask it again. Day by day, he decided. They would pass their time together day by day and see what changes the wind across the lake brought.

They walked quietly along the beach for some time, Cadderly leading Danica to one of his favorite places. The shoreline jutted sharply out into the water in a small, tree-covered peninsula with banks only a foot above the water level. A single path, barely a foot wide, led the way into the thick tangle, ending at a small clearing right in the center of the peninsula. Although they were barely a half-mile from the bustle of Carradoon, and barely a half-mile from the island section as well, it seemed to Cadderly and Danica that the world had disappeared beyond the shelter of those trees.

Danica looked slyly at Cadderly, suddenly suspecting the reason he had brought her out here.

But Cadderly had other ideas. He led Danica down

another narrow path, to the very tip of the peninsula, beside a small pool formed by the waves whenever a large boat passed by. Cadderly, indicated a mossy stone and bade Danica to sit.

Cadderly walked the perimeter of the pool, muttering something under his breath that Danica could not make out. She soon came to understand that the young priest was chanting, a magical spell, most likely.

Cadderly halted the walk. His body swayed gently, a willow in the wind, he seemed, and his arms moved about in graceful circles. Danica's eyes settled on Cadderly's holy symbol, the single eye-and-candle design set in the center of his wide-brimmed hat. She felt a pulse of power from that emblem; it seemed to glow with some inner strength.

Cadderly's arms waved again as he reached low in front of him and swung them slowly out wide to either side.

The water reacted to his call. The center of the pool bubbled with sudden energy, then rolled outward, great ripples moving to every edge. Danica moved her feet in close to her, thinking that she was going to get splashed, but the water did not break the edges of the pool. As the waves crested, there came a great hissing sound and the water vaporized, rolling up into the air to form a grayish cloud.

More water rolled out to be consumed, and when it was done, just a few small puddles remained where the pool had been. The cloud hovered for a few moments, until the pull of the wind broke it apart to nothingness.

Danica blinked in amazement and looked to Cadderly, who stood very still, staring at the mud-and-puddle pit.

"You have become powerful," she remarked after some time had passed. "For a nonbeliever."

Cadderly glared at her but could not sustain any anger in the face of her disarming smile. Through his smile, though,

Danica recognized the young man's torment.

"Perhaps it is just a variation of a wizard's magic, as you fear," she offered, "but perhaps the strength does come from Deneir. You seem too quick to deny what others of your order—"

"My order?" Cadderly was quick to interrupt, his tone both sarcastic and incredulous.

"Your holy symbol vibrated with power," Danica replied. "I witnessed it myself."

"A conduit to the energy, much like the tome on my desk," Cadderly said more sharply than Danica deserved. He seemed to understand that, and his tone softened considerably as he continued. "Whenever I call on the magic, I merely recall some of the words in that book."

"And it is a book of Deneir," Danica reasoned.

Cadderly shook his head. "Do you know of Belisarius?" he asked.

"The wizard in the tower to the south?" Danica said.

Cadderly nodded. "Belisarius has a similar book—a spell book. If he attached a god's name to it, would it then become a holy book?"

"It is not the same," Danica muttered, frustrated.

"I do not know," Cadderly said finally.

Danica looked to the lake behind her, to the gently lapping waves against the many small rocks at the peninsula's tip, determined to change the subject. Then she looked at the muddy hole, somewhat disconcertingly. "How long will it take to refill?" she asked, clearly not happy with the results of Cadderly's display. "Or must it wait for the next rain?"

Cadderly smiled and bent low, scooping a few drops of the remaining water into his cupped palms. He pulled his hand in close to his chest, again muttered some words under his breath.

"As the graceful rain must fall!" he ended, then he threw

his hands out before him, threw the water to the air above the muddy pit. A tiny cloud appeared, hovering and churning in the air, and a moment later, a steady stream of water poured forth, splashing into the mud.

Before Danica ended her first burst of laughter, the pool had returned, as full as when she had first seen it.

"You find this humorous?" Cadderly asked, narrowing his gray eyes and thumping his fists against his hips so that he seemed a caricature of wounded pride.

"I find you humorous," Danica retorted, and Cadderly's expression revealed that he was truly hurt.

"You have all the proof right before you," Danica explained, "more proof than the vast majority of ordinary people will ever know, and yet you remain so filled with doubts. My poor Cadderly, so damned by the unending questions of his own intelligence!"

Cadderly looked to the pool he had magically evaporated and then refilled, and chuckled at the irony of it all. Danica took his hand then and led him back to the clearing at the center of the peninsula. Cadderly thought to keep going, down the other narrow path and back out to the wider beaches, but Danica held tight to his hand and did not continue, forcing him to turn about.

They were alone in the sun and the breeze, and all the world seemed peaceful. Danica smiled mischievously, her almond eyes telling Cadderly without the slightest doubt that it was not yet time to leave.

*   *   *   *   *

It was nearly twilight when Cadderly and Danica made their way back to the Dragon's Codpiece. Farther down Lakeview Street, fatherly Ivan watched their progress. The dwarf was much more at ease than he had been, and the safe return of Cadderly and Danica told him that his suspicions might be unfounded, that he was acting as silly as a mother hen.

But was it a coincidence, just a moment later, when a beggar came to the end of the alleyway next to the Dragon's Codpiece, and appeared to be watching the young couple as intently as Ivan?

Ivan sensed that the man meant to go after the two, and the dwarf started to make his way slowly up the street. He didn't have his great axe with him—it wasn't considered proper to stand about on one of Carradoon's streets so obviously armed—but he was wearing his deer-antlered helmet. If this beggar made a move against Cadderly, Ivan resolved to gore him good.

Cadderly and Danica turned into the inn, and the beggar leaned casually against the wall. Ivan stopped, perplexed and feeling very foolish. He looked all about, as if expecting everyone else on the street to be pointing at him and chuckling, but no one had apparently noticed anything unusual about his stalking advance.

"Stupid dwarf," he muttered under his breath. "What're ye getting so anxious about? Just a poor man, looking for a bit of coins." Ivan stopped and scratched his yellow beard curiously when he looked back toward the alleyway.

The man was gone.

* * * * *

Danica giggled, but Cadderly was not amused at the knock on his door—not at that particular moment.

"Oh, go and answer it," Danica whispered to him. "It is probably the innkeeper's son, whom you have been worried over the whole of the day!"

"I do not want to go," Cadderly replied, pouting like a child. This brought another chuckle from Danica, who pulled the bedclothes up tight about her neck.

Groaning with every move, Cadderly pulled himself out of bed and eased over to the door, wrapping himself in his discarded cloak.

"Rufo?" he asked as he cracked the door open. The hallway was dark, the candles in the great chandelier atop the stairs having long since died away. Only the glow from the hearth room's fireplace offered any light at all. Still, Cadderly could not mistake Rufo's tilting posture.

"My greetings," the angular man replied. "And my apologies for disturbing you." Cadderly blushed deeply, a sight the angular man obviously enjoyed.

"What do you want?"

"You are needed in the hearth room," Rufo explained, "as soon as you can."

"No." The answer seemed simple enough, and Cadderly moved to shut the door, but Rufo stuck his foot in the way.

"Headmaster Avery will return with a delegation from the Ilmater chapel," Rufo lied, for he knew well that Headmaster Avery was snoring contentedly back in their room.

Cadderly looked back over his shoulder to the balcony doors, to the blackness of the night. "What time is it?" he asked.

"It is very late," Rufo admitted. "The priests of Ilmater wish this done in private. They seek information about the deaths of their acolytes at the Edificant Library during the time of the chaos curse."

"I have already written my testimony—"

"Avery asks that you come," Rufo pressed. "He has not required much of you, certainly less than he asks of me." Obvious resentment rang clearly in the angular man's tone. "You can do this much for him, impudent Cadderly, after all the headmaster has done for you."

The argument seemed solid enough. Cadderly groaned again, then nodded. "Ten minutes," he said.

Danica's giggling renewed as soon as the door was closed.

"I will not be gone long," Cadderly promised as he pulled on his clothes.

"It does not matter," Danica replied coyly. "I am certain I shall fall asleep immediately." She stretched languidly and rolled to her side, and Cadderly, cursing his luck, left the room.

He, too, must have been sleepy, for he didn't even notice the weasel-like man—was it a man?—behind a slightly opened door, watching him go.

* * * * *

"Cadderly?" Danica uttered the question, but she heard it as though someone else had spoken the words. A smell of exotic flowers permeated the room.

Somewhere deep in her mind, she was surprised that she had fallen asleep so soon. Or had she? How long had Cadderly been gone? she wondered. And what was that smell?

"Cadderly?" she asked again.

"Hardly."

The word should have sounded like a warning to the woman—she knew she should open her eyes and find out what in the Nine Hells was going on . . . but she couldn't.

She felt a thumb, a gloved hand, she believed, pressed against her eyelid, and then her eye was forced open, just a crack. Danica tried to focus her thoughts—why was she so sleepy?

Through the blur, she saw herself in a small mirror. She knew that the mirror was hanging around someone's neck.

Whose neck?

"Cadderly?"

The laughter that came back at her filled her with dread, and her eyes popped open against the permeating drowsiness, suddenly alert.

She saw Ghost for just an instant, too briefly to strike

out, or even to cry out. Then she fell back into her own
thoughts, into the blackness that suddenly became her
own mind, and she felt a burning pain throughout every
inch of her body.

Danica did not understand what was happening, but she
sensed that it was not good. She felt herself moving away,
but knew that her body was not moving.

Another blackness loomed in the distance, across a gray
expanse, and Danica felt herself pulled toward it, compelled
to sink into it. The first blackness, her mortal coil, was left
behind, far behind.

Few in all of Faerûn would have understood, but few in
all of Faerûn were as well versed in meditation as Danica.

Her identity!

Someone was stealing her very identity!

"No!" Danica tried to cry out, but control of her body's
voice was almost gone by then and the word came out as an
indecipherable whimper.

Danica focused her will, dismissed the continuing smell
that she now suspected was some sort of sleeping poison.
She located that approaching blackness and pushed against
it with all her mental strength, understanding that to enter
it was to be lost.

A moment later, she felt another presence, similarly wandering out of body.

Her thoughts screamed a thousand protests at it, but it
did not respond; it just kept making its way for the blackness that Danica had left behind.

* * * * *

"Where are they?" Cadderly asked impatiently when he
came down into the hearth room. The fire burned low and
the place was empty, except for him and for Rufo, sitting
nervously at a table in the far corner.

"Well?" Cadderly growled as he moved over and took a seat opposite the angular man.

"Patience," Rufo replied. "It will not be long."

Cadderly leaned back and threw one arm over the back of the chair. By his estimation, it had already been too long. He looked at Rufo again, noting a subtle undercurrent of nervousness in the angular man. Cadderly dismissed the feeling and any suspicions it started to encourage, reminding himself that Kierkan Rufo was always nervous.

The young priest closed his eyes and let the minutes slip past, let his thoughts linger back to Danica and the pleasures and implications this day had brought. He would never leave her again, of that much he was sure.

Cadderly's eyes popped wide.

"What is it?" he heard Rufo ask loudly. Cadderly studied the man, saw Rufo blink.

Heard Rufo blink!

The fire crackled so powerfully that Cadderly thought the whole wall would be aflame, but when he turned to regard the hearth, the embers barely seemed to glow with their last flickers of life.

A fly buzzed by the bar. Gods! Cadderly thought, the thing must be the size of a small pony!

He saw nothing there.

And then he was aware of that song again, playing softly in the back of his mind. Instead of trying to figure all of this out, Cadderly wisely just allowed himself to feel.

Something—some danger?—had put him on his guard, and he had subconsciously replayed a page from the tome, enacted a magical spell to heighten his hearing.

"What is it?" Rufo asked him again, more urgently. Cadderly did not look at the man, just held a hand up to silence him.

Breathing.

Cadderly heard the steady inhale and exhale of breath a

few tables away. He looked over but saw nothing.

But there was something, someone, there! Shifting his probe, Cadderly felt the magical energy.

"What are you saying?" he heard Rufo ask, and he realized only then that his lips were moving, forming the words from yet another page of the *Tome of Universal Harmony*.

Cadderly saw a silvery outline of a young man, recognized the stringy locks of hair hanging down to one side of the invisible intruder's head.

Rufo shoved him roughly, forcing his attention.

"What?" the angular man demanded.

Cadderly started to rebuke him, then stopped and instead locked his intent gaze on Rufo.

* * * * *

Danica calmed her thoughts; she had to beat the other presence to the void of her physical mind. She turned her spirit about, willed her mind to connect fully with the tiny part of her that she had left behind, the part that had forced her mouth to utter that pitiful sound. She sensed the other presence pushing at the blackness then, nearly entering her form.

She felt a burning sensation.

Danica saw too many things in the next instant for her to possibly sort through them. She saw, most clearly, murders, dozens of murders. She saw Night Masks.

Night Masks!

The assassin band, the scourge of Westgate, had killed her parents. She saw a clan of giants, through the eyes of a giant.

She saw the other giants die at her own giant hands.

She saw Cadderly, on the road to Carradoon, huddled at his desk over the *Tome of Universal Harmony*, crouched behind the protection of his partly opened door.

To her horror, Danica realized that she was recalling someone else's memories, had connected with the small part this other identity had left behind on its journey to take her body! And that this person, whoever it might be, had been close to Cadderly on several occasions.

Night Masks!

Let me out! her thoughts protested.

The other identity cried out to her in rage and agony and disbelief. She heard no words, but understood its meaning acutely, understood that her focused rage could push her back to where she belonged.

Let me out!

Danica pushed against the foreign blackness with all her mental strength, called upon her rage in combination with her years of mental training. The burning intensified, then abated, and Danica felt a physical presence once more—her own body.

The smell returned and Danica felt a cloth pressed against her face. Giving in to her warrior instincts, she locked her fingers into a gouging position and cocked her arm for a strike.

She fell hard against the floor, but she didn't realize it.

* * * * *

Shadows, evil, misshapen things, grumbled and growled from the angular man's shoulders, their demeanor toward Cadderly obviously hostile. Rufo reached out across the small table to touch Cadderly again, but the young priest slapped his hand away.

"Cadderly!" Rufo responded, but the young priest sensed clearly that the man's apparent concern was a facade. Before Rufo could move again, Cadderly pushed against the table, slamming its other edge into the angular man's belly.

Cadderly honestly did not know what to do, did not know whether he was being warned or misled.

"Tell Avery that he can find me in the morning," the young priest said, rising and spinning about to survey the room. He sensed that the invisible wizard was long gone.

"Avery will not like that," he heard Rufo say, but more acutely, he heard a thump from somewhere upstairs that he knew instinctively was his own room.

Danica!

Cadderly bounded across the floor to the stairs, but then he was moving slowly, as if in a dream, barely able to put one heavy foot in front of the other.

The song played in his head; he instinctively pictured a page from the great book, a page describing focused magical energies, describing how to dispel such malevolent collections of magic.

A moment later he was moving again normally, free of whatever magical bonds had been placed on him. The door to his room was closed, as he had left it, and all seemed as it should.

Cadderly burst through the door anyway, to find Danica, her breathing rapid, sprawled upon the floor, tangled in a pile of blankets next to the bed. Cadderly knew she was alive and not seriously hurt as he held her in his arms.

The young priest surveyed the room. The notes from the song seemed more distant to him now and all seemed calm, but still the young priest wondered if someone had come in during his absence.

"Cadderly," Danica breathed, suddenly coming awake.

She looked about her, confused for a moment, pulled the blankets high and brought her arms in close—actions that struck Cadderly as curious gestures.

"A terrible dream," Danica tried to explain.

Cadderly kissed her gently on the forehead and told her that everything was all right. He placed his chin atop

Danica's head and rocked her in his arms, his own smile widening with growing security.

Danica was unharmed. It had been only a dream.

Fifteen

A Good Day to Die

A s the night wound on toward morning, the guests in half of the eight private rooms at the Dragon's Codpiece slept soundly.

Bogo Rath was simply too agitated to think of sleeping. Knowing what was to come, and knowing that he had played a part in the prelude to the actual assassination, the young wizard thought through the potential problems facing him that morning. Would Kierkan Rufo remain loyal? And even if the priest did, would the odd and angular man be able to carry out the mission Bogo had set before him? Things could get very troublesome at the Dragon's Codpiece very quickly if a certain headmaster from the Edificant Library was not dealt with properly and efficiently.

Bogo understood the unmerciful Night Mask organization well enough to realize that Ghost would hold him responsible if Kierkan Rufo failed. The wizard paced his small room, taking care to keep his footsteps as quiet as possible. He wished that Ghost would come to him then, or that one of the approaching band would at least make contact to let him know how things progressed.

The young wizard resisted an urge to crack open his door, remembering that if he interrupted at an inopportune moment, he might well share Cadderly's grim fate.

In his own room, Ghost sat staring out his window, bitter and full of rage. He hadn't slept at all that night, after Danica's mental discipline had defeated his attempted possession. He had wanted to be close at hand when the assassin band roared in; he had even been forced to go to the band that night and change the orders. Danica must die beside her lover.

For all the unexpected twists, the assassin remained confident that Cadderly would die that day, but even if the young priest fell easily now, this had been a messy execution, filled with complications and unexpected losses. Vander had killed one man; five others were missing in the foothills of the Snowflakes.

And young Cadderly was still very much alive.

And very much awake. In his room, the young priest sat at his table, dressed for the coming day and reading through the pages of the *Tome of Universal Harmony*. The hearth room had shown Cadderly many surprises earlier that night, and he searched for an entry that might help explain the sudden heightening of his senses, particularly his hearing.

Danica sat cross-legged on the floor beside the bed in quiet meditation, allowing the priest his needed privacy and taking some for herself. Hers was a life of discipline, of private challenges and trials, and though it was a bit early, she had already begun her daily morning ritual, working her inner being, stretching her limbs, and clearing her mind in preparation for the coming day.

Danica had discovered no answers for her strange experience earlier that night, and, truthfully, she hadn't sought any. To her, the encounter with the unknown other mind remained a dream; since nothing else traumatic or dangerous had occurred, the explanation seemed to satisfy.

* * * * *

"The sun has not peeked over the rim!" Headmaster Avery protested, managing with some difficulty to roll his bulky form out of bed.

"That was Cadderly's wish," Kierkan Rufo reminded him. "He desired secrecy, and I believe what he might have to say will be worth the effort."

Avery struggled to clear his throat of its nighttime phlegm and draw in a profound breath, never taking his curious stare off the angular man.

Rufo struggled even harder to remain calm under that searching gaze. He kept his breathing steady; so many things depended on his facade now. And beneath the calm front, turmoil boiled in Rufo. He honestly wondered how it had come down to this, how he had been led to such a dramatic point. He had been used by Barjin when the evil priest had invaded the library several months before; he had been the one who had kicked Cadderly down the secret stairway, nearly leading to the library's downfall.

Rufo had never quite forgiven himself—no, not forgiven himself, but rather, had never quite been able to justify the action to himself. Self-forgiveness would imply that he held guilty thoughts for that treacherous act, and by this time, the angular man held none. With every event that had come after Barjin's invasion, Cadderly had become more Rufo's rival, more his bane. In Shilmista, Cadderly had emerged a hero, while Rufo, through no fault of his own (at least, none that he would admit, even to himself), had become a scapegoat.

Bleary-eyed, Avery stumbled across the floor and pulled

on his clothes. Rufo was glad to be released from the head-master's gaze.

"Are you coming down with me?" Avery asked.

"Cadderly does not want me there," the angular man lied. "He said he would meet with you alone in the hearth room before Fredegar began his work."

"Before dawn," Avery muttered distastefully.

Rufo continued to stare at the portly headmaster's back. How had it gotten this far? Rufo didn't hate Avery—on the contrary, the headmaster had acted on Rufo's behalf many times over the last decade.

But that was behind them now, the angular man reminded himself. Shilmista had undeniably changed Rufo's life course, but now, looking at vulnerable Avery, the angular man had to pause and consider just how drastically.

"Well, I am off for the hearth room, then," Avery announced, moving to the door.

He wasn't even carrying his mace in the loop on his belt, Rufo noted. And he hadn't yet prayed and prepared any spells.

"Truly I wish Cadderly would be more conventional," Avery remarked, his obvious fondness for the young priest showing through, and that only strengthening the treacherous Rufo's resolve. "But, then, that is his charm, I suppose." Avery paused and smiled, and Rufo knew the portly man was engaged in some private recollection of Cadderly.

"Meet me in the hearth room for the morning meal," Avery instructed. "Perhaps I will be able to persuade Cadderly to dine with us."

"Just what I desire," the angular man muttered grimly. He moved to the door and watched Avery descend the sweeping stairway to the dimly lighted hearth room.

Rufo closed the door softly. His part was done. He had set events into motion, as the young wizard had instructed him to do. Avery's fate was the headmaster's own to deal with.

The angular man leaned back against the wall, desperately trying to dismiss his growing guilt. He recalled Avery's recent treatment of him, of the terrible things the headmaster had said to him and the threats to drive Rufo from the order.

For Kierkan Rufo, so consumed by resentment, guilt was not a difficult emotion to overcome.

* * * * *

Half asleep in the common room of the inn two doors down from the Dragon's Codpiece, his head resting on the ledge of the alley window, Pikel heard a distinct whistle. The dwarf's grogginess held fast only for the few moments it took Pikel to remember what his brother would do to him if Ivan caught him asleep on his watch.

Pikel stuck his head out the window and took in a deep breath of the chilly predawn air.

Another whistle sounded, from the alley on the other side of the building he was facing.

"Eh?" the dwarf questioned, his instincts telling him that the whistles were not random, more probably a signal. Pikel hopped up from his seat and ran to the front door, throwing aside the locking bar and hopping out onto the inn's front porch.

He saw shapes moving out of the alley beyond the nearest building, shapes moving onto the veranda of the Dragon's Codpiece, slipping quietly through the open door.

Pikel started forward to better investigate when a movement close beside him stole his attention. A large man rushed up to him, sword slicing wildly. The first hit bounced off the dwarf's armored shoulder, not penetrating but leaving a painful bruise.

"Oooo!" Pikel exclaimed in surprise, backpedaling the way he had come. The man kept right with him, flailing away viciously. Pikel had no weapon—he had left his club back in his room, not really believing Ivan's growing suspicions that dangers were lurking just outside.

The green-bearded dwarf believed them now, with this man hacking away at him, driving him backward with every step. Blood rolled down one of Pikel's arms; he took a glancing hit across the cheek that drew a thin red line.

The beating continued relentlessly, and Pikel, nearly across the common room, had little distance left to run.

* * * * *

The lockpick had been silent. Headmaster Avery, his heavy eyelids drooping, didn't even realize that anyone had entered the Dragon's Codpiece until the assassins were upon him.

Then they were beyond him, slipping up the stairs as quietly as shadows.

Cadderly looked up from the *Tome of Universal Harmony* and glanced over his shoulder at Danica.

"What is it?" the woman asked, her meditation interrupted by the sheer intensity of the young scholar's stare.

Cadderly lifted a finger over pursed lips, beckoning the woman to be silent. Something had called out to him, a distant song, a voice of impending danger. He took up his spindle-disks and his walking stick and started to rise, facing the closed door.

He hadn't even left his chair when the door burst open and dark shapes stormed in.

Danica was still sitting cross-legged when the first assassin, sword in hand, rushed at her. The killer came in low, gaping in disbelief as Danica's coiled legs sprang, her momentum lifting her into the air. She tucked her legs under as she rose, clearing the low strike, then descended on the bending man.

Her legs locked around his neck as she came down, clamping tightly, and she jerked herself to the side violently, dipping into a full bend and throwing her full weight right under the bending man.

The assassin saw the room spin, but his body had not turned.

* * * * *

Cadderly whipped his walking stick across in front of him and was amazed when he heard something—a crossbow quarrel, he realized—tick off it and fly harmlessly wide. He swung again in a wide, shoulder-level arc, this time offensively, as two men bore down on him. Instinctively, Cadderly dropped to one knee and snapped his spindle-disks straight out ahead of him.

The ducking Night Mask came down right in line with this second weapon, catching the adamantite disks on his forearm.

Cadderly expected the man to immediately retaliate, for the young priest had not yet learned of the power of Ivan's forging. Cadderly stared as the man's arm folded—it seemed as though he had grown a second elbow!—under the power of the blow.

But pausing to gape with a second enemy so near was not a wise choice. By the time Cadderly realized his error, realized that a spiked club was on its way down to crunch his head, he knew that his life was at its end.

* * * * *

Pikel managed to keep close enough to his pursuer so that the man hadn't been able to extend his long arms and get in a serious hit. Still, the dwarf said "Oooo!" repeatedly, feeling the sting of a dozen razorlike slashes.

Pikel's first thought was to go for the stairs, but he dismissed the idea, realizing that if he started up, he would rise to his enemy's level and lose his desperately needed advantage of being down below the man's optimum striking area. The dwarf veered to the side, backpedaling faster, nearly tumbling over in the effort.

The man stayed with him, every step.

The killer stopped suddenly, and Pikel realized that he could not do likewise, leaving the dwarf wide open for a full-force roundhouse. "Oooo!" Pikel screamed, desperately hurling himself backward through the air. He collided heavily with the wall before he had gotten very far, and the assassin's sword whipped across just under the breastplate of the dwarf's fine armor.

Pikel didn't even have the time to cry out for this newest wound. He bounced back off the wall and charged forward wildly. The assassin held his sword level in front of him, and Pikel would have impaled himself, except that he grabbed the sharp blade with his bare hand and turned it aside.

Then Pikel was up against the man. He released the sword almost immediately and wrapped the man's arms in his own, pushing with all his strength, his stubby, muscled legs pumping frantically.

Now the killer was backpedaling and Pikel driving forward, gaining speed and momentum. The dwarf could hardly see around the larger man. He aimed for the open door but missed, two feet to the left.

The inn suddenly had a second door.

*　*　*　*　*

Danica hit the floor harder than she would have liked, but she managed to scramble back under her victim fast enough so that the next closest Night Mask inadvertently sliced his sword into the back of his still-standing companion.

Out the other side, Danica ran to the foot of the bed, hooked the post in one arm, and spun right around, hopping up onto the mattress. A Night Mask came up on the bed as well, at the other end, bearing down on the apparently unarmed woman.

Danica kept low and kicked straight out. She could hardly brace herself amidst the tangle of blankets, so her kick was not fierce, but neither could the assassin brace himself, so it did not have to be. The man stumbled in the tangle and lurched over. Danica came up under him, hooking her arm under and behind his shoulder and heaved him away, using his own momentum to launch him over the foot end of the bed.

She was up, grabbing the blankets as she went, knowing the sword-wielder was too close. Instinctively she lifted the tangle of cloth out in front of her, smiling grimly as she felt it absorb the weight of the coming blow.

Caught in, and concerned with, the impromptu web, the assassin didn't even realize Danica's next attack until her foot connected solidly with his belly.

The agile monk let herself drop as the man lurched over, using the spring of the bed to lift her right back up, her forearm slamming against the stooping man's face. Danica's second arm, coiled against her chest, snapped out under the first, thumping into the man's throat, then she reversed the angle of her first arm, flying high over her head in its follow-through, and came down diagonally at her stunned victim, blasting against his collarbone. He flew to the side, and Danica, temporarily free of any immediate threat, was not pleased by what she saw beyond him.

Again using the spring of the bed, the young woman leaped out, diving between the posts at the foot of the bed. She heard a heavy thump distinctly as a crossbow quarrel hit the wall right behind her.

The man she had thrown this way was back up and turning back to the fight, but hardly prepared as Danica's shoulder-block launched him over the table and crashing into the wall.

* * * * *

"Stop!" The word came from somewhere deep inside Cadderly. He wasn't even aware of the magical strength it carried until the killer above him, already beginning his stroke, pulled his spiked club to a halt and stood perfectly still. The weapon hovered just a few inches above Cadderly's head.

The command had no lasting power, and the assassin came out of it quickly, snarling and lifting his club for another strike.

Still purely on instinct, Cadderly lashed out in two directions at once, slamming his walking stick against the side of the man's knee, and heaving his spindle-disks straight ahead, to collide with the crumbling killer's chest and send him flying backward.

"The balcony!" Danica cried, and Cadderly, seeing the group of killers—some cocking crossbows—still coming in the door, could hardly disagree.

Danica hooked his arm as she passed and threw open the door.

The song had started again in Cadderly's head, somehow passing through the confusion and the many noises.

He grabbed Danica's hair and jerked violently backward just as the woman took her first step out of the room. Fully caught by surprise, Danica fell back.

Cadderly snapped his spindle-disks across her angled torso, to meet head on with a thrusting dagger coming the other way.

Ivan's disks easily won the contest, bending the dagger blade and crushing the hand that held it.

Cadderly recoiled quickly, felt the sting as the disks snapped back into his own hand, and then whipped them straight back, this time hitting the wounded Night Mask in the chest, driving him over the railing.

The assassin reached out as he tumbled, grasping futilely at the rail. His hand hooked the balcony just enough to allow him to continue in his spin, to put his legs straight out under him so that when he fell the twenty feet to the ground, he landed flat on his back.

And he lay very still.

* * * * *

Pikel shook the splinters from his beard and hair.

"Me brother!" The call, though emphatic, sounded distant, and then was accentuated by the crash of shattering glass and splintering wood as Ivan, hearing his brother's distress, ran full speed down the inn's second story hallway and flung himself headlong through the window above the inn's front door.

He crashed down with a groan, two feet to the right of Pikel and the stunned assassin, showering the two of them with glass and shards of broken wood.

The killer, up first, his back bleeding from many gashes, turned around to discern this newest threat. He saw the lower half of Ivan—the dwarf's upper torso having plummeted right through the raised wooden decking—but he knew by the way the dwarf was flailing and cursing that Ivan would not be held captive long.

He almost got his sword up before Pikel grabbed him by the ankles and yanked his legs out from under him.

Pikel continued to pull, dragging the man away from Ivan. Rage blinded the green-bearded dwarf. "Ooooooo!" he growled, winding up, beginning his spin, and locking the man's feet under his arms.

The Night Mask twisted and turned to get at the dwarf, but Pikel's footing was sure and his spin quickly gained enough momentum to force the man out straight.

"Ooooooo!"

The man bounced and flailed, and had all that he could handle in just keeping a hold on his sword.

"Ooooooo!"

Now the only part of the Night Mask making any contact with the ground was his arms as he struggled to find a handhold, to find something to grab on to.

"Ooooooo!"

Pikel spun furiously; the man, narrowly missing porch posts and the inn's wall, heartily joined in his scream.

Ivan, back up, watched in disbelief that soon turned to amusement. The dwarf laid his brother's club aside, spat in both his hands, and took up his huge double-bladed axe.

The killer noticed Ivan's preparations and gave a half-hearted swing of his sword, not even coming close to hitting the mark. His arm still extended, he slammed his wrist against the porch support as he came around, his sword flying harmlessly out into the street.

Ivan tightened his grasp on the axe. He started to swing, but the man was by him.

"Gotta lead him," the dwarf reminded himself, taking a bead as the circling target came around again. He saw the Night Mask's face go ghastly pale, saw the most profound look of horror the tough dwarf had ever witnessed.

Slam!

Distracted by a rare onset of sympathy, Ivan's timing was not so good and he buried his axe deeply into the wooden decking.

Pikel didn't even notice his brother or the axe, didn't notice that the killer's scream had dissipated in a breathless gasp of terror, and had no idea of how he would stop this spin, or stop the world from spinning in his dizzy head.

"Ooooooo!"

The weight was gone suddenly and Pikel twirled into the wall. He looked down to the empty boots, still held tightly under his arms.

The poor assassin took out the closest supporting pole and crashed through the railing, breaking under the top rail and skidding along through the thin, carved balusters. He bounced along for several feet, then came to an abrupt halt, his hip driving onto the pointed edge of a broken beam. There he lay, half on the porch and half hanging out over the cobblestone street, groaning softly.

"Nice boots," Ivan remarked, running past Pikel and tossing his brother the tree-trunk club he had brought along. Ivan started for the fallen man, then veered away, hearing a scream as someone went toppling over a balcony—Cadderly's balcony—of the Dragon's Codpiece, two doors down.

Both dwarves breathed a sigh of relief when they rushed past the unmoving form of the fallen man, glad that it was not Cadderly or Danica who had gone for such a tumble. But the continuing sounds of battle twenty feet above them told them that their friends were not out of trouble just yet.

The door to the inn was closed again, and barred, but such had never stopped the Bouldershoulder brothers. Actually, coming into the hearth room with a dislodged door in front of them proved a good thing for the dwarves, for several crossbow quarrels greeted their entrance, thudding harmlessly into the oaken barrier.

* * * * *

A quarrel ripped past Cadderly's shoulder, drawing a line of blood along his arm. Night Masks bore down on him from behind; two others waited on the balcony, a sword and a heavy axe gleaming dully in the predawn light.

Still holding Danica by the hair, Cadderly pulled the young woman to her feet. Immediately, she became a blur of motion, snapping a burst of kicks and punches at the already wounded men who were closing from behind. She landed several solid hits, enough to force one of the assassins to back off. But the other caught Danica around the waist and his momentum carried both of them across the narrow balcony to the rail.

Danica got one hand up onto her attacker's face, her fingers seeking out the man's vulnerable eyes. One of the Night Masks on the balcony, though, forewarned of this extraordinary woman's prowess, found a devilish answer. A single swing of his huge axe broke apart the railing that was supporting both Danica and her attacker.

They pitched over the side together, Danica releasing her grasp on the man's face and swinging both her arms wildly to find a handhold.

Cadderly saw her fall away, his face locked in a stare of helpless denial.

A crossbow quarrel smacked into the back of the young priest's thigh. He turned about as he sank to the deck, sheer rage splayed clearly on his usually calm features.

Without even thinking of the movement, Cadderly lifted a clenched fist toward the bowman and uttered, *"Fete!"* the elven word for fire, the command word for his magical ring.

A line of flames shot out from Cadderly's hand, seeking his attacker, immolating the man in a burning shroud.

With a mental shriek of revulsion, Cadderly ended the fire. He spun about again, his walking stick leading, and got a solid hit on the swordsman. He didn't really care how badly he had hurt the man; all he wanted was to get the man out of his way, to clear the path to the axe-wielder who had sent Danica away.

Again, inexperience had led Cadderly to an unwise single-mindedness. Before he ever got near to the axe-wielder, strong hands grabbed at his shoulders and drove him to the side railing.

* * * * *

Ivan threw the heavy door aside, meaning to charge right to the stairs. A gruesome sight off to the side slowed him, though, for just a moment, and when he resumed his charge, his fury had heightened tenfold.

Pikel, too, thought to head straight for the stairs. "Uh-oh," he mumbled and he ran to the right, for the cover of the room's bar instead, for several dark shapes knelt in formation on and above that staircase, all holding deadly crossbows.

Pikel dove over the long bar, coming to a crashing halt along the narrow walkway behind, up against kegs of thick ale. To the dwarf's surprise, he was not alone, and he just managed to convince Fredegar Harriman that he was not an enemy a split second before the terrified innkeeper bonked him over the head with a full bottle of brandy.

A quarrel ricocheted off the blade of Ivan's axe; another struck the dwarf on the head, stunning him, though his fine helmet managed to deflect the thing up between the deer antlers. Perhaps that particular quarrel knocked some sense into the thick-headed dwarf, for Ivan wisely cut to the side, skidding in around the staircase and scrambling for cover underneath it. He slammed hard into one of the structure's supports as he rushed in, getting all tangled up with it. By the time the dwarf figured out that it was just an ordinary wooden pillar and not some lurking enemy, he had battered it to pieces.

Ivan blushed, thinking himself incredibly foolish. Then he looked around, noticing the other four supports—one more on this side, two on the opposite side and one in the middle—and a wide and wicked grin spread over his face.

*   *   *   *   *

Danica caught hold of the feeble trim along Cadderly's balcony, and her strong hands would not let go, despite the nagging weight of the Night Mask, still clutching at her waist.

The woman wriggled and squirmed, freed up one foot, and slapped it back and forth across the stubborn man's face.

Only a dozen feet from the ground, the attacker wisely let go, dropping heavily but unharmed, on the cobblestones.

Danica's thoughts of climbing back up to join Cadderly on the balcony lasted only a moment, until the trim split away on one end from the main frame, sending Danica on a swinging ride around the corner of the balcony.

Instinctively, she kicked out and leaped before the trim broke away altogether, latching on to the sill of a window near the building's corner, opposite from where she had left Cadderly. Unable to break her momentum, Danica was forced to leap out again, farther from the fight, but this time landing with a more solid handhold and foothold on a gutter running up the side of the building, just around the corner.

By the time she managed to peek around, the balcony was crowded with black-and-silver-outfitted assassins. She didn't see Cadderly at first amid that throng and could not pause long enough to sort him out, for one crossbowman put her immediately in his sights and two other assassins came over the rail, walking the ledge toward the gutter.

Danica scrambled the ten feet or so to the rooftop. Only as she pulled herself over did she realize that she had somehow badly twisted her knee, probably in the struggle over the railing.

"Cadderly," she mumbled over and over; this scenario reminded her vividly of when she had left the young priest to join the fray in Shilmista, when she had been forced to trust in Cadderly to take care of himself.

She started across the roof, thinking to go right above the balcony and leap down upon the enemy. She turned, though, hearing the gutter groan under the weight of a pursuer.

"Do come up," Danica muttered grimly, thinking to clobber the fool as soon as he poked his head over the roof's edge. It never occurred to her that this well-prepared band might already have someone planted on the roof.

She heard the crossbow click behind her.

"A valiant fight, Lady Maupoissant," said a baritone voice at her back, "but a futile effort against the skill of the Night Masks."

* * * * *

Cadderly's walking stick flew away when he collided with the railing. He hardly kept his bearings as he spun over, but did manage to loop one arm about the railing.

It seemed a wasted effort, though, for the Night Mask clubbed at that arm mercilessly, determined to drop the young priest over the side.

Cadderly's first instinct told him to just drop—the fall probably wouldn't kill him. He realized, though, that another assassin loomed below, and he would be easy prey before he ever recovered from the fall.

None of it seemed to matter when the second Night Mask, the axe-wielder, joined the first at the railing above him.

"Farewell, young priest," the man said evilly, lifting his cruel weapon to split Cadderly's head wide.

Cadderly tried to utter a magical command at that man, but he could do no more than groan as the club connected again against his already wounded shoulder.

The young priest glanced around desperately, only a brief moment left open to him. He saw a tiny ledge along the building a few feet away, behind him, and for some reason he did not understand, a memory of Percival, the white squirrel, came to him, an image of Percival skittering happily and easily along ledges at least that thin back at the Edificant Library.

There was no way that any man could make that leap to the ledge, as twisted as Cadderly was. Yet somehow, he was there, and not holding desperately. Hand over hand, foot over foot, the young priest ran along the ledge.

"Get him!" he heard one of the frustrated and astonished assassins yell from behind, and then the other called for a crossbow.

Cadderly came up fast on the corner, with no intentions of turning aside. The alley was only about eight feet wide at this point, but the only apparent handhold on the building across the way was several feet higher than his present perch. By the time Cadderly registered this fact in the still-dim morning light, though, it was too late for him to alter his course.

He leaped, soared, impossibly high and impossibly far. Hardly slowing, he found himself scrambling easily up the side of the other building, disappearing over the top before any crossbowman back on the balcony could begin to get a shot at him.

* * * * *

Pikel peeked up over the bar to see one of the assassins bearing down on him, the other two leaning over the far side of the staircase, trying to get a shot at Ivan.

The green-bearded dwarf hopped up, club in hand, ready to meet the challenge.

"Here," came Fredegar's call behind him. Pikel glanced back to see the brandy bottle, now stuffed with a burning rag, coming for him.

"Oo oi!" Pikel cried, too startled to catch it, as Fredegar had intended. The dwarf did get a hand off his club fast enough to tap the bottle over him, though, and he spun about immediately and slammed the slow-moving missile with his club, creating a small fireball and showering the approaching assassin with glass shards and flaming liquid.

"Oo oi!" Pikel squealed again, this time happily, as the man fell away to the floor and rolled about desperately to get the stubborn flames off his robes. When the assassin finally got back up, he ran screaming for the door, having no more heart for the fight.

The dwarf hopped up on the bar, then fell back again as the bowmen on the stairs took note of him.

* * * * *

Cunning Ivan's only mistake was that he saved the center support for last. Not until he knocked it out, with a single powerful swipe of his axe, did the grinning dwarf realize that he was standing directly under the heavy structure.

The stairs, and the two surprised Night Masks standing on them, came tumbling down.

Only one of the assassins had regained his feet when Ivan finally managed to burst through the pile of broken wood. The dwarf came up with a roar and tried to swing his axe, only to find its head caught fast on a random beam.

The assassin, bruised but not too hurt, grinned at him and pulled out a short sword.

Ivan tugged mightily, and the axe pulled free, coming

across so swiftly that neither the dwarf nor the assassin even realized its movement as it struck the assailant, cutting cleanly through the man's belly.

"Bet that hurt," Ivan mumbled with a helpless, almost embarrassed shrug.

*　*　*　*　*

Again Pikel hopped up on the bar, and again he reconsidered, seeing a pair of dark shapes rush out of Cadderly's room into the aisle above, right to the lip of the fallen stairway.

The frustrated dwarf groaned loudly—these two also carried those wretched crossbows.

Pikel realized that he wasn't their target, but he knew, too, that Ivan, standing unsuspectingly right below the ledge, was.

Sixteen

Scramble

Night Masks.

The words stung Danica's heart as surely as could the crossbow quarrel aimed her way. Night Masks. The band that had killed her parents; the wretched, evil assassins of Westgate, the town where Danica had been raised. The questions that rushed into the young woman's mind—Had they come for her? Were they working for the same enemy that had sent Barjin and the invading army into Shilmista?—were no match for the bile, the sheer rage, that climbed up the young woman's throat.

Slowly, she turned to face her adversary, locking his gaze with her own. He was a curious sight, bleeding in several places, leaning to one side, and struggling to draw breath, with half of his face swelling in a grotesque purple bruise and wooden splinters sticking from his hair, face, and arms. And for some reason, the man was barefoot.

"I will not ask for a surrender," the assassin slurred, waving the weapon. "Not after the dwarves . . ." He shook

205

away the frightening memory of the fight at the other inn, dropping several splinters to the roof with the effort.

"You shall be offered none," Danica assured, barely able to spit the words through gritted teeth. A growl escaped her lips as she dove to the roof and rolled.

The crossbow fired and Danica felt something thud against her side, though she was too enraged to know the seriousness of the wound or even to realize the pain. She came up near where the man had been, to find that he had taken flight.

Danica was on him in a few strides. He spun to face her, and she leaped into him, grabbing him tightly. Her knee moved repeatedly, each blow connecting on the man's groin.

She hit him a dozen times, grabbed his hair and ears and yanked his head back from her, then pulled it forward and drove her forehead in to meet it, splattering the man's nose and knocking out several teeth.

She kneed him a dozen more times and butted him again. Her fingers raked the beaten man's face; she drove one finger right through his eye.

Night Masks!

Danica jumped back from the doomed man, spinning a circle kick that snapped his head to the side violently and forced him into a series of stumbling steps. Somehow he did not fall down, though he was hardly conscious of his surroundings.

Danica leaped high behind him, lay herself flat out, planted both feet on the man's back, and sent him in a running takeoff over the roof's edge.

She pulled herself back to her feet, saw that two men had gained the roof by the gutter, though neither had summoned the courage to charge the furious woman.

Too many emotions assaulted the wounded and weary monk. The appearance of the assassin band, the knowledge

that these were Night Masks, sent her mind careening
down a hundred corridors of distant memories. More
recent memories, too, like the strange dream of the previous night, when she had, for a moment, entered the consciousness of her mental attacker.

What had happened to Cadderly? Danica's fear multi-
plied when she learned the identity of the killers. Had the
Night Masks again taken the love from Danica's life?

She fled, her eyes filled with tears, her arm and side
throbbing. Up the sloping rooftops, across the uneven
angles, leaping the small gaps, the young monk went.

The two killers followed her every step.

* * * * *

Ivan looked down, an inch to the side, to the neat hole
the crossbow quarrel had drilled into the lumber pile.
Slowly, the dwarf lifted his gaze to the men standing ten
feet above him, one leaning over the broken ledge, smiling
grimly, with a cocked crossbow pointed Ivan's way.

Sheer desperation shoved new heights of insight into
the mind of Pikel Bouldershoulder. Ivan—his brother!—
was about to die! Pikel's eyes darted all about, taking in a
surrealistic view of the grim scene.

Bar . . . pile . . . dead man (guts, yech) . . . struggling men
. . . Ivan . . . precipice . . . crossbowman . . . chandelier . . .

Chandelier? Chandelier above the leaning man.

They had to bring the thing down to light the candles,
Pikel reasoned. The dwarf whipped his head about, his
gaze coming to rest on the crank, conveniently located at
the back of the bar.

The assassin standing over Ivan paused long enough to
wave good-bye to the helpless dwarf.

Pikel could have just pulled the pin out of the crank to
set the spindle spinning, but now was not the time for

finesse. With a "Whoop!" to try to distract the crossbowman
a moment longer, the green-bearded dwarf hopped from the
bar to the shelving along the wall, crashing aside scores of
mugs and bottles, the shelves breaking away under his
weight.

"Ooooooo!" he wailed as he slammed his club against
the crank. Spindle and all broke out from the wall, hanging
stubbornly by a single peg. Pikel, on his knees beside Fredegar, looked at it as though it had tricked him, but then,
with a loud popping noise, the last peg gave and the whole
assembly rocketed up into the air.

"What?" the confused crossbowman asked.

His companion behind him gasped.

The chandelier took the crossbowman on the shoulder,
spinning him over the precipice.

He crashed into the wood pile beside Ivan, the stunned
dwarf nodding, stupefied. As though the gods had decided
to play some macabre joke, Ivan heard the distinctive click
a moment later as the crushed man's crossbow, pressed
harmlessly between the man and the broken stairs, fired.

"Hee hee hee," chuckled Pikel, standing again to watch
the spectacle. He forgot that the spindle above him was fast
unwinding, and fast dropping, and he was back to his knees
when it ricocheted off his skull.

"Oooo."

"Set the rope!" he heard Ivan cry, and, shaking away his
dizziness, Pikel wrapped the rope in his arms.

Ivan grasped his axe handle in his teeth (not an easy
thing to do!) and started up. He noticed that the remaining
assassin in the pile behind him was getting to his feet, so he
jumped back down to the raised end of a plank lying between him and the man. Ivan's end snapped down and the
end under the crawling assassin went up, slamming the
man under the chin. He groaned and rolled away, grabbing
at his shattered jawbone.

That done, Ivan leaped up again, stubby arms pulling him up the rope to the level of the other crossbowman. To the side, he noticed that Pikel was similarly climbing.

Ivan rushed on, finally getting his head high enough so that he could see the other man.

It was not a pleasant sight.

For the second time in the last few moments, Ivan Bouldershoulder stared into the wrong end of a readied crossbow.

Pikel made the ledge and let go of the rope, realizing only then that he had not secured it below him.

Ivan dropped like a stone. The crossbow fired, harmlessly high. And the stubborn assassin on the first level, his jaw grotesquely shattered, realized his folly in going to the rope under the climbing dwarf.

As he sat atop the man, atop the pile of broken stairs, Ivan, for perhaps the first time, thought it was not such a bad thing to have a scatterbrained brother.

* * * * *

Still on all fours, the young priest skittered fast and sure-footed along the edge of the adjoining building. His spindle-disks clung tightly to his hand, hanging to the end of their cord and bouncing along the building's side. Cadderly hardly noticed them, and had no time to stop and replace them in any event. Nor did the young priest note that the pain was no more in his wounded thigh.

He spotted Danica, running weakly away from him, limping, and then he spotted the two black-robed killers in pursuit, gaining on the stumbling woman with every stride.

Cadderly came up on the other side of the building, where the alley opened perpendicularly to a wide lane of craft stores called Market Square. Two merchants, up at dawn to prepare for the coming day, spotted the young priest and stared, then pointed up and called out something that Cadderly did not bother to decipher.

Too enraged to think of his movements, Cadderly slipped headfirst over the side of the building, going down hand over hand. A banner had been strung along thick ropes across the alley as a sign for one of the craftsmen's shops.

Hand over hand, foot over foot, Cadderly ran across the tightrope. He heard a shout of disbelief from the street below, didn't even realize that it was aimed his way. Back on the many-angled roof of the Dragon's Codpiece, the young priest charged off, nothing but Danica in his thoughts.

He spotted her a moment later—she had leaped across the narrow alley to the next building—stumbling over the crest of a dormer, going headlong. The two men went over right behind her.

"No!" the young priest tried to call out, but his word came out as a strange, squealing sound.

Never slowing, his eyes focused straight ahead, Cadderly flew over the short alley expanse.

One of the black-robed killers emerged from the region Danica had entered, in full flight. Cadderly feared he was too late.

* * * * *

The remaining man in the corridor darted into Cadderly's room, brushing aside the smoke and stench of charred flesh that blocked the doorway.

Pikel grabbed the rope again, and Ivan began to climb, his efforts aided by his brother's hauling movements toward Cadderly's door.

Pikel drove on, much relieved when he saw Ivan's stubby hand come over the lip of the hallway. But then four shapes emerged from Cadderly's room.

Pikel instinctively let go of the rope. He winced at Ivan's diminishing wail and the dull thump as Ivan landed again on the assassin at the bottom of the rope. Pikel couldn't worry about it, though, not with four killers just a few strides away.

But the Night Masks were no longer interested in battle. Seeing the stairs gone, they sought other avenues of escape. One grabbed the rope and, without even testing to see if it was secured, leaped over the precipice. The others ran the other way down the hall, scrambling over the railing wherever they found high spots—tables mostly—where they could get down.

Pikel thought to give chase, but he paused when he heard a door creak open, heard chanting. The next thing the green-bearded dwarf knew, he was lying several feet from where he had been standing, a sharp and burning pain in one side, and his shocked hair wildly dancing on end.

Me brudder. The words cried out in Pikel's mind over and over, a litany against the swirling dizziness, a reminder that he could not remain up here, lying helplessly on the floor.

Ivan heard the man land heavily beside him, and he felt the other one squirming slowly beneath him. The dwarf opened one heavy eyelid to see the assassin standing over him, sword in hand.

The thrust came before the dwarf could react, and Ivan thought he was dead, but the assassin struck low, beneath Ivan.

Ivan didn't question his luck. He struggled to a sitting position, trying to locate his axe, or anything else he might use against the standing killer.

Too late. The assassin's sword came up again.

"Me brudder!" Pikel cried as he flew over the precipice.

The assassin dove away, rolled to his feet, and followed his companions out the door.

Pikel hit Ivan full force.

Ivan groaned as he waited patiently (he had no choice in the matter) for Pikel to crawl off him. "If ye're looking for thanks, keep looking," Ivan grumbled.

* * * * *

Cadderly was too late in getting to the scene—for the sake of the other assassin.

The young priest relaxed as soon as he crested the steep roof. Danica was below him, in a valley between several gables. The remaining assassin was there, too, kneeling before Danica, his arms defenselessly by his sides and his head snapping to one side and the other, blood and sweat flying wide, as Danica landed blow after blow on his face.

"He is dead," Cadderly remarked when he got beside the young monk.

Danica, sobbing, slammed the man again, the shattered cartilage of his facial bones crackling under the blow.

"He is dead!" Cadderly said more emphatically, though he kept his tone calm and unaccusing.

Danica spun about, her face contorted with a mixture of rage and sorrow, and fell into his arms. Cadderly stared curiously as he wrapped his own arms about her, and Danica jumped back, staring at the young priest in disbelief.

"What—?" she stammered, backpedaling even farther, and Cadderly, noticing the change for the first time, had no answers for her.

His arms and legs, covered in white fur, had become those of a squirrel.

Seventeen

Mentor

Turn it back," Danica pleaded, her voice edged in desperation, her hands trembling at her sides. Cadderly stared helplessly at his squirrel-like limbs, without the slightest idea of how to begin to reverse the process. "I cannot," he admitted, as much to himself as to Danica. He looked helplessly to her, his gray eyes wide with disbelief and horror. "I cannot."

Danica moved to him, or tried to, until the pain in her side sent her lurching over. She grasped at the bloody wound in her abdomen just above her hip, and slumped to one knee.

Stubbornly, Danica got back to her feet, one hand held out in front of her to keep her concerned lover at bay.

"That must be tended," Cadderly pleaded.

"With squirrel arms?" Danica's retort stung the young priest more than she had intended. "Turn your arms and legs back to human, Cadderly. I beg you."

Cadderly stared long and hard at his limbs, feeling deceived, feeling as though his god, or the magic, had led him astray. Danica stood before him, needing him, and he, with the limbs of a rodent, could do nothing for her.

The young priest searched his memory, let page after page of the *Tome of Universal Harmony* flip through his thoughts in rapid succession. Nothing openly hinted at what he had done, at this transformation, miraculous and damning, that he had somehow brought upon himself.

But while Cadderly found no direct answers, he did begin that distant harmony, that sweet, inspiring song where all the mysteries of existence drifted past him, waiting to be grasped and deciphered. The song rang out a single word to the young priest, the name of the one person who might help him make sense of it all.

"Pertelope?" Cadderly asked blankly.

Danica, still grimacing, stared at him.

"Pertelope," he said again, more firmly. He turned his gaze to Danica, his breath coming in short gasps. "She knows."

"She knows what?" the young woman asked, wincing with every word.

"She knows," was all Cadderly could answer, for in truth, he did not really know what information the headmistress might have for him. He sensed only that the song was not lying to him, was not leading him astray.

"I must go to her."

"She is at the library," Danica argued. "It will take you three . . ."

Cadderly stopped her with an outstretched palm. He closed his mind to the stimuli around him and focused on the song again, felt it flow across the miles, calling him to step into it. Cadderly fell in with the tune, let it carry him along. The world became a dreamscape, surreal, unreal. He saw the gates of Carradoon and the western road leading into higher ground. Mountain passes zipped along beneath his consciousness, then he saw the library fast approaching, came upon the ivy-strewn walls and passed right through them . . . to Pertelope's room.

Cadderly recognized the tapestry on the back wall, to the side of the bed, the same one he had stolen so that Ivan could use it in making a replica of the drow crossbow.

"I have been waiting for you to come to me," he heard Pertelope say. The image of the room shifted and there sat the headmistress on the edge of her bed, dressed as always in her long-sleeved, high-necked black gown. Her eyes widened as she regarded the presence, and Cadderly understood that she saw him, with his rodent limbs, though he had left his corporeal form far behind.

"Help me," he pleaded.

Pertelope's comforting smile fell over him warmly.

"You have found *Affinity*," the headmistress explained, "a powerful practice, and not without its dangers."

Cadderly had no idea what Pertelope was talking about. Affinity? He had never heard the word used in such a way.

"The song is playing for you," Pertelope remarked, "often without your bidding." Cadderly's face revealed his startlement.

"I knew it would," Pertelope continued. "When I gave you the *Tome of Universal Harmony*, I knew the song would begin to play in your mind, and I knew that you would soon find the means to decipher the mysteries hidden within its notes."

"I have not," Cadderly protested. "I mean, things are happening around me, and to me—" he looked helplessly at his own limbs, translucent replicas of his corporeal form, "—but they are not of my doing, not of my control."

"Of course they are," Pertelope replied, drawing his attention away from his polymorphed limbs. "The book is the conduit to the magical energy bestowed through the power of Deneir. You summon and guide that energy. It comes to your call and bends to your will."

Cadderly looked down helplessly, and doubtingly, at his deformed body. He knew Pertelope could see his problem, and wondered if Danica could as well, back on the rooftop in Carradoon. Those squirrel limbs flew in the face of what the headmistress was saying, for if Cadderly could control the magic, as Pertelope insisted, then why had he remained half a rodent?

"You have not learned complete control," the headmistress said to him, as though she had read his mind, "but you are still a novice, after all, untrained and with mighty powers at your fingertips."

"Powers from Deneir?" Cadderly asked.

"Of course," answered Pertelope coyly, as though Cadderly's next remark would come as no shock whatsoever to her.

"Why would Deneir grant me such powers?" the young priest asked. "What have I done to warrant such a gift?"

Pertelope laughed at him. "You are his disciple."

"I am not!" Cadderly said, and he gave a horrified expression, realizing that he had offered that admission to a headmistress of his order.

Again, Pertelope only laughed. "You are, Cadderly," she said. "You are a true disciple of our god, and of Oghma, the brother god, as well. Do not measure fealty in terms of rituals and attendance to duties. Measure it by what lies in your heart, by your morals and your love. You are a scholar, in all your inquisitive mind and in all your heart, a blessed scholar. That is the measure of fealty to Deneir."

"Not according to Avery," Cadderly argued. "How often he has threatened to throw me out of the order altogether for my indiscretions concerning those rituals you so quickly dismiss!"

"He could not throw you out of any order," Pertelope replied. "One cannot be 'thrown out' of a religious calling."

"Religious calling?" Cadderly replied. "If that is what you must label it, then I fear I was never in the order to begin with. I have no calling."

"That's absurd," replied Pertelope. "You are as attuned with the precepts of Deneir as any person I have ever mit. That, my young priest, is what constitutes a religious calling! Do you doubt the powers you have begun to unlock?"

"Not the powers," Cadderly replied with typical stubbornness, "but their source."

"It is Deneir."

"So you say," answered Cadderly, "and so you are free to believe."

"You will, too, in time. You are a priest of Deneir, a follower of a god who demands independence, the exercise of free will, and the exercise of intellect," Pertelope continued, again as though she had read Cadderly's mind. He had to wonder if Pertelope hadn't played through this scenario herself many years ago.

"You are supposed to question—to question everything, even the existence of the gods and the purpose of being alive," Pertelope continued, her hazel eyes taking on a faraway, mystical look. "If you would follow blindly from ritual to ritual, you would be no better than the cattle and sheep that dot the fields around Carradoon.

"Deneir does not want that," Pertelope went on, calmly, comfortingly, and looking directly back at the frightened young priest. "He is a god for artists and poets, freethinkers all, else their work would be no more than replicas of what others have deemed ideal. The question, Cadderly, is stronger than the answer. It is what accomplishes growth—growth toward Deneir."

Somewhere deep inside, Cadderly prayed that Pertelope was speaking truthfully, that the apparent wisdom of her words wasn't just the feeble hope of one as confused and desperate as he.

"You have been chosen," Pertelope went on, bringing the conversation back to more concrete terms. "You hear the song and will come, over time, to decipher more and more of its notes, to better understand your place in this confusing experience that we call life."

"I am a wizard."

"No!" It was the first time the headmistress had appeared angry during the conversation, and Cadderly wisely did not immediately reply. "Your magical gifts are clerical in nature," Pertelope asserted. "Have you done anything beyond those enchantments you have witnessed other priests casting?"

Cadderly thought long and hard. In truth, everything magical he had done in some way, at least, replicated clerical spells. Even this *Affinity* was not so different from the shape-changing abilities exhibited by the woodland priests, the druids. But still, his powers were different, Cadderly knew.

"I do not pray for these spells," he argued. "I do not get out of my bed in the morning with the notion that I should be able to create light this day, or that I will find need to turn my arms into a squirrel's paws. Nor do I pray to Deneir, at any time."

"You read the book," Pertelope reasoned, stealing Cadderly's building momentum. "That is your prayer. As far as selecting spells and memorizing their particular chants and inflections, you have no need. You hear the song, Cadderly. You are one of the chosen, one of the few. I had suspected that fact for many years, and came to understand just a few weeks ago that you would take my place."

"What are you talking about?" Cadderly asked, his near panic only intensified by the fact that Pertelope, as she spoke, had begun to unbutton her long gown. Cadderly gaped in amazement as the headmistress peeled the garment off, revealing a featureless torso covered by skin that resembled the hide of a shark, covered not with skin, but with sharp pentacles.

"I was raised from childhood on the Sword Coast," the headmistress began wearily, "near the sea. My father was a fisherman, and often I would go out with him to tend the nets. You see, I found affinity with the shark, as you have with squirrels—with Percival in particular. I came to marvel at the graceful movements, at the perfection of that oft-maligned creature.

"I already explained to you that *Affinity* is a practice that is not without its dangers," Pertelope went on, giving a small, ironic chuckle. "You see, I too fell prey to the chaos curse. Under its influences, I assumed my affinity with no regard for safety, no practical restraints at all."

Cadderly winced to think that this wonderful woman, always a dear friend to him, had suffered by the curse that he had brought upon the library.

There was no malice, no blame, edging Pertelope's voice as she continued.

"The change I enacted is permanent," she said, rubbing a hand along her arm, the denticles drawing several lines of blood on her human palm. "It is painful, too, for my whole body is part human and part fish. The very air is poison to me, as would be the waters of the wide sea. I have no place left in this world, my friend. I am dying."

"No!"

"Yes," Pertelope replied easily. "I am not young, you know, and have labored long on this confusing path we call life. The curse killed me, do not doubt, and I have struggled to hang on for the very purpose that is before me this day. You, Cadderly, are my successor."

"I will not accept it."

"You cannot avoid it," answered the headmistress. "Once begun, the song never ends. Never."

The word sounded like the bang of a drum to Cadderly,

suddenly terrified of what horrors he may have unlocked in the pages of that awful book.

"You will come to know the limitations of your powers," Pertelope went on. "And there are indeed limitations." She looked disconcertingly at her own destroyed arms as she spoke, making her point all too clear. "You are not invincible. You are not all-powerful. You are not a god."

"I never said—"

"Humility will be your preservation," Pertelope promptly, sharply interrupted. "Test the powers, Cadderly, but test them with respect. They will drain you and take a bit of you with them whenever you summon them. Exhaustion is your enemy, and know that enacting magic will inevitably weary the spellcaster. But know, too, that if Deneir has chosen you, he will demand of you."

Pertelope smiled warmly, revealing her confidence that Cadderly would be up to meeting the challenge.

No reciprocal smile found its way to Cadderly's face.

* * * * *

"Do you plan to go somewhere?" Ghost whispered to Bogo Rath, seeing the young wizard in the upstairs hall of the Dragon's Codpiece with a sack in hand. The assassin stepped out of Cadderly's room and motioned for Bogo to follow him to his own room.

"The city guard has been called," the wizard explained. "They will swarm all about this place."

"And find what?" Ghost replied with a snicker, thinking it an ironic statement, given that he had just deposited Brennan's body in Cadderly's room. "Certainly nothing to implicate either one of us."

"I hit the green-bearded dwarf with a lightning bolt," Bogo admitted.

"He did not see you," Ghost retorted. "If he had, you

would be dead. Both he and his brother are up and about, downstairs with Fredegar. They would have come back for you long before this if the stupid dwarf suspected you had launched that magic."

Bogo relaxed a bit. "Did Cadderly and Danica get away?"

Ghost shrugged, unable to answer. He had seen little beyond the carnage left in the wake of the violence. "Temporarily, perhaps," he answered at length, and with as much conviction as he could muster. "But the Night Masks have been set on the trail now. They will not stop until the young priest is dead."

"Then I am free to return to Castle Trinity," Bogo reasoned hopefully.

"If you try to leave now, you will invite only suspicion," Ghost replied. "And if Cadderly has managed to elude the assassins, he will likely return here. This is still the best seat at the game, for those who have the courage to play to the end."

The last words sounded clearly like a threat.

"Aid the city guard in their investigation," Ghost continued, a sudden ironic smile crossing his features. He was the artist, he privately reminded himself, already weaving new webs of intrigue. "Tell them you possess some knowledge of magic, and that you believe a bolt of lightning was set off in the upstairs corridor. When the dwarf confirms your story, you will be viewed in a favorable light."

Bogo eyed the assassin doubtfully, even more so when he remembered that Kierkan Rufo was still about, carrying information that could certainly damn him.

"What is it?" Ghost asked, seeing his mounting concern.

"Rufo."

Ghost chuckled evilly. "He can say nothing without implicating himself. And he, by all of your descriptions, is too much a coward to do that."

"True enough," Bogo admitted, "but I am still not

certain of our wisdom in remaining at the inn. We have underestimated Cadderly and his friends, it would seem."

"Perhaps," Ghost said in reluctant agreement, "but do not complicate the error by overestimating the priest now. For all we know, Cadderly might lie dead in an alley."

Bogo hesitated, then nodded.

"Be gone," Ghost instructed, "back to your room, or to aid in the investigation, but say nothing to Rufo. Better that the cowardly priest be left alone to stew in his guilt and terror."

Again Bogo nodded and then was gone.

Ghost's confidence disappeared as soon as he was alone. This had been a complicated visit to Carradoon, had not been a clean kill. Even if Cadderly was dead, the toll had been horrendous, with more than half of the dedicated Night Mask band killed.

Ghost really was no longer sure that remaining at the Dragon's Codpiece would bode well for either himself or Bogo, but he feared the consequences of trying to slip away with the city guard, and two rambunctious dwarves, snooping around. He moved to his door and cracked it open an inch, curious to see what might be transpiring outside.

He watched carefully for Rufo, thinking that if the treacherous priest made any dangerous moves, he might have to kill him.

No, it had not been without complications, but that was part of the fun of it all, was it not? It was a new challenge for the artist, an intricate landscape for the filling canvas.

Ghost smiled wickedly, taking comfort in the fact that he wasn't in any personal danger—not while he had the *Ghearufu*, and had Vander as a waiting and helpless host on the outskirts of town.

*   *   *   *   *

Cadderly was relieved to see Danica still up and conscious when he rejoined his corporeal form on the rooftop beside the Dragon's Codpiece. The young woman's face remained contorted in pain. A crossbow quarrel protruded from her right side, hanging from skin and tunic and surrounded by a widening crimson stain.

Cadderly did not immediately go to her. He closed his eyes and forced the song back into his thoughts. The notes drifted past until Cadderly recalled that part of the song, that page in the tome, he had been hearing back on the balcony when he had enacted the change to the squirrel form.

Danica whispered to him softly, sounding more concerned for his own safety than for her own. With some effort, Cadderly pushed her words away, concentrated on the music. His mouth moved in silent prayer, and when he at last opened his eyes, Danica was straining to smile and his arms and legs were back to normal.

"You found your answers," the young woman remarked.

"Along with more questions," Cadderly replied. He pulled his spindle-disks from their tight hold on his finger and tucked them away, then moved beside his love.

"You were speaking," Danica said to him, "but not to me. It sounded like half of a conversation, the other half—"

"Was with Pertelope," Cadderly explained. "I, or at least my consciousness, was back in the library." He hardly noticed Danica's stare, was more interested in her sorely wounded side.

When he recalled the song this time, it sounded more distant to him, required more effort to get near it. Pertelope's warnings of exhaustion welled up in him, but he pushed his mounting fears away; Danica's health was more important.

Cadderly focused on the dangling quarrel as much as on the wound it had caused; his thoughts were as much on destruction as on healing. His chant was uttered through gritted teeth.

Danica grunted and winced. Black smoke wafted from her wound. Soon a small cloud of the stuff covered her side.

The quarrel was his enemy, was Danica's enemy, Cadderly determined. Poor Danica, dear Danica.

When the smoke dissipated, gone, too, were the crossbow quarrel and the wound.

Danica straightened and shrugged, not knowing how she could possibly thank Cadderly for what he had done.

"Are you injured?" she asked, concerned.

Cadderly shook his head and took her arm. "We must be gone," he said, his tone absent, as though he was talking more to himself than to Danica. "We must go and sit together, privately, and try to sort through the turns fate has shown us." He cocked his head, turned his attention to the growing tumult in the awakening lanes around the Dragon's Codpiece, particularly to the clip-clap of many hooves echoing from every direction.

"The city guard is about," Danica replied. "They will require information."

Cadderly continued to pull her along.

"We have nowhere to go," Danica argued as they neared the building's back edge, many soldiers coming into sight along Market Square.

Cadderly wasn't listening. His eyes were closed again and he was deep in some chant, deep in song.

Danica's eyes widened one more time as she felt herself become something less than substantial. Somehow Cadderly kept his grip on her arm and together they simply blew away, off the rooftop, riding the currents of the wind.

* * * * *

Bogo Rath slipped out of the Dragon's Codpiece a short while later, rushing briskly past the dwarves and the bereaved innkeeper in the hearth room. After brief consideration, the frightened young wizard decided that Ghost's presumptions were not worth risking his life over, and he decided, too, that departing the inn after such tragedy could not be viewed as a suspicious act.

The only thing the city guardsman asked of him as he passed through the hole where the front door had been was that he remain in town.

Bogo nodded and pointed to an inn a few doors farther up Lakeview Street, though the wizard had no intention of staying around for very long. He would go to the inn and get a room, but would remain in Carradoon only until he had studied the spells that would allow him to leave quickly and without the possibility of being stopped.

Eighteen

Reflections on the Water

The morning light was still new, and the mist had not yet flown from the waters of Impresk Lake. The great three-arched stone bridge connecting the mainland to Carradoon's island section loomed ghostly. It towered above Cadderly and Danica as they drifted in a small rowboat, quiet with their thoughts and the lap of the gentle waves against the prow.

The weather was fitting to Cadderly's grim mood. He had killed a man, had burned him to a blackened ball, and had knocked another from the balcony, leaving him for dead as well. There had been no real choice, Cadderly knew, but he could not easily dismiss his guilt. Whatever the reasons, he had killed a human being.

He tried hard to not think of the man's family, children perhaps, waiting for a father that would never return.

Danica, too, sat quietly, deep in thought, at the small boat's prow. More accustomed to battle than her somewhat innocent companion, the young woman was more concerned with what had precipitated the vicious attack. What had brought the Night Masks upon her and Cadderly?

Cadderly took up the oars and gave a single stroke, reversing the drift and pushing the boat farther out from the imposing bridge. He let the oars hang in the water and turned about on the bench seat to face Danica.

"Night Masks," Danica muttered grimly.

Cadderly looked at her; the name meant little to him.

"From Westgate," Danica explained. "They are among the deadliest killers in all the Realms. We were fortunate to escape them, and I now believe I have escaped them twice."

Cadderly's expression showed that he still did not understand.

"On our journey down from the library," Danica continued, "the dwarves and I were attacked by a band of five."

"Many bandits have been reported on the roads during these troubled times," Cadderly remarked.

Danica shook her head, certain that there was a connection between the attack on the road and the one in Cadderly's room.

"Why would an assassin's guild from Westgate come after us?" Cadderly reasoned.

"Us?" echoed Danica. "No, they are after me, I fear. It was the Night Masks who killed my parents, years ago. Now they have come to finish the job."

Cadderly didn't believe a word of that explanation. He sensed that—if Danica's theories about the identity of the killer band were correct—there was more at work here than the completion of a decade-old vendetta. Cadderly contemplated his own experiences of the last few days, thought of his meeting with Rufo in the hearth room and the presence of the invisible wizard. And what had happened, he wondered, back in his own room that night?

He looked at Danica quizzically. "I found you on the floor, terrified. Tell me about your dream."

"I do not remember much," Danica admitted, and her tone revealed that she did not really see the point of it all. Cadderly was determined, though. He thought for a moment, then took out his crystal-centered spindle-disks.

He held them up before Danica's eyes and set them spinning. Even in the dim light, the crystals flickered with reflective fires. "Concentrate," Cadderly begged the woman. "Let the crystal into your mind. Please, do not use your meditative talents to block me now."

"What will this tell us?" Danica argued. "It was just a dream."

"Was it?"

Danica shrugged—it was a dream that contained references to the Night Masks, after all—and relaxed, focusing her gaze on the spindle-disks. Cadderly watched her intently, then closed his eyes and thought of the sacred tome, heard the song playing the words to a simple spell of hypnosis.

Danica sank deeper, her shoulders visibly slumping, as Cadderly quietly chanted. His words became prying questions that Danica heard only subconsciously.

Cadderly, too, allowed the hypnosis to fall over him, used it to achieve complete empathy with Danica.

The questions rolled out of his mouth, though he was barely aware of them. And Danica answered, as much with her posture and her facial expressions as with mere words.

Danica blinked her eyes open; Cadderly followed her lead. Neither of them knew how much time had passed, but Cadderly understood then, beyond any doubt, that Danica's nighttime experience had indeed been an important clue.

"It was not a dream," he announced.

Cadderly recalled what Danica had imparted to him under the hypnosis: the sense of departure from a black sphere that the young priest knew represented her identity. The image reminded the young priest vividly of his own telepathic experiences with the imp Druzil and the wizard Dorigen. Might those two be behind all this?

Cadderly dropped a hand into his pocket to feel the amulet he had taken from Rufo in Shilmista Forest, an amulet that Druzil had given Rufo to improve telepathic contact between the two. With the amulet, Cadderly had been able to sense the imp's proximity, and he took comfort that it had not signaled Druzil's presence in many weeks, not since the large battle in the forest.

But who then? he wondered.

Dorigen remained a distinct possibility.

"Possession?" he muttered, using the word as a catalyst for his thoughts.

Another image struck Cadderly then, an image of Nameless, the beggar on the road, and the horrible, shadowy shapes writhing atop his shoulders. He remembered, too, that night when Brennan had come to his room, projecting the same vile aura. Perhaps the song of Deneir had not lied to him; perhaps the attempt on Danica was not his enemy's first try at possession.

Cadderly winced, remembering Fredegar's worries that young Brennan had not been seen since that night. He tried to recall clues as he took up the oars for another single stroke against the drift.

"What is it?" Danica asked. Her tone revealed her understanding that Cadderly's mind had unlocked some of the secrets.

"They have not come for you," the young priest answered with certainty, looking over his shoulder. "They were here before you, around me, close to me." Cadderly exhaled deeply, fearing for Brennan and Nameless, and let his gaze drift across the water to the gray outline of the great bridge. "Too close."

Danica started to reply—something comforting, Cadderly knew—then she stopped and cocked her head curiously.

Cadderly began to turn his whole body about, to fully face Danica, understanding that something was wrong and fearing that the young woman had come under some mental assault.

Danica spun about, rocking the boat so suddenly that Cadderly, though he was seated near the center, almost went over the side.

"Stubborn!" Danica cried. Her hand snapped in front of her just in time to grab the wrist of the man who had tried to drive a dagger into her back. Holding tight, Danica leaped to her feet, stretched her attacker's arm to the limit, and pulled him farther over the bow.

She gave her attacker's arm a quick, violent twist and brought her free hand over the back of his fingers, jerking the man's hand back toward his wrist.

Cadderly tried to get about in the rocking boat to go to Danica's aid, but all he wound up doing was stumbling over the boat's center seat and slamming himself on the side of the head with one of the oar handles.

He realized that the stumble was a good thing, though, as a knife soared up over the side of the boat and whipped across above his head. Reacting instinctively to the threat, Cadderly forearmed the oar, freeing it from its lock to tumble into the water near the unseen attacker.

The young scholar got his spindle-disks looped onto his finger. The boat rocked, and he looked back the other way, across the boat, to see still another assassin coming up over the side.

Danica held her balance easily in the rocking craft. She continued her vicious press on the caught man's hand, finally forcing him to release his dagger.

She wasn't done with him yet.

Night Masks!

Danica's foot snapped out wide, coming back around the man's head and forcing his chin over the prow rail. Holding him tightly against the wood, Danica yanked his arm back out over the water. She locked his elbow so that he could not bend the limb and pressed straight down.

The man's eyes bulged as the bow pressed his throat up under his jaw.

Cadderly's off-balance throw soared lower than he had hoped, but while he did not get the man's head, he did get a few fingers—and the top plank of the boat. Wood splintered, the remaining oar flew off, and so did the assassin, clutching his blasted belly as he fell away into the lake.

Free of the weight, the boat rocked back so far that Cadderly feared its other side would dip under the water where the knife-thrower waited.

The young priest realized how vulnerable he was, and how vulnerable Danica was! They needed a distraction, something to allow them to get their bearings.

Water did come in over the broken side of the boat when it rocked back again, but Cadderly took no note of it, intent on the wounded man fumbling in the water with the floating oar. The shape of the oar caught the young priest's attention.

With one foot planted in the rocking boat, and with the choking man struggling frantically against her, Danica amazingly held her balance.

The struggling killer tried to come up over the side, but Danica jammed his arm down mightily, dislocating his shoulder.

The man could not even grimace at the obvious pain. His face went blank, weirdly serene. Danica understood. She brought her foot back around, released its hold on the man's head, and let him slip under the water.

Her sensibilities returned to her then, her sheer rage at the presence of the Night Masks temporarily sated by the reality of the kill. Others were about—Danica realized for the first time that others were likely about!

She turned and, to her horror, saw Cadderly disappear under the water in the grasp of a killer. Another boat, with several men in it, approached from behind; Danica did not know if they were friend or foe—until a crossbow quarrel cut the air beside her face.

Instinctively, she dove to the floor of the boat. She knew she had to get to Cadderly, but how? If she went under the water, how could she hope to stop this approaching menace?

A scream to the side turned Danica about, to peek over the broken plank. There floundered the wounded Night Mask, the one Cadderly had hit with his spindle-disks, fighting desperately to free himself from the clutches of a long, thick constrictor—a snake about the same size as one of the boat's oars.

The man somehow broke free and began swimming with all speed toward the approaching boat. The snake slithered off in pursuit, slipping under the water as it went.

Despite the peril, Danica could not help but smile. She knew that the appearance of this snake was no natural coincidence; she knew that Cadderly, and that mysterious power, had struck again.

Danica got up to her knees. The other boat was closer now; she could see a man in the prow leveling a crossbow her way. She jerked up, as though she meant to stand, then fell flat and heard the whistle of the high-flying bolt.

Now she had time to get over the side, into the water after Cadderly. Before she moved out of the boat, though, the water churned and the Night Mask appeared, his face contorted in terror and the second snake, the second oar, wrapped about his shoulder and chest. He reached for the boat, then slapped at the water and the beast.

Then he was gone.

Again the water churned, a short distance to the side. Up came Cadderly, impossibly fast, his body breaking out of the water impossibly high.

He was standing on the water! And still wearing his hat, the holy symbol set in its front glowing furiously.

Danica nearly laughed, too amazed to react any other way. Cadderly took in a few gulps of air, seeming more surprised than Danica.

He looked back toward the approaching boat—the swimming man had just about met it by then—and saw that the crossbowman was preparing another shot.

"Get in!" Danica cried, thinking Cadderly too vulnerable standing on the water out in the open. Cadderly seemed not to hear her. He was chanting, singing actually, and waving one hand slowly to and fro.

Danica looked back to the other boat, saw the man leveling the crossbow—and saw Cadderly standing in the open, vulnerable.

She scrambled to the side, grabbed at a piece of broken wood floating in the small pool at the bottom of her boat. She came up throwing, skimming the wood sidelong so that it spun and swerved . . . and plopped harmlessly into the water a dozen feet to the side of the approaching craft.

But the crossbowman had flinched, had looked her way.

A sudden swell erupted in the calm lake, near where Danica's wood had disappeared. The water reared up and rolled, as if aimed, toward the enemy boat. The crossbowman had set his sights on Cadderly again when the wave collided against the side of his boat. Not even bracing himself at the time, the man lurched over the side and nearly lost his weapon.

At first, Danica wondered how the little piece of wood had so disrupted the stillness of the lake. She realized it was no more than coincidence, though, and she turned to the true source of the swell. Cadderly, still standing calmly, sung his soft song and waved his hand back and forth.

Another swell rose and crashed against the enemy boat, turning it about so that it was facing the bridge.

Cadderly smiled; another swell turned the boat so that it was facing the shore, directly away from him.

"Come," Cadderly said to Danica, extending his hand. "Before they get their bearings."

Danica at first misunderstood, thinking that Cadderly wanted her to help him into the boat. He resisted her pull, though, beckoning her to go to him.

The assassin who had pulled Cadderly under the water bobbed to the surface face down. The snake that had been wrapped about him became an oar again at Cadderly's command and floated benignly, a harmless piece of flotsam.

"Come," Cadderly reiterated, tugging Danica. She jumped onto him and wrapped herself about him.

Cadderly looked about, then ran for the island. Danica watched over his shoulder, taking note that his footsteps did not splash the water. Rather, the burdened young priest left depressions in the lake surface, which quickly reverted to the natural water shape, as though he was running across soft ground.

Behind them, the enemy boat finally straightened and the crossbowman pulled the swimmer up over the side. The oar that had been chasing him bobbed up over the waves.

Danica kissed Cadderly on the neck and rested her weary head on his shoulder. The world had gone crazy.

Cadderly came to the shore mumbling, thinking out loud. He kept chugging along but slowed under the weight of his burden when he hit more solid ground.

"Cadderly . . ."

"If those are professional assassins," he was saying, "we must assume they were hired by our enemies, by Dorigen perhaps."

"Cadderly . . ."

"Someone has made the connection to us," Cadderly continued, undaunted. "Someone has determined that we are, or at least that I am, a threat to be eliminated."

"Cadderly . . ."

"But how long have they been hovering about me?" the young priest muttered. "Oh, Brennan, I pray I am wrong."

"Cadderly!"

Cadderly looked right at Danica for the first time since he had left the lake. "What?"

"You can put me down now," Danica replied.

She hit the ground running, grabbing Cadderly's wrist and tugging him along. They heard the enemy boat skid to shore through the brush behind them.

"Stubborn," Danica said, looking over her shoulder gravely.

Cadderly knew she wanted to turn and finish the fight.

"Not now," he begged. "We must get back to the inn."

"We may never get our enemies so out in the open again," Danica reasoned.

"I am weary," Cadderly replied. And indeed, the young priest was. The song no longer played in his head, but was replaced by a severe headache, the likes of which young Cadderly had never before experienced.

Danica nodded and sped on. They crashed through a hedgerow, into the back yard of one of Carradoon's finer estates. Dogs began to bark from somewhere nearby, but Danica did not veer from her path through another hedgerow and into another open yard.

Several people, older merchants and their spouses, stared at the fleeing couple incredulously.

"Get to cover and alert the city guard!" Cadderly called to them as he followed Danica past. "Thieves and murderers pursue us! Call out the city guard and send them to the bridge!"

The couple burst through another row of bushes,

coming out onto a wide, flat cobblestone lane, running between lines of beautiful manor houses, between lines of staring, curious people.

Not a horse or wagon was seen on the bridge at this early hour, something Cadderly took comfort in as he and Danica started across. The young priest would have hated to place anyone directly in the path of his deadly pursuers, and he knew by the continued bark of distant, unseen dogs that the Night Masks had not given up the chase, were only a few minutes behind.

Cadderly skidded to a stop when they came to the high point in the first of the bridge's three arching supports. Danica started to question him, but was stopped by his conniving smile.

"Watch for the assassins," he said to her as he fell to his knees. He used his soaked cloak to trace a square on the stone of the wide bridge.

"The first page I ever looked at in Headmistress Pertelope's book always amazed me," he explained, not slowing in his work. "I knew it was a spell, similar to one I had seen in the book of Belisarius."

The square completed, two lines of wetness running parallel across the structure, Cadderly rose and led Danica a few dozen steps farther along.

Cadderly called up the song and began to chant, knowing the words intimately. He had to stop, though, and rub his temples to relieve the throbbing the powers caused.

They will drain you and take a bit of you with them whenever you summon them, Pertelope had warned him. *Exhaustion is your enemy . . .*

"They are on the bridge!" he heard Danica say, and he felt her tug at his arm, trying to hurry him along.

It could not be helped. Cadderly fought through the pain and weariness, forced the song into his mind and to his lips.

What is the bond that holds the stone?
A bond that wetness breaks.
What are you without the bond?

Danica knocked him to the ground; he barely heard the crossbow quarrel pass them by.

Still he sang, his concentration complete.

Seep, my water, seep
Through the bond, so deep.

The leading assassin stumbled suddenly, lurched forward as though his feet had been ensnared, fell face down onto the bridge . . . and sank into the mud that the section of bridge had become.

Danica and Cadderly heard splashes below as chunks of mud and stone dropped into the lake. Another assassin hit the area but managed to fall back, knee-deep in the collapsing morass.

The man who had gone in headlong screamed as he dropped out the bottom, plummeting the twenty feet or so to the churning lake.

The entire section Cadderly had marked off slipped down right behind him.

Four stunned assassins stood at the edge of the fifteen-foot gap separating them from their intended quarry, staring in disbelief.

"She said that Deneir would demand of me," Cadderly remarked to Danica, rubbing his throbbing temples. "And he will again, when we get to the inn."

"You have come into some faith?" Danica asked as they fled, leaving behind the frustrated assassins' curses and the clip-clap of many horses coming onto the bridge, bearing city guardsmen.

Cadderly looked at Danica as though she had slapped

him. He calmed and shrugged, having no recourse against her logic.

They heard the shouts of guardsmen and killers as the trapped assassins, one by one, dove for the cover of the water.

The way was clear, all the way back to the Dragon's Codpiece, to dead enemies and dead friends.

Nineteen

Sorrow and Divine Joy

S houts continued to follow Cadderly and Danica after
they left the bridge and made their way onto Lakeview Street. The mist was fast flying, burned away by
the steamy rays of the rising sun.

Carradoon had awakened to a travesty.

Lakeview Street was jammed with curious citizens and
city guardsmen. Many heads turned to regard the young
priest and his escort, Cadderly's wide-brimmed hat drooping on all sides from its soaking. Pointing fingers turned
the companions' way as well, and soon a horseman, a city
guard, pushed his way through the throng to stop in Cadderly's path.

"Are you a priest of the Edificant Library?" came the
guardsman's blunt and gruff question.

"I am Cadderly, of the Order of Deneir," the young priest
replied. He turned to Danica and shrugged, embarrassed
and almost apologetic, as soon as he had spoken the last
few words.

"We are making our way back to the Dragon's Codpiece, the inn of Fredegar Harriman," Danica explained, tossing Cadderly a sidelong glance, "to check on the friends we were forced to leave behind."

"Forced?" Cadderly and Danica knew the question was a test. The guardsman's eyes remained narrow and searching as he continued to scrutinize them.

"You know what occurred," Cadderly replied without hesitation.

The guardsman nodded gravely, apparently satisfied with the explanation. "Come, and quickly," he bade them, and he used his horse to nudge aside any who stood to block the couple's progress.

Neither Cadderly nor Danica enjoyed that stroll down Lakeview Street, fearful that among those many watching eyes loomed some belonging to their assassin enemies. And even more fearful to the companions, considering the guard's grim tone, loomed the possibility that the victory back at the inn had not been without cost.

Their fears did not diminish when they passed the inn two doors down, where Ivan and Pikel had been staying, to find that the front rail, the window above the door, and the wall beside the door all had been smashed apart. The innkeeper, sweeping glass and wood shards from his front porch, regarded the two suspiciously, not looking away and not blinking once as they passed.

Cadderly paused and sighed deeply when the Dragon's Codpiece came into sight. He spotted the balcony of his room, the place he had used as a sanctuary from the harshness of the world for the past several weeks. The front rail lay in the street; one plank, the one that had supported Danica's ride to safety, hung out at a weird diagonal angle. There were no bodies in the street (thank the gods!), but Cadderly saw a crimson stain on the cobblestone beneath his room, and a larger one halfway across the wide street.

Danica, apparently sensing his distress at the sight, hooked her arm around his and lent him support. To her surprise, Cadderly pulled away. She looked at him, to see if she had done something wrong, but his return stare was not accusing.

He stood straight and tall, took another deep breath, and squared his shoulders.

Danica understood the significance of those simple acts, understood that, this time, Cadderly had accepted what he had been forced to do. This time, he would not run away, as he had in Shilmista; he would meet the threat head-on, strike back against those who meant to strike at him. But could he do so, Danica wondered, without ghosts like Barjin's hovering beside him for the rest of his days?

Cadderly walked past her, then smiled and waved when "Oo oi!" sounded from the door of the Dragon's Codpiece and Pikel Bouldershoulder stepped onto the front porch. The dwarf held Cadderly's lost walking stick high above his head and waved excitedly with a heavily bandaged hand.

Danica waited a moment longer and let Cadderly get far ahead of her, considering the perceived shift in the young priest's demeanor. This continuing stream of violent events was forcing Cadderly to grow up, to thicken his hide, in a hurry. Violence could be a numbing thing, Danica knew; no battle is ever harder to accept and fight than the first, no killing blow made with more reluctance than the first.

Watching her lover stride confidently to join Pikel, the young monk was afraid.

By the time Danica caught up to Cadderly, he stood silently inside the inn with both dwarves (to her relief) and with a teary-eyed Fredegar Harriman. Danica held in check her elation at Ivan and Pikel's good health, though, for she followed Cadderly's gaze to a table in the hearth room, to Headmaster Avery's sprawling corpse. The chest was torn wide and revealed a gaping hole where the heart should have been.

"My Brennan," broken Fredegar was saying. "They killed my poor Brennan!"

Cadderly let his gaze drift about the sacked room, to the broken stairwell, the shattered chandelier atop its rubble; to the charred floor beside the long bar; to a young, unmarked body gently laid beside that bar; and to the row of six corpses, one of them still releasing wisps of smoke from under the cloth that covered it.

"Four of them, at least, got away," Ivan informed them.

"You will find another one on the roof," Danica remarked.

"Oo oi," Pikel chirped, snapping his stubby fingers and motioning for one of the guards to go and check.

"Maybe only three got away," Ivan corrected.

"Seven got away," Cadderly said absently, remembering the three men who had assaulted him and Danica from the water, and the four others in the pursuing boat.

Ivan shook his yellow-bearded face, then grumbled, "Well, there's a pack of trouble for ye."

Cadderly hardly heard the dwarf. The young priest walked slowly across the cluttered floor toward the body of the man who had served him as a father for as long as he could recall. Before he got there, though, a tall man, a city soldier, intercepted him.

"We have some questions," the man explained gruffly.

Cadderly eyed him dangerously. "They will wait."

"No," the man retorted. "They will be answered when I say. And fully! I'll brook no—"

"Leave." It was a simple word, spoken quietly and in controlled tones, but, to the city guardsman, it struck like a thunderbolt. The man stood up very straight, glanced about curiously, then headed for the front door. "Come along," he instructed his fellow soldiers, who, after exchanging surprised glances, obeyed without complaint.

Ivan started to say something to Cadderly, but Danica put a hand on the dwarf's shoulder to stop him.

Cadderly wouldn't have heard Ivan anyway. The young priest moved beside Avery's torn body and wiped a tear from his gray eyes. Avery had gotten in the way of something that really did not concern him, Cadderly suspected, and the notion brought disgust to the young man, brought yet another layer of guilt to his growing burden.

But it wasn't guilt that drove Cadderly now; it was sorrow, a grief more profound than any he had ever known. So many images of Avery's life flowed through the young priest. He saw the portly headmaster on the lane outside the Edificant Library, trying to enjoy a sunny spring day but continually hampered by Percival, the white squirrel, who dropped twigs on him from the branches above. He saw Avery at Brother Chaunticleer's midday canticle, the headmaster's face made content, serene, by the melodious song to Avery's cherished god.

How different that fatherly face seemed now, its mouth open in a final scream, an unanswered plea for help that did not come.

Most of all, Cadderly remembered the many scoldings the headmaster had given him, Avery's blotchy face turning bright red with frustration at Cadderly's apparent indifference and irresponsibility. It took the insidious chaos curse for the headmaster to finally admit his true feelings for Cadderly, to admit that he considered Cadderly a son. In truth, though, Cadderly had known it all along. He never could have upset Avery so completely and so many times if the headmaster had not cared for him.

Only now, standing beside the dead man, did Cadderly realize how much he had loved Avery, this man who had served as father.

It occurred to Cadderly that Avery should not have been down in the hearth room at such an early hour, especially not dressed so informally, so vulnerably. Cadderly digested that information almost subconsciously, filing it away with the myriad other facts he had collected and scrutinized since his flight from the assassin band.

"My Brennan, too," Fredegar blubbered, coming to Cadderly's side, draping an arm over Cadderly's shoulder to lean on the young priest.

Cadderly was more than willing to give his gentle friend the needed support, and he followed the innkeeper's lead across the floor toward the bar.

The contrast between Brennan's body and Avery's was startling. The teenager's face showed neither horror nor any signs of surprise. His body, too, seemed intact, with no obvious wounds.

It appeared that he had simply, peacefully, died.

The only thing Cadderly could think of was poison.

"They could not tell me how," Fredegar wailed. "The guardsman said he wasn't choked, and there's no blood anywhere. Not a mark on his young form." Fredegar panted desperately to find his breath.

"But he's dead," the innkeeper said, his voice rising to a wail. "My Brennan is dead!"

Cadderly shuffled to the side under the weight as Fredegar fell into him. Despite his sincere grief at the sight of Brennan, the death had raised a riddle that Cadderly could not leave unanswered. He remembered the horrible shadows he had seen dancing atop Brennan's shoulders that night at supper. He recalled Danica's story, her dream, and knew beyond doubt that someone, something, had possessed the young man, then discarded him.

Perhaps some lingering trace of what had happened remained to be seen. Perhaps telltale shadows remained on Brennan's shoulders. Cadderly opened his mind, let the song of Deneir into his consciousness again, despite the continuing, painful throb in his head.

Cadderly saw a ghost.

The spirit of Brennan sat atop the bar, looking forlorn and lost, staring with pity at his distraught father and with disbelief at his own pale body. He looked up at Cadderly, and his nearly translucent features twisted with surprise.

All the material world around the spirit became blurry as Cadderly allowed himself to fall more into Brennan's state.

Poison? his mind asked the lost soul, though he knew he had not spoken a word.

The spirit shook its head. *I have nowhere to go.*

The answer seemed so very obvious to Cadderly. *Go back to your father.*

Brennan looked at him with confusion.

The song played louder in Cadderly's throbbing head, its volume becoming ferocious. The young priest would not let it go, though, not now. He saw Brennan's spirit tentatively approach the corpse, seeming confused, hopeful yet terribly afraid. To Cadderly's eyes, the room around the spirit went dark.

Everything went dark.

"By the gods," Cadderly heard Danica whisper.

"Oooo," Pikel moaned.

A thump on the floor beside him jolted Cadderly awake. He was kneeling on the hard floor, but, beside him, Fredegar was out cold.

In front of him, young Brennan sat up, blinking incredulously.

"Cadderly," Danica breathed. Her shivering hands grasped the young priest's trembling shoulders.

"How do you . . . feel?" Cadderly stammered to Brennan.

Brennan's chuckles, as much sobs as laughter, came out on a quivering, breaking voice reflecting astonishment, as though he really didn't know how to answer the question. How did he feel? Alive!

The young man looked to his own hands, marveled that they again moved to his command. Fists clenched suddenly, and he punched them up into the air, a primal scream erupting from his lips. The effort cost the lad his newfound physical bearings, though, and he wobbled and swooned.

Ivan and Pikel rushed to catch him.

Cadderly steadied himself suddenly, his gaze snapping back across the room, to Headmaster Avery. The determined young priest rose briskly, brushed Danica aside, and stalked to the corpse.

"They took out his heart," Danica said to him meekly.

Cadderly turned on her, not understanding.

"That is their usual method," the young monk, familiar with the dark practices of the wretched Night Masks, replied. "It prevents an easy recalling of the spirit."

Cadderly growled and turned back to Avery, back to the task at which he would not fail. He called up the song, forcefully, for it would not readily come to his weary mind. Perhaps he should rest before continuing, he thought as the notes continued on a discordant path. Perhaps he had pushed the magic too far this day and should rest before delving back into the spiritual world.

"No!" Cadderly said aloud. He closed his eyes and demanded that the music play. The room blurred.

Avery's ghost was not about.

Cadderly, though his material body did not move, looked all about the room. He saw marks of blackness, supernatural shadows, on the floor beside the bodies of the dead assassins and sensed a brooding evil there.

The spirits were gone, and Cadderly got the impression their journey had been forced, that they had been torn away.

Would they receive punishment in an afterlife?

The thought did not bring compassion to Cadderly. He stared hard at the puddles of residual blackness. He thought of recalling one of those lost spirits, to question it about Avery's spirit, but dismissed the notion as absurd. The fate awaiting these souls had nothing to do with what awaited the goodly headmaster.

With sudden insight, Cadderly reached with his thoughts beyond the parameters of the room, sent out a general call to the heavens for his lost mentor's departed spirit.

The answer he received did not come in the form of words, or even images. A sensation swept over Cadderly, an emotion imparted to him by Headmaster Avery—he knew it came from Avery! It was a calmness, a contentment beyond anything Cadderly had ever experienced, divine.

A bright light gave way to nothingness. . . .

Ivan and Danica helped the young priest to his feet. Cadderly, coming fully from his trance, looked at Danica with a most sincere smile.

"He is with Deneir," Cadderly told her, and the joy in his voice prevented any reply.

Cadderly realized that his headache had flown. He, too, had found contentment.

"What do ye know?" Ivan asked him, and Cadderly understood that the dwarf was not speaking of Avery's fate. Danica also looked at the enlightened young priest curiously.

Cadderly did not immediately answer. Pieces of this puzzle seemed to be falling from the sky. Cadderly looked over to the dead assassins, then looked to Brennan and Fredegar, in the thick of an unabashed hug.

Cadderly knew where he would find more of those tumbling puzzle pieces.

* * * * *

The passing hours came as reassurance to Ghost, who sat quietly in his room, going about his day as routinely as he could. Massacres were certainly not a common thing in Carradoon, but these were troubled times and Ghost was confident that the news would grow stale soon enough. Then young Cadderly would become vulnerable to him once more.

Thoughts of abandoning the mission had crossed the assassin's mind soon after he had learned that Cadderly had escaped—and that many of his Night Masks had not. He dismissed those thoughts, though, choosing instead to personalize this kill even more. He would get Cadderly, get him through one of his friends, and the young priest's death would be all the sweeter.

Ghost was a bit dismayed when he saw Bogo depart, more because he wanted Bogo to serve as a scapegoat if Cadderly and his friends closed in on the truth than for any practical services the wizard might provide.

The wicked man looked out his window at the afternoon sun's reflection on quiet Impresk Lake. He saw the bridge to the island clearly, saw the masons huddled out there, in boats and on the structure itself, studying the wide break.

Ghost shook his head and chuckled. He had already contacted Vander telepathically, back at the farm, and knew that Cadderly had precipitated that break. Four men had returned to the farm—four out of fourteen.

Ghost continued to stare at the gaping break in the great bridge. Cadderly had beaten them; Ghost was impressed.

But he was not worried.

* * * * *

Every detail of the battle scene—Avery's presence in the hearth room, where he should not have been; the curious, continued absence of Kierkan Rufo, who had come down from his room only long enough to identify Avery's body and answer the city guards' few questions; even the peculiar scorch mark on Pikel's tunic registered clearly in Cadderly's mind—came together in the overall picture he was forming.

He spoke with Brennan, though the young man's recollections were foggy at best, dreamlike. That fact alone confirmed Cadderly's suspicions of what had happened to Danica. The young priest made a point of telling Brennan to keep out of sight, and bade Fredegar to not tell anyone that his son was alive again.

"We must press on quickly," Cadderly explained to his three companions, gathered around him in an out-of-the-way room. "Our enemies are confused for now, but they are stubborn and will regroup."

Danica leaned back in her seat and placed her feet on the table in front of her. "You are likely the most weary among us," she replied. "If you are ready to continue, then so are we."

"Oo oi!" Ivan piped, before Pikel got the chance. The yellow-bearded dwarf offered his surprised brother an exaggerated wink, and Pikel promptly tugged hard at Ivan's beard.

Although it took him and Danica several moments to quiet the boisterous brothers, Cadderly was glad for the distraction, for the break in the exhausting tension.

"You have spoken with the guard?" Cadderly asked Danica when order was finally restored.

"Just as you suspected," the young woman replied.

Cadderly nodded; another piece fell squarely into place. "The wizard will not be there for long."

"But are ye ready to battle the likes of that one?" Ivan had to ask.

Cadderly chuckled and stood, straightening his trousers, still moist from his dip in the lake. "You make it sound as if I am going alone," he quipped.

Ivan was up in an instant, bouncing his huge axe atop one shoulder. "Can't trust that type," the dwarf explained, wanting to clarify his atypical hesitance. "Dangerous sort."

"Can't trust an angry priest, either," Cadderly retorted, taking up his walking stick and sending his spindle-disks into a few short up-and-down snaps.

"Dangerous sort," Danica finished for him, and after the sights the young woman had experienced that day, the tremendous magical powers Cadderly had revealed, the words were spoken without any hint of sarcasm.

Twenty

I Telled Ye So

Bogo Rath paced anxiously in his small room. He kicked a basket aside and watched a cockroach skitter across the floor, seeking the shadows under the bed.

"Flee, little bug," the young wizard remarked.

Bogo flipped his stringy brown hair to one side and ran his fingers through it repeatedly. He was the little bug.

He looked out the window, which was too small to get any real view, but enough to tell him that the afternoon light finally was beginning to wane. Bogo meant to leave the city at twilight, disguised among the host of beggars that departed Carradoon every evening.

Outside the gates, he could conjure a magical mount, and his ride to Castle Trinity would be swift and unhindered. The thought of getting far from Carradoon, from the young priest and his cohorts, appealed to Bogo, but the thought of facing Aballister did not. Even worse, if Ghost succeeded in finishing the task, the assassin's return to Castle Trinity would cast an unfavorable, cowardly light on Bogo.

"Boygo," he muttered. He figured he had better get used to hearing the name. Aballister and Dorigen would not soon let him forget his cowardice. The lone consolation for the young man was the fact that he had arranged the library headmaster's death.

The cockroach skittered back out for an instant, zipped across the floor and under the folds of the oversized curtain.

"That will silence them!" Bogo said to the roach. Especially Dorigen, who had been so humiliated in Shilmista Forest.

A smile found its way through the tension on Bogo's boyish face. He had killed a headmaster!

A glance at the window told him it was time to start for the western gate. He selected the components for a spell that would alter his appearance and placed them in a convenient pocket, then took up his pack.

He put it right back down when he heard chanting in the hall.

* * * * *

"Fire and water," Cadderly said in an intense, monotone voice. "Fire and water, the elements of protection. "Fire and water."

Danica and Pikel stood in front of the young priest, between Cadderly and the door. Danica flipped her hair out of her face and looked to the stairway, to the top of the crouching, nervous innkeeper's balding head. Every so often, the man peeked over the top stair, fearful for his property.

Still, Cadderly had easily convinced the man to let the three up the stairs to Bogo's room. Danica looked to Cadderly again, who chanted more forcefully now with his eyes closed and his hands waving up and down in front of him, creating a magical tapestry. The young priest had shaved his beard before they had left the Dragon's Codpiece, and now he appeared much like his old self.

And yet, he did not. Danica couldn't explain it, but somehow Cadderly appeared more confident with every move. His encounter—whatever had happened—with Avery's spirit had put a sense of calm on top of that growing confidence as well.

Danica hadn't questioned him about it, but she sensed that Cadderly now walked with the knowledge that his god was with him.

"Fire and water," Cadderly chanted, "the elements of protection." As one of his hands came up, he loosed a few drops of conjured water against the door. As the other came up right behind, Cadderly sent from it a gout of flame.

The fire hit the wet door with a hiss, the signal for Pikel.

"Oo oi," the dwarf chirped and slammed his club like a battering ram against the door. The weapon popped cleanly through the thin wood, creating a fair-sized hole but not forcing the door open. As the dwarf retracted his club, Danica realized Pikel's mistake. She reached over the dwarf, turned the handle, and easily opened the door—out.

"Oh," the deflated Pikel remarked.

Bogo's chanting from inside the room joined Cadderly's continuing prayer when the door came open. The wizard held a small metal rod in front of him, a conductive component that Danica had seen before.

Pikel had, too, and both he and the woman dove to the side, expecting a burst of lightning.

Cadderly didn't move, didn't flinch. An almost transparent, slightly shimmering field of energy appeared in the open portal.

Bogo's blast struck it with fury, the lightning driving hard against the barrier, sizzling and throwing multicolored sparks, sending a spider web of green and orange energy across the breadth of Cadderly's field to burn at the door jamb. When it had ended, a tiny pool of water lay at the base of the intact defensive field.

Wide-eyed, the frightened wizard began another spell, as did Cadderly.

Bogo pulled another component and began a fast-paced chant.

"Sneeze," Cadderly commanded.

Bogo complied, and his spell was disrupted.

The stubborn wizard growled and began again.

"Sneeze."

"Damn you!" Bogo cried, wiping the wetness from his face.

"You could not be farther from the truth," Cadderly replied calmly. "Shall we continue to play the game?

"Dispel!" Cadderly cried suddenly, his face twisting to an angry glare. The shimmering field in the doorway disappeared, and Danica and Pikel burst into the room.

Bogo realized his mistake; he should have continued to "play" as the young priest had called it, continued to force Cadderly into a defensive posture in the hopes that his spell repertoire would outlast the priest's.

Danica came straight ahead, dove, came up in a leap, and jolted forward with her landing, too fast for the surprised Bogo to react. He threw his arms out defensively, and the monk promptly wrapped them, bringing her arms up through the wizard's, then down and around, locking Bogo fast.

He did twist one wrist, though, cutting a line of blood on Danica's sleeve.

An invisible dagger!

Danica's foot shot up between her and the close wizard, crunching Bogo's nose. Dazed, Bogo offered no resistance as Danica released his other arm, cupped her free hand over the back of his clenched fingers and yanked his hand back toward his forearm, pulling his arm in the other direction at the same time.

The wizard's face contorted in agony. He tried to hold his only weapon, but Danica's foot came up again; her hand continued to pull.

Pikel joined her a moment later. "Oo," he said glumly, disappointed that the fun was already over. He heard the clang as the unseen dagger hit the floor, and he looked down for it, scratching his green-dyed hair curiously.

Cadderly walked to the bed and motioned for Danica to lead her prisoner to it. "You can let him go," the young priest offered.

Danica gave a quick, painful jerk as she released Bogo's arms, and she pushed the wizard, knocking him to a sitting position.

"We must talk, you and I," Cadderly demanded quietly.

Bogo glared up at him from the bed, an impotent threat, but Danica cuffed him anyway, on the ear.

She scowled and showed Cadderly her cut arm in answer to his surprised expression, and that seemed to satisfy the young priest's nagging conscience.

"Dorigen sent you," Cadderly said to the man.

"No."

Cadderly looked at him curiously. "I have ways of telling when you lie," he warned.

"Then you detect nothing," Bogo replied.

"You were with the Night Masks, but you are not a part of their guild," Cadderly remarked.

"You will die," Bogo promised, drawing another cuff from Danica.

"Why have they come for me?" Cadderly asked. With no answer forthcoming, he added, "I could speak with your corpse, if that would please you."

For the first time, Bogo seemed afraid. The sincere calmness of Cadderly's tone gave weight to the threat, the promise, Bogo knew and, because he wanted to grow to be an old wizard, he replied. "You got in the way," the young wizard stammered, "at the library and in the forest. You forced Abal—" Bogo stopped abruptly.

"Who?" Danica demanded, putting her face right up to Bogo's.

"Aballister," Bogo admitted, "Dorigen's mentor, my mentor."

Cadderly looked to Danica, concerned. Dorigen had been a powerful adversary. How strong might her mentor be?

"I came only to observe," Bogo went on, "as I was told."

"Oh?" Pikel cut him short, stepping past Danica, pushing her aside, and displaying the scorched hole in his leather tunic, the hole Bogo's lightning had made back at the Dragon's Codpiece.

The blood drained from Bogo's face, and his growing desperation forced him to a desperate act. He shoved his hand into a pocket, grabbed a handful of pebbles, and flung them to the floor.

A burst of minor explosions went off, blowing in rapid succession and shooting variously colored puffs of smoke into the air. The pops did nothing to the companions, other than distract them. With a quick chant, Bogo diminished to the size of a cat and slipped between Cadderly and Pikel.

Cadderly tried to call out but could not decide fast enough whether he should shout for his friends to stop Bogo or cry out a warning to the wizard. Danica finally pushed past him and Pikel, following the wizard's expected path to the door.

They heard the door close—the smoke began to clear and Bogo, outside the room and man-sized again, began a new chant.

Danica stopped, wisely not going through the portal.

From behind the door they heard Bogo cry out in terror.

The friends heard a shuffle of feet, a sickening thud, then something heavy slammed against the door.

Cadderly shook his head and looked away. The tip of Ivan's double-headed axe protruded through the door, dripping crimson. As if that weren't macabre enough, Bogo's fingers, grasping helplessly and twitching, reached through the circular hole Pikel's club had made in the door. Pulled by the unbalancing weight, the door slowly creaked open.

Pikel walked past Danica and opened the door the rest of the way, peeking around it and saying, "Oo" as he regarded the hanging wizard.

"I telled ye ye couldn't trust a wizard," Ivan, standing a dozen feet down the hall with his hands on his hips, asserted. He strode up to the door and motioned for the group to come out of the room.

The young priest couldn't help but look over at the dead young wizard, a man probably not even as old as Cadderly. "We never asked his name," Cadderly remarked.

Ivan kicked the door closed, spat in his hands, and put one boot up beside Bogo for leverage. "Wondering what to put on his stone?" he asked gruffly.

Danica watched the young priest closely, looking for any signs of weakness. This time, though, Cadderly appeared to control his emotions and accept the guilt.

"Just wondering," he answered Ivan, giving a resigned shrug as though he had pushed the incident from his mind. "Get the body back in the room," Cadderly instructed the dwarves. He shook his head at the irony of one of his earlier statements, which he had made merely to scare his prisoner.

He could indeed speak with Bogo's corpse.

* * * * *

There was only the lake and the empty street. Carradoon quieted considerably as twilight neared, and the interest in the outrageous events at the Dragon's Codpiece had dissipated quickly. Only a few guests had remained at the battered inn, and with Cadderly and his companions out of the building, the place was quiet—too quiet for Kierkan Rufo.

The angular man stood in front of his room's small window, the tilt of his stance making him appear almost like a diagonal crosspiece to the glass. Many minutes passed; Rufo did not move.

He had gone too far this time, he realized, had crossed the line to the dark side of his nature. He doubted he could ever step back. He stood in reflection now, trying to follow the course that had led to this horrible position. It had begun in the library, when he had met evil Barjin and, on the priest's command, had sent Cadderly tumbling down the stairs to the hidden catacombs.

Rufo could excuse himself of that indiscretion, and all of the other members of his order, including Cadderly, had excused him as well. In the elven forest, Rufo had betrayed his companions once more, but he had redeemed himself, had come through in the end to provide his companions with the information they needed to ultimately win out. As in the library, the efforts of Cadderly and the others had averted disaster, had helped to cover Rufo's weaknesses.

Now Avery lay dead downstairs. Rufo had put the headmaster in the path of an assassin band. Rufo had stepped over, had crossed the line.

He tried to justify his actions, told himself repeatedly that he had been given no choice, that the assassins would have killed them all if he had not cooperated.

The facts did not support his excuse. Cadderly, Danica, and the dwarves (where had those two come from, anyway?) had won, had chased off the band. If Rufo had

gone to them soon after his initial meeting with the young
wizard, their victory would have been more swift.

Avery would be alive.

The angular man whimpered and turned from the
window, suddenly feeling very vulnerable. "He deserved
his fate," Rufo muttered grimly, reminding himself of the
way Avery had treated him since the trouble in Shilmista.
Avery would have held him back in his ascension through
the Order of Deneir; the headmaster had even threatened
to have him removed from the library! That was not justice,
Rufo's sensibilities argued, not when the headmaster held
all the power and Rufo could only stand and let Avery's
whims determine his fate.

By the time Rufo had crossed the small room and collected his pack, anger had replaced his guilt. He had struck
back at Avery in the only way he could, and now it was
done. No one suspected him; the conspiring wizard had
already fled, and Rufo had easily deflected the city guards'
questions. Even more comforting, Cadderly apparently had
taken the guards' conclusions for truth, for the priest hadn't
asked Rufo a single question concerning the tragic events.

Rufo had to hide his smile as he paid Fredegar (from
Avery's purse) for the time spent in the inn. He explained
to the hospitable innkeeper that he had to return at once to
the Edificant Library and report the tragic loss.

It was getting dark outside when he exited the Dragon's
Codpiece, dark like the path Kierkan Rufo had stumbled
down.

* * * * *

The four friends left the other inn a short while later,
Cadderly tossing the fearful innkeeper a bag of coins to
cover the damages and the cost of disposing of Bogo's
body.

"Where do we go?" Ivan asked, impatient, now that he knew where other enemies might be, to get on with the fighting.

"Back to the Dragon's Codpiece," Cadderly replied evenly.

"What do we do when we get there?" Ivan said, not sounding happy about the choice.

"We wait," Cadderly answered, trying to calm the volatile dwarf. "We have struck hard this day and this night. All of us need some rest." Cadderly believed the words; his extensive use of magic had drained him, and he wanted nothing more than to spend the next hours in peace. After what he had learned from Bogo's spirit, though, the young priest wasn't confident he would get his wish.

The air was chill outside as the night grew dark and the first stars made their appearance.

Cadderly knew it would be a long night.

Twenty-One

Pikel Bait

Cadderly paid his friends' banter little heed. He sat by his small table, beside the *Tome of Universal Harmony*, pushing the pieces of this mental puzzle closer together, seeking information from every memory he could summon. His contemplations were not purely for reasons of information gathering, though.

Cadderly lingered on the image, the sensation, of Avery's spirit, on the divine joy he knew the dead headmaster had found. The young priest's doubts, which had followed him through all of his spiritually bereft life, could not penetrate the holy barrier of that sensation. Cadderly's logic, founded on information he could see and test with his own senses, seemed ridiculous when compared with the perceived smile of Avery's ghost.

The foundation of Cadderly's existence had been violently shaken, and yet, the young priest felt no remorse and no sense of loss. Quite the opposite—the mystery of it all gave Cadderly a sense of hope beyond anything he had known. Rather than deny what he had felt, the young priest would simply have to expand his foundation to include these wonderful new revelations.

Cadderly's unconscious chuckle turned Danica and Ivan, who sat on the bed, toward him, and their stares, in turn, awakened the young priest from his musing. Cadderly shrugged, not knowing how to begin to explain.

"Peoples," Ivan grumbled, but Danica nodded to the young priest, as though she understood the resolutions Cadderly was finding.

Dear Danica, Cadderly thought, and he did not doubt she knew, or that she approved.

*   *   *   *   *

Pikel crept along the first floor of the Dragon's Codpiece, slipping in and out of the shadows in search of the cupboards. It was late, and the dwarf was hungry, having missed three out of four meals during the course of the exhausting day.

"Hee hee hee," the dwarf tittered when he found biscuits and sweet dough. He dropped the amulet Cadderly had given him into a pocket and rubbed his plump hands together briskly, his cherubic dimples revealing his glee.

The dwarf sported an armload of food as he ascended the makeshift stairway to the second level, each step on the stairs that he and Ivan had put back together helping him to justify his filching.

His smile disappeared before he got back to Cadderly's room, though, and, as a puny human approached him a moment later, half a biscuit fell out of his mouth.

*   *   *   *   *

Danica and Ivan struggled on the bed, the young woman proving, to Ivan's disbelief, that her concentration could prevent Ivan from taking her hand down in wrist wrestling. The mighty dwarf, his bright red face framed by his yellow beard, pushed and yanked vigorously to the side, but the woman's arm, tiny compared to Ivan's gnarly and corded muscles, did not budge an inch.

"You have met your better," Cadderly remarked to Ivan, which only set the dwarf into a deeper frenzy. He hopped up on his toes and pushed with all his strength, moving the bed several inches, but Danica's position remained unchanged.

The sudden and somewhat loud scrape of the bed set off silent alarms within Cadderly. The young priest had made no secret of the fact that he and his friends were back at the inn, but he didn't want to give his potential enemies too much information.

"Quiet!" he whispered harshly, and, remembering Pikel, he closed his eyes and sent his thoughts to the missing dwarf. He expected to find the same sensations—hunger mostly—waiting for him, but when Cadderly made contact, through the power of the telepathy-enhancing amulet, his eyes popped wide open. The sensations were vague, as expected, but instead of distant thoughts of muffins and ale, Cadderly visualized hunched black shadows.

It was not Pikel on the other end! Images of dead Brennan, and of poor Nameless, filtered through Cadderly's rising sense of panic. The young priest abruptly broke contact and jumped from his seat.

"I'll get ye yet!" Ivan snarled at Danica, oblivious to Cadderly's alarm. Danica, though, facing Cadderly's way, did not miss his actions. Ivan tugged her arm to the bed as she came from her meditative state, the dwarf growling victoriously until he noticed that Danica was paying him no heed.

Danica scrambled over the bed, past Ivan. The dwarf turned about to see her and Cadderly exit the room, and realized then that the trouble likely involved his absent brother. Not pausing even long enough to locate his axe, Ivan half-crawled, half-ran out the door in pursuit.

* * * * *

Poor Pikel had never felt so weak! He stared dumbfoundedly at himself, or at his body at least, or at whatever this monster was that had stolen him.

Holding the weakling body by the throat in one hand, Ghost heard the rumble down the hall and realized that Pikel's friends would soon be on him. The thought brought an evil chuckle to his dwarven lips. He slapped aside Pikel's skinny arm and reached into one of his pockets, producing a small packet.

"Oooo," Pikel wailed, and he nearly swooned, thinking the item to be some horrible magical thing and suspecting that his life was at its end, as Ghost brought the packet up between them. But Ghost broke the packet over himself, over the dwarvish trappings, instead.

"Eh?" Pikel queried, for the imposter dwarf's face was covered in blood, blood from the packet.

With one arm Ghost lifted the puny form from the ground and hurled Pikel across the room, where he slammed into a wall and slumped to the floor.

Ghost, too, fell back, leaning heavily on the wall perpendicular to the door, and groaned.

* * * * *

Enraged Ivan grabbed both Cadderly and Danica by the backs of their tunics and hurled himself past them as soon as he discerned where Cadderly was leading them. The dwarf, without his deer-antlered helmet, hit the door head first, bursting into the room.

Staggering, Pikel lifted a shaking finger and pointed accusingly across the room, to the slender human form crawling about the base of the wall.

"Me brother!" Ivan roared, and he charged across, hands leading to throttle the weakling killer.

Danica, too, followed the imposter dwarf's trembling finger, but Cadderly came into the room more slowly, warily, paying full attention to the apparently wounded dwarf.

He had brought the song of Deneir into his thoughts. He saw the shadows crouched on Pikel's—on the imposter's!—shoulders.

"Ivan!" he cried, and, trusting in the song, he whipped his adamantite spindle-disks straight into the dwarf's face.

The dwarf flew back against the wall; real blood mingled with the fake on the green-dyed beard. "Oooo," he moaned. Across the room, Ivan let go of the weakling and came rushing back to throttle the new target.

Cadderly hadn't released the dwarf from his knowing gaze. He watched the shadows break apart, then melt down into Pikel's shoulders.

Ivan caught his brother in both hands and hoisted him off the floor, slamming him against the wall.

"Oooo," Pikel moaned again.

"Hold, Ivan," Cadderly said calmly. "Pikel is back where he belongs."

Cadderly nodded to Danica, and she turned about to face the assassin again, ready to spring at him in an instant.

"You have nowhere to run," Cadderly said to Ghost. He walked up to join Danica. "I know you."

"Shouldn't have made the damn disks so fine," Cadderly heard Ivan say behind him, to Pikel's continuing groans. The young priest looked back briefly to see Ivan tending Pikel's bloodied face.

When he turned back, the shadows were gone from the puny assassin's shoulders. Cadderly's gaze darted all about the room, fearing that the man had stolen one of his friends' identities once again. His three companions appeared the same to him, though, looking to him for direction and with confusion now, apparently recognizing the young priest's sudden distress.

"Who are you?" Cadderly muttered under his breath when he turned back to the weakling man. He let the song of Deneir sound louder in his mind, studied the aurora of this new identity.

He felt a cold wind, pictured a rocky, forlorn shore backed by towering mountains. Huge ice floes dotted the bay, waves breaking against their invulnerable sides, and a giant ship sat quiet in the calmer waters near the shore, awaiting the mighty arms that could pull its monstrous oars.

Cadderly looked into the weakling man's face and saw true fear and unexpected resignation.

Danica sensed that the puny man was about to dart for the door, and she tensed for a spring to intercept him. A whisper came into her ear, though, a magical message from Cadderly. She looked at her companion curiously.

The little man broke for the door. Danica went for him, as did Cadderly, the two getting conveniently tangled, enough for the man to get by.

Ivan dropped Pikel hard to the floor, wincing at his brother's ensuing groan.

"Halt!" Cadderly cried, looking to the fleeing man. That command was not aimed for the weakling, though, and it carried the weight of considerable magical energy.

Ivan stopped in spite of himself and the man rushed out the open door. Danica halfheartedly took up the chase, as Cadderly had instructed. She came out the front door of the Dragon's Codpiece a few moments later, saw the man turning a corner one way, and purposely went the other, to return empty-handed after an appropriate amount of time had passed.

Back in the room, Ivan stood staring in disbelief at Cadderly, tapping one heavy boot impatiently on the wooden floor.

"More waiting?" the yellow-bearded dwarf asked gruffly.

Cadderly smiled and nodded. "Not too long," he promised, and the young priest believed the claim. The puzzle was nearly complete.

Twenty-Two

Striking Back

W**ell I'll be a smart goblin,"** Ivan whispered, peering over the back edge of the roof of the building adjacent to the Dragon's Codpiece. Market Square was bustling, usual for this time of the day, but the dwarf had picked out one figure clearly, a tilting, angular man making his way through the crowd.

Danica, following the dwarf's pointing finger to spot Rufo, was over the side in an instant, picking her way down into the alley and quickly falling into step some distance behind the man.

"I'd have thought that one'd be long gone from here by now," Ivan remarked to Cadderly, who sat farther from the edge, the *Tome of Universal Harmony* open in front of him and his eyes closed. The young priest shook his head, not at all surprised.

"Rufo would not dare the trails alone," Cadderly explained, the same argument he had used when Fredegar had told the friends Rufo intended to go back to the library.

"It is likely that he has found refuge within the city, in the temple of Ilmater perhaps."

Ivan and Pikel shrugged at each other, neither willing to dispute Cadderly's logic. Their young friend had been leading them through the continuing mysteries as if he knew all the answers, or knew where to find them. Pikel shrugged again and crossed the roof to watch over Lakeview Street, while Ivan continued his scan of Market Square. They had been on the roof for more than a day, waiting with all the patience that could be expected of dwarves.

Danica returned a few minutes later, easily scaling the back of the building. "He is with the priests of Ilmater," she reported.

Cadderly nodded silently, not opening his eyes, not breaking the trance he had spent hours attaining.

"He knew that," Ivan remarked dryly, the dwarf starting to feel like a pawn in somebody else's chess game. Under his breath Ivan muttered, "Damned cocky priest knows everything."

"Not yet," Cadderly replied, drawing another disbelieving shake of the head from Ivan. There was no way that Cadderly, twenty feet away, could have heard his remark.

Defeated, Ivan went back to watch for the escaped assassin, for Kierkan Rufo, or for anyone or anything else that might give the friends a clue.

Not that he believed Cadderly needed any.

*   *   *   *   *

As soon as he regained control of his giant form, Vander began to pace the barn nervously, stretching his huge arms out wide. He had nearly been caught, and, honestly, the firbolg didn't know how he had moved that weakling body fast enough to get out of the room and out of the inn.

He had spent a miserable night on the streets of Carradoon, fearful that Ghost would never give back his true form and continually looking over his shoulder, expecting to find Cadderly, the woman, or the two fierce dwarves, bearing down on him.

But now he was back, at the farm and in his familiar body. He peeked out the door at the quiet house and empty yard, not sure whether the four remaining assassins were still around.

Four remaining assassins! At least eleven of the killers were dead, with five others missing. Ghost alone walked the streets of Carradoon, except, perhaps, for the wizard, Bogo Rath. And Cadderly, now surrounded by powerful allies, remained alive and alert.

In their last spiritual passing, though, Vander had sensed clearly that Ghost remained confident, had sensed that the little man was actually enjoying the challenge of this difficult chase.

Ghost had been in trouble before, had lost entire bands of killers only to turn the tables and bring the intended victim down. He was confident, cocksure, the quality of a true warrior.

Of course, the firbolg's admiration of the little man was tempered by the knowledge that Ghost's confidence was rooted in the fact that the weakling had a quick way out of any situation. With Vander a safe distance from the fight, Ghost always had a quick and easy escape route.

How convenient.

* * * * *

"What is it?" Danica posed the question just a moment after Cadderly opened his eyes for the first time in several hours. The young priest had searched the city, had reached out with detection spells to locate the particular magical emanations of the strange item the evil little assassin carried.

"A shift in the power," Cadderly explained absently, his thoughts still firmly locked on the *Ghearufu*.

Ivan, a few feet away but overhearing the conversation, waggled his bearded face in disbelief. "If ye know where the damn thing is—" he began.

"I do not," Cadderly interrupted, "not exactly. Our enemy is in the city, somewhere south of here or, I should say, our enemy has just returned to the city."

Danica cocked her head curiously, pushed the stubborn lock of hair from her face.

"He departed the city while we had him cornered back in the room," Cadderly tried to explain, "magically. The man who physically ran away, or at least the spirit of the man occupying the killer's body, was not the same conniving person that captured Pikel."

Ivan waggled his face again, too confused to offer any remarks.

"Now he has returned to Carradoon," Cadderly went on.

"And we are to find him?" Danica stated as much as asked, and she was surprised when Cadderly shook his head.

"What would we gain?" the young priest asked. "Our enemy would only flee once more."

"What're ye thinking, then?" Ivan huffed, tired of Cadderly's cryptic clues. "Are we to sit here and wait for them killers to find us?"

Again Cadderly shook his head, and this time the action was accompanied by a wide and wicked smile. "We're going to catch our tricky friend from behind," he explained, thinking of the farmhouse that Bogo Rath's spirit had described to him. "Are you ready for a fight?"

Ivan's dark eyes popped wide at the unexpected invitation, and his response pleased his brother. "Hee hee hee."

* * * * *

"There!" Cadderly whispered harshly, pointing to a window under the spreading limbs of a wide elm tree. "Someone walked by that window, inside the house." Cadderly scanned the farmyard, wondering where Danica's stealthy progress had put her. The young monk was nowhere in sight, had disappeared into the shadows.

"Time for going," Ivan said to Pikel as he hoisted his great axe.

Pikel grabbed his brother's shoulder and cooed, pointing plaintively to the tree.

"I'm not for going up another tree," Ivan growled, but his anger couldn't hold out against Pikel's pitiful expression. "All right," the gruff dwarf conceded. "Yerself can get up the tree."

Pikel hopped at the news, and his wide smile disappeared under his helmet as the cooking pot dropped over his face. Ivan roughly adjusted it, realigned his own deer-antlered helm, and pushed his brother off.

"Ivan," Cadderly said gravely before they had gone two steps. The dwarf turned a sour expression back to the young priest.

"Do not kill anyone if it can be avoided," Cadderly said firmly, "as we agreed."

"As yerself agreed," Ivan corrected.

"Ivan." The weight of Cadderly's tone brought a frown to the dwarf.

"Damn boy's taking all the fun out of it," Ivan remarked to Pikel as the two turned and headed off once more, skittering, hopping, crawling, falling over one another, and, somehow, finally getting to the base of the wide elm.

Cadderly shook his head in disbelief that the dwarven racket hadn't alerted the whole countryside of their presence. He continued to shake his head as Pikel clambered up onto Ivan's shoulders, reaching futilely for the lowest branch. The green-bearded dwarf hopped up, dropping his club on Ivan's head, but managed to grasp the branch. Hanging by his fingers, his feet wiggling wildly, Pikel would never have gotten up, except that Ivan promptly returned the club, slamming it against Pikel's rump and nearly launching him over the thick branch.

"Oooo," Pikel moaned softly, rubbing his seat and taking the club from Ivan.

Cadderly sighed deeply; the dwarven brothers were better at defense than at stealthy attack.

* * * * *

The one guard for the four remaining Night Masks shook his head in disbelief, too, watching the dwarven escapades. He crouched in the tight and smelly chicken coop, one leg up on the wall-to-wall-perching bench, and peered through a crack in the old boards, a crack wide enough for him to level his crossbow and take aim. He figured Ivan for the tougher foe, and thought that if he could take out the dwarf on the ground, the one in the tree would be in serious trouble.

Squawk!

The startled Night Mask spun about frantically and fired, seeing a flurry of movement. The air was full of chickens—one less when the crossbow quarrel cut through—but in the dim light and close quarters, the birds seemed like one ominous, feathered foe to the man.

He got hit twice, on the face and neck, and felt the liquid oozing under his tunic. He grabbed for the wounds, hoping to stop the flow of blood.

The relieved man nearly laughed aloud when he found the blood was really eggs . . . until he realized that someone, behind the barricade of flapping chickens, must have thrown them at him. The man snarled, dropped his cross-bow, and drew out a slender dagger.

The chickens quieted quickly. He saw no enemy in the small coop.

The bench, the man thought; his enemy had to be under the bench. His smile disappeared and his mouth dropped open as he started to bend.

Under the bench and, maybe, behind him.

A hand slapped across the man's mouth; another grabbed his weapon hand. His eyes opened wide, then closed tight at the searing pain as his own knife pierced his throat, under the chin, and slid unerringly to his brain.

Danica dropped the man aside and turned to regard the dwarven brothers. Ivan was under the farmhouse window by this time, with Pikel carefully picking steps in the tree right above him. It was a recipe for disaster, Danica knew, and she figured she had better get back outside and into a new position, just in case.

She paused before stepping over the dead assassin and considered the kill. Cadderly had prompted an agreement that no man would be slain if it could be avoided, and Danica, though she, like Ivan, had thought the agreement absurd, felt some pangs of guilt for not honoring the spirit of her lover's wishes. Perhaps she could have taken this guard out without killing him.

Danica felt no sympathy for the man she had killed, though. She, above all the others in her party, understood the motives and methods of the assassin band, and she reserved no mercy for anyone who would don the silver-and-black mask of the amoral guild.

* * * * *

Ivan, directly under the window, looked up in frustration as Pikel sought a secure perch in the tree branch's shaky outer reaches. Finally, when Pikel seemed on solid enough footing, Ivan placed the edge of his axe against the house and ran it slowly down the wall, scraping and bumping over each shingle.

A moment later, a curious face peered out beside the curtain. The man, sword in hand, straightened, seeing nothing there, and gradually peeked over the sill.

"Ha!" he cried, spotting Ivan. Above, a branch cracked.

"Me brother," Ivan explained, pointing up.

"Oh," the confused assassin replied.

"Ooooooo!" Pikel roared, swinging down like a pendulum, his club thick end out, like a fat lance, and securely braced. The man tried to get his sword in front of him, but got slammed in the chest and went flying away as if he had been sitting in the basket of a giant-cranked catapult.

"Come on!" Ivan cried, hopping up to the windowsill and pulling himself in beside his upside-down brother.

Pikel shrugged helplessly; things had not gone exactly as planned. The branch had snapped and Pikel's thick ankle was firmly stuck in a fork, leaving him hanging helplessly.

"Come on," Ivan, now inside the room, said again. He grabbed Pikel's free hand and tugged, dragging the dwarf halfway into the room.

"Uh-uh," Pikel tried to explain.

Thinking his brother was just being stubborn, Ivan dropped his axe, grabbed with both hands, and yanked with all his strength. Pikel came into the room, the bending, grasping branch being pulled in right behind him.

* * * * *

Vander held the barn door firmly, supporting it tightly against its hinges so that it would not creak so loudly as he gingerly cracked it open. He couldn't see the fight at the window from his angle, but he did see the trembling branches of the elm above the corner of the farmhouse roof. That, and the previous squawking of the chickens, told the giant beyond doubt that intruders were about.

Vander stopped, staring incredulously at a ball of fire hovering in the air a few feet above him, just outside the barn door. The firbolg tensed, sensing the danger, sensing that if he moved, the pausing magic would go off.

Why was the spellcaster waiting?

Slowly, Vander leaned back into the barn.

A line of flames roared down from the fireball, scorching the ground at the firbolg's feet. Vander dove to the barn floor, pulling the door closed behind him, fearing that the magic would follow him in.

Black smoke rose from the bottom of the door.

Everything went pitch black.

The stubborn firbolg rose to his feet, knowing that he had to get out the door, out of the trap.

Everything went absolutely silent.

Vander growled and eased one foot in front of the other, toward the door. He had no way of knowing if the flames remained, but he had to find out.

He heard no sound, but it seemed as if the ground rushed up in front of him, twirling dust nipping at his eyes and forcing him to fall back. He tripped over unseen crates and crashed silently to the dirt.

The disoriented firbolg's vision returned in the blink of an eye, the magical darkness dispelled. Vander heard the snap of wood as a plank broke under his hand, and he heard, too, a whirling sound above him that alerted him a moment before he tried to rise.

The firbolg stared helplessly at the air only inches above his head, at the air that had suddenly filled with magical manifestations of whirling blades.

Vander heard the door creak open and looked across his body to see a young man in a wide-brimmed blue hat.

"The blades will cut," the young man said evenly.

The trapped Vander didn't doubt it for a minute.

* * * * *

"Oooooooo!"

Danica, making her way toward the far side of the farm-house, heard Pikel's cry as the branch holding Pikel flew out of the window.

When the pliable branch reached its end and reversed direction, Pikel's ankle slipped free and the dwarf went sailing, turning a perfect two-and-a-half back somersault to land headfirst into a pile of dust.

"I told ye not to let go!" a frustrated Ivan, holding Pikel's club, shouted from the window.

Pikel shrugged, adjusted his cooking pot, and rushed back to join his brother.

Together, the dwarves crept across the small room. It had two doors, both fortunately closed, one along the wall to their right, and the other directly across from the window, leading to one of the front rooms.

"Makes a nice rug, that one," Ivan remarked, heading for the front room and stepping over the back of the clobbered Night Mask, who was lying spread-eagle and face down on the floor, his arms flung out wide.

Instinctively, Pikel, wearing open sandals, wiggled his gnarly toes as he crossed the man's back behind Ivan, and the green-bearded dwarf nodded, surprised at just how good a rug a clobbered human might make.

"Ye know they know we're here?" Ivan asked when he reached the door.

Pikel quickly shrugged, as though that fact hardly mattered.

Ivan nodded his agreement and looked to the wooden door, his smile widening under his yellow-haired face. "Ye remember the charge at the inn?" he asked slyly.

The door burst from its hinges, crossbows clicked, and Ivan and Pikel, behind the impromptu shield, smiled wickedly to see the two darts protruding through the wood.

"These men is so predictable!" Ivan declared, and he flung the broken door aside, showing the dwarven brothers that they had entered a kitchen.

Pikel swerved left, toward a man caught between the charge and the wall who was trying to squeeze through the room's tight window. Ivan bolted right, in chase after the other assassin, heading for the growing daylight beyond the open door.

Pikel considered the struggling man's predicament for just a moment, then slammed his heavy club at the window's top frame, collapsing it to further ensnare the man.

"Hee hee hee." Thoroughly enjoying himself, the dwarf pulled the kitchen table over, unlaced the man's boots, and retied them around one of the table legs.

The remaining man stopped abruptly and swung about, thinking to catch his dwarven pursuer off guard by the sudden change in tactics.

Ivan was too crafty for that simple trick. He skidded to a halt, lifting his huge axe to easily deflect the slicing sword blade.

The assassin twirled the weapon up above his head and came in again with it, furiously, angling it left then right to poke holes through the dwarf's defenses. He scored a hit on Ivan's side, but Ivan turned with the thrust, pressing the top of his axe against the thin blade and slamming it against the wall.

The assassin fell back, holding only the hilt and first two inches of his snapped sword.

Ivan looked to the severed strap on the side of his armored suit. A single metal plate hung out an inch, but the

ssassin's hit had not come close to penetrating the dwarf-
orged armor.

"Was it worth it?" Ivan asked in all seriousness.

The assassin snarled and flung his broken sword at the
mpertinent dwarf, then turned and darted out the door.

Ivan batted the missile away and broke into a charge. He
love for the man's ankles but came up short and bumped
lown off the front of the porch.

The Night Mask never looked back as he rushed for the
stable. He leaped atop an unsaddled horse, set the beast
nto a dead run, and flew over the fence rail.

Ivan groaned, angered that one had escaped, and rolled
o his back—and saw Danica kneeling on the farmhouse
roof, crossbow loaded and level.

"Ye ever use one of them things?" the surprised dwarf
asked.

Danica fired. The fleeing assassin's head snapped forward, the quarrel entering at the base of his skull. He held
his seat for a few moments longer, then drifted off the
horse's side, dropping to the dust as the steed ran on.

"Yup," answered Pikel, coming to the door behind Ivan.

Twenty-Three

An Offer He Couldn't Refuse

W here's the big one?" Ivan asked when he, Danica, and Pikel found Cadderly standing in the farmyard, leaning against a young tree.

Cadderly pointed to the barn. "He is occupied," the young priest explained wryly, his gray eyes turning up at their corners with his satisfied grin. "Not hurt, but not in any mood to fight back."

Danica nodded. "Then your guess was right," she remarked, her voice unmistakably revealing her distaste. "The band was led by a giant."

Cadderly recalled the images he had seen on the little assassin's shoulder back in the Dragon's Codpiece. The *aurora* change had revealed much to the observant young man, had told him the identity and, more importantly, the demeanor of the assassin band's gigantic leader.

"Dead giant." Ivan snickered hopefully.

"No," Cadderly answered him.

"Soon?" Ivan asked.

"I do not think so," Cadderly replied. The young priest looked around the yard, to the chicken coop, to the window by the tree, and to the corpse lying in the dust by the road. "I did not want these men killed," he remarked sharply.

Ivan looked to Danica. "Better to let that one get away," the dwarf whispered with obvious sarcasm.

Cadderly heard the comment and locked a deep frown on the yellow-bearded dwarf.

"It was a fight, ye . . ." Ivan began to protest, but he threw his thick hands up in disgust, snorted "Bah!" and stomped away. A few strides off, beyond the nearest corner of the house, he caught sight of the lone living Night Mask, wedged tightly in the kitchen window and no longer struggling against the pressing weight.

"There ye go, lad," the dwarf bellowed. "Me brother held out some mercy for yer foolhardy wishes." The other three moved over to join Ivan, to see what the dwarf had discovered.

"What'll ye do with him?" Ivan asked Cadderly when the young priest saw the trapped man. "Do ye have some questions ye need to ask this one? Or are ye going to give him to the city guard, ye merciful fool?"

Cadderly regarded the dwarf curiously, not understanding Ivan's anger. His ensuing question sounded clearly as an accusation. "Are you so eager to kill?"

"What do ye think the city guard'll do with him?" Ivan balked. "Ye forgetting yer fat friend, sprawled across a table with his heart cut out? And what of them that lived in this place? Do ye think the farmer and his family'll be coming back anytime soon?"

Cadderly averted his gaze, stung by the honest words. He preferred mercy, hated killing, but he could not deny Ivan's observations.

"Ye bring us out here and ask us to fight with half our hearts," Ivan blustered, spittle glistening the bottom edges of his thick mustache. "If ye're thinking that I'm one to risk me own neck to give a few more days of life to that scum, then ye're thinking wrong!"

Confusion dictated Cadderly's next move. He brought the song up in the recesses of his mind, heard the flow of Deneirian magic, and found a point where he could join in that sweet river. He had stepped fully into the spirit world several times—in Shilmista Forest, to bid farewell to Elbereth's gallant horse; in the Dragon's Codpiece, to find Brennan's wandering spirit and learn the truth of Avery's heavenly bliss—and now he found the journey short and not so difficult.

As soon as he arrived, as soon as the material world faded into indistinct grayness behind him, he heard the desperate screams of lost souls.

Leaving his corporeal body standing with his unknowing friends, Cadderly willed his spirit toward the corpse lying in the road, the man Danica had shot from the horse. The young priest ended his trek abruptly, though, terrified by the images. Huddled, shadowy things, shapes akin to those growling pools of darkness he had seen on the shoulders of evil men, encircled the doomed assassin's spirit. The dead man noticed Cadderly then and looked to him desperately.

Help me, came his silent plea.

Cadderly did not know what to do. The growling, shadowy things tightened their ring, dark claws reaching out for their victim.

Help me!

Cadderly willed his spirit toward the man, but something, his fears, perhaps, or his knowledge that it was not his place to interfere, held the young priest's spirit firmly in place.

Shadows grabbed the doomed assassin. He twisted and jerked about frantically, but the dark grip did not relent, did not release him.

Help me! The cry tore at Cadderly's heart, horrified him and filled him with sorrow all at once.

The shadows melted into the ground, taking the man's spirit with them. Only the spirit's legs remained visible, kicking futilely.

Then they, too, were gone, pulled down to eternal hell.

Cadderly found himself back in his corporeal form, his eyes open wide, sweat beaded on his forehead.

"What're ye thinking?" Ivan demanded.

"Maybe I was wrong," Cadderly admitted, looking at Danica as he spoke the words, looking for judgment in her knowing gaze.

Danica grabbed him by the arm and put her head on his shoulder. She understood the trial Cadderly had just undergone, the realization once again that war precipitated cruel actions, that their survival against this unmerciful foe demanded a resolve equally vicious.

"But he goes back to the town," Cadderly went on firmly, pointing to the man trapped in the window. "The city guard will decide his fate. He cannot harm us now, and we have no cause to kill him."

Ivan, deadly in battle but certainly no merciless killer, readily agreed. He and Pikel immediately started for the man.

"Not now," Cadderly called to them, turning them about. "Will the window hold him?"

The dwarves turned to study the broken structure.

"For a hunnerd years," Ivan decided.

"Hee hee hee," Pikel chuckled and patted his trusty club, the compliments to his mighty clubbing bringing a blush to his cherubic, fuzzy cheeks.

"Then let it hold him," Cadderly said to them. "We have other business." The young priest turned and nodded to the barn door, realizing that his spell of whirling blades would not last. If they did not get to the giant soon, they would likely wind up in yet another fight.

On Cadderly's command, Ivan and Pikel each took hold of one of the barn doors and pulled it wide. The dwarves remained behind the doors, out of sight, for Cadderly knew that most giants were not particularly fond of the bearded folk and that the sight of the brothers might send this one into a rage that would be quieted only by the monster's death.

Vander wasn't up for any fight, though. Vander wasn't up at all. He lay on his back, helpless below the magically conjured blades. The firbolg lifted his head at the sound of the opening doors and looked across his prone form to see Cadderly and Danica regarding him.

Cadderly studied the giant intently, studied the forms on Vander's shoulders. He saw again the wide mountains, the great boat in the iceberg-dotted bay, and he knew this was the same being (the same spirit at least) that the assassin had switched bodies with when Cadderly and the others had cornered the evil little man.

"I will release you," the young priest promised, "on your word that you will attack neither me nor my companions."

Vander growled at him.

"By my estimation, we have no quarrel with you, mighty giant," Cadderly went on, "and we want none. It may be that I can aid you in your struggle."

The growling stopped, replaced by an honestly perplexed expression.

"Aid it?" Ivan bellowed from behind the shielding door. "Ye didn't say nothing about aiding any stupid giant!" Before Cadderly could react, the dwarf stormed around the barn door, axe in hand, Pikel rushing in from the other side to join him.

"Ivan!" Cadderly started, but Pikel's sincere, "Oo oi!" and the look of amazement on Ivan's face stopped the young priest completely.

"Let him up," Ivan snapped at Cadderly, giving the man a push. "Ye got no cause to keep one o' his kind in the dirt!"

"Well met, good dwarves," the giant said unexpectedly.

Danica and Cadderly exchanged stunned stares and helpless shrugs, Danica blowing away a lock of her hair and blinking.

"Let him up, I say!" Ivan demanded, pushing Cadderly once more. "Can't ye see the flames of his beard?"

Cadderly mouthed the words silently as he regarded the prone giant, wondering what the red color of this one's beard had to do with Ivan's apparent approval of the monster. Cadderly had seen Ivan and Pikel go after giants with wild abandon in Shilmista Forest. What made this one so different?

"He ain't no giant," Ivan explained.

"He looks pretty big to me," the disbelieving Danica remarked.

"He's a firbolg," Ivan answered impatiently, "a friend o' the land—and a friend of the elves. We'll forgive him that, since firbolgs and dwarves get on well, too."

Ivan seemed to be winding up for a long dissertation on the subject of firbolgs, and would have continued, but Cadderly motioned for him to stop, needing nothing further. The images, the *aurora* of this strange giant, made perfect sense to Cadderly now, and he understood, too, beyond any doubts, why one of this being's honorable weal would be in league with an evil wretch.

The giant was a prisoner.

A wave of Cadderly's hand removed the magical blades. Vander growled at the indignity of it all, took up his huge sword, and got to his feet. For a moment, it seemed to Cadderly and Danica that the monster would attack, but Ivan and Pikel, nodding and smiling, walked right into the barn and struck up a conversation—in a voluminous, grumbling language that sounded like the roll of boulders down a rocky mountainside.

The giant, talking with the dwarves, kept his sword up in front of him and seemed even more nervous when Cadderly and Danica joined their companions.

"He's not to trusting us," Ivan whispered to Cadderly. Then, louder, he announced, "His name's Vander."

"If we had wanted you dead, I would have lowered the blades," Cadderly reasoned.

Vander's thick lips curled back, his giant teeth showing white through the red tresses of his beard.

"Don't ye insult the thing!" Ivan warned harshly. "Don't ye ever tell a firbolg that ye could've beaten it unless ye've already beaten it!"

"Where are my associates?" Vander demanded, his huge sword hovering in the air only a few short strides from the companions. Cadderly realized then that the firbolg could probably take one great step forward and cut him in half before he even began to form a defense—and what defense could Cadderly put up against so monstrous a beast, anyway?

"They are dead, except for one," Cadderly answered as firmly as he could, determined to show no signs of weakness, though he was less than confident of how the giant would take the news.

Vander nodded, seeming none too upset.

It was a good sign, Cadderly noted, a piece of the puzzle that fit exactly. "I came here to find you," the young priest explained, "to speak with you about our common enemy."

There, he had put things out in the open. His three friends stared at him, still not in the know about Cadderly's revelations.

"Ghost," Vander replied. "His name is Ghost." Danica and the dwarves looked to each other and shrugged.

"Together we can beat him," Cadderly promised.

Vander snickered, a curious sound indeed, coming from the giant. "You know little of him, Cadderly," he replied.

"I am still alive," Cadderly argued, not surprised at all that the giant had figured out his identity. "Can the same be said for most of Ghost's associates?"

"You know little of him," Vander said again.

"Then tell me."

Cadderly bade his friends to clean up the yard and set a watch from the house. The companions, particularly Danica, didn't seem anxious to leave their friend beside a dangerous giant, but Vander said something to the dwarves in that mountain language, and Ivan immediately took hold of Danica's arm.

"He gave me his word," Ivan explained. "A firbolg never breaks his word." Cadderly's nod further assured his concerned lover, and she left with the dwarves, looking back over her shoulder every step of the way.

"You should be wary," Vander said as soon as the others had left.

Cadderly looked at him curiously, wondering if the giant had just threatened him.

"I will not go against what I have promised," Vander assured him, "but Ghost can take my body when he chooses, and you would be an easy kill if your guard was down."

"Then we must act quickly," Cadderly replied, no tremble in his voice. "I know Ghost took your body and left you in his boots when we had cornered him in the inn. And I know, too, that the possession can be blocked."

Vander shook his head doubtfully.

"Danica, the woman you just met, blocked him," Cadderly replied. "Together, you and I can do the same. I have spells, and this." He held up the amulet he had taken from Rufo in Shilmista Forest, the imp's amulet that Cadderly had claimed as his own, that allowed the young priest to easily contact the mind of another. "The amulet will allow me to join with you in your struggle."

Vander eyed him suspiciously, but Cadderly could see he had at least intrigued the beleaguered giant.

They talked for a short while longer, then went to the farmhouse to coordinate the defenses with the others.

They found the dwarves hard at work freeing the captured Night Mask from the broken window.

The man at last slipped back to the kitchen floor, shakily finding his feet. He would have offered no resistance, so obviously outnumbered, except that he spotted Vander out of the corner of his eye, standing beside the outside door. With a jerk, the man pulled free of Ivan's halfhearted hold, punched the surprised dwarf in the eye, and rushed for the door.

"Master!" he cried hopefully.

"That one's going to be trouble," Ivan muttered.

There came a great swoosh as Vander's sword cut the air and cut the man's torso cleanly in half.

"Nope," Pikel said to Ivan, both of the tough dwarves wincing at the gruesome sight.

Vander shrugged against the stunned stares that lingered on him from every direction. "If you knew him as well as I," the firbolg explained, his tone casual, "you would have killed him long before now."

"Not like that," Ivan protested, "not when me and me brother got to clean the mess up!"

Cadderly closed his eyes and fell back out of the room, back to the relative clean of the wider yard. He wondered if he would ever get as accustomed to such violence as his sturdy, battle-hardened companions.

He hoped he would not.

* * * * *

Vander took the companions to the graves of the murdered farm family, explaining grimly that he had, at least, forced the assassins to properly bury the victims.

Danica looked quizzically at Cadderly, and the young priest knew she was wondering if he meant to go straight after the spirits of the departed, to resurrect the family.

Cadderly shook his head, more a gesture for himself than to Danica. Such actions were not so simple, he knew, and he did not have time to make an attempt. Also, Cadderly, still bone-weary from his exhausting use of magic over the previous two days, was determined to save what little power remained in him. Confident that he would soon be tested again, the young priest decided to open himself to the song only when absolutely necessary.

Besides, the horrible memories of the shadowy things pulling the assassins' doomed souls to eternal torment were too fresh in Cadderly's mind for him to want a return trip to the realm of the dead.

That afternoon, the farm was quiet once more, showing no signs that any trouble had occurred.

Watching the fast-westering sun, Cadderly led the firbolg back to the barn. If Ghost was coming for Vander, telepathically or physically, it might well happen soon.

Cadderly set his spindle-disks spinning, let their crystalline center catch the lamplight and disperse it into a myriad of dancing shapes and flickers. The willing giant slipped in to the hold of the mesmerizing crystal and let Cadderly into his thoughts. Vander put a hand into his pocket and clutched at the amulet Cadderly had given him, as though the closer contact would improve the joining of their minds.

A short while later, Cadderly sat quiet, out of sight, in one of the small stalls within the barn, enjoying the majestic images playing in his mind at the firbolg's mental recounting of his frosty, rugged homeland.

Twenty-Four

Layers of Treachery

The call drifted on the silent winds of the dimension where dwelled only the mind. It drifted inexorably toward the farm on the outskirts of Carradoon and the firbolg that had served for so long as this caller's waiting vessel.

Cadderly sensed the fear in the unseen giant, knew that Ghost had come a-calling.

Stand easy, the young priest imparted telepathically to Vander. *Do not let your fear or your anger block me from our joining*.

Cadderly knew that the profound fear, far beyond what he would have expected from a mighty and proud giant, had not diminished, but Vander mentally reached back to him, strengthening their bond.

Ghost's call meandered in; Cadderly drove it away.

Vander? the distant assassin questioned.

Like a mirror, Cadderly offered no response other than to turn the telepathic question back on the winds.

Vander!

Anger. Cadderly felt that above all else. The young priest smiled in spite of the importance of his task, pleased by the confirmation that he had somewhat unnerved the little assassin.

Then the call was no more, but Cadderly, suspecting the killer who had been so dogged in pursuing him would not give up this important link so easily, did not let his guard down.

Vander hissed; Cadderly heard it distinctly.

"Fight!" the young priest cried, aloud and mentally. Ivan and Pikel moved to the stall door, weapons ready, as Cadderly had instructed. If the assassin found his way into Vander's identity, the dwarves would set upon him before he could sort out his surroundings.

But Cadderly had no intention of letting Ghost in, not while the trickster had his body as an open escape route, safely away in Carradoon. The young priest conjured an image of the spinning spindle-disks, shared it with Vander, and together they studied the hypnotic dance, remembered the specific defensive chants Cadderly had taught the giant.

Other, more evil sensations assaulted them, cluttered their space with the anger of another will. Cadderly prayed that Ghost would not understand the joining, would not realize that Vander had an ally beside him.

Cadderly watched and chanted, and the firbolg, though his anger rose dangerously, managed to keep Cadderly in his mind.

Together, they drove the would-be possessor away.

* * * * *

"You defy me?" Ghost asked in the dark alleyway. Above anything else, the assassin, vulnerable without

Vander, knew this type of defiance could not be tolerated.
Vander was his out, his desperate escape from any situation. He could not allow the firbolg to somehow, somewhere, find the strength to turn his distant intrusions
away.

Somehow? Somewhere?

The little assassin breathed a deep sigh. What was going
on at the farm? he wondered. He feared that Cadderly
might be involved, but how could that be? Certainly Vander,
if an attack had come, would have called out to Ghost?
Might Cadderly and his friends have taken the farm so
quickly that the firbolg never got the chance?

Ghost dismissed the thought. Vander was still alive;
Ghost had recognized the receptacle at the other end of his
telepathic call. He told himself he was being paranoid, a
dangerous state of mind for a killer living on the edge of
artistry and disaster. Vander had denied him before, after
all, from a distance, where the *Ghearufu*'s power was not
quite the same.

In a few hours, Ghost could call upon the firbolg again
and get back in. Vander would not be able to keep up his
mental defenses for very long. An evil grin spread across
the wicked man's face as he considered the boundless possibilities for punishment.

The smile did not last long. His mind was clouded by
doubts. Things were too unusual this time, and there was
simply too much at stake for Ghost to readily accept that
Vander had found a moment of strength to keep him out.
The assassin had not located Cadderly and the young
priest's friends in many hours.

"To the farm," the assassin decided quietly. He would go
to the farm, punish Vander, and regroup his forces.

He slipped out of the alleyway and approached an armed
man sitting comfortably on a fine horse.

"Your pardon, gentle sir," Ghost said meekly to the city

guardsman. The assassin was wearing his mismatched gloves.

No need to take chances.

* * * * *

Up on the farmhouse roof, wearing the black-and-silver domino mask and nondescript clothes of a Night Mask, with the cowl of a black cloak pulled low, Danica watched the riders—two men on one horse—moving steadily down the road. The monk leveled her crossbow when the two entered the farmyard. She recognized the man on the back as the same assassin they had found at the Dragon's Codpiece. Danica's first instincts, her initial anger, prompted her to shoot the man from the horse, but Cadderly had warned her against such actions, warned her that the man might not be what he seemed.

Another factor urged Danica to hold her shot: the man in control of the horse wore the uniform of a Carradoon guardsman.

"He is a friend," the assassin on the back of the horse called out, seeing Danica atop the roof.

Danica smiled under the cowl, glad that her disguise had apparently fooled the pair.

"Friend," the guardsman said. He brought the horse into the yard, said something Danica could not hear to the other man, and dismounted, heading straight for the barn.

Danica was confused and worried. Cadderly had expected the weakling assassin to come in and confront Vander, not bring a city guardsman. She still held tight to her crossbow, still wanted to put a quarrel into the evil little man's androgynous face.

To her further surprise, the guardsman did not go into the barn; rather, he moved to the gutter along one corner and began to scale it. He was halfway up the tall structure before the man on the horse took serious note of him, and Danica thought his reaction—wide-eyed and pale—a curious thing.

"What in the Nine Hells is going on?" the young woman whispered quietly. She looked about the yard to see if Ivan or Pikel had slipped out of the barn, to try to discern if anyone inside had any idea about the strange events in the yard.

The guardsman made the edge of the roof. Danica looked up to see him, and she pulled her cowl tighter, fearing that the man had climbed only to give him a better view of her position, a better view of her.

He paid her little heed, though. He wore mismatched gloves and stood on the edge, looking down at his companion, who, by this time, was off the horse.

"You have outlived your usefulness," the guardsman explained. He laughed wildly, clapped his hands, and dove headlong off the roof.

His laughter turned to a shriek, then a groan as he hit, then silence.

Danica breathed hard, not beginning to understand what had just occurred. She looked down to the man standing beside the dead guard, saw that it was he who now wore the strange gloves. He looked up to her, shrugged his shoulders, and bolted for the barn door. By the time he got there, the gloves were gone.

*   *   *   *   *

"You resisted my call," Ghost said to Vander. "We have discussed this matter before."

"This kill is . . . ugly," Vander stammered in reply, obviously nervous in facing the man who had been his tormentor for so long. The firbolg gnawed his thick lips under his bushy red beard, wishing that his newfound allies would rush out and end this taunting nightmare.

"I am not speaking of young Cadderly!" Ghost retorted. "He will be dealt with in time, do not doubt. I have come here to speak only with you, the one who dared to resist my call!"

"I did not . . ."

"Silence!" Ghost commanded. "You know that to resist is to be punished. I cannot complete my task with an unwilling associate out here, safely from the town."

Unwilling vessel, Vander corrected, but he wisely held the thought to himself.

Ghost took a few steps across the barn floor, peering out through a crack in the side boards. "Do you remember your brother?" he teased, referring to the firbolg he had killed when Vander had run away from him, had run all the way back to the distant Spine of the World Mountains.

The wicked little assassin turned about, smiling even more widely when he noticed Vander's great hands clenched in helpless rage at the giant's side.

* * * * *

Ivan peeked through a crack in the stall's wall, then looked back, concerned, to Cadderly and Pikel.

The young priest, intent on his telepathic connection with the firbolg, did not notice the dwarf at all. He felt Vander's mounting rage, a blocking emotion that diminished their bond. Things had gone pretty much as Cadderly had expected, but he was no longer certain of how he should react. Even across the miles from Carradoon, Ghost's intrusion had been difficult to fend off. How would he and Vander fare now, with the sneaky assassin standing just a few feet in front of the firbolg?

Calm, he imparted to the firbolg. *You must remain calm.*

* * * * *

"Punishment," Ghost purred, putting one finger to his pursed lips. He fingered something in his other hand, something round and gold, though Vander could not discern exactly what it might be.

"I never told you this before," the assassin went on, smoothly, "but I did more to your son, poor boy, than take his arm."

Vander's eyes widened. His great hands twitched, trembled, and his roar shook the walls of the wooden barn.

"Time to go?" Ivan dared to ask aloud under the cover of that prolonged growl.

Cadderly's mind was filled with a wall of red, the manifestation of Vander's uncontrollable rage. The young priest was out of contact with the firbolg, he knew, and he knew, too, that by the time he managed to contact his ally once more, the disaster might well be complete. He uncoiled his legs beneath him and accepted Pikel's arm to hoist him to his feet. Neither his spindle-disks nor his enchanted walking stick offered him much hope in defeating a giant, so he clenched his hand, the hand with the enchanted ring, and reached inside his cloak for the wand.

"No!" he cried out, leading the dwarves into the main area of the barn. Cadderly calmed immediately, though, as did Ivan and Pikel behind him, when he regarded the scene, a scene that Vander apparently had well in control.

The firbolg, panting and growling, held the puny assassin in the air by the throat, shaking him hard, though the man was obviously already dead.

"Vander," Cadderly said quietly to calm the giant's rage.

The firbolg paid him no heed. With another roar of outrage, he folded the assassin in half, backward, and hurled him against the barn wall.

"He will return!" the giant wailed. "Always, he comes back for me! There can be no escape!"

"Like a damned troll," Ivan remarked from beside the firbolg, his voice reflecting sympathy for the beleaguered giant.

"Troll?" Cadderly whispered, the word inspiring an idea.

The young priest held his clenched fist out before him, barked the word, "*Fete!*" and sent a line of fire at the corpse.

He kept his concentration firm, determined to burn whatever regenerative powers he could from the wretch, determined that Vander would at last be free. He glanced sidelong at the firbolg, took note of Vander's satisfied expression, then noticed, curiously, that Vander was wearing a golden ring.

Curious indeed, Cadderly thought as he turned back to the charred body, for he was just thinking of looking for such an item on Ghost's blackened form.

Cadderly searched his memory in an instant; Vander had worn no rings.

Aurora.

"Ivan!" Cadderly cried, ending his flames and spinning about. The giant moved as well, whipping out his huge sword, with Ivan standing unsuspecting right beside it.

Cadderly proved the quicker. "*Mas illu!*" he screamed as he drew the wand. A burst of colors exploded in the firbolg's face. Blinded, the giant continued his swing, aiming for where Ivan had been.

The dwarf, warned and then blinded by the blast, fell back. He heard the tremendous rush of air as the sword passed, taking off his helmet and clipping him enough to send him into a roll.

"I knew I'd get me chance!" the stubborn dwarf growled when he at last righted himself. Never shying from a fight, Ivan took up his axe and charged back in.

Danica slipped into the barn, discerned immediately what was going on, and fired a quarrel into the firbolg's belly.

The giant howled in pain but was not deterred from parrying Pikel's powerful charge, deflecting the overbalanced dwarf to the side, where he collided with a beam.

The giant feigned a sword thrust, then kicked out instead, sweeping Ivan aside once more.

Another quarrel caught him, this time in the shoulder, but again he seemed to hardly take note of it.

Danica was back at the door, Ivan and Pikel off to the sides, leaving Cadderly as the closest target. The young priest's first instincts told him to use his ring, to drive the beast back with a line of flame until his friends could regroup.

He realized the grim consequences for Vander, though, for the poor, proud firbolg who had been trapped in the weakling body and tossed aside like so much garbage. The magical ring had no power to restore burned flesh, and if this body was charred, like the assassin's corpse across the room, the firbolg would never reclaim it.

The giant lurched, popped in the back of the knee by Pikel's rebounding charge. With a grunt, the beast reached around and grabbed the green-bearded dwarf, hoisting him up into the air.

Pikel stared into the outraged giant's bloodshot eyes, then promptly stuffed his foot up the beast's flaring nostril and waggled his gnarly and smelly dwarf toes.

Half-sneezing, half-coughing, the disgusted giant hurled Pikel into the far wall and wiped his arm across his face. When he looked back at Cadderly, he found himself staring down the end of that slender wand. Thinking another attack forthcoming, Ghost snapped his eyes shut.

"*Illu,*" Cadderly said calmly, and the whole barn lit up with the brightness of a midday sun in an open field. Cadderly's aim had been perfect, though, and soon the glow of his wand's magic restricted itself to the firbolg's face, particularly to the giant's eyes.

Whiteness? When Ghost opened his eyes, he saw only whiteness, glaring and blinding. The whole damned world had gone white! Or perhaps, Ghost wondered, more curious than afraid, he had been transported to some other place.

Another stinging crossbow bolt dove into his belly, driving that notion away.

The roar shook the walls once more, and the light-blind giant charged ahead, toward the unseen bowman, flailing his sword wildly. He slammed into the edge of the open barn door, dislodged the thing, and continued out.

Danica danced quickly away, determining her role in this fight. Another quarrel sliced into the giant, lured him ahead.

Ghost felt a club slam the back of his knee again, this time slipping through his great legs and tripping him as he tried to spin and react. Down the giant sprawled, shattering a water trough with his face and arms.

Something heavy and sharp, an axe, perhaps, sliced into his ankle; a crossbow quarrel entered his shoulder, clicking off his huge collarbone.

Somehow the stubborn wretch managed to stand and stagger forward. His already wounded ankle took a hit from the heavy club.

He turned about, sword leading, but the dwarf was already out of reach and the mighty weapon smacked hard against a small tree, uprooting it. Growling with rage, Ghost heard scuffling feet as the enemy continued to flank him, to encircle him.

He tried to call for the *Ghearufu*, even though he knew his own body was inaccessible, and knew that, even if he managed to hold enough concentration to summon the thing, Cadderly would somehow follow his spirit's

movements. He couldn't get to it anyway; the hits were
coming too fast, from every direction.

He jerked about, one way and then another, leading with
his low-cutting sword each time. Fury became his only
defense, and he was confident that he was swift enough to
keep his enemies at bay. Only weariness would slow him,
and he hoped he could continue the blind assault until the
infernal whiteness left his eyes.

Another quarrel whistled in, taking the giant in the lung
this time, and Ghost heard the wheeze of his life's-breath
spurting out through a bloody hole.

He swung again, and again, frantic and dizzy. He overbalanced, roaring and wheezing. He tried to step forward,
but his badly gashed ankle would no longer support him,
and he lurched ahead, bending low.

Right in line for the waiting Ivan.

The axe chopped into the firbolg's backbone; Ghost felt
the burning flash, then felt nothing at all below his waist.
His momentum carried him one more long step forward,
an awkward gait on stiff, unsupporting legs, and he
tumbled and turned, crashing hard into the base of the
huge elm at the side of the house.

There was only whiteness, pain, numbness.

Ghost heard the three friends shuffle near him but had
not the strength to lift his sword in defense. Above all else,
he heard the bloody wheeze at his side.

"Got him," Ivan remarked as Cadderly rushed up to join his
friends. "Ye wanting us to tie him down afore ye talk with him?"

The young priest, stone-faced, did not reply, understanding that the loss of a physical body did not end the threat of
Ghost's evil. He walked to the side of the helpless giant,
took his spindle-disks in hand, and hurled them with all his
strength right into the firbolg's temple.

The battered monster jerked once, weirdly, then slipped
to the ground at the side of the tree.

Danica, holding her crossbow low, gaped openmouthed at her lover's uncharacteristic lack of mercy.

"Take out your bolts," Cadderly instructed her, "but do not remove his ring!"

The last image the young priest saw was that of his friends exchanging confused glances, but he had no time to explain.

Spirits were waiting for him.

* * * * *

Cadderly followed the flow of Deneir's song into the netherworld without hesitation. The material world blurred to him; his friends appeared as indistinct gray blobs. As he had expected, the young priest saw the spirit of Ghost sitting near the fallen giant's body—on one of the lower limbs of the elm, actually—the spirit's head resting in its translucent palm, waiting patiently for the magical ring to open the receptacle for its return.

Cadderly knew then that he had two choices: go back and remove the giant's ring, or go and find the rightful owner of the soon-to-be-restored body. He willed himself to the barn, leaving his corporeal body standing impassively beside his friends.

Vander's spirit crouched inside the barn, terribly afraid and uncertain.

You also? came his thoughts to Cadderly.

I am not dead, Cadderly explained, and he beckoned for the firbolg to follow him, showed his lost friend what he must do.

Together, the two spirits set upon Ghost with a vengeance. They could do no real damage to the assassin's ghost, but they mentally pushed him away, combined their wills to create a spirit wind that increased the distance between the evil spirit and the recovering body.

You'll not stop me, the wretch's spirit told them, its thoughts burning into their minds.

Cadderly looked back, saw a glowing ring form beside the firbolg's massive form. *Go,* he bade Vander.

The giant's spirit rushed away; Ghost's spirit followed quickly.

Cadderly held up a hand. *No,* he commanded, and Ghost slowed almost to a stop as he passed the young priest's mental barrier. Cadderly's spirit arms wrapped about him, further delaying him, and the young priest, both his corporeal and spirit forms, smiled as Vander's spirit narrowed like a flying arrow and slipped through the glowing ring, entering the waiting giant form.

You are lost, Cadderly told the assassin, releasing his mental hold.

Ghost didn't hesitate; he rushed for the only other waiting, spiritless receptacle.

*   *   *   *   *

"Shave me if this one ain't alive again!" Ivan growled, lifting his axe dangerously above the firbolg's head. "He lifts one o' them big arms, and I'm gonna give him a headache . . ."

Danica grabbed the dwarf's arm to quiet him, explaining that the firbolg, alive or not, was in no position to threaten anyone. The reassurance sent Pikel skittering up beside the giant head, the curious dwarf bending low to watch the reawakening.

A strange mewing sound from Cadderly turned them all about. The young priest's body trembled, one eye twitched wildly, and his mouth contorted as if he were trying to say something but could not control his actions.

Ghost had gotten there first, had slipped into Cadderly's waiting shell. Cadderly rushed in right behind, felt the burning pain of rematerializing, and felt, too, that he was not alone.

"*Get out!*" he finally managed to shout, aloud and telepathically. Ghost did not respond, other than to push at Cadderly's spirit. The young priest felt the burn begin again and knew it signified that he was slipping back out of his form.

But to be pushed out then was to lose himself forever. Cadderly called on his recollections of mental battle, of his experience with the imp, Druzil, back in the forest, and called, too, upon the song of Deneir, hoping to find in its notes some clue that would give him an edge.

But Ghost, too, had experiences to call upon—three lifetimes of exchanging spirits with unwilling victims.

What it came down to was a test of willpower, a test of mental strength.

Ghost didn't have a chance.

"*Out!*" Cadderly screamed. He saw his friends, clearly for a moment, then slipped back to the spirit world and saw Ghost's stunned form, floating helplessly away.

You have not won, came the defiant assassin's promise.

Your connections are gone now, Cadderly argued. *You have no magical ring upon a corpse to give you a hold in the material world.*

I have the Ghearufu, the sinister spirit retorted. *You cannot know its strength! There will be other victims about, foolish priest, weaklings who will lose out to me. And then I will come again for you! Know that I will come again for you!*

The threat weighed heavily on Cadderly, but he didn't believe Ghost's promises were likely. A black spot appeared on the ground, accompanied by a growl, confirming Cadderly's suspicions.

Your connections to the material world are gone now, Cadderly reiterated, seeing the other spirit's confusion.

What is it? Ghost cried to Cadderly, his panic showing clearly.

A black hand shot up from the ground, grabbed the evil spirit's ankle, and held it fast. Frantic, Ghost struggled to pull away, the effort tripping him to a sitting position.

Black hands grabbed his wrists; growling shadows rose all about him.

* * * * *

Cadderly blinked his eyes open to see his concerned friends, Danica and Ivan holding him by the arms, and Pikel studying his face. He felt unsteady, thoroughly drained, and was glad for the support.

"Eh?" the green-bearded dwarf piped curiously.

"I am all right," Cadderly assured them, though his shaky voice weakened his claim considerably. He looked to Danica, and she smiled, knowing beyond doubt that it was indeed Cadderly standing before her.

"The giant's alive again," Ivan said with wonder.

"It is truly Vander," Cadderly assured them. "He returned through the power of the ring." He drew a deep breath to stop the world from swimming in front of his eyes. His head throbbed more painfully than he ever remembered.

"To the barn," he instructed, and he stepped out of Danica and Ivan's grasp and took a step forward.

He pitched sidelong to the dirt, overcome.

* * * * *

It took the young priest many minutes to orient himself when he again found consciousness. He was in the barn—the stench of burned flesh told him that more than the blurry images dancing before his half-opened eyes.

Cadderly blinked and rubbed his bleary orbs. His three friends were with him; he realized he had not been unconscious for very long.

"They just appeared," Danica explained to him, leading his gaze to the items—a small, gold-edged mirror and mismatched gloves adorning the charred and broken corpse by the wall.

"*Ghearufu*," Cadderly said, remembering the name Ghost had given the thing. The young priest stared closely at the item, felt a sensation of brooding, hungry evil. He looked around to his friends, concerned. "Have any of you handled it?"

Danica shook her head. "Not as yet," she replied. "We have decided that the best course of action would be to bring the item to the Edificant Library for further study."

Cadderly thought differently, but he nodded, deciding it best not to argue. "Has the firbolg awakened?" he asked.

"That one'll be out for days," Ivan answered.

Again, Cadderly thought differently. He understood the regenerative powers of the magical ring and was not surprised, a moment later, when Vander, hearing the discussion, walked into the barn.

"Shave me," Ivan whispered under his breath.

"Oo oi," Pikel agreed.

"Welcome back," Cadderly greeted the giant. "You are free from Ghost—you know that—and you are free, too, to go your way. We shall escort you as far as the Snowflakes—"

"You should not make such an offer so easily," the firbolg's resonant voice interrupted, and Cadderly wondered if he had misjudged the giant, if perhaps Vander was not so innocent after all. The others were apparently thinking the same thing, for Ivan and Pikel put their hands to their weapons, preparing for another fight.

Vander smiled at them all and made no move toward his

great sword, belted at his side. "I know where lies Castle Trinity, your true enemy," the firbolg explained, "and I pay my debts."

Epilogue

The temple priests regarded Cadderly and his three companions curiously as they made their bouncing way to the guest rooms.

Rufo heard the racket and opened his door to see what was going on.

"Hello to yerself, too," Ivan growled at him, putting a hand on the angular man's chest and shoving him back into his small room. The other three came in right after the dwarf, Danica closing the door behind her.

"Are you surprised to see me . . . alive?" Cadderly asked, sweeping his blue cape dramatically from his broad shoulders.

Rufo stammered the beginnings of several words, not really knowing where to begin this unexpected conversation. Dozens of questions and fears assaulted him, stealing his voice. How much did Cadderly know or suspect? he wondered. Where was the young wizard, or the rest of the killers?

"The assassins are no more," Cadderly told him confidently, as if reading Rufo's thoughts. "And the young wizard, too, is dead."

"Got that one good," Ivan whispered to his brother, and Pikel gave the great axe, strapped to Ivan's back, a respectful pat.

"Dead," Cadderly reiterated, letting the word hang in the air ominously, "like Avery."

Rufo's chalky, sharp-featured face paled even more. Again he started to reply, to concoct some lie about the headmaster's fate, some tale that would allow him an alibi for his crimes.

"We know," Danica assured him before he got the first words past his thin, dry lips.

"I did not expect this of you," Cadderly said, hooking his walking stick into the crook of his elbow. "Even after the events at the library and in Shilmista, I trusted that you would find a better path to tread."

Rufo ran his bony fingers through his matted black hair. His beady, dark eyes darted all about. "I do not know what you are referring to," he managed to say. "When Avery was found dead, I decided that I, too, would not be safe at the inn. I searched for you, but you were not to be found, so I came here, to be among my friends of Ilmater."

"You were afraid?" Danica asked sarcastically. "Did you fear your cohorts would cheat you?"

"I do not understand," Rufo stuttered.

Danica slapped him across the face, knocking him to a sitting position on his bed. The monk started forward, her expression an angry grimace, but Cadderly quickly intercepted her.

"Why else would you be afraid?" Cadderly asked Rufo, to clarify Danica's last statement. "If not for your cohorts, then who would threaten you?"

"He knew we'd catch him," Ivan put in, grabbing Rufo's arm with an ironlike grasp.

"You err!" Rufo stammered desperately. All the world seemed to be closing in on him. Ivan's clenching hand felt like the jaws of a wolf trap. "I did—"

"Silence!" The command from Cadderly quieted the blustering man immediately and turned his friends' incredulous stares to him. Rufo slumped in his seat and lowered his eyes, thoroughly defeated.

"You led Avery to his death," Cadderly accused him bluntly. "You betrayed me in the library, your friends in the forest, and now Avery. Do not expect forgiveness this time, Kierkan Rufo! The headmaster is dead—his blood is on your hands—and you have crossed into an area from which there is no return." Images of those awful, growling shadows assaulted Cadderly. He closed his eyes and took a few deep breaths to steady himself but found himself imagining Rufo's impending fate, of the hungry, evil things that would drag the fallen priest down to eternal torment.

Cadderly shuddered and opened his eyes. "Hold him," he instructed the dwarves.

"What are you doing?" Rufo demanded as Pikel grabbed the arm opposite the one Ivan held and the two locked him steady on the bed. "My friends will hear! They will not allow this!"

"Ilmater?" Ivan queried. "Ain't them the ones dedicated to suffering?"

"Yup," his brother answered.

"Well, with the hollering ye're about to do," Ivan snickered to Rufo, thoroughly enjoying the angular man's distress, "they're likely to build a statue to ye."

Rufo bit Pikel on the arm, but the tough dwarf just grimaced and did not let go. Danica was around the bed in an instant. She grabbed Rufo's hair and jerked his head back viciously. Between that strong hold, and the dwarves at either side of him, Rufo could only watch and listen.

Cadderly was chanting quietly, his hands moving through specific motions. He extended one finger to point toward Rufo, its end glowing white with heat.

"No!" Rufo cried. "You must let me explain!"

"No more lies," Danica hissed from behind.

Rufo screamed and twisted helplessly as Cadderly's enchanted digit branded his forehead, burned the curse of Deneir—the likeness of a single, broken candle above a closed eye—into the man's skin.

It was over in mere seconds, and Danica and the dwarves let Rufo go. He slumped forward, whimpering, not so much for the continuing pain (there was little), but for the knowledge of what Cadderly had just done to him.

Branded. He smelled the foul odor and knew it would follow him, would magically ward people away from him, for the rest of his days.

"You must never hide your mark of shame," Cadderly said to him. "You are aware of the consequences."

Indeed, Kierkan Rufo was. To hide the lawful brand of Deneir caused the lingering magic to burn deeper into one's forehead, to burn to the brain, resulting in a horrible, agonizing death.

Rufo turned an angry gaze up at Cadderly. "How dare you?" he growled with every ounce of defiance he could muster. "You are no headmaster. You have no power—"

"I could have given you over to the city guard," Cadderly interrupted, the simple logic cutting Rufo short. "Even now I could tell them of your crimes and let them hang you in the street. Would that be preferable?"

Rufo looked away.

"If you doubt my ranking in the order," Cadderly continued, "doubt that I have the power to cast such judgment over you, then simply cover the brand. We will learn soon enough if you are correct." Cadderly removed his widebrimmed hat and held it out to Rufo. "Let us see," he prompted confidently.

Rufo shoved the hat aside and staggered to his feet.

"Highest Priest," he said hopefully when his door

opened and a thick-jowled, bald-headed priest, wearing the red skullcap denoting high rank in the Ilmater order, peered in. Behind the man stood a dozen or more disciples of the temple, aroused by Rufo's agonized screams.

"They heared his yells and thinked he joined their order," Ivan whispered to Danica and Pikel, and the three, despite the gravity of the situation, could not hide their chuckles.

The Ilmater priest sniffed the air, his face twisting against the foul smell. He looked hard at Rufo, at the brand, then turned to Cadderly and asked, no anger in his tone, "What has transpired?"

"They have betrayed me!" Rufo cried desperately. "They—he—" he pointed to Cadderly, "—led Headmaster Avery Schell to his death! And now he tries to blame me, to divert attention from himself!"

Cadderly did not grow excited at the ridiculous claim.

"Would Deneir have granted me the magical brand if the tale rang at all of truth?" he asked the Ilmater priest.

"Is it authentic?" the lean priest asked, motioning to the wicked mark.

"Do you care to test it?" Cadderly asked Rufo, again extending his hat. Rufo stared at it for a very long time, at the Deneirian holy symbol set in its front center, knowing this to be the critical point in his life. He could not accept the hat and put it on—to do so would bring about his death. But refusing strengthened Cadderly's claims, showed Rufo to be an honestly branded outcast. He paused for a long moment, trying to concoct yet another excuse.

His hesitation cost him any chance of explaining.

"Kierkan Rufo, you must be gone from here," the Ilmater priest demanded. "Never again shall you be welcomed in any hall of Ilmater. Never again shall any priest of our order show you any kindness or respect."

The finality of the words sounded like a peg in Rufo's coffin. He knew there would be no point in arguing, that the decision was final. He turned, as if to move for his chest of belongings, but the Ilmater priest would brook no delays.

"Now!" the man shouted. "Your possessions will be dumped into the alley. Be gone!"

Ivan and Pikel, always ready to lend a hand, grabbed Rufo by the arms and roughly heaved him forward. Of the many witnesses, not a single one offered a word of protest.

Branded priests had no allies.

* * * * *

Cadderly had only one more task to complete before he would consider his business in Carradoon at its end, and he found assistance from a local cleric residing outside the lakeside city's tall walls. The aged priest led Cadderly and his four companions—with Vander traveling in his magically reduced state, as a red-haired and red-bearded barbarian warrior—to a small grave in the churchyard.

Cadderly fell to his knees before the grave, not at all surprised, but filled with pity and grief.

"Poor dear," the gentle old priest explained. "She went out in search of her lost husband and found him, dead, on the side of the road. Alas for Jhanine and her children." The priest waited a few moments, then nodded to the companions and took his leave.

"You knew this man?" a perplexed Danica asked, crouching beside Cadderly.

Cadderly nodded slowly, hardly hearing her.

Danica took Cadderly's arm. "Will you go for him?" she asked, a bit sourly, but with all sympathy.

Cadderly turned to her, but his eyes were looking to the past, to his exchange on the road with the unfortunate leper. *Could you cure them all?* Nameless had asked him. *Are all the world's ills to fall before this young priest of Deneir?*

"This makes no sense, and borders on irreverence," Danica remarked, misconstruing Cadderly's silence. "Where next after here? To the graves of the unfortunate farmers and the city guardsman?"

Cadderly closed his eyes and withdrew from Danica's stinging logic. He had already tried to resurrect the farmers, and the unfortunate guardsman, privately, before they had left the farm. The spirits of the farmers were not to be found, and the guardsman would not come to Cadderly's call. The effort had cost Cadderly dearly, exhausted him and taken, he knew, a little bit of his life energy forever.

"How many thousands will Cadderly recall to populate the world?" he heard Danica ask. He knew her sarcasm was not intended to be mean, only practical.

He knew Danica could not understand. This act of resurrection was not as simple as it had seemed when Cadderly had brought Brennan back from the dead. Cadderly had come to learn, painfully, that resurrection was a God-given blessing, not a magical spell. Whatever powers the young priest possessed, he could not defeat ultimate fate. Many conditions had to be met before resurrection could be granted, and many more before the spirits of the dead would heed the call and return to the world they had departed. So many conditions, and Cadderly couldn't even begin to sort through them, couldn't begin to question the divine decisions beyond his mortal understanding.

Wisely, he did not ask Deneir to grant him this act.

"My powers are for the living," he whispered, and Danica quieted, confident that he had come to understand what must be. He said a prayer for Nameless, a plea to whatever gods might be listening to judge the lost man fairly, to grant him the peace in death that had been so unfairly stolen from him in life.

Cadderly never did learn the beggar man's real name and he preferred it that way. He and his friends went back to the priest who had shown them the grave, bearing a fair amount of gold they could spare for the deserving Jhanine, but it was Vander who threw in the largest gift: Aballister's purse of gold, the advance sum given the Night Masks for Cadderly's execution.

"Do you mean to cure the ills of the world?" Danica asked Cadderly again, after the companions had left the priest's small house beside the graveyard. She looked to him pleadingly, fearful for her love, fearful that this new weight of responsibility would break him.

"I will do what I can," Cadderly replied stubbornly. "It is the most that can be asked of us, and the least that any of us should be willing to give."

A chill breeze blew in from the west, a reminder that winter was not far away. Cadderly looked into it, sought the lines of trails on the distant Snowflake Mountains, the paths that led to the Edificant Library.

Maybe it was time to go home.